"I am Spock," he said.

His name appeared to spark immediate recognition in Sorent, as well as in most, if not all, of her fellow officers. That did not surprise Spock, since his efforts—and all efforts—to unify the Vulcan and Romulan peoples had been deemed illegal long ago by the Romulan government.

"Remove your hood," Sorent ordered. "Slowly."

With care, Spock reached up and pulled the cowl of his robe backward, revealing his face. Once again, he saw recognition in Sorent, as well as in others. Behind him, he heard a faint trill, and he suspected that both the inner and outer doors had just been sealed. Four more security officers scrambled from behind the counters to join Sorent and J'Velk. Past the left-hand counter, Spock saw a door open and a uniformed man emerge, the colored rank strip on his arm identifying him as a protector, the highest field-office grade in Romulan Security.

"You are the Vulcan who preaches for the reuniting of Romulus with your people," Sorent said. "Am I correct?"

"I *advocate* for such a reunification, yes," Spock said. He watched as the protector stepped up to observe the proceedings.

"And this is?" Sorent asked, gesturing at Spock's prisoner.

"I do not know," Spock said, "but he tried to kill me."

STAR TREK®
TYPHON PACT

ROUGH BEASTS OF EMPIRE

DAVID R. GEORGE III

Based upon *Star Trek*
created by Gene Roddenberry
and
Star Trek: Deep Space Nine®
created by Rick Berman & Michael Piller

POCKET BOOKS

New York   London   Toronto   Sydney   Tzenketh

Pocket Books
A Division of Simon & Schuster, Inc.
1230 Avenue of the Americas
New York, NY 10020

This book is a work of fiction. Names, characters, places, and incidents either are products of the author's imagination or are used fictitiously. Any resemblance to actual events or locales or persons, living or dead, is entirely coincidental.

First Pocket Books paperback edition January 2011

POCKET and colophon are registered trademarks of Simon & Schuster, Inc.

For information about special discounts for bulk purchases, please contact Simon & Schuster Special Sales at 1-866-506-1949 or business@simonandschuster.com.

The Simon & Schuster Speakers Bureau can bring authors to your live event. For more information or to book an event, contact the Simon & Schuster Speakers Bureau at 1-866-248-3049 or visit our website at www.simonspeakers.com.

Cover art and design by Alan Dingman

Manufactured in the United States of America

10 9 8 7 6 5 4 3 2 1

ISBN 978-1-4391-6081-7
ISBN 978-1-4391-9165-1 (ebook)

To Marco Palmieri,
Who came into my life as an editor,
Plying his craft with artistry and optimism,
But who turned out to be something even more important:
A good man and a good friend

Inevitable as the dusk must fall,
The shadows gather beneath birds of prey;
The nightmare drops again, ensnaring all
Within the dark veil of ego and sway.

Covering the land in surrounding gloom,
Forces alight in the murky city,
And staring and waiting, they promise doom,
Seek weakness and vantage, offer no pity.

Their hour come around, slouching toward the throne,
They clamber over fellows, reaching ever higher,
Seizing all wealth and power for their own,
Battling each other, these rough beasts of empire.

—RABAN GEDROE,
notes accompanying
her painting *Affairs of State*

I

The Fell of Dark

I wake and feel the fell of dark, not day.
What hours, O what black hours we have spent
This night! what sights you, heart, saw; ways
   you went!
And more must, in yet longer light's delay.

—GERARD MANLEY HOPKINS

1

The blade tore through his flesh with cruel ease.

Agony erupted in Spock's midsection, a red-hot ember blazing at the center of an instantly expanding inferno. He grabbed for the knife protruding from his abdomen, for the hand that wielded it, but as he staggered backward a step under the assault, he reflexively threw his arms wide in an attempt to retain his balance. He knew he had to prevent himself from falling, vulnerable, before his unknown, half-seen attacker. Loosed from his grip, Spock's handheld beacon clattered to the rocky ground, its narrow beam sending long shadows careering about the subterranean remnants of the ancient Romulan settlement. In silhouette, visage concealed by darkness, his assailant loomed above him, broad-shouldered and a head taller.

Spock struggled to concentrate, understanding on the heels of the ambush that he likely would have little time to defend himself. Seeking to rule the pain screaming through his body, he focused on the other details of sensation. He felt the cool metal of the knife against his now-exposed right side, even as his blood rushed warmly from the newly opened wound. He smelled the musty scent of age and abandonment that swathed the underground ruins, commingled with the fetid odor of the modern city's sewer system, which ran nearby. The electric tang of copper filled his mouth.

Spock had tasted death before, and recognized it. Intense memories surged in a flash through his mind. *Piloting the faltering* Galileo *above Taurus II, the heat in the smoky main cabin climbing as the shuttlecraft and its crew began plummeting back into the atmosphere. On the planet Neural, hearing the report and then feeling the strike of the lead projectile as it penetrated his back, mangling his viscera. In the Mutara Nebula, repairing* Enterprise's *warp drive, and suffering the lethal effects of extreme radiation as he did so.*

But then the images slipped, melting away in a flat wash of color. The past faded from Spock's mind as quickly as it had arisen, and thoughts of the future suddenly seemed unreachable. Only the excruciating present remained, and only at a remove. Loss of consciousness beckoned, and beyond it—with no ready receptacle for his *katra*—so too did nonexistence.

The would-be assassin closed the small distance, the single pace, that Spock had put between them. The attacker seized the handle of the knife and twisted the blade within the ragged wound, doubtless searching for vital organs. With the pain intensifying, Spock reversed course and reached with his mind for his physical distress, embraced it, clung to it as a means of preventing himself from passing out. He summoned his strength to fight back, only to discover that he had already taken hold of the hand clutching the weapon. As a Vulcan, even at his advanced age—a year short of his sesquicentenary—he possessed corporal might exceeding that of the individuals of many humanoid species. He could not fend off his assailant, though, perhaps owing to his compromised condition—or more likely, he thought, because his adversary enjoyed commensurate bodily prowess.

Romulan, Spock thought, though in the inconsistent lighting, could not be certain. But the conclusion followed, considering the aversion of the Romulan government—of *both* Romulan governments—to his efforts to reunify their people with their Vulcan cousins. It also made sense given his current location, deep beneath Ki Baratan, the capital city of Romulus, and the very heart of the Romulan Star Empire. Few natives, let alone outworlders, knew of even the existence of the old dug-out structures, much less how to access them. Buried by both history and the foundations of the present-day metropolis, much of the belowground, stone-lined tunnel system had been converted long ago into sewage conduits.

A patina of perspiration coated Spock's face as he strained to push his attacker's hand away, to drive out the knife from where it had breached his body. He could do no more than keep his assailant at bay, but he felt his own vigor continuing to wane and knew that he would soon fold. A haze once more drifted across his awareness. He didn't know how much longer he could remain conscious.

On the threshold of desperation, Spock peered past his attacker and gauged their distance from the far wall, ascertaining their position within the passage. Then with all the force he could bring to bear, he swiftly raised one hand and brought the side of it down against his assailant's wrist. The blade jumped within Spock, causing a fresh wave of pain to slice through the lower part of his torso. At the same time, his attacker cried out, his yelp echoing through the tunnel, his hold on the haft of the knife slackening. Spock quickly retreated one long stride, then another, and a third and fourth. Stopping where he judged necessary, he steeled himself and yanked the weapon from his body. More blood issued from the wound, the warm, green plasma saturating his clothing.

Spock reseated the knife in his grasp, its point outward, arming himself. His attacker faced him but made no immediate move other than to reach up and wrap his other hand around his injured wrist. For a moment, stillness settled over the tableau. Spock could hear his own tattered breathing, could feel the rapid throb of his heart.

He knew he would have to act. Though the confrontation had reached a standstill now that he held a weapon, he could not in his condition maintain that impasse for long; soon enough, he would falter. For the same reason, retreat seemed as unlikely a solution.

Spock tightened his grip about the knife, preparing to engage the enemy. But then a tendril of irritation reached him, a fragment of emotion carried into his mind by an empathic projection—a *strong* empathic projection. At once, Spock realized that he had not been assaulted by a Romulan. He also saw how the truth underlying that fact could aid him with the rudimentary plan he had formed.

He lifted his arm and whipped it downward in a single, rapid motion, hurling the knife at his foe. Light glinted along the blade as the weapon passed through slivers of illumination. Spock's attacker nimbly jumped aside, turning to watch the flight of the knife as it shot past and disappeared into shadows untouched by Spock's lost beacon. For an instant, the face of Spock's assailant became visible in a patch of reflected light: a bald skull, mottled flesh, large pointed ears curling outward from his head, raised brow and cheekbones surrounding sunken eyes, a jagged line of teeth.

The Reman did not chase after the knife, but spun back around, his features receding once more into the gloom. He reached for no other weapon that he might be carrying, but he bent his knees and tensed his body, obviously about to spring toward his prey. Spock knew that the Reman would require nothing but his hands to complete the slaying he'd begun.

With virtually no time and no other opportunity left to him, Spock willfully surrendered his mental discipline. His own fears, both intellectual and emotional, soared within him. Though Spock had long ago accepted the reality—indeed, the necessity—of the feelings his mind generated, and though he regularly allowed himself to experience what he imprecisely regarded as his "human half," he still sustained considerable control over his internal life. As he faced his own mortality directly and without restraint, though, a surfeit of powerful emotions threatened to overwhelm him.

Instead of battling his fear, Spock latched onto it. He searched for and found the anger accompanying it: anger at the violence perpetrated against him, anger that his death would forestall his attempts at reunification, anger that he would be forcibly and permanently removed from the lives of those about whom he cared. Then he deliberately dropped his mental guard, pulling down the defenses he maintained about his mind that protected him from external forces.

He immediately felt the full, robust empathic presence

of the Reman. Spock allowed it to sweep over and through him, to buffet and suffuse him with impatience, frustration, and a determination to kill. Rather than battling against it, Spock added to it, layering it with his own anger. As the redoubled emotions grew into a rage, he redirected it to his attacker.

The Reman flinched, cocking his head to one side for a second. Then he launched himself forward, his body uncoiling as though released from great pressure. He came at Spock fast, lifting his hands before him as he closed the gap.

Spock remained motionless, calculating that he would have but one chance to save himself. He judged the speed at which the Reman moved, the man's long gait devouring the distance between then, and still Spock waited. He watched the long, bony fingers his assailant clearly meant to wrap around his neck.

Finally, with the tips of the Reman's curved fingernails nearly upon him, Spock moved. He threw himself backward onto the ground, simultaneously pulling his knees in toward his body. The pain emanating from his midsection swelled to almost unimaginable proportions, and his vision began to cloud at the margins. Still, he willed himself not to stop.

Unable to halt his momentum, the Reman overbalanced, but as he fell forward, his fingers found their target and encircled Spock's throat. Spock felt the touch of his assailant's cold, clammy hands on his neck, along with the weight of the Reman's body descending atop him. Their gazes met at close range, their faces mere centimeters apart.

Spock thrust his legs upward. His feet connected with

the Reman's hips, causing a massive jolt of agony to rip like lightning through the center of Spock's body. But the action continued his attacker's momentum, and the Reman hurtled over and past him.

Spock felt his assailant's hands jerk free from around his throat, then heard a meaty crunch as the Reman's head struck the near side of the tunnel. Under normal circumstances, Spock would have found the sound repugnant, but in this case, it proved satisfying, and a cause for hope. The Reman slumped to the ground, his right boot coming down hard on Spock's face. Spock felt the cartilage of his nose splinter and blood spurt from his nostrils.

He waited, not to learn whether or not he had incapacitated his attacker, but because he could do nothing else. He felt enclosed within his pain, unable to escape its unrelenting clutches. If the Reman recovered and resumed his assault, there would be no struggle.

For minutes, both combatants remained still. Gradually, Spock focused on the frayed whispers of his own breathing. As best he could in his depleted condition, he raised his mental defenses and reestablished control of his emotions. He sought to rein in his pain, but met with only limited success.

When at last he felt capable, Spock pushed himself up from the tunnel floor. Dirt clung to the blood on his hands and clothing. Beside him, the Reman did not move.

Once he'd stood up fully, Spock applied pressure to his wound. It still bled, and would until he either received medical treatment, or perished. He possessed no means of sending for assistance. Not long ago, the praetor had sent capital security forces into the tunnels beneath the city in search of the Reunification Movement. Several of Spock's comrades had been lost, tracked down via their own communicators. As a result, those in the Ki Baratan cell had agreed in the short term to cease carrying the devices.

Spock regarded the man who had attacked him. Half-covered by shadows, the Reman lay prone, one arm bent awkwardly beneath him. A dark pool had formed by his head. Though the movements of his chest seemed shallow, he continued to breathe.

Spock considered ending the Reman's life—via *tal-shaya*, or by taking a rock to his head, or simply by smothering him. Beyond having to answer the moral questions raised by such a choice, Spock didn't believe he currently possessed the strength to do so. Instead, he followed the lone beam of light in the tunnel to its source and retrieved his handheld beacon. Then he resumed his trek to the present location of his Reunification cell.

Spock had walked nearly half a kilometer before he collapsed, unconscious, to the ground.

2

Benjamin Sisko raced to the tactical console and studied the readouts there. On the long-range sensor board, he quickly spied the telltale indicators of ships approaching the planetary system at high velocity. "How many?" he wanted to know.

Lieutenant Cavanagh operated her controls, obviously working to distinguish individual warp signatures. When she looked up, the grave expression on her young face presaged her answer. "Six, Captain."

Six, Sisko echoed to himself, though he said nothing aloud, making sure that he in no way betrayed his concerns. He knew that the crew of *New York,* who had suffered through such difficult circumstances recently, would look to him not only to provide their orders but to set a tone. They barely knew Sisko—he had replaced their fallen captain just three weeks ago—but especially during the current crisis, they would have to rely on his leadership.

"Time to engagement?" he asked, his mind speeding through the possible strategies and tactics that his small defense detail could employ. *Six ships,* he thought again, sensing around him the rising anxiety of the crew. No number of Borg vessels would have brought calm to the bridge of *New York,* but for Starfleet forces to be outgunned two to one would severely compromise their chances not only to succeed in defending Alonis but even to survive the coming battle.

"Depending on how close they get before pulling out of warp," Cavanagh said, consulting her panel again, "estimating between seven and twelve minutes."

Sisko nodded, certain that if the Borg could make it to Alonis within seven minutes, they would. "Take us to battle stations," Sisko ordered. "Red alert." As acknowledgment, Cavanagh's fingers marched across her console, initiating the call to general quarters. The shipwide klaxon blared at regular intervals, in concert with the flashing of the red lights ringing the circumference of the bridge. The overheads dimmed and shifted, bathing the command center in a dull crimson hue.

To Cavanagh, Sisko said, "What's their formation?"

This time, the lieutenant didn't need to check the tactical displays. "Two cubes in front, two in the middle, two in the rear."

Sisko nodded again, calculating that the Borg would not attack in such a configuration. "Maintain sensor contact, Lieutenant," he said. "I want to know when they break formation and how. I also want to know the instant they drop to impulse speed."

"Aye, sir."

Sisko strode to the center of the *Nebula*-class starship's compact bridge, to where the command chair perched at the front of the raised, upper section. Before him, past the crew seated at the conn and ops stations, a great purple-and-white arc filled the bottom of the screen, the world of Alonis, crowned by a panoply of stars. Off to port, sunlight gleamed off one of the two starships that had accompanied *New York* on its mission.

Reaching down to the right arm of the command chair, Sisko tapped a control surface, silencing the klaxon. "Sisko to engineering," he said, voice slightly raised. Not for the first time, he couldn't call to mind the name of the ship's chief engineer. He had no trouble recalling his appearance, though: a roughly cylindrical body nearly two meters tall, tapering slightly in the middle almost like an hourglass, colored a rich green, with a row of fingerlike tentacles a third of the way up, and a second row of longer, wider tentacles a third of the way down. Prior to Sisko's assignment to *New York,* he hadn't known that any Otevrel had joined Starfleet.

"Engineering," responded a tinny, mechanical voice, clearly the result of filtering through a portable translator. *"Relkdahz here. Go ahead, Captain."*

"Commander Relkdahz," Sisko said, intentionally addressing the chief by name in an attempt to impress it upon his memory. "How many photon torpedoes have you upgraded?" In the hours since the Borg had launched their invasion and had begun to overrun Federation space, Starfleet's commander in chief had disseminated plans for the modification of weapons and defensive systems. Though perhaps a case of too little, too late, the changes—at least in initial, limited use—had proven effective for other ships as they fought the relentless enemy.

"Five, sir," Relkdahz said.

"Just five?" The words escaped Sisko's lips before he could suppress them. He at once regretted the question, which would hardly rouse confidence in the bridge crew.

"The transphasic modifications are complex, Captain, and we're understaffed down here," Relkdahz explained.

Understaffed and *inexperienced,* Sisko thought. The terrible incident that had claimed the life of *New York*'s captain six weeks ago had also killed seven others and seriously injured nearly half the engineering staff. Their replacements had been both fewer in number and culled primarily from the ranks of Starfleet personnel only recently graduated from the Academy. "Understood," Sisko said. "Good work," he added, trying to mitigate the disappointment he'd voiced.

"We did *complete the upgrades to the shields,"* Relkdahz said.

Sisko felt his eyebrows lift in surprise. "Excellent," he said, genuinely pleased. Anything that enhanced the *New York* crew's ability to sustain combat against the Borg could make a difference. "Sisko out." He descended the two steps to the front half of the bridge, where he stood between the personnel at conn and ops. "Commander Plante," he told the operations officer, "raise the *Kirk* and the *Cutlass.*" Intership communications normally would have fallen under the purview of tactical, but Sisko wanted Cavanagh's attention fully on the Borg.

"Yes, sir." Sisko watched as Plante called up a comm interface onto her panel, then worked it to complete his order. He peered up at the main viewer and waited. There, the world of Alonis hung in space, a beclouded indigo jewel in the night. Beneath its violet waters, Sisko knew, teemed a civilization of billions. The Alonis had joined the Federation four and a half decades ago.

And I've been sent here to save them, he thought. *As though helping for years to protect and preserve Bajor and its people hasn't been enough for one career, one lifetime.*

Sisko recoiled from the bitterness he suddenly felt, uncertain to whom it had even been directed. After a moment, a split-screen view of the commanding officers of *U.S.S. James T. Kirk* and *U.S.S. Cutlass* appeared on the screen, the image of the planet vanishing. Sisko could only hope that when the Borg finally arrived, the actual world of Alonis didn't disappear as readily.

Captain Elias Vaughn sat in the command chair aboard *U.S.S. James T. Kirk* and acknowledged his orders from Captain Sisko, the officer in charge of the defense force. Vaughn had ordered the klaxon off and the lighting returned to normal, but red alert panels continued to pulse on and off around the bridge. On the main viewer, Sisko stared back at him from the left half of the screen, Captain Rokas from the right.

Vaughn detected a distinct difference in the aspects of the two starship commanders. While both projected a seriousness of purpose, Rokas exuded a quiet self-assurance that, if not entirely justified in light of the imminent Borg attack, at least seemed a healthy conceit. The slight flush of her blue skin, the almost imperceptible tension in the bifurcated ridge that ran down the center of her face, bespoke an adrenal rush as she anticipated leading the *Cutlass* crew into battle.

"Yes, sir," Rokas said, also acknowledging her orders. *"We'll stop them,"* she added, underscoring her obvious con-

fidence that the trio of Starfleet crews would find a way for their vessels to protect Alonis and its people. Ben Sisko, on the other hand, appeared—

Lost, Vaughn thought, unable to come up with another way to describe the faraway expression deep in his friend's eyes. He doubted anybody else could see past Sisko's commanding presence and sober manner, but Vaughn could, and what he saw troubled him. He hadn't spoken to Sisko on a consistent basis over the past two years, since transferring out of the Bajoran system, from Deep Space 9 to *Kirk.* They'd occasionally exchanged subspace messages in that time, and they'd seen each other once, about a year ago, during that bad business on Bajor's first moon. Back then, Vaughn had noted an undercurrent of anxiety in his friend, but he'd ascribed that at the time to the necessity for Sisko to function during the incident as the Emissary of the Prophets.

On the main viewer, Sisko said, *"Stick to the plan as best you can, for as long as you can. We'll only get one chance at this."*

Vaughn knew that almost a decade and a half ago, at the Battle of Wolf 359, Sisko's first wife—not to mention his captain and many of his shipmates aboard *Saratoga*—had perished at the hands of the Borg. Vaughn understood that pain all too well, having lost Ruriko, the mother of his daughter, to the Collective. Given the present situation, it seemed reasonable that those terrible memories, that anguish, could explain the distance he perceived in Sisko, but he didn't think so. Nor did he believe that his friend simply missed and worried about his family. Vaughn might not have known Sisko for that long or spent that much time with him, but they'd shared some intensely personal experiences. Consequently, they'd grown close, coming to know each other quite well. Something else troubled Sisko—something more, even, than the looming Borg onslaught.

And if we survive this, Vaughn thought wryly, *I'll be sure to ask Ben about it.*

"Good luck," Sisko concluded before signing off. The main screen reverted to a view of Alonis, with *New York* and *Cutlass* suspended silently in space above it. Vaughn also discerned one of the half-dozen defense platforms orbiting Alonis. All around the Federation, such planetary protections had failed utterly to repel the Borg, quickly reduced to slag by the advancing cubes.

In the distance, sunlight glimmered off other metal surfaces that Vaughn couldn't differentiate but that he knew belonged to a flotilla of Alonis civilian craft, hanging back as a last line of defense should the Starfleet crews fail in their mission. Those small ships, with minimal defenses and little or no armaments, would be wholly unable to slow the Borg even for a moment. Still, Vaughn understood the need for those Alonis crews to make their stands. In the right circumstances, everybody tilted at windmills.

Beside Vaughn, Commander Rogeiro stood from the first officer's chair. "Adjust screen," he said. "Let's see the Borg approach." His words came cradled in his light but distinctive Portuguese accent.

At the tactical station situated on the rear, elevated arc of the bridge, Lieutenant Magrone tapped at his controls. On the viewer, an empty starfield replaced the planet, platform, and ships. "Two minutes, ten seconds from their probable arrival," Magrone noted. "Transphasic torpedoes prepped and loaded for launch. Shields up, transphasic shields at the ready." While the *New York* crew had cobbled together five upgraded torpedoes, and the smaller complement of *Cutlass* had managed just four, the *Kirk* engineering team had churned out an even ten.

Vaughn knew that many captains claimed their crews were the best in the fleet, and he assumed that a majority of those probably even believed it. Vaughn never made such statements about the personnel aboard *James T. Kirk*, but then he didn't have to: the *Akira*-class vessel carried with it a reputation worthy of the heroic and wildly successful twenty-third-century starship captain whose name it bore. For years, even before Vaughn had taken command, the crew had recorded one achievement after another, from exploratory missions, to diplomatic assignments, to military engagements. With *Kirk* as part of the task force, Starfleet might just save the Alonis.

Vaughn glanced to his left, to where Counselor Glev sat. The gaze of the Tellarite's deep-set eyes met his own. "The crew are ready, Captain," he said, without Vaughn having to inquire.

During the two years of Vaughn's command of *Kirk,* the crew had continually adjusted to him, and he to them, so much so that they often foresaw his orders before he issued them, surmised his questions before he asked them. Indeed, he'd even recently taken to facetiously accusing his executive officer of possessing hidden telepathic talents. In a Starfleet career that had spanned more than eight decades and comprised hundreds of assignments, Vaughn's time aboard *Kirk* had ended up the most satisfying of all.

"Short-range sensors now picking up the Borg,"

Magrone announced. "They're decelerating. Estimating fifty seconds to contact."

"Formation?" Vaughn asked.

"Unchanged," Magrone said. "They are—wait. They're altering course . . . stretching out into a single line . . . the cubes are spreading farther and farther apart."

Of course, thought Vaughn. That way, the three Starfleet ships wouldn't be able to attack the cubes en masse. Where the Borg had once sought to assimilate Federation vessels and crews—to assimilate the whole of the UFP, really—they now apparently intended only to destroy it. The Collective had always maintained the futility of resistance to it; in its contacts with the Federation, it evidently had reached a threshold beyond which it had replaced its imperative of assimilation with that of extermination. The cubes arriving at Alonis would doubtless confront *Kirk, New York,* and *Cutlass* as necessary, but they had come bent on the destruction of the civilization on the planet.

"Attack plan delta," Vaughn ordered. When the Borg ships had initially appeared on long-range sensors, exposing their numbers, the captains of the three Starfleet vessels had coordinated their tactics, formulating several plans, the choice of which to use dependent upon how the cubes deployed.

"Plan delta, aye, sir," replied Lieutenant Commander T'Larik from the conn, even as she worked her controls to bring the ship about. *Kirk* sprang to life as the thrum of the impulse drive spread through the deck.

Vaughn stood up beside Rogeiro. "The timing's got to be perfect," he told his exec. "The transphasic torpedoes may only work the first time."

The commander nodded, then turned and strode up the starboard ramp toward the tactical station. "Are you tracking each cube's course and velocity?" he asked. "How far apart will they be when we meet them?"

"Far enough that we'll only be able to cross the path of one before reaching a second," said Magrone.

"Calculating the drop now," announced Lieutenant Dunlap from the operations console.

"The *Cutlass* and the *New York* are making their runs," Rogeiro said, reading from the tactical station. "The *Cutlass* is headed for the sixth cube, *New York* for the third."

Vaughn peered at the main viewscreen. The stars moved left to right as *Kirk* continued its long sweep to port. He could not see any of the Borg vessels, but the presence of the relentless enemy seemed palpable. Several moments passed in silence.

"Nineteen seconds to intercept the second Borg vessel," said Magrone. "Ten seconds until we cross the path of the first."

"Initiating high-frequency burst," Dunlap said. "Preparing to drop transphasic torpedoes." The silver-haired operations officer counted down from five. "Torpedoes away," he said, "seeded behind us."

On the viewer, looking ahead of his ship, Vaughn spotted movement, a distant, shadowy image streaking opposite the direction of the stars. As *Kirk* neared, the form resolved into the peculiarly generic shape common to most Borg vessels. "They're powering weapons," Magrone said.

"Commence shield nutation," Rogeiro said. Although the engineering teams aboard *Kirk* had modified the shields to employ transphasic harmonics, Captain Sisko had elected to hold the advanced defenses in abeyance at the start of the conflict. Instead, they would utilize a method of shield projection that had in the past stopped the Borg—at least for a short time.

"The Borg are firing," Magrone said, raising his voice. "The—"

If any words followed, Vaughn couldn't hear them over the thunder of the attack. He lost his footing and tumbled to the deck as the ship shuddered. A spray of sparks erupted from somewhere along the aft curve of the bridge.

"Shields down to eighty-three percent," called out Rogeiro.

"Stay on target!" Vaughn yelled, still sprawled on the deck. The lights flickered, went out, came back on again.

Vaughn scrambled to his feet and lurched over to the conn, where Lieutenant T'Larik had somehow remained in her seat. As her fingers dashed across the controls, Vaughn peered at her navigational readout, which depicted the flight paths of *James T. Kirk* and its foes. As the first Borg ship neared *Kirk*'s impulse wake, the second converged with the Starfleet vessel itself. "Stay on target," Vaughn said again, looking back toward tactical.

Rogeiro stood there alone, Magrone no longer at his side. Behind the exec, along the bridge's outer bulkhead, Vaughn saw that one of the supplementary stations had exploded. *Shrapnel,* Vaughn thought, automatically attempting to account for whatever must have felled his tactical officer.

"Firing torpedoes," Rogeiro called, and then warned, "Hold on."

The ship jolted again as another barrage landed. Vaughn

grabbed for the conn station and managed to keep his feet. The lights went out again and this time did not come back, replaced instead with the red glow of emergency lighting. "Status of the first two Borg ships?"

At tactical, Rogeiro searched for an answer. "The torpedoes worked," he finally said. "The second ship was destroyed, and the first—" He operated a few more control surfaces. "Also destroyed," he said.

Vaughn almost couldn't believe the report. Starfleet Command had detailed the efficacy of transphasic torpedoes against the Borg but had also cautioned that the weapons would probably fail in short order to withstand the Collective's ability for rapid adaptation. The *Kirk* crew had sown four of their upgraded torpedoes in the path of the first Borg cube, masking them with a high-frequency communications signal. They then timed their assault on the second cube to coincide with the first cube's collision with the weapons, providing the crews of neither vessel any time to adapt.

"And the others?" Vaughn asked. With fewer torpedoes, the crews of *Cutlass* and *New York* had only enough to fire directly on the Borg ships, but they had coordinated their attacks with those of *Kirk*.

"Scanning," Rogeiro said. Vaughn girded himself for bad news, but then his first officer said, "The third cube has also been destroyed."

The portside doors in the aft bulkhead parted, revealing Ensign Ni-Jalikreii. The Efrosian nurse surveyed the bridge for a moment, then quickly moved over beside Commander Rogeiro. Ni-Jalikreii ducked down, out of sight, behind the tactical console, no doubt to tend to Lieutenant Magrone.

"The sixth cube shows faltering shields, but it's still operational," Rogeiro said.

Damn, Vaughn thought. Three cubes wiped out, but three remaining. And since the crew of *Cutlass* hadn't destroyed the vessel upon which they'd fired, that likely meant that their attack hadn't occurred simultaneously with those of *Kirk* and *New York.* However short the additional time it had taken for *Cutlass*'s torpedoes to land, the interval had allowed the rest of the Borg squadron to adapt to Starfleet's new transphasic weaponry.

"T'Larik, bring us about," Vaughn said, gazing down at the conn officer. "Head us for the nearest cube."

"Aye, sir," she said.

Vaughn turned toward the main viewscreen to see the starfield whirling to one side. After a moment, the scene steadied on the orb of Alonis. A dark cube hung above it. As Vaughn watched, a fiery red beam streaked forth from the Borg vessel, aimed at the planet.

"They're firing on Calavet," said Rogeiro.

The third most populous city on the planet, Vaughn knew, Calavet housed more than thirteen million inhabitants. "Load unmodified photon torpedoes alongside the transphasics," Vaughn said, since he knew that *Kirk* carried only two more of the upgraded weapons. "Ready on main phasers, random resonance frequencies." At one time or another, the Borg had adapted to each of those weapon systems, but Vaughn hoped that hitting them with everything would make a difference.

"Sir, the *New York* is firing on the fourth cube," said Lieutenant Dunlap. "They've raised their transphasic shields."

"Then raise ours," Vaughn replied, looking over at the ops officer. For a second, Vaughn took strength from his own order, from the added layer of defense that would be erected around his ship. Then he peered back at the main viewer.

In the distance, a second red beam erupted from another Borg cube, slicing through the atmosphere of Alonis and deep into its violet waters.

"Fire!" Sisko yelled, raising his voice to be heard over the clamor of the Borg attack. He stood beside the command chair, gripping its back to keep his balance as the sickly green streak of energy pounded into *New York*. He didn't hear any acknowledgment of his order, but on the main viewscreen, he saw the ship's phasers leap into the void until they found the fourth Borg cube. The beams flashed through random color changes as Cavanagh adjusted their resonance frequencies on the fly. Still, the Borg vessel continued discharging its weapons, a red energy ray piercing an Alonis ocean and into a city, a green one tracking with *New York* as it raced toward the cube.

"Phasers reduced the Borg's shield strength by sixty-five percent," Cavanagh said, "but they are now having no effect."

"What about *our* shields?" Sisko said. The *Nebula*-class ship trembled beneath the Borg offensive, a heavy drone feeding back through the shield generators, but the damage sustained seemed minimal.

"Transphasic shields holding steady at ninety-three percent," Lieutenant Commander Plante confirmed from her ops console.

Good, Sisko thought. Until they could eliminate the Borg weapons, they would need the shields in order to interfere with the Collective's assault on the Alonis. "Cease fire and alter course to juxtapose the *New York* between that ship and the planet."

At the conn, Ensign Jaix glanced up from his panel. "Sir, the Borg are *firing* on Alonis."

"And we have to stop them from doing so," Sisko told the young Catullan officer, his voice hard.

"Yes, sir," Jaix said. "Altering course." A quaver in his voice made him sound both chastened and scared.

"Lieutenant Wilkes," Sisko said, looking over at the environmental-control station on the periphery of the bridge, to his left.

"Sir?"

"I want all outer sections along the top of the primary hull evacuated at once," Sisko said. "See to it."

"Yes, sir," Wilkes said, turning back to her controls.

Sisko watched the Borg ship slide toward starboard on the main viewer as *New York* rounded the cube, to the side facing the planet. The nearest of the Alonis orbital defense platforms came into view, its hull blackened by a Borg attack, its weapons left mute. "Interpose us between the cube and the planet. Show them the top of the primary hull." Though such a maneuver would render the saucer section of the ship vulnerable, it would also better protect the flattened secondary hull, which housed the engineering section as well as the twin nacelles. All three structures depended from the bottom of the saucer.

On the screen, Sisko saw the green energy beam stop

firing. At once, a relative quiet descended about the bridge. It didn't last.

"Moving into the line of fire," said Jaix, his inflections divulging his uncertainty.

The Borg ship filled the main viewscreen. *New York* shook violently as the primary hull made contact with the red energy beam. A loud whine pervaded the bridge—and, Sisko thought, probably the entire ship.

"Shields down to eighty-five percent, but holding steady there," said Plante. "Hull temperature is rising beneath the beam."

"Captain," Cavanagh said, her tone urgent. "The Borg have locked onto us with a tractor beam." The ship quaked again, harder. "They've deployed a cutter."

Sisko knew from Starfleet's encounter with the Borg at Wolf 359 that the indefatigable enemy used a cutting beam to carve off sections of the ships it battled and to extract those sections for study. *But they're done studying the Federation,* he thought. *As soon as our shields go down, they'll simply slice us apart.*

"Shields down to seventy-one percent," said Plante. "Seventy . . . sixty-five."

"Fire all weapons," Sisko ordered. "Include the transphasic torpedo with the photons." The crew of *New York* had utilized four upgraded torpedoes to destroy the third Borg vessel, leaving them with just one of the advanced weapons.

"Aye," said Cavanagh.

Even through the noise and vibration of the Borg attack, Sisko felt the launch of the torpedoes through the deck plating. He peered at the viewscreen to watch the red bolts speed toward the Borg vessel. They reached their target quickly, detonating in several concentrated blasts, with a pair of phaser shots attempting to exact their own tolls. The green tractor beam collapsed first. A second later, both the red beam meant for the planet and the white cutting beam guttered and then went out.

"Borg shields down to nineteen percent," Cavanagh called out.

As though loosed by *New York*'s attack, a torrent of green pulses suddenly shot from two points on the cube. "Hang on," Sisko said, tightening his own grip on the back of the command chair. The bolts rocked the ship. Barely able to stay on his feet, Sisko looked upward and through the transparent-aluminum dome that crowned the bridge. Through it, he could see the threatening form of the Borg cube, spewing forth its destructive venom. "Jaix, get us out of here," he yelled.

"Our shields just failed," Cavanagh said, the sound of fear tingeing her voice for the first time.

She should be scared, Sisko thought. *One more energy pulse, maybe two—*

"Jaix!" Sisko shouted, looking over at the conn, seeing the ensign's fingers flying across his controls.

"Sir, the helm is not responding," Jaix said, his voice on the edge of panic.

"Power conduits burned out when the transphasic shields overloaded," Plante said, searching for answers at ops.

"Reroute to auxiliary power," Sisko said. "I don't care if you have to get out and push, get this ship moving." Dreading what he would see, he peered up once more through the bridge's transparent dome. The Borg cube seemed to hover above them, like the head of a hammer about to be brought down with crushing force.

But nothing happened.

"What's—"

The Borg vessel suddenly flew apart in a tremendous explosion. Sisko looked back down at the main viewer to see sections of the cube hurtling in all directions, and beyond it, the apparent source of its destruction: *James T. Kirk*. He turned and sprinted the few paces over to the tactical station. "How long?" he asked, gazing down at one of the readouts, where numbers that could only be velocities tracked the fragments of the Borg ship twisting through space.

"Twenty seconds," Cavanagh calculated.

"Jaix?" Sisko said, knowing that the thrusters would not be able to move the ship out of danger in time. "Plante?"

"Power junctions have fused shut," said Plante. "I can't complete a circuit for auxiliary power."

Sisko dashed back to the command chair, where he reached for the intraship comm control on the right arm. "All hands," he told the *New York* crew, "brace for impact." On the viewer, smaller and larger sections of the demolished cube turned end over end, several sizable fragments growing large on the screen as they drew nearer.

Sisko looked upward again, through the bridge's hemispherical peak, in time to see a large fragment of the Borg vessel's outer structure slam into the top of *New York*'s primary hull. The sound of the collision boomed through the air, a sound like no other Sisko had ever heard on a starship. Even as he stumbled and fell to his knees, he kept his gaze locked on the transparent dome. A crack appeared, followed by an electric-blue flare as an emergency force field automatically snapped into place.

The ship bucked again, and again, coincident with the roars of other impacts on the hull. "Three more pieces," said Cavanagh. "None of them as big as the first."

Sisko rode out the crashes of the Borg debris against *New York*'s hull, then rose back to his feet. He padded down to the front portion of the bridge. On the main viewscreen, the starfield turned slowly. "Status," Sisko said as he stepped up between ops and the conn.

"The ship is tumbling toward Alonis," said Ensign Jaix, "but I can stop us with thrusters."

"Do it," Sisko ordered, then looked to Lieutenant Commander Plante.

"Four hull breaches reported, all contained," Plante said. "But one of the Borg fragments penetrated the starboard nacelle."

"So the warp drive is out," Sisko concluded.

"And the impulse engines," Plante added. She peered up at him from her station. "We're dead in space."

U.S.S. James T. Kirk advanced on the fifth Borg vessel. After Vaughn's crew had destroyed the first two cubes and had helped their counterparts aboard *New York* finish off the fourth, only two of the enemy ships remained. Both had opened fire on Alonis.

"Where's the *Cutlass*?" Vaughn asked. He sat in his command chair, while his first officer continued to stand in at tactical. After Nurse Ni-Jalikreii had treated Lieutenant Magrone, she had overseen his transfer to sickbay.

"The *Cutlass* is still fighting the sixth cube," Dunlap replied from the ops console.

Vaughn nodded. He could take his ship to join *Cutlass*'s battle, but both of the remaining cubes needed to be stopped. Though it would take longer than for a multiplicity of ships, even a single Borg vessel could lay waste to the population of Alonis. And since arriving, the fifth cube had gone completely untouched by the Starfleet force.

"The instant we're in range, open fire," Vaughn said. The crew had used their final two transphasic torpedoes in the barrage they had launched against the fourth Borg vessel, leaving them with only their standard complement of weapons. They would randomize the frequencies of their phaser blasts, but Vaughn understood that victory would likely require more radical measures.

"Fifteen seconds," T'Larik said, interpreting the data from her conn readouts.

Vaughn eyed the magnified image of the fifth Borg cube on the main viewer, his gaze drawn to the red beam cutting through the atmosphere and into the waters of Alonis. He felt a visceral response. Down on the planet, he knew, people were dying—dying for no better reason than that a number of Federation citizens had dared to resist the attempts of the Collective to assimilate them.

Hatred welled up within Vaughn. Though he grew up with a wanderlust and a yearning for exploration, his dreams had been interrupted too often by death. After decades in intelligence, years in which he had actively safeguarded the hopes and desires of trillions, he'd finally found the courage for genuine self-examination, and the strength to revisit his own youthful aspirations. Leaving the shadows of both the intelligence business and his own misguided attempts at self-preservation, he had joined Deep Space 9 as Kira Nerys's first officer, had taken *Defiant* on a months-long journey of discovery into the Gamma Quadrant, and had along the way rediscovered the core of his own being. His three years aboard DS9 and, to an even greater extent, his two years leading the crew of *James T. Kirk* had been the best of his career—of his *life*.

But a combination of circumstance and necessity had brought him and his crew to Alonis. Reports from across the Federation painted a grim picture of the Borg invasion. Whole worlds and populations had already been devastated, and the two remaining cubes sought to visit the same fate on the planet and people below. Whatever the cost, Vaughn could not allow that to happen.

"Five seconds," T'Larik said.

Vaughn saw the Borg vessel unleash its weaponry in a confusing array of colors. Red and white beams flashed toward *Kirk* alongside green pulses of energy. Vaughn had just enough time to think that he had never read any reports of such an attack, but then the Collective had little experience against transphasic shields. Clearly, they sought to adapt.

The Borg salvo landed even before *James T. Kirk* could fire its own weapons. Inertial dampers failed for a moment as the ship pitched violently backward. The kick threw Vaughn from his chair. He landed hard against the deck and felt his right shoulder give way. He opened his eyes to darkness, and in that second, thought that he had been blinded. But then he picked out the glow of the conn, and then of other stations around the bridge. Only the emergency lighting had failed.

Vaughn heard Rogeiro's voice, and it took the captain a moment to decipher his words through the din: "Firing weapons!"

Vaughn neither felt nor heard *Kirk*'s phasers and photon torpedoes let loose, but when he looked up at the main viewscreen, he saw a volley of destructive energy smash into the near side of the Borg cube.

Almost *smash into it,* Vaughn thought, even as Rogeiro called out his own verdict.

"No effect." The Borg shields held against the Starfleet weaponry.

"Keep firing!" Vaughn yelled, though as he looked at the main viewer, *Kirk*'s phasers and photon torpedoes showed no signs of abating. Vaughn tottered to his feet, but as he stepped forward in the dim light provided only by the instrumentation around the bridge, he tripped and went down again. He landed with his legs draped over a body.

"Transphasic shields down to seventy percent," said Rogeiro. The Borg learned quickly.

Vaughn pulled himself from atop Lieutenant Commander T'Larik, then reached down and felt for a pulse at her neck. He found her heart rate, weak but present, obviously slowed by whatever injury had felled her. When he pulled his hand back, his fingertips came away tacky with T'Larik's blood.

The ship rocked again as the Borg weapons stormed the shields and once more momentarily disrupted the inertial dampers. Vaughn climbed to his feet, then stepped over to the conn and dropped into T'Larik's chair.

"Shields down to forty-eight percent," Rogeiro called out. "Phasers and photon torpedoes ineffective."

Vaughn searched the displays for the information he needed. He knew what he had to do, and realized that he'd prepared himself for his moment ever since the assignment to protect the people of Alonis had been handed down to him and his crew. He reached up and altered *Kirk*'s course, decelerating as he set the ship on a deep curve to port, away from the fifth cube. The Borg weapons tracked with them, continuing to devour *James T. Kirk*'s defenses.

"Shields at thirty-six percent," said Rogeiro.

Vaughn punched in a sharp course change, then shifted the engines back to full impulse and tacked hard to starboard. The bridge quieted at once as the Borg weapons lost their target. Vaughn adjusted the ship's path again, turning to port and then quickly straightening out. He looked up to see the Borg vessel nearly filling the main viewscreen.

The cube's weapons shut down for a moment, then bounded out again and once more caught *Kirk*. Vaughn heard an explosion somewhere behind him on the bridge, but he ignored it. Instead, he monitored his ship's course, making small adjustments as the Borg weapons took their toll not just on *Kirk*'s shields but on all its systems, including the impulse drive.

The ship rumbled as though it might come apart, and still Vaughn kept it aimed directly at the center of the cube. He watched intently as the distance indicator plummeted toward zero, his hand on the conn's pitch control. In his head, he estimated the timing of his desperate maneuver.

At the last possible moment, he pulled *Kirk*'s bow upward, taxing the inertial dampers with the rapid movement.

The Borg weapons broke off again, leaving only the strained whine of the impulse engines to fill the bridge. Vaughn peered at the main viewer in time to see the cube disappear from the bottom of the screen, and for a brief but terrible interval, he thought he had miscalculated.

Then *James T. Kirk* collided with the Borg vessel.

Vaughn had never heard a louder or more horrifying sound. The inertial dampers failed utterly, and Vaughn flew from his seat at the conn. He felt pain in his knees as they struck the console, then saw the stars and a tiny arc of Alonis rushing toward him. He had only enough time to think of his daughter—*Prynn!*—before his head plowed into the viewscreen. Then he collapsed to the deck, motionless.

Sisko watched helplessly from the command chair as the drama played out on *New York*'s main viewer. Battered by the fifth Borg cube, its shields failing, its weapons firing futilely, *James T. Kirk* executed a suicidal dash toward the enemy vessel. Voices and movements quieted around the bridge, and Sisko became vaguely aware that the crew around him also looked on, for the moment halting their efforts—no longer to continue fighting, but simply to keep *New York* intact. They all watched as *Kirk* pursued its kamikaze run.

At the last second, the *Akira*-class vessel swept upward, its primary hull passing over the Borg vessel by the narrowest of margins. *Kirk*'s warp nacelles, depending from the ship's aft section, sheared off as they impacted the upper edge of the cube, the drive structures shattering and then exploding. The red beam aimed at the planet ceased, and a series of smaller blasts bloomed on the surface of the Borg vessel. Its main drive amputated, the crippled primary hull of *Kirk* spun away into space, clearly no longer under power.

"Captain," Cavanagh said from the tactical station, her voice low. Before she could say more, the Borg resumed their attack on Alonis, the red energy beam beating down once more on the planet. Perhaps a third of the cube had been demolished by *Kirk*'s attack, and still its remaining drones sought the annihilation of a people they had likely never even met.

Sisko felt helpless, unable to lead the battered hulk of the starship he commanded back into battle. But a sense of abandonment also closed in around him, as though Vaughn had somehow chosen to leave him alone out there, a powerless witness to the eventual obliteration of an entire civilization. Sisko could think of no orders to give the crew, no words of solace to lead them forward.

On the main viewscreen, far past the fifth Borg cube, another explosion intruded on the eternal night of space. Sisko waited, not wanting to ask the question to which he already knew the answer. Cavanagh made the announcement, her voice barely above a whisper.

"The *Cutlass* has been destroyed."

Just visible in the distance, the sixth cube recommenced its attack on Alonis.

Some sense beyond failure clutched at Sisko, and another question occurred to him: *Why am I still alive?* He knew that beneath the violet seas of Alonis, in beautiful underwater cities that he had never visited but had read about, genocide threatened. It made no sense that he should be there, a willing combatant, subdued but not killed. It felt wrong, and yet it also made him feel less isolated.

Tentatively, he reached into his mind, into his spirit, for that which he had known before. When nothing came to him, he discarded his caution and opened himself up completely. And still, nothing came.

I am alone, he thought, not for the first time.

On the viewer, the last two Borg vessels continued to rain destruction down upon the populace of Alonis. Sisko thought to switch the screen off, to spare himself and the crew the horrible sight of the extermination. When the Borg had completed their task, he had no doubt that they would also take the time to finish the destruction of *New York* and *James T. Kirk.*

Still a Starfleet captain, Sisko issued the orders he knew he must. "Back to work, people," he said as gently as he could. "We have to get this ship moving if we can." Slowly and deliberately, the crew returned to their jobs, though Sisko would have been surprised to find a single one of them who believed that they would live out the day.

Five minutes later, unaccountably, the Borg ended their attack.

3

The great hall bore no name. Assigning it an appellation would have run counter to the nature of its purpose. Any members of the Hundred called to a summit knew where and when to assemble, details closely guarded by clan elders and passed on to younger generations only as needed.

Durjik made sure to arrive early—not so early that the camouflaged approach and entrance had not yet been opened by a gatekeeper, but far enough before the gathering that he could observe most of the attendees enter. He sat nearer to the entryway than not, in one of the outer rings of seats. Arranged concentrically in the circular space, the chairs sat divided into quadrants by a pair of perpendicular aisles that crossed at their midpoints, where a small platform allowed for the elevation of a single speaker at a time. The place smelled slightly sour from disuse, a combination of dust and stale air that would take more than the occasional meeting to diffuse.

At first, members of the Hundred arrived sporadically, in twos and threes. Durjik noted wryly that although none came clad in expensive or regal garments befitting their station, most nevertheless bore themselves in a manner that would have permitted even a casual observer to identify them as belonging to one of the five-score families whose wealth and power had controlled the Empire for millennia. In a sense, they reflected their surroundings: deep in the hills surrounding Ki Baratan, hewn out of solid rock, the vast room impressed not by its negligible trappings, but by its very character. Modest wall hangings and floor coverings served only the practical function of reducing the echoes off stone surfaces, but the extent of the space, the height of the ceiling, measured well out of the ordinary.

Large casements set into the top of the eastern arc of the room provided the only illumination, most brightly at a specific time of day, shortly after dawn. Sunlight streaming through the windows would describe a golden box high on the curve of the wall opposite, which would travel downward as the hours wore on, until it at last reached the floor and then disappeared entirely. Even on overcast days, the box of light, though barely visible, would define the span of the congress.

Eventually, Durjik saw the hall filling almost to its capacity of five hundred. Though for most assemblies, clans dispatched one or two members to represent their interests, it appeared that for the current meeting, many families had sent four or five of their number. Durjik's own clan, the Rilkon, had settled on the intermediate figure of three. As the start of the summit neared, he saw his great grandfather, Orvek, dodder through the room's single doorway, accompanied by Orvek's daughter, Selten. Durjik made no attempt to draw their attention, and they ended up sitting in another section, some distance from him.

Of all those gathered, Durjik saw no face he did not recognize—at least visually. He understood, though, that some of the attendees wore miens designed to conceal their additional, hidden identities and their true interests; they acted not only for their clans but for the praetor, or for the Tal Shiar, or even simply for themselves. Durjik himself served more than one loyalty, including that of the Rilkon, of himself, and of his new allegiance, though, in the end, he would argue that with respect to his political actions, he undertook all that he did for the sake of the Romulan Star Empire itself.

As the flow of people into the hall fell to a trickle and then stopped altogether, Durjik glanced up to the crown of the western wall. What had begun earlier as a thin line of sunlight had grown into the large rectangle of light that would demark the beginning and end of the forum. The room quieted as a sense of communal anticipation swelled. Durjik, too, waited to see who would rise first to speak.

Over the course of the past eight or ten days, word of the summit had propagated throughout the Hundred, though, unusually, neither who had called it nor why. But as the news circulated that Tal'Aura had committed Romulan military assets to the Federation's war with the Borg, the opinion prevailed that the praetor herself had set the meeting, probably so that she could seek out validation and support for her actions. Her decision to fight alongside Starfleet and Klingon forces had proven unpopular, with many thinking it traitorous.

Durjik believed something different. While he despised the imperialism, duplicity, and hypocrisy of the United Federation of Planets, he had also educated himself enough about the Borg threat to know that the Collective would not stop at the UFP's borders. Especially given the current

divisions within the Empire, Romulus could not hope to
stave off assimilation or destruction if it stood alone. Durjik
hated the Federation, and he distrusted both Tal'Aura and
Tomalak—their intentions and their competences—but he
felt no compunctions about backing the temporary alliance
to which the praetor had agreed if it meant the continued
existence of his people.

The creak of old, overtaxed hinges reached Durjik's
ears. He swung his gaze back to the door to see the gatekeeper, an older man from the Vorken family, pushing the
large stone slab closed. Just before it shut, a lean figure
sidled lithely through the opening.

The door shut with the loud scrape of stone against
stone, followed by a definitive thud. Durjik watched with
some amusement as many heads turned toward the sound,
then slowly swiveled as they followed the progress of the man
who'd just entered. He strode purposefully down an aisle
toward the center of the room, seeming to take no notice of
the wealthy and powerful figures massed about him. Unlike
his prospective audience, and in violation of convention, the
man wore aristocratic clothes: a silver-and-black suit, cut
broadly across the shoulders and adorned with senatorial
ensigns, which seemed intended to convey the impression of
both the martial and political skills of its wearer.

Tomalak reached the small platform at the center point
of the hall and stepped up onto it without hesitation. "My
friends," he said at once, his voice raised to a volume sufficient for the entire audience to hear. "And my enemies,"
he added, rather disarmingly, Durjik thought. "As must be
obvious, I have come to you today not only as a member of
the Hundred, but as proconsul to our praetor."

Some rumblings went up, and Durjik heard a woman two rows in front of him mutter something about Tal'Aura not being *her* praetor. He understood the sentiment. More than a year earlier, Tal'Aura had been one of the few legislators not present when Shinzon had launched his attack on the Senate, decimating it and declaring himself praetor. Durjik had been both appalled and impressed by his hubris, and had sympathized with his desire to take the Empire to war against the Federation. But Shinzon, a clone of a human starship captain and raised in the brutal conditions of the Reman mines, had grown unstable, and he'd failed in his crusade.

As the most powerful senator left alive, Tal'Aura had stepped into the power vacuum. Suspicions about her possible complicity in assassinating the bulk of the Senate had gone unproven, and had mostly faded away as she held the government together with laudable tenacity. In due time, her de facto status as the accepted leader of the Empire had become a matter of law, by her own declaration and with only meager opposition.

"It was Praetor Tal'Aura who called for this meeting," Tomalak continued, turning slowly so that he faced everybody in the hall. More rumblings coursed through the assembly, louder. It did not appear to trouble the proconsul. "Our praetor has sent me here to assure you that she wants what you want, what *all* Romulans want, no matter the world on which they live or who proclaims to be their leader." A few shouts of support rang out, but most stayed quiet, their skepticism evident.

The reference to Commander Donatra—*Empress* Donatra—lacked subtlety, but Durjik assumed it achieved

Tomalak's objective. After Shinzon's death, Tal'Aura's assumption of power, and the Remans' successful quest for independence from Romulus, Commander Donatra and the considerable military faction loyal to her had taken control of the Romulan breadbasket worlds. The maneuver had failed to wrest Tal'Aura's authority from her, instead resulting in the sundering of the Empire. Donatra, under the title of empress, had declared the worlds her forces held to be their own sovereign nation, dubbed the Imperial Romulan State.

Durjik could not imagine that any Romulan—whether a member of the Hundred, an officer in the military, or merely a civilian—approved of the fissure. Although life in the Romulan Star Empire had calmed of late, the limited availability of foodstuffs, the vulnerability brought on by a seriously reduced military, and the uncertainty of a government still considered provisional by many, all kept the population on edge. Tomalak—and by extension, Tal'Aura—clearly aimed to take advantage of such fears.

"Praetor Tal'Aura wants a strong and secure Romulus," the proconsul went on. "Our people should not know privation, should not live afraid that they cannot be protected from foreign attack, should not be separated brother from brother and sister from sister because planets once our own have been taken from us." Tomalak's voice rose as his words met with a number of cheers. "The praetor wants the Romulan Star Empire to climb once more to preeminence, to stand as the undisputed power in this region of space, safe and inviolate."

Political applause lines, Durjik thought, and indeed, the words produced the obviously desired effect. But surely

Tal'Aura had not sent Tomalak to the Hundred in an attempt simply to elicit this brand of mindless, nationalistic support. Though even the ruling class could engage in such insipid flag-waving, anybody at all could ring the bell of blind patriotism; inciting such fervor would not necessarily translate into sustained, reasoned backing, and the praetor must know that.

On the small stage, with all eyes upon him, Tomalak waited for the ovation to fade. When the hall had grown quiet again, the proconsul lowered his voice, lending a subdued weight to his next words. "Praetor Tal'Aura has a detailed plan to achieve these goals, and to do so quickly."

Durjik felt his eyes narrow involuntarily. While he assuredly subscribed to the vision of a strong and united Romulan Empire, he saw no ready means of accomplishing this anytime soon. As a result, Tomalak's claim gave him pause. The silence around him implied that others shared his uncertainty.

"Our praetor has taken steps to ensure the return of Romulus to galactic prominence," Tomalak said, engaging in a bit of hyperbole; the galaxy was a big place, much of it far removed from the Romulan Star Empire. "But because some of what Tal'Aura proposes is unprecedented, she feels that she cannot, that she *should* not, take further action unilaterally. She therefore seeks the cooperation and guidance of the Romulan Senate."

Durjik blinked. Had Tal'Aura, through her proconsul, just offered to share her autocratic power? Had she actually *requested* it?

"For some time now, Praetor Tal'Aura has shouldered alone the burden of responsibility in governing the

Empire," Tomalak said. "She has done this selflessly and without complaint."

Durjik allowed himself a small grin at the notion of an altruistic dictator.

"If the praetor must, she will continue to lead alone," Tomalak said. "But she would prefer that the Hundred reconstitute the Senate." Murmurs spread immediately through the hall. So much time had passed since the mass killing that had bled the Empire of Praetor Hiren and almost all of its senators that the idea of repopulating the Senate had long ago lost any sense of urgency. At first, after Shinzon and then Tal'Aura had taken over, few had any appetite for placing themselves in what had so recently before become a killing field—and those who had such a craving had been quickly silenced, in one way or another. Once Donatra had cleaved the Romulan state in two, plunging the Empire into a condition of rampant nutritional deprivation and overall hardship, the ruling class had found even fewer reasons to lead; hungry and scared, the proletariat would have welcomed a new group of men and women to blame for their woes.

If Tal'Aura truly does want the Senate reseated, Durjik thought, *is that why? So that she can deflect responsibility for the present state of the Empire, for the deep wounds inflicted upon the Romulan people?*

On the central platform, Tomalak waited for the whispers to quiet. When they did, he said, "The praetor submits to you, and to all the members of the Hundred, that public confidence would rise greatly from a fully functioning government. Further, Tal'Aura herself needs the help of the Senate to follow her vision and to make Romulus whole again." Tomalak turned slowly once more, as though endeavoring to emphasize the importance of Tal'Aura's proposal. Then without another word, he stepped from the stage and paced back down the aisle along which he'd entered. Normally, the hall remained sealed during the course of a gathering, but by the time Tomalak reached the door, the gatekeeper had already pulled it halfway open. The proconsul slipped sideways through it as agilely as when he'd entered.

Durjik surveyed the room, looking for the members of Tomalak's own clan, whom he'd seen earlier, but he could not spot them. He wondered if they or someone else would stand and take the platform, and whether that speaker would champion the praetor's entreaty or rebuff it. *Surely we must meet her challenge,* Durjik thought. No matter Tal'Aura's agenda, he could conceive of no reason short of madness that would have her call for the resumption of the Senate, only to destroy it again. And while the praetor did not lack for ambition or a talent for treachery, she did not strike him as mad.

Still, Durjik found it difficult to credit the motives Tomalak had attributed to her. He didn't know what she really wanted, but he thought he needed to find out. Once, long ago, Durjik had been selected by his family to serve in the Senate, which he had done for some years. *Perhaps,* he thought, *I need to make that happen again.*

4

Spock awoke with a suddenness that startled him. Even asleep, even unconscious, the Vulcan mind marked time. But he retained no sense of the past minutes—or hours, or days, or however long it had been since his last waking thoughts. He'd been unaware and then aware, with no feeling of transition whatsoever.

Anesthesia, Spock surmised, opening his eyes in darkness. He flexed his fingers and tested his surroundings, finding that he lay supine atop a soft, flat surface, no longer facedown on the hard, uneven ground of the tunnels beneath Ki Baratan. He recalled the attack on him, as well as his narrow escape. He'd lost consciousness, likely the result of blood loss brought on by the knife wound he'd endured. The fact of his continued existence implied that he'd been found and his injuries treated.

Carefully, Spock tensed and moved different parts of his body. He felt a general stiffness in his muscles and an overall weariness, but no pain. His clothes had been removed in favor of a light smock, and a blanket covered him.

With even more caution than he'd utilized with his physical self, Spock examined his mind. Though he'd passed out after the assault, he would not have become entirely insensible. Sounds, scents, and tactile sensations still would have impressed themselves upon his brain.

Spock closed his awareness to the input of his body—the darkness before his eyes, the damp chill against his face, the undercurrent of putrescence assailing his nostrils—and searched for whatever perceptions had reached his unconscious mind. He went back to the tunnels through which he'd walked, back to the attack. Memories of his bodily distress replayed, and the ebb and flow of his consciousness during the confrontation returned to him, as did the struggle afterward to get away. He felt himself collapsing to the ground and waited for what came next. Pain and weakness prevailed, his mind a diminishing speck of light in the blackness of encroaching death. He faded to a point where it seemed impossible that he would continue to live for even a single moment more.

And then confronted by the threat of eternal night, a sound, a hum, somewhere along the limits of discernment. Perhaps an artifact of memory, an aural impression from the past. Spock pursued it, grappled with it in an attempt to bring it into even the barest focus.

Corthin, he thought, hearing his comrade's voice uttering a lone unintelligible syllable somewhere in the emptiness. But then even that paled, vanishing into the void. Spock floundered, the recollections of his unconscious mind not merely unapproachable but invisible, hidden in some recess of his brain that he could not access. He felt frail and unfocused.

"Spock."

He whirled in the barren landscape of his being, hunt-

ing for the remembrance, grasping for it without knowing
its source. Only then did he realize that the voice had come
to him not from within, but from without.

"Spock," the voice repeated.

He opened his eyes, emerging from his mental shadows and, at last, into light. Corthin crouched beside him,
her position telling him that the bedroll upon which he
lay rested on the ground. Past her shoulder, he could see a
panel suspended from the stone ceiling, providing the small
cave with dim illumination. A black curtain hung across
the room's one small opening.

"Spock, can you hear me?" she asked gently.

It required a moment for him to find his voice. "Yes," he
said, the word coming out in a dry whisper.

Corthin nodded, apparently satisfied. A native of Romulus, she had joined the Reunification Movement three years
earlier. A schoolteacher by trade, she had dedicated herself
to the idea that the Romulan and Vulcan people should seek
understanding, cohesion, and ultimately, integration. She
had demonstrated her commitment to those ideals time and
again, becoming a trusted right hand for Spock and, of late,
offering flashes of her own leadership abilities.

"Do you need some water?" she asked. She wore con-
servative Romulan clothing, including black slacks and a
long-sleeved ultramarine blouse.

Spock nodded, and Corthin reached to her side for a
covered cup. She held a dispensing tip to his lips and he
drank. The cool liquid felt strangely foreign in his mouth
and throat, but also instantly refreshing.

After setting the cup aside, Corthin said, "You were
attacked."

"Yes, I remember," Spock told her, his voice no longer rasping.

"When you didn't return by the time expected, we sent people out to search the tunnels for you." She looked down for a moment, clearly battling her emotions. "I found you. You'd lost a great deal of blood. I placed you in a stasis field and—"

"Stasis," Spock said, concerned about the usage of such a device, which consumed a considerable amount of power. Though minerals in the rock strata beneath Ki Baratan could and often did interfere with sensors, they did not provide comprehensive cover, particularly for communications signals and higher-powered equipment. In recent years, first under Praetor Hiren, and later under Shinzon and Tal'Aura, Romulan Security forces had ventured beneath the capital city to locate and apprehend members of the Reunification Movement. Over time, more than a half dozen had been taken into custody; of those, at least three had been executed, though none since Tal'Aura had taken control of the government. As a precaution, Spock and his compatriots had abandoned even carrying devices that could compromise their freedom, though they still maintained caches of equipment for use in exigent circumstances.

"Yes, stasis," Corthin said. "You were in critical condition. With your injuries, I couldn't risk moving you, and I didn't know how long it would take for Shalvan to reach us." A skilled Romulan physician, Shalvan had joined the Movement more than a decade ago, not long after Spock had first come to Romulus.

Spock did not argue the point with Corthin. With no

hint of ego, he understood his importance to the cause of reunification. "How long since the attack?"

"Two days," Corthin said. "The knife punctured your heart. Shalvan had to operate."

Two sets of footsteps sounded behind Corthin, and Spock watched her glance up over her shoulder. Above her appeared the doctor himself, the dark circles below his eyes combining with his gray hair to make him appear even older than his advanced years. D'Tan took up a position beside him, the young man's stone-faced countenance not completely masking his concern for Spock.

"How are you feeling?" Shalvan asked. The doctor squatted down and reached for Spock's wrist, presumably to assess his pulse. The physical contact occurred coldly, Shalvan's mental barriers obviously in place.

"I am fatigued, and my muscles are not entirely flexible," Spock said, "but I am pleased to be alive."

"As you should be," Shalvan said. "You would not have lived much longer had Corthin not found you when she did."

Spock acknowledged Corthin's deed with a slight bow of his head in her direction. Then he began to push himself up in preparation to stand. Corthin and Shalvan both moved to stop him.

"The surgery went well, Spock," Shalvan said, "but you are not sufficiently recovered to walk."

"That may be," Spock allowed, "but since powered equipment was employed in my recovery, we must relocate in order to ensure that we avoid detection."

"We've already moved twice," Corthin said. "Once

prior to your surgery, and once afterward. We're under the far northwest corner of the city now."

"I see," Spock said. Satisfied, he allowed Shalvan to help him lower himself down. As he lay back, he realized that the simple act of trying to prop himself up had exhausted him. "What is my prognosis?"

"You'll make a complete recovery," Shalvan said, touching the flat of his hand to Spock's forehead. "But your body has undergone serious trauma, first from the wounds and then from invasive surgery. You will require at least another five to seven days of bed rest."

Spock received the news with equanimity. In his younger days, he might have been inclined to push himself to best the doctor's forecast, but Spock acknowledged the limitations of his age. Though still strong, his body did not convalesce as swiftly as it once had.

With a promise to have a meal delivered to Spock and to check on him again shortly, Shalvan exited the cave. Once he had, Spock looked to Corthin. "I was attacked by a Reman," he told her.

"We know," Corthin said, peering over at D'Tan.

"I discovered the assassin," the young man said, his final word laced with contempt. For all his efforts on behalf of reunification and his staunch preference for the Vulcan way of life, he had not yet learned how to fully govern his Romulan passions. "I should have left him to die."

"Then he is alive," Spock said, seeking confirmation from Corthin. For the moment, he chose not to address D'Tan's aggressive attitude. As tired as he felt, he had trouble enough concentrating on one train of thought.

"Yes," she said. "He suffered a fractured skull and an epidural hematoma, but Shalvan operated on him. He has already largely recovered."

"You're holding him, then?" Spock asked.

"Under constant and redundant guard," D'Tan offered. "He won't be going anywhere."

"We're keeping him away from our present location," Corthin said. "We searched him for comm and tracking devices. We didn't find any, but if he's not acting alone, his accomplices could come looking for him."

"Has he told you why he attempted to kill me?" Spock asked.

"The cur refuses to speak," D'Tan said. "He will not even provide his name, much less whether or not he is doing the bidding of others."

"In the interest of your safety," Corthin said, looking at Spock, "I think we must assume that the assassin has allies or employers. If that is not correct, then the danger to you has ended by virtue of your thwarting the attempt on your life and our subsequent capture of the assassin. If it is, then you are clearly still at risk."

"I have been at risk since joining the cause of reunification," Spock said. "The Romulans have taken me into custody on more than one occasion, and have even threatened my execution."

"Are you suggesting that Tal'Aura's government is behind this?" Corthin asked, her tone doubtful.

Spock closed his eyes for a few seconds, fighting his fatigue. "No," he finally said, looking up again at Corthin. "Considering the tumultuous relationship between the Romulans and the Remans, an affiliation between the two seems unlikely." Since Shinzon's death more than a year ago, the Remans had continued their revolt against their Romulan enslavers, eventually accepting the status of Klingon protectorate, settling first on the continent of Ehrie'fvil on Romulus, and then on their own world of Klorgat IV. "But the simple fact of enmity between the Romulans and the Remans does not mean that the two do not share political imperatives."

Corthin tilted her head to one side, her brow furrowing. "I understand why many of my people oppose the reunification of Romulus and Vulcan," she said, "but why would the Remans oppose it? Why would they care at all?"

"Because," D'Tan said slowly, realization evidently dawning on him, "the reunification of the Vulcans and Romulans would probably entail the reintegration of the Romulan Star Empire and the Imperial Romulan State."

"And a reinvigorated Romulan Empire might not be in the best interests of the Remans," Corthin concluded. "But did this assassin take action on his own, or as part of an organized Reman plot?"

"I do not know," Spock said, "but I believe it is essential that we find out."

"We will," D'Tan said. "*I* will." He darted from the room, his sense of purpose plain.

Spock watched him go. "D'Tan claims devotion to the Vulcan way of life, and yet he sometimes displays a regrettable lack of emotional restraint."

"He is still young," Corthin said.

"Indeed," Spock agreed. "Too young, I think, to interrogate the Reman." When Corthin nodded hesitantly, Spock said, "Violence would not serve our purpose."

"No, of course not," Corthin said. "I will supervise the process. I'll enlist the aid of Dorlok and Venaster."

Both men, Spock knew, had served in the Romulan military and possessed some experience in such matters. He gave his approval, then told Corthin that he needed to rest.

"Of course," she said. "As you are able, I'll keep you informed of our progress."

"Very good," Spock said. He watched Corthin depart— she darkened the lighting panel on her way—before allowing his eyes to slip closed once more. He pondered again, as he had for the past couple of months, just how the Romulan schism would impact the Movement. Thus far, he and his comrades had modified little in their word-of-mouth efforts to draw more people to their cause. As sleep pulled him down into its pliant folds, Spock thought that maybe the time had come for a different kind of action.

5

"We need you, Ben."

From across the room, Sisko looked over at the admiral, who had turned back on his way out the door, apparently to tender one last entreaty. "I understand," Sisko said, more to head off further conversation than for any other reason, but in truth, he did understand. At the Azure Nebula, the crews of *Enterprise*, *Titan*, and *Aventine* had defeated the Borg—had defeated not just some number of cubes, but the entire Collective, and if he could believe the reports, not only for the near term, but permanently. Victory, though, had not come soon enough either to save the sixty-three billion killed during the invasion or to prevent the destruction of more than forty percent of Starfleet. Admiral Walter didn't have to build a case that Sisko should remain on active duty; the terrible devastation rendered the need for experienced officers self-evident.

But I don't know if I want to be needed, Sisko thought. *Again.* To Walter, though, he said, "I'll consider it . . . discuss it with my wife."

The admiral continued to stand silently in the doorway, his gaze measuring. His waist had spread some and his hair had gone white in the nearly three decades since Sisko had first met him. The irregular scar crawling from his right eyebrow and up his forehead hadn't changed from those days, though; even dermal regenerators had been unable to restore George Walter's flesh to its natural state. The jagged streak of pale skin acted as a disquieting reminder to Sisko that the two had served during the last Federation-Tzenkethi war. Sisko had witnessed the infliction of the wound that had caused the disfigurement, an image that for months afterward had returned to him in nightmares.

For an awkward moment, he thought that the admiral might step back into the room and renew his appeal. Sisko had agreed to reactivation in Starfleet solely for the duration of the Borg crisis; once the peril had passed, he'd intended to doff his uniform and return home to Bajor. Perhaps Walter believed that his willingness to leave his civilian life in Kendra Province for a starship assignment *once* meant that he could be convinced to do so again. The admiral himself had recruited him for the battle against the Borg, traveling all the way to Bajor to make his pitch in person.

Maybe he feels he has to say more because he doesn't think that I'll really consider his offer, Sisko thought. *Or maybe he doesn't trust that I'll talk with Kasidy about it.* The admiral had met Kasidy when he'd visited their home, and had likely sensed the tension between the couple.

Sisko didn't know what else to say, and he had no desire to hear more than he already had. Fortunately, Admiral Walter chose to offer nothing more. The single-paneled door slid closed behind him with a whisper.

Sisko exhaled heavily, unaware until that moment that he'd been holding his breath. He turned away from the door and gazed through the large picture windows set into the two outer walls of the room. The spectacular views visible in both directions attested to the fact that he'd been assigned VIP quarters at the base.

Crossing the large living section, Sisko peered out across the beautiful violet waters of Alonis. Starbase 197 did not just sit at the western edge of the main landmass on the planet, but slipped away from it and into the surf; half of the facility had been constructed on dry ground, and half beneath the waves. An aquatic species, the Alonis had evolved enough technologically to provide for their cultural desire to explore. They had first fashioned rebreathing suits and land-based methods of transport to allow them to travel the ten percent of their world not submerged beneath the oceans. Not satisfied to stop there, they had continued striving, until in time they'd discovered the means of thwarting the gravitational pull of their world, ultimately developing faster-than-light drive and making contact with other species.

And more than eleven thousand of them died yesterday for no good reason, Sisko thought. The death toll could have been far greater, he knew, but that would afford little salve to those who had lost friends, neighbors, colleagues, and loved ones. Though grateful that their society and the Federation would go on, the Alonis mourned the tragedy that had befallen so many, on their world and beyond.

Trying to clear his head, Sisko stood quietly staring out across the water for several minutes, until the sun dipped below the horizon, the great orb linking up with the yellow-orange column of light it cast across the surface of the purple sea. The mix of colors dazzled, and he thought about how much Kasidy would appreciate the view. A pang of guilt overcame him, and he knew that he had to compose a message to his wife. Kasidy deserved more than the simple note he'd already sent her, the few words he'd recorded and transmitted to let her know that he hadn't been killed or seriously injured during the combat with the Borg.

It had been almost a full day since Sisko and the surviving crew of *New York* had abandoned the starship to the first repair teams. While an Alonis tug towed the vessel to the nearest dock—one of several orbiting structures that had endured the Borg attack—all of *New York*'s personnel transported down to the planet surface, to Starbase 197. Once Sisko reached the quarters allocated to him, he sent quick word to Kasidy of his survival and general good health. He then lay down, wanting merely to rest for a few minutes, judging that the adrenaline still coursing through his body wouldn't allow him to sleep. He'd woken up twelve hours later.

After replenishing himself with a sizable breakfast, the captain had been called into one meeting after another. Starfleet Command debriefed him, asking for details of the battle against the Borg waged by *New York*, *James T. Kirk*, and *Cutlass*. Sisko also wrote and filed accounts of the confrontation, checked in with the base's infirmary, and updated crew casualty lists. When he could, he read some of the reports coming out of the Azure Nebula, essentially seeking confirmation of something he found difficult to credit, namely that the Collective had been vanquished for good.

With the sun halfway out of sight, Sisko glanced out the great window to his left and saw lights starting to come on across the skyline of Lingasha, the largest nonmarine city on Alonis. Pulling himself away from both vistas, he walked over to an inner wall, sat down at a sleek, modern desk, and touched a control pad to bring up the lighting in his own quarters. Facing the companel on the desk, he said, "Computer, record a message to Kasidy Yates, Kendra Province, Bajor." Accompanied by a quick sequence of electronic tones, the symbol of the United Federation of Planets winked off from the display, replaced by the word RECORDING.

"Kasidy," Sisko began, but then he immediately found himself at a loss for how to continue. "Kas," he tried again, "I wanted to tell you . . ."

What? Sisko thought. He didn't really *want* to tell his wife what he knew he must, and he certainly couldn't do so via subspace. For the moment, he would simply have to give her more than he already had, for despite Kasidy knowing that he had made it safely through his mission, she would remain concerned about him. Despite her opposition to his returning to Starfleet, even for a short time, and regardless of whatever else had transpired between them of late, he knew that she still loved and missed him. And though he also knew that in the end it would come to nothing, he loved and missed her too.

He could not even think about his four-year-old daughter, Rebecca. Or his son and daughter-in-law.

"Computer," he said, "cancel recording." As the UFP standard reappeared on the readout, Sisko decided to take on another uncomfortable task, one that he'd specifically requested from Starfleet Command. "Computer, record a message to Lieutenant Prynn Tenmei at Deep Space Nine." After the companel indicated its readiness, he proceeded.

"Lieutenant, this is Captain Sisko. I don't know if you're aware, but I accepted reactivation to Starfleet within the last month in order to help fight the Borg threat. I was part of a task force detailed to protect the Alonis. Your father's ship was also one of those assigned." He found himself unable to keep from hesitating and looking down for a moment, though he knew such cues would telegraph his intention to deliver bad news. "The *James T. Kirk* bore a great deal of battle damage. I'm sorry, but your father was critically wounded. He suffered a traumatic head injury. His body is alive, but . . ." Again, Sisko looked away from the monitor, sad not just for Tenmei's loss but for his own. ". . . but the doctors report no brain activity."

Sisko paused again, this time to gather himself before he went on. "Lieutenant . . . Prynn . . . I want you to know that Captain Vaughn fought heroically. I know that may sound trite, but it's true. His last act was a brave, desperate attempt to save the people of Alonis without sacrificing the lives of his crew. Though it may not mean anything to you right now, I intend to nominate your father for the Medal of Honor."

Searching for more to say, Sisko placed his palms flat on the desk and leaned forward slightly, as though he could push himself physically and emotionally closer to Tenmei. "I can't say that I knew Elias particularly well, but I felt extremely close to him. I considered him a friend—a *good* friend—and I feel his loss deeply. I know that you and he had a stormy relationship at times, but he was so happy that the two of you finally left all that in the past. He loved you very much." The words felt inadequate, but he still believed them necessary.

"Starfleet Command and the medical staff here at Starbase One-nine-seven will be in touch," Sisko concluded. "If there is anything I can do for you, Prynn, I'll be happy to help." He reached up to the companel and stopped the recording with a tap to a control surface.

Before transmitting his message to Lieutenant Tenmei, Starfleet required that he inform her commanding officer about what had taken place. He ordered the computer to make another recording. When the companel signaled ready, he said, "Commander, this is Captain Sisko. I'm—"

A small green light flashed in the top right corner of the screen, specifying the receipt of a transmission. Sisko paused his recording, then called up a readout. He saw that the message had been sent by his son, but not from the home Jake shared with his wife, Korena, on Bajor; it had been dispatched from Earth. Sisko touched a control to begin playback of the message.

"Dad, it's Jake," the young man said. Now in his mid-twenties, he'd filled out physically, broadening across his chest and shoulders. He appeared tired, his easy smile absent from his features. *"I tried to reach you before Rena and I left Bajor, but with the Borg trouble, I didn't have any luck. I don't even know how long this will take to reach you."* He gave the date he'd recorded the message, three days earlier. Behind him, Sisko could see only a plain, white wall, unadorned by any decoration that identified Jake's location—a clue in itself. A knot of anxiety formed in Sisko's stomach.

"Dad, Grandpa's sick. Alžbeta found him when she came to the restaurant and it was closed." A local college student, Alžbeta waited tables in exchange for Creole cooking lessons. *"He was upstairs in his apartment, unconscious. He was taken to Orleans Parish Hospital, where he's improved a bit,*

but . . ." Jake paused, making Sisko think of his own message to Prynn Tenmei. *"Aunt Judith and Uncle Samuel are both here, and Uncle Aaron is on his way from Cort,"* Jake went on. *"I know what you're doing is important, Dad, but if you can get here, you should. It's serious."*

Sisko closed his eyes and dropped his head. A vise seemed to tighten around his heart. He barely heard Jake say that he loved him. When he looked up again, the message had ended.

That quickly, Sisko's priorities changed. His father's health had fluctuated often through the years, and so Jake's message had not been entirely surprising—but it still hurt. Sisko would arrange travel to Earth at once, and send a message to let Jake know that he'd be coming. And because he would not be returning to Bajor right away, he could no longer put off contacting Kasidy.

Sisko pushed back from the desk, intending first to find Admiral Walter, hoping that the senior officer would both hasten Sisko's detachment from Starfleet and find him swift passage to Earth. As Sisko paced toward the door, he peered out the back window again, out over the waters of Alonis. The sun had set completely, he saw, the arriving night turning the picturesque purple ocean to black.

6

Gell Kamemor walked into the stronghold's library with a demeanor that she hoped members of her clan would consider dignified. Called on to preside over the small gathering, she wished to project a decorous bearing, but she also meant her deliberate stride to cover the slight limp she'd acquired two days earlier. Though nobody found fault with a woman nearly a century and a quarter old keeping fit, some would have thought it unseemly for her to engage in a sport as physical as *voraant*.

Kamemor stepped up to the head of the large, elegant conference table and waited for the members of her extended family, the Ortikant, to take their seats. Many of the seventeen invited today had already taken their places, but several others stood huddled in small groups about the room, talking in hushed voices that seemed perfectly appropriate to their surroundings.

Kamemor didn't much care for Stronghold Ortikant, but she appreciated the old-fashioned library. Hardbound volumes lined the long side walls from floor to ceiling, the antique pages filling the room with the pulpy aroma of aged paper. Opposite the tall, ornamented doors through which Kamemor had just passed, a huge stone fireplace embellished the far wall. Flames crackled in the hearth, providing the room with heat, a necessity on this chill evening.

Other than the discreet placement of portable lighting panels throughout the edifice, the stronghold had not been modernized in recent times. One of the oldest extant structures on Romulus, it stood atop the highest elevation in Rateg, overlooking the city with what Kamemor had always considered regal malevolence. In ancient times, her forebears had ruled the surrounding territory with despotic force. The great, gray-walled fortress, cold and unapproachable, had functioned as more than a symbol for the tyranny of the Ortikant clan; its curtain walls and battlements had helped keep the ruling family secure and in power.

After the last of those present took their place at the table, Kamemor did so as well, seating herself in the oversized, throne-like chair reserved for the clan elder. She had not particularly welcomed the designation as her family's matriarch, but when it had come, just prior to her last birthday, she'd understood and accepted the responsibility. Though hardly the oldest member of her lineage, she had been deemed by a plurality of her clan as the worthiest successor to her great-grandfather, Gorelt, after his death.

"Jolan tru," Kamemor said, offering the conventional Romulan salutation. She folded her hands together on the dark hardwood of the tabletop, bowed her head, then recited the words passed down through the generations of her family. *"Ihir ul hfihar rel ch'Rihan. Ihir ul Ortikant. Ihir dren v'talla'tor, plek Rihannsu r'talla'tor."* We are the noble clan of Romulus. We are the Ortikant. We meet to live, so that Romulans will live. Kamemor delivered the shibboleth with ease, by virtue of having heard it uttered so often by Gorelt,

but she did not relish doing so. While more proud than not of her family and its heritage, she did not judge them better than any other Romulan clan, whether one of the Hundred or not. Such chauvinism served no one and, in her experience, often fomented the next level of bias: blind nationalism.

Kamemor opened her eyes and looked up to see every gaze in the library focused upon her. "As you know, we have assembled here tonight at the behest of Praetor Tal'Aura," she began. "Five days ago, the praetor requested, via Proconsul Tomalak, that the Hundred replenish the Senate. Since then, debate within and among the clans has been extensive. We are meeting to determine how the Ortikant will proceed, either by choosing our senator or by refusing to so choose. Because of who we are, our decision will unquestionably help define the course of the Romulan government." Kamemor did not have to explain to anybody present the preeminent position of the Ortikant, not only as one of the Hundred, but as one of the wealthiest and most powerful clans within that group. From its earliest days, her family had forged a long record of successfully reaching beyond its sphere of influence and thereby expanding that influence, first across Romulus, then throughout the planets of the Empire, and ultimately well beyond the borders of Romulan space. Over the last three centuries, the Ortikant had dealt with the Gorn, the Tholians, the Ferengi, the Tzenkethi, the Federation, and even, from time to time, the Klingons.

"I invite your thoughts," she finished.

Midway down the table on the left, Anlikar Ventel spoke up. Kamemor had no closer blood relation at the gathering than Ventel, the grandson of her sister. Though he was several decades younger than she, his deeply lined face and gray, unkempt hair imparted to him a much older appearance. "It seems well past time to restore our government to something more functional than a dictatorship," he said. "Does it not?"

"More functional?" asked Minar T'Nora, a short, elegant woman with a completely denuded scalp. She sat toward the far end of the table, across from Ventel. "I'd argue that Tal'Aura has the Hall of State functioning exceedingly well. You cannot legislate and rule more efficiently than with a bureaucracy of one."

"Efficient, perhaps," Ventel replied, "but also dangerous. Tal'Aura is not omniscient. If she should err, if she should take Romulus down the wrong path, what then, with no strong countervailing force to correct her mistake or to hold her in check?"

"Neither is Tal'Aura immortal," offered Ren Callonen, a contemporary of Kamemor's sitting directly to her right. Kamemor barely knew her. "What if she should meet her own demise? Who would replace her? Are any of us sanguine about the prospect of Praetor Tomalak?"

General grumbles rose around the table, speaking to the distaste many held for the proconsul. The discussion spontaneously broke down into little knots of comment and conversation among all assembled. For the moment, Kamemor remained quiet, wanting the debate to unfold without her sway. She had never met Tomalak, but since his assumption of the position of proconsul, she had educated herself on his personal history. As a longtime member of the Romulan Imperial Fleet, he had risen to positions of military authority not quickly, but with a steady progress throughout his career. Kamemor had concluded from his record that he possessed a middling intellect but had succeeded to the extent that he had as a result of cautious planning and a talent for subterfuge. While she did not believe that military service necessarily implied a lack of fitness to hold the highest office of government—Sorilk, her son, had spent more than a decade in the Imperial Fleet—Kamemor mistrusted belligerence, a trait too often present in the martial class, and almost certainly a major component of Tomalak's personality.

As voices quieted, T'Nora brought the conversation back to the matter at hand. "If the Hundred are to rebuild the Senate, would we not then be placing members of our families in immediate danger?" she asked. "Rumors abound that then-Senator Tal'Aura supported Shinzon and his Reman accessories, and that she even might have abetted the assassinations of Praetor Hiren and almost all of her own colleagues. If true, then what's to prevent her from taking the same action against a new Senate? What good will it do our government or our people to experience another such tragedy?"

From the very far end of the table, on the left, a quiet male voice said, "Are we to base the form of our government on rumor?"

The youngest clan member at the gathering, perhaps a third of Kamemor's age, Xarian Dor impressed. Immaculately dressed in a dark suit, handsome, with sharp features and black, penetrating eyes, he projected confidence. His reputation as a keen negotiator and quick thinker preceded him, with word of his trade successes percolating throughout the family. Most recently, he had secured favorable terms with a Ferengi art merchant, and had also obtained a lucrative deal with the notoriously obdurate Ivvitrians. Prior to the assassination of Praetor Hiren and the Senate, Kamemor had worked with Dor on a soil-reclamation project in Venat'atrix Territory. She'd found him bright and hardworking, though she knew that he did have detractors; they pointed to his youth and inexperience, along with a reticence to share information and an occasional inflexibility.

"Dor is right," Ventel said. "There is no proof of Tal'Aura's collusion with Shinzon."

"No," agreed Roval D'Jaril from beside T'Nora. "But she did kill Admiral Braeg."

"Braeg took his own life after committing treason," Callonen said.

"After being imprisoned for the crime, and then found guilty of it, by Tal'Aura," T'Nora said. "But there is a vast difference between sedition and dissent. He died because he opposed Tal'Aura."

Nobody disagreed. A heavy stillness settled, and everybody seemed to take a breath. Into the quiet, Xarian Dor said, "Is it not always important to fight tyranny, no matter the risk?"

"But is there even a risk?" Ventel said. "Whether or not Tal'Aura aided Shinzon, suspicion has fallen upon her, so would she really chance murdering new senators?"

Ren Callonen nodded in agreement. "And it was Tal'Aura herself who asked the Hundred to renew the Senate. Why would she do that if not to strengthen her government?"

"Perhaps to demonstrate the *appearance* of being a

thoughtful leader," T'Nora suggested, "in order to elicit support from the people."

"She already has enough support," D'Jaril said. "Since Braeg's death, there have been few incidents of civil unrest."

"People aren't supportive," Ventel said. "They're scared. And hungry."

"It comes to the same thing," D'Jaril said. "Whether the people are supportive of her praetorship or resigned to it, Tal'Aura maintains a strong position. Right now, she controls the whole of the Romulan Star Empire."

"*Half* the Empire," noted Dor.

Again, nobody disagreed. Peering around the table, Kamemor saw spirits flagging. Not wanting to lose the point to which the debate had flowed, she opted to continue it along. "In the assembly of the Hundred the other day," she said, "Proconsul Tomalak avowed that Praetor Tal'Aura supported one Empire, undivided."

"With her as its leader, no doubt," Callonen scoffed.

"No doubt," Kamemor agreed. "But is there anybody here tonight who does not champion unifying the Romulan people?" Not a single voice rose in opposition. "We must then work toward that goal. Whatever Praetor Tal'Aura's reasons for calling for the renewal of the Senate, whatever the scope of her power, if we refuse to rejoin the government, then we are abdicating our responsibilities— to our family, to our people, to the Empire itself. Of practical importance, if we do not accept the authority being *offered* to us now, we will likely have to *fight* for it later. It is therefore my opinion that we must accept the course of action set us by Praetor Tal'Aura. I believe that we must name a representative to the Senate."

Kamemor waited for argument and received none. "Do we require more debate?" she asked. "T'Nora?"

T'Nora spoke as though chastised. "No," she said. "The Empire must be made whole."

"Very well," Kamemor said, pleased. "Then we must select a senator." The people attending the gathering had been chosen by family elders—Kamemor included—not just to deliberate the matter of the praetor's call to action, but if necessary, to name a senator from their midst.

Anlikar Ventel stood from his chair. His fingertips brushing the top of the table, he said, "Elder Kamemor, I submit that you would serve as a worthy representative of the Ortikant."

Surprised by the suggestion, Kamemor felt her eyes widen. "I am honored by your confidence in me," she told Ventel, "but I did not mean to imply that I sought the position."

"Nor *did* you imply it," Ventel said, still standing. "But you are eminently qualified. I do not need to recapitulate your own record for you, but I wish to ensure that everybody here knows how well you have served the Romulan people. You have been a professor of higher education, an ambassador, a military liaison, a city administrator, and a territorial governor. You have a reputation for loyalty to the Romulan people, but not unreasoned loyalty. You are also known for your open and straightforward approach to politics." Apparently finished, Ventel took his seat again.

Kamemor almost didn't know how to respond. Though a public official for most of her adulthood, she had not even considered assuming the role of senator. Rarely in any meeting had she felt so stunned. "Again, I am honored by your approbation," she managed to say. "But while it is true that I have spent a great deal of my professional life in the arena of public affairs and politics, I am now essentially retired."

"Leaving you free to serve the Empire in any capacity whatsoever," Ventel replied, evidently undeterred.

Kamemor shook her head from side to side. Peering down both sides of the table, she saw at least a few other faces radiating approval of Ventel's proposition. *How could I not have foreseen this?* she wondered. Had the family elders maneuvered her into the matriarchal role specifically so that she would be placed in this position?

Why not? she thought. Ventel had not exaggerated her qualifications, nor had he been wrong to point out that no other responsibilities stood between her and a seat in the Senate—and not just because of her retirement. She had lost her wife, Ravent, a decade ago to Tuvan Syndrome—well, Ravent had died a decade ago, but Kamemor had lost her to the ravages of the neurological disease years before that. And their son had been gone for half a century, Sorilk surviving his tour of duty in the Imperial Fleet, only to perish in an industrial accident at a chemical plant back on Romulus.

Kamemor looked back over at Ventel. "If called upon to serve, I will not refuse," she said. "But surely there must be other candidates to consider . . . somebody not already removed from public life, somebody younger, somebody with political ambitions . . ." She let her voice trail off to silence, hoping that she had not unduly emphasized the middle criterion; Kamemor knew her own preference for the family's next senator, but wanted the selection to come free of her matriarchal influence.

"You will permit your candidacy, then?" Ventel said.

"Yes," Kamemor said, but then quickly asked, "Have we other nominations?"

Curiously and without explanation, Lisker Pentrak, who'd said almost nothing during the gathering, put forth the name of Minar T'Nora. Kamemor knew little about Pentrak, and so could only deduce that he aspired to having all points of view represented in the list of nominees, including fears about a repopulated Senate. Kamemor could not imagine that T'Nora would even agree to serve in such a capacity, considering her distrust of the praetor. Oddly, though, she did not object to Pentrak's nomination.

For her own part, Kamemor held little regard for either Tal'Aura or Donatra, both of whom had contributed to the sundering of the Empire. Further, despite the praetor's stated desire for a unified Romulan state, she doubted that Tal'Aura would actually work to pursue that goal. Kamemor could only hope that a new Senate would.

Finally, Ren Callonen recommended Xarian Dor. Kamemor kept her emotions in check, not wanting to reveal the satisfaction Dor's nomination brought her. Her concealment lasted only as long as it took for the gathered clan members to make their individual choices, when Kamemor cast her lot for Dor.

7

When Spock entered the dimly lighted cavern for the first time, the prisoner did not even glance up at him. Dressed in a pale blue coverall, the Reman sat on the ground atop a bedroll, his back against the cave wall. His arms encircled his steepled legs, and his forehead rested against his knees. A metal shackle bound each of his wrists, the cuffs attached by monofilaments to opposite rock faces. His breathing did not appear shallow enough to indicate sleep, so Spock watched, silent and motionless, to see if he would stir.

Spock did not reach out with his mind to search for the Reman's consciousness, nor open himself up to receive any empathic impressions. Eight days had passed since the failed assassination, six since Spock had first awoken after surgery, but he still did not feel entirely recovered from his experiences. So he simply waited. Two full minutes passed before the prisoner finally looked up, his expression mixing curiosity and confusion; he'd obviously heard Spock enter, but then had heard him neither leave nor move.

The Reman said nothing.

Spock knew that, though held captive in awkward circumstances, the assassin had been tended with as much care as possible. Though he was restrained, the lengths of monofilament allowed him some freedom of movement within the cavern. The lighting had been kept low to accommodate the general photosensitivity of most Remans. Dr. Shalvan had surgically repaired his head wounds; his soiled, bloodied clothes had been replaced; and he'd been fed regularly. Corthin had overseen his interrogation, which had been conducted by Venaster and Dorlok. Because of its immoral nature and dubious effectiveness, torture had not been employed; rather, a range of techniques had been used for the questioning, though none had yet proven successful. The Reman had said virtually nothing, refusing even to give his name.

Making eye contact with the prisoner, Spock stated his own name, then asked, "Who are you?"

The Reman held Spock's gaze a moment longer, then dropped his forehead back onto his knees. Spock closed his eyes and directed his mind, not to the prisoner, but back to the assassination attempt, to the moment he had let down his mental guard and had connected empathically with his attacker. He searched within his memory of the Reman's emotions for a name. When he found none, he sought any other detail that might be of use.

Opening his eyes, he saw the Reman's position unchanged. "You do not hate me," Spock declared. "You were determined to kill me, but not motivated by some personal enmity." He paused, exploring what he had detected of his attacker's psyche. "Why, then?" he asked. "What actions have I taken for you to believe that I should die?"

Again, the Reman did not look up or say anything, or give any indication at all that he had even heard the questions. Trusting that he could not improve upon the efforts of his compatriots to extract information from the assassin, Spock knew that he could add but one distinction to his interaction with the man who had tried to kill him. As both the leader of the Reunification Movement and the intended target, he told his would-be murderer what he would do with him if he did not cooperate.

And still the Reman said nothing.

Spock turned and left, intending to follow through with his threat.

"You want to do what?" D'Tan asked sharply, apparently incredulous, accurately reflecting Corthin's own reaction.

"I wish to turn the Reman over to the Romulan authorities," Spock repeated. He stood at one end of the cavern, addressing several leading members of the Reunification cell that worked out of Ki Baratan. While Corthin listened quietly along with Dr. Shalvan, Dorlok, and Venaster, D'Tan voiced his objection.

"That makes no sense," he told Spock with unrestrained indignance. He raised his hands into the air, palms up, clearly a gesture of his frustration.

"On the contrary," Spock said evenly, "informing the Romulan authorities of the crime and remanding the perpetrator to them makes complete sense."

As Corthin attempted to understand why that might be so, she paced slowly toward Spock and D'Tan. The flat soles of her shoes crunched along the ground. "I understand the practicality of what you propose," she said. "We're obviously not going to kill the Reman, and we are not set up to keep him as a prisoner." Since finding the assassin, they'd had to improvise his detention, which had necessarily claimed some of their already limited resources, including their time. In addition to providing the Reman with food, water, clothing, and medical care, they'd had to commit personnel to continuously guarding him.

Corthin stopped beside D'Tan as Spock went on. "Additionally, keeping anybody captive as we have violates Romulan law."

D'Tan barked out a derisive laugh, which Corthin interpreted and translated into words. "That seems a curious position to take," she said, "given that the Romulan government has declared the very existence of our Reunification Movement a violation of the law."

"Granted," Spock said. "But that declaration can be revoked, or another made to supersede it."

"Is that what you hope to accomplish?" Dr. Shalvan asked from the rear of the cave. Corthin stepped aside so that Spock could see him. "Do you seek legitimization of the Movement by offering up the assassin as some sort of conciliation to the Romulan authorities?"

"What if he's working *for* the authorities?" asked D'Tan.

Corthin thought that idea unlikely. "It's difficult to imagine a Reman acting on behalf of the Romulan government," she observed. "A government that kept the Reman people enslaved and confined to unspeakable living conditions for centuries."

"Actually, Tal'Aura's autocracy granted the Remans their freedom," Spock said.

"During an attack on Romulus by the Remans," D'Tan said, "and only after the Federation got involved."

"Nevertheless," Spock said. "But whether or not it seems improbable for the Reman to have acted in concert with the Romulan government, I submit that it is irrelevant."

"Irrelevant?" Venaster asked from beside the doctor. "You're talking about the possibility of handing an assassin over to those employing him."

Spock walked between Corthin and D'Tan to the center of the cave, where everybody gathered around him. "Let us assume for a moment that Tal'Aura did retain the services of the Reman. Returning him to her would not harm us in any material way. We have kept him apart from our operations, so he would be unable to provide any useful information about us. We would free an assassin, but such operatives are easily replaced." Spock paused, then continued his argument. "Regardless of why the Reman attacked me, or for whose purpose he did so, turning him over to the authorities would demonstrate the Movement's fidelity to Romulan law, and it would relieve us of the burden of detaining him."

Logical, Corthin thought. *But incomplete.* In her time with Spock, she had grown accustomed to the thoroughness of his reasoning, as well as the foresight with which he examined possible courses of action. It seemed to her that, in transferring custody of their prisoner to the Romulans, Spock had some objective in mind other than simply obeying the law. "If we do as you suggest, there's no guarantee that the authorities will even believe our story about the Reman," she said. "They might just as likely think we are attempting to plant a terrorist in their midst." She saw D'Tan and Dorlok nod their agreement with her. "You've told us why your proposal is not a bad idea," she said to Spock, "but why is it a good idea? What do you seek to achieve?"

"I wish to open a dialogue with Praetor Tal'Aura."

Corthin expected a surprised reaction from the others, perhaps even another outburst from D'Tan, but everybody remained silent for a moment. Spock's assertion did not shock Corthin because she had lately sensed his dissatisfaction with the progress of the Movement. Since the attack on him, he had spoken to her several times about augmenting their methods; establishing communication with the praetor would clearly mark such a new direction.

"Why would you want to speak with Tal'Aura?" Dr. Shalvan finally asked. "She has continued Hiren's program of hunting our people down. Under her regime, Vorakel and T'Solon were captured."

"Captured, but not executed," Spock said. "They remain imprisoned, awaiting trial. And the sweeps for our people have become less frequent under this praetor. If I am able to speak with her, I will attempt to negotiate for their release."

"Does that seem reasonable?" D'Tan asked, his voice more measured than it had been earlier. Corthin could see that Spock's proposal concerned him deeply.

"It may prove more reasonable than you think," Spock said. He folded his hands before him and slowly made his way back to the front of the cave, Corthin and D'Tan parting to allow him past them. "As I said, the sweeps for Reunification sympathizers have occurred less frequently during the past few months, which may indicate a softening of the praetor's stance. Indeed, considering the current state of affairs, the praetor may even be persuaded to completely reverse her position."

"Tal'Aura suspiciously survived the murders of Hiren and most of the Senate, then later seized power, and now rules essentially as a dictator," Shalvan said. "She does not seem the type open to persuasion."

Corthin agreed with the doctor, but Spock had mentioned the "current state of affairs," and she thought she understood why. "The divided empires," she said. "For the eventual reunification of Romulans and Vulcans to take place, the Empire itself must unite."

"Precisely," Spock said, turning back to face everybody. "Although the praetor may not support our ultimate goal, she certainly must support uniting all Romulans."

"And we now have more adherents to our cause than we have ever had before," Corthin reasoned along with Spock. "If Tal'Aura allows us to bring the Movement out of the shadows, it could help her focus public opinion on restoring a unified Empire."

"Yes," Spock said.

"I don't know," said the doctor. "I'm not convinced that we can trust Tal'Aura."

"Nor have I suggested that we should," Spock said. "But if for even a short while our aims coincide, it stands to reason that both parties can benefit."

"Do you suppose that is why you were attacked?" D'Tan asked. "The Remans have only recently gained their freedom, at least in part thanks to the Romulan schism. A united Empire does not stand to be in their best interests. Could the attempt on your life have been a means for the Remans to disrupt our Movement, in order to make it less likely that we would aid Tal'Aura?"

"Possibly, but again, it is irrelevant to how we proceed,"

Spock said. "Are there continued objections to turning the Reman over to the authorities, and to my opening talks with the praetor?" Corthin watched as Spock looked in turn to each of those present. Only D'Tan spoke up.

"I don't think it's a good idea," he said simply.

"Noted," Spock said. He waited for any other response but received none. "Very well," he said.

Corthin understood that Spock regarded the silence of the others as tacit approval of his plan, and that he would look to obtain a similar endorsement from the rest of the Movement's leadership. She wondered, though, if Spock considered such consent irrelevant as well. Although he often sought the opinions and advice of others, he also sometimes exhibited a calculated single-mindedness, choosing his own counsel over that of the aggregate.

Corthin agreed with the logic Spock had just voiced, but she still held grave reservations about what he had proposed. She'd said nothing because it would not matter. Before long, she knew, Spock would make his argument to Tal'Aura. Corthin could only hope that the praetor would not have him hauled away in irons.

Or executed.

8

Sisko walked out of the Uptown public transporter facility into the crisp New Orleans evening. Though darkness had not yet descended, the sun had already set, allowing the modest afternoon warmth to begin bleeding off. With the end of winter still several weeks away in North America, Sisko had known what sort of weather to expect. He moved off to the side of the large marble terrace that fronted the transporter terminal, set down his duffel, and pulled on his lightweight brown jacket over his civilian clothes.

Before moving on, Sisko took a moment to peer down the wide stairway that led to St. Charles Avenue. The antique-style streetlamps that marched along below the elevated maglev rail had already come on in the gloaming. The great, twisting forms of southern live oaks lined the boulevard, with an occasional southern magnolia interspersed among them.

Sisko breathed in deeply, and though the magnolias would not bloom until springtime, their citrusy scent returned to him in memory. During the summer months, he knew, the sultry air would hang heavily throughout the Crescent City, laden with the aromas of both flora and food. Sisko had spent so much time in New Orleans during his life that he imagined he could detect the savory smells of the Cajun and Creole dishes he had grown up eating, and that he relished still: gumbos and jambalayas, étouffées and brochettes, bisques and rémoulades.

The scents of home, he thought.

The idea brought him up short.

Discomfited, Sisko tried to put the notion out of his mind. He grabbed up his duffel and headed down the steps. At street level, he turned left, in the direction of the fading sunlight and Audubon Park. As he fell in among the people strolling along the avenue, though, the feeling of "coming home" welled up within him once more.

That's not a bad thing, he told himself. More than likely, what he felt stemmed from his father's unexpected return to health. Five days earlier, when Sisko had departed Starbase 197 after receiving Jake's message, he hadn't known if he would ever see his father alive again. Sisko replied to his son, letting him know that he would get to Earth as quickly as he could, but with so many Starfleet vessels lost to the Borg and so many private ships pressed into humanitarian service, he ended up having to make his journey piecemeal. Less than twenty-six hours ago, while aboard *U.S.S. Vel'Sor,* the third of four different starships he took on his trip, he heard from Jake again. With Sisko so much closer to Earth, they spoke with each other in real time.

On the companel in Sisko's small cabin aboard *Vel'Sor,* Jake had looked exhausted, but his smile had returned. Although the doctors concluded that they could do little for Joseph Sisko other than to make him more comfortable, the old man actually rallied—enough, at least, that the medical staff agreed to release him from the hospital. When Jake contacted *Vel'Sor,* he did so from the apartment above the elder Sisko's restaurant.

And since Dad's still here, Sisko thought, *no wonder this place feels like home.*

He crossed Soniat Street and glanced at the expansive grounds to his left, and at the Beaux Arts mansion that had graced the site since its construction in the early nineteen hundreds. Sisko had always loved the look of the beautiful old building, with its wide, columned porch on the first floor, the ornate railing enclosing the upstairs porch, the detailed brackets beneath the eaves, the paired dormers rising from the red-tiled roof. The venerable structure had somehow survived the numerous natural and man-made disasters that had struck the Gulf Coast through the centuries. Originally erected as a private residence, it later served as a public library for more than a hundred years, until falling into disuse during the dark days of the post-atomic horror. After decades of neglect, local residents eventually restored it to its former glory and converted it into a museum showcasing the works of regional artists. Sisko had reached his twenties before he'd come to appreciate the contents of the building as much as he did the building itself.

As he continued along St. Charles Avenue, he realized that his easy familiarity with New Orleans, combined with the ongoing presence of his father in the city, made the place come alive for him in a way no other had for some time. He had resided in many other locations—San Francisco, Starbase 137, New Berlin, *Livingston* and *Okinawa* and *Saratoga,* Deep Space 9 and Bajor—and he had eventually adopted a sense of belonging in each of them. He'd even accepted his stay with the Bajoran Prophets in the Celestial Temple, for a period of time he could not define but that the outside world had perceived as about eight months.

In the four-plus years since his return from that other-space and other-time, Sisko had lived with Kasidy and Rebecca in Kendra Province, in the house that he had planned, and that Kasidy and Jake had built during his absence. And they had been happy there—at least until recently. But then something happened. He couldn't be precisely sure just when it started, or how, but of late, he had begun tracing it back to the accident.

Eighteen months ago, their friends and neighbors Eivos Calan and his wife, Audj, had died in a house fire. Kasidy took the loss hard, as did Sisko. Something more clicked within Sisko, though, something he couldn't classify at the time, but which affected him very deeply. It went beyond sorrow, beyond loss, something stoking a dread within him that he could neither articulate nor share.

In part, that undefined emotion had driven him to join the archeological teams working at B'hala. The revered Bajoran city had been lost for twenty millennia, until Sisko himself had unearthed it during his command of Deep Space 9. Eivos Calan, at the time a prylar in the Bajoran religious hierarchy, started toiling at the site immediately after its rediscovery. Years later, he even supervised Jake, who, for a few months during Sisko's time in the Celestial Temple, chose to volunteer at the B'hala dig as a means of feeling closer to his father. Sisko supposed that his own decision to enlist in the excavation reflected similar emotions with respect to Calan, with whom he'd grown close.

Although Kasidy had claimed to understand Sisko's

need to help at B'hala, she'd been opposed to it. She pointed to the "unusual brain activity" that led him to the lost city in the first place, and which almost killed him. Quite simply, she said, the city scared her.

Sisko had enrolled with the archeologists anyway. Kasidy seemed to resent him for it, and so before long, he quit. He resented her for that. They agreed to put the incident behind them, but bitterness remained within him, and he could see that it remained within her too—that, and more.

Kasidy had never mentioned the Ohalu text, a very old book of prophecies recovered from the ruins of B'hala. The ancient manuscript—it antedated the city itself—identified their daughter as the "Infant Avatar," whose birth would usher in a new age for Bajor. A year ago, that prophecy contributed directly to the abduction of Rebecca, and nearly to her death. Though Kasidy voiced no accusations, Sisko knew that she blamed him, at least in some measure, for bringing upon them an almost unbearable ordeal, and to the brink of what would have been a crushing loss. If he hadn't found B'hala, they never would have come so close to losing their precious Rebecca.

But those events, and all of the thoughts and feelings they had wrought, failed to completely define the trouble between Kasidy and Sisko. What happened and what they felt contributed to it, exacerbated it, but also masked it. Only very recently had Sisko come to fully recognize the issues at the heart of it all, and the source of his terrible dread.

But maybe now everything will be all right, he thought as he walked along St. Charles Avenue. He'd left Kasidy and

Rebecca only temporarily, to protect the Federation against the Borg; he'd always intended to return to them. But after the unthinkable losses throughout the Federation, after what had taken place aboard *James T. Kirk* . . .

And then he thought of his father, released from the hospital, back at home in his own bed. *Maybe it'll be all right now,* he told himself again. *Maybe I don't have to talk with Kas after all.*

With a start, Sisko realized that he hadn't been paying attention to his surroundings. He stopped and stepped to the side of the pedestrian walkway, then took a moment to orient himself. He saw that he had almost reached Arabella Street, and so after resettling his duffel on his shoulder, he headed up to the next corner and turned left. Not more than a couple of kilometers ahead, he knew, the Mississippi River made its southernmost approach past the city. Much closer than that stood his destination.

In the firmly entrenched dusk, islands of light centered around the lampposts, chasing away shadows from the narrow street. With satisfaction, Sisko saw that little, if anything, had changed in the neighborhood. The news kiosk still occupied the far corner, the movie theater and the playhouse still filled the second block down on the right, and in the middle of the third block on the left, Mr. Roby's bookstore still adjoined Sisko's Creole Kitchen.

A warm feeling enveloped Sisko as he approached the restaurant. It didn't surprise him to see the place mostly dark. Normally, yellow neon illuminated the outsized name *Sisko's* on the sign above the front doors, with blue neon outlining the entire sign. Though his father always strived to keep the restaurant open during regular lunch and dinner hours, he also did not like turning over its operation to anybody else. Until the elder Sisko fully recovered from his infirmity, it seemed likely that his eatery would remain closed.

Lights shined from the downstairs windows, and also from one of the rooms on the second floor. As he heard the clip-clop of a horse drawing a carriage down the street, Sisko reached for the right-hand knob on the double doors. It turned beneath his touch, and he pushed into the restaurant.

Inside, only the lights in the foyer had been left on. The soft yellow glow did not penetrate too deeply into the main room, leaving its far corners shrouded in gloom. Chairs had been placed atop all but one of the tables, as though somebody had wanted to sweep the floor. On that one open table, which seated eight, Sisko saw glasses, dinnerware, napkins, and half-eaten plates of food, as though the meal there had been consumed in haste.

Sisko set down his duffel and moved to the right, to the base of the steps that rose to the second story, to his father's apartment. He saw light leaking into the stairwell from an upstairs room. "Hello?" he called, though not so loudly that he would wake his father should he be resting.

Footsteps immediately met his greeting, hurrying toward the second-floor landing. The tread fell lightly, certainly not that of Jake or either of Sisko's brothers. He waited to see who would emerge from the apartment.

When Azeni Korena appeared, alone, Sisko knew at once that the situation had changed since he'd last spoken with Jake. "Mister Sisko," she said, seeming flustered. She and Jake had been married for almost four and a half years, and she had become as much a member of the family as anybody born into it. Sisko had even invited her to call him *Dad,* though probably because she'd lost her parents in her youth, she preferred *Mister Sisko*—an appellation that he at least favored over *Emissary.*

Korena rushed down toward him, the heels of her shoes banging loudly on the wooden steps. "I'm sorry," she said as she descended, "I didn't hear you come in." She reached the bottom of the stairs and stopped just a pace from Sisko, anxiety revealed in her aspect.

"I didn't knock, I just let myself in," he said, pretending to himself that Korena's disquiet came from not having met him at the door. "I didn't mean to startle you."

"No, it's not that, it's—" she began. She reached out and took his hand in her own, and the sadness on her face told him that he could pretend no longer.

"What's happened?" he asked her quietly.

"I'm sorry," she said, her voice quivering, her eyes glistening. "Your father passed away."

Sisko staggered backward a step, and Korena grabbed at his arm to steady him. "When?" he managed to say. He felt as though he couldn't breathe, as though he'd been punched in the gut and had the wind knocked out of him.

"This morning," Korena said. Tears slipped down her face, leaving quicksilver trails on her cheeks.

"This morning," he repeated. His father had been dead for hours and he hadn't known, he hadn't *felt* it.

"Jake wanted to wait until you were here to tell you," Korena explained. "He wanted you to be with family."

"Where is Jake?" he asked. "Is he here?" He looked past Korena to the stairs.

"No." She still had hold of his arm, and she squeezed, as though trying to hold him up both physically and spiritually. "I'm sorry . . . we expected you later."

"Where is Jake?" Sisko wanted to know, and then he recalled that his sister and brothers had come to New Orleans as well. "Where is everybody?"

"They're at the hospital, making arrangements," Korena said. "When . . . when . . ." The words seemed to catch in her throat.

Sisko stepped forward and hugged Korena to him. As she sobbed into his shoulder, he closed his eyes, causing his own tears to spill down his face. *So many losses,* he thought. The tens of billions killed by the Borg, including eleven thousand on Alonis, the entire crew of forty-seven aboard *Cutlass,* thirty-one on *James T. Kirk,* and nineteen on *New York.* Elias. Calan and Audj.

And now my father, Sisko thought. If he hadn't been convinced before, he was now: *it* had begun. And he knew in his heart that if he didn't run, there would be no stopping it.

9

Proconsul Tomalak stood in the conference room and peered out through the large, round port. Situated just above the equator of the sphere that formed the main body of Typhon I, the room looked out over one of the six spiral arms that encircled the space station. Tomalak thought that the facility fulfilled well the intent of its designers, who had meant it to evoke the form of the galaxy. Each arm represented a founding member of the Typhon Pact, with docking ports specially fitted for their ships and an internal environment designed specifically for their species. The central globe provided a more generic setting, adapted to accommodate all of the pact members well, if none of them perfectly.

It's certainly not perfect for Romulans, Tomalak thought. He pulled his black suit jacket tighter about him and fastened it closed, trying to ward off the chill he felt. The lower temperatures might be to the liking of the Breen or the Kinshaya, but Romulans generally favored warmer climes. *At least I don't need an environmental suit.*

From his vantage, Tomalak could see two of the station's spiral arms. The one to his right, belonging to the Gorn, had yet to be completed, and as the proconsul watched, tiny, space-suited figures and small labor craft buzzed about the half-finished structure. Work also continued on another of the arms, that of the Breen—currently out of Tomalak's sight—as well as on the interior of the central sphere. While several of the powers that would make up the Typhon Pact had begun discussing an alliance more than a year ago, it had only been within the last half-year that a general, albeit still unfinalized and still unratified, agreement had been reached among five of them; the sixth, the Tzenkethi Coalition, had only recently decided to join. That so much of the space station had been finished already represented a monumental achievement.

As Tomalak gazed out the window, he monitored the conversation behind him. Representatives from four of the other five Typhon Pact nations—all but the Tzenkethi—had arrived for the summit. While the Kinshaya envoy, Patriarch Radrigi, remained conspicuously mute, the Gorn, Tholian, and Breen diplomats filled the room with a discordant olio of hisses, chirps and clicks, and electronic warbles. Tomalak's translator provided him the dialogue rendered in High Rihan, though he heard nothing of interest to him. Predictably, most of the current conversation centered around Tholian Ambassador Corskene complaining about the Tzenkethi's tardiness.

Speaker Alizome Vik Tov-A would arrive soon, Tomalak knew, otherwise he might have shared in Corskene's displeasure. Only moments ago, Tomalak had watched through the port as the marauder ferrying Alizome from Coalition space docked at the tip of the Tzenkethi arm of the station. The great ship impressed the proconsul. Its elongated body essentially resembled a teardrop, smooth and seamless in flight, though several hatches had swung open aft to allow various gangways and umbilicals to connect to the station. Tzenkethi script fell across the hull like flowing water, which seemed like abstract art to a nonreader of the language. Tomalak found the vessel's profile far more interesting than the black spheres of the Kinshaya or the angular, wedge-shaped craft of the Tholians, and less overwhelming than the complicated ship designs of the Gorn, Breen, or even the Romulans.

"I cannot tolerate this laggard behavior," Corskene announced. Tomalak heard the skitter of her six legs on the deck. Although Tholian individuals possessed both male and female characteristics, Corskene had introduced herself with a feminine title.

Tomalak turned to see that the Tholian ambassador had moved away from the round conference table after rising from the cushioned disk on which she'd been sitting. Half the seats around the table comprised such disks, for use by the Tholians, Kinshaya, and Tzenkethi. "We will wait a bit longer," Tomalak told her, quietly but with authority. While Praetor Tal'Aura had agreed in principle for the Romulan Star Empire to join the Typhon Pact in equal standing to the other members, he understood that his people would mean more than that to the nascent alliance. Even with the rending of the Empire by Donatra and her forces, the extent of Romulan technological, scientific, and military accomplishments would contribute strength to the Pact at a disproportionately higher level than the resources of the other nations. Consequently, and despite the fact that Tomalak knew Romulus would still benefit from the union, he considered his people "more equal" than their new allies.

"Wait longer?" Corskene said. Her white polygonal eyes

shined brightly through the faceplate of her black environmental suit. "Did you intend that as an order, Proconsul Tomalak?"

"An order?" Tomalak said, stepping toward the table and forcing a thin smile onto his face. "No, of course not," he lied. "But the complexities of these negotiations have required a great deal of time and effort. I would hate to see them derailed in haste, particularly for such a minor offense."

"It is not a 'minor offense,'" Corskene protested. "It marks a pattern of behavior. Indeed, the Tzenkethi Coalition was *late* to the treaty." When first approached about the possible alliance, the Tzenkethi had declined—at least until the Federation had hired the Breen to help protect against the Borg, something the Tholian Assembly itself had intended to do, and which the Tzenkethi viewed as an example of Federation imperialism.

"The Tzenkethi were not *late,*" said Tomalak. "They were simply the last to agree to join the Pact. That differs from not appearing at the appointed time for a summit. In any case, the Tzenkethi vessel carrying their representative has docked at the station. I'm sure we can expect her shortly."

"I need not point out that the time scheduled for the start of our meeting has already passed," said Corskene.

"No," hummed the Breen ambassador, Vart, "you need not."

Corskene turned her sterile gaze toward Vart, who wore an environmental suit with a snout-nosed helmet, which, as best Tomalak could tell, all Breen wore when away from their homeworld. An uncomfortable silence suddenly filled the room as the Tholian appeared to measure Vart. With the Breen's words passing through the electronic transmitter of his helmet, and then through a language translator, Tomalak could not tell whether he'd intended his comment as agreement with Corskene, or as criticism of her complaints; the proconsul suspected that Corskene could not tell either.

Just as Tomalak prepared to step in to prevent any sort of quarrel from erupting, the circular door to the conference room wheeled into the bulkhead. All eyes turned toward the entrance as the silence in the room lingered. The Tzenkethi representative stepped inside.

Alizome stood tall and lean, humanoid in every respect, but not *just* humanoid. Like all Tzenkethi, she embodied physical perfection in a way that defied explanation. The bodily proportions of every member of her species seemed without flaw, their movements graceful and languid. They possessed bones only along their spines, the rest of their skeletons instead consisting of differentiated, fluid-filled sacs that could keep their forms rigid, but that also allowed for a considerable range of motion in their limbs and digits. Their large, colored pupils—in Alizome's case, bright green pupils—filled their eyes, endowing their faces with a striking appearance. And their flesh—

Although Tomalak had encountered a number of Tzenkethi throughout his life, he had never grown accustomed to the soft radiance that emanated from them. He didn't know whether their luminescence resulted from a chemical or an electromagnetic process. Nor did he know of any definite limits to their range of colors, though he had only witnessed Tzenkethi radiating from a pale yellow to a midrange green. Alizome shined a stunning golden hue.

Perhaps most amazingly, the corporeal Tzenkethi form inspired awe in a broad range of other species. Tomalak himself felt their allure, but he had seen individuals of such physically disparate races as the Tellarites, the Terixans, the Koltaari, and even the Klingons, exhibit similar attraction. As if in voiceless testimony of that reality, none of those present in the conference room spoke, all of them—Tomalak included—apparently bewitched by the appearance of a woman with whom they had dealt on numerous other occasions.

Obviously accustomed to such reactions, Alizome addressed the group. "You are all here," she said matter-of-factly. "Good. Let us finalize the agreement to join forces." Though the words that emerged from Tomalak's translator sounded straightforward, they came tempered by the lyrical nature of Alizome's voice, which conjured the sound of wind chimes.

At last, somebody else spoke. "You're late," said Corskene, not hiding her disapprobation.

Alizome turned her head slowly to look directly at the Tholian ambassador. "I am not interested in your tiresome grievances," said the Tzenkethi, her musical tones unable to mask the harshness of her statement.

"And I am not interested in your disrespect," said Corskene. Rather than continuing the argument, though, she signaled her capitulation by returning to her seat, sending her six legs around the disk and then settling her body atop it. The Kinshaya representative, Patriarch Radrigi, sat in the same way on his seat, though he had only four legs.

Alizome walked slowly to the conference table, moving with a delicate elegance. She sat down on an unoccupied disk as any bipedal humanoid typically would, but then pulled her legs up onto the seat as well, curling them around the left side of her torso. The shift in position gave her the appearance of having been cut in half, and yet she retained her appeal.

Tomalak sat down as well. He picked up his data tablet from the table and activated it with a touch of his left index finger to the security scanner. He quickly glanced at the document that appeared. "I can start," he told the others, "by stating that the praetor has agreed to the sharing of our cloaking technology."

"Excellent," said Skorn, the Gorn Ambassador. The Tzenkethi and Breen representatives nodded their accord, and the Kinshaya flared his wings slightly to indicate his approval. Corskene gave no visible sign of her assent, but Tomalak felt certain that his news pleased her.

Ever since the agreement in principle had been reached among the five, and now six, prospective Typhon Pact members, they had worked on fleshing out the details of their alliance. Most insisted that the Romulan Star Empire must share, among other items, their ability to cloak their starships. Praetor Tal'Aura had waited to grant this until Imperial Fleet scientists had achieved a breakthrough in the next generation of the technology. While the newest iteration of the invisibility screen would not be installed on Romulan vessels, it sufficed for the praetor that should the Typhon Pact not endure, the Empire would gain an immediate tactical advantage over their former allies by virtue of having already devised a more-advanced cloaking technology.

From that point, the conference proceeded apace. The representatives reached a consensus on mutual defense and a common currency. They discussed policy with respect to the United Federation of Planets and the Klingon Empire, as well as other political entities. The six nations promised to share weapons and defensive systems, agricultural advances and machinery, and food and medical provisions. Overall, the negotiations satisfied Tomalak, with the last two items supplying the proconsul with much of the benefit Romulus needed to obtain from its participation in the Pact in the near term. Donatra's stranglehold on the Romulan breadbasket worlds dramatically impacted the availability of food and medicine within the Empire, a situation that would only grow more dire as long as the Romulans remained a divided state.

When finally Tomalak departed the space station aboard the vessel *Khenn Ornahj,* he carried with him a copy of the finalized treaty terms. He would take it to the newly reconstituted Senate, where he believed it would meet with swift approval. He expected that within days the Typhon Pact would rise as the preeminent power in the region. From there, it would be only a matter of time before a reunited Romulan Star Empire ruled the Pact, and with it, the Alpha and Beta Quadrants.

10

Standing at the top of the rough-hewn staircase, Spock pressed his ear against the cold stone surface and listened. When he heard nothing for two full minutes, he reached up and pushed against the wall. The hidden door swung slowly open, and he passed quickly through the gap, into a storeroom. Within, crates, bags, and other containers of merchandise filled numerous freestanding shelves, while stacks of ornate frames and large data canvases leaned against the far wall. Once Spock confirmed the space was vacant, he looked back and signaled silently to Venaster and D'Tan. The two men followed him inside, directing their prisoner before them.

Spock closed the secret entrance to the Ki Baratan underground, then took a moment to scrutinize the Reman. They had dressed him as they had themselves, in a traditional Romulan robe, its oversized cowl hiding his features in the depths of its folds, though the dark-brown, loose-fitting garment could do nothing to disguise his considerable height. A monofilament wrapped around the Reman's waist and concealed beneath his robe bound him from behind to D'Tan. The virtually invisible strand measured long enough to permit both to walk comfortably, but not so long that it would provide much slack.

Spock gestured to Venaster. On cue, the former military officer drew a disruptor from beneath his own robe. Now out of the underground, he activated the energy weapon, then displayed it to Spock, allowing him to see that he had adjusted it to its highest stun setting. He then positioned it back inside his clothing.

Spock nodded his approval. Despite such provisions, he fully expected the prisoner to attempt an escape at some point during their transport of him. Though considerably shorter than the Reman, Venaster possessed both a solid physique and an abundance of security experience. Spock trusted him to maintain their custody of the prisoner.

Wending between the tall shelves, Spock made his way to the room's conventional entrance. There, he cast his gaze through an eyehole. The convex lens made it possible for him to see the entirety of the store's single main room. T'Coll, the owner of the establishment and a sympathizer of the Reunification Movement, sat behind a counter, atop a stool. Spock saw several customers moving about, and so he indicated to Venaster and D'Tan that they would have to wait.

Seventeen minutes passed before the store cleared. When it did, Spock pulled open the door and stepped into the shop. The others followed.

Shelves and display cases offered up a variety of large and small art pieces, including items such as sculptures and decorative blown glass. Both framed and unframed paintings and prints blanketed the walls, while a few data canvases of various dimensions cycled through their repertoires, their brushstrokes and textures changing along with the pigments. Spock distinguished most of the works as products of Romulan artists, though he espied a few of off-world provenance.

Spock peered over at T'Coll, who glanced up from the data tablet on which she worked. The middle-aged woman gave no reaction at first, but then she hopped down from her stool and ducked down behind the counter. When she stood back up, she held out a cloth bag, obviously weighed down by its contents. Spock walked over and accepted it from her. Reaching into the bag, he extracted a small bronze figurine of a kneeling man looking down, a hand raised to the side of his forehead as though deep in thought. Spock recognized it as a reproduction of a famous work by a renowned Romulan artist, Raban Gedroe.

"Thank you for acquiring this for me," Spock said, depositing it back in the bag. In reality, the item would serve as a subterfuge. Should T'Coll's shop be under surveillance by Romulan Security, Spock would simply look like a customer.

"Jolan tru," said T'Coll.

Spock replied in kind. Then he turned back toward the others and nodded once. With a touch to the back of the Reman's shoulder, D'Tan headed the prisoner toward one of the shop's two public entrances. Spock fell in beside Venaster and trailed them outside.

Since the sun had risen a couple of hours earlier, the dawn fog, carried inland from the Apnex Sea by a marine layer, had yet to dissipate. The overcast sky veiled the city in shades of gray. Peering toward the government quarter, Spock saw wisps of vapor obscuring the tips of the spires there, as well as the dome capping the Hall of State's rotunda, the structure at the very center of Ki Baratan.

D'Tan and his charge headed right along Via Chula, a thoroughfare that paralleled the circumference of the circular city. Venaster swung out to the left, a pace behind the two, clearly prepared to act if the Reman tried to break free of his captivity and flee. Spock took up a similar position to the right of D'Tan. None of the men spoke.

The march to the nearest security office required only a quarter of an hour. When the group turned from Via Chula onto Via Colius, a straight avenue that traversed the city radially, the facility came immediately into view. The silver ensign of Romulan Security—a raptor holding a shield in its talons—showed prominently on the two-story building's black façade. Spock renewed his focus on their prisoner, certain that he would fight for his freedom before they reached their destination.

But that didn't happen.

As the Reman walked through the front door of the security office, D'Tan surreptitiously detached the monofilament from where it connected to the harness around his waist. Then he stepped back, allowing Spock to hand him the cloth bag with the sculpture in it. Spock then entered the security office behind their prisoner. As planned, D'Tan and Venaster would wait outside.

In turning the Reman over to the Romulan authorities, and in finding a means of requesting an audience with the praetor, Spock wanted to put only himself at risk. Many of his comrades had attempted to dissuade him from such a course, several even volunteering to substitute for him. They argued that his importance to the Reunification Movement should preclude him from intentionally placing himself in harm's way. Spock agreed in general, but contended that because of his prominent position in the Movement, his participation would generate the best possible chance, both of securing a meeting with Tal'Aura and of establishing a rapprochement with her government.

Spock remained two paces behind the Reman as they navigated a narrow foyer, then passed through a second, inner door. Spock remained alert to the possibility of an escape effort, but again, none came. Inside, they entered a large lobby, surrounded on three sides by tall counters, behind which sat security personnel. A bank of monitors directly ahead displayed various public locations throughout Ki Baratan, most notably several views of the building in which Spock stood. He readily picked out the figures of Venaster and D'Tan on Via Colius.

Numerous security officers at the counters looked up as a pair stationed on either side of the door quickly closed in on Spock and the Reman. Each wore a snug, dark-gray uniform, the Romulan Security sigil emblazoned on the right breast, their name listed beneath it in matching silver characters. A thin, colored insignia marched down the outside of the right arm, denoting rank. As well, each carried an energy weapon on their hip.

"Stop," demanded the officer to Spock's left. He read her name as Sorent, her rank as sentry.

Both Spock and the Reman stopped. "I wish to report a crime," Spock said from within the hood of his robe, "and to remand into your custody the malefactor who committed the offense. I suggest that you regard him as dangerous."

"What is the nature of the crime?" Sorent asked.

"Attempted assassination," Spock said. He heard movement to his right, and he looked to see that the other sentry, a man named J'Velk, had drawn his weapon.

"Whose assassination?" Sorent asked.

Spock turned back to her. Unlike her partner's, he saw, her firearm remained on her hip. "My own," he told her. He saw that the conversation had captured the attention of the security officers behind the counters.

Sorent nodded, her manner one of disbelief. "And who are you?" she asked.

"I am Spock," he said. His name appeared to spark immediate recognition in Sorent, as well as in most, if not all, of her fellow officers. That did not surprise Spock, since his efforts—and all efforts—to reunify the Vulcan and Romulan peoples had been deemed illegal long ago by the Romulan government.

"Remove your hood," Sorent ordered. "Slowly."

With care, Spock reached up and pulled the cowl of his robe backward, revealing his face. Once again, he saw recognition in Sorent, as well as in others. Behind him, he heard a faint trill, and he suspected that both the inner and outer doors had just been sealed. Four more security officers scrambled from behind the counters to join Sorent and J'Velk. Past the left-hand counter, Spock saw a door open and a uniformed man emerge, the colored rank strip on his arm identifying him as a protector, the highest field-office grade in Romulan Security.

"You are the Vulcan who preaches for the reunifying of Romulus with your people," Sorent said. "Am I correct?"

"I *advocate* for such a reunification, yes," Spock said. He watched as the protector stepped up to observe the proceedings.

"And this is?" Sorent asked, gesturing at Spock's prisoner.

"I do not know," Spock said, "but he tried to kill me."

Spock detected puzzlement in the expressions of most of the security officers, though Sorent seemed less bewildered by the situation and more suspicious. "You," she said, walking over to the prisoner, "remove your hood."

The Reman did so, his hand slowly moving up to the cowl of his robe and pulling it back. As his face became visible, somebody—Spock did not see who—gasped in apparent surprise. Though the Reman made no threatening moves, two security officers rushed toward him, grabbing for his arms.

"No!" yelled Sorent, but too late.

The Reman roared and threw off the security officers, one of them staggering backward into the central counter and crumpling to the floor. J'Velk raised his weapon, but the Reman saw it and batted it from his hand. As two more security officers raced in, Spock saw Sorent step back and take aim with her own disruptor, clearly prepared to stun everybody in order to disable the Reman. Before she could fire, though, she lowered her weapon, and Spock saw why: to his surprise, the protector had also entered the melee.

The Reman fought wildly, throwing another officer to the side, then wrapping his hands around the throat of another. J'Velk jumped in and pulled at the Reman's arm, obviously wanting to free his colleague. The protector tried to wrench the Reman's other arm free.

Spock glanced around and saw more security personnel coming forward. The Reman whirled around, loosing his grip on the one Romulan's throat and tossing him into the advancing officers. With another bellow, he flung both J'Velk and the protector away from him. For a moment, he stood alone in the center of the security office, his head darting around as though searching out the source of the next assault. Spock waited for the piercing sound of a disruptor, and had enough time to wonder if the weapon that would fire the shot had been set to stun or kill.

But then the Reman collapsed.

Spock looked around confusedly, sure that he had heard no discharge of any weapon. As a strange silence rose in the security office, he saw that others appeared perplexed as well, including Sorent. When the Reman did not move, she handed her disruptor to the nearest officer and said, "If he moves, fire, even if you have to hit me." That at least told Spock that she had adjusted her weapon to a stun setting.

Cautiously, Sorent approached the Reman. She stood over him for a few seconds, observing, before finally bending down and taking hold of his hand. She felt at his wrist for a pulse.

"He's dead," she announced, but then she seemed to notice something. She leaned in closer, then pushed back the sleeve of the Reman's robe and turned over his arm. Near his elbow, on the underside of his forearm, a square patch had been applied to his flesh. All around it, jagged, dark-green lines twisted in myriad directions below the skin.

"A toxin of some kind," Sorent concluded. "He killed himself."

Again, Spock felt a wave of confusion wash over him. The Reman had made no attempt to escape on the way to the security office, but then had killed himself when the

Romulans sought to physically detain him? For the first time, he wondered if mental illness might have played a role in all that had transpired, from the attempt on his life to the death of the Reman. In his empathic contact with his would-be assassin, he had perceived no psychosis in him, but that did not preclude the existence of such a condition.

As Spock pondered the situation, the Romulans around him began moving again. Sorent stood and ordered the removal of the Reman's body, while other security officers assisted their injured colleagues. Still others returned to crew their stations behind the counters.

And in the midst of the sudden activity, Spock was taken into custody.

11

As Sisko strode through the spacious atrium of Starfleet Headquarters in San Francisco, he kept his head down. He hadn't visited the facility in years, hadn't spoken in the intervening time to but a handful of Starfleet personnel outside of Deep Space 9 and the Alonis task force, but he remembered many of the people who had offices in the complex. More to the point, they would remember him, not just for their personal encounters with him, but for what had come later. Even people he didn't know would remember what had come later. Even with him dressed in civilian clothes, many would recognize him as the Starfleet captain revered by Bajorans as the Emissary of the Prophets. The officer who survived on the front lines of the Dominion War, only to disappear into the Bajoran Wormhole for months afterward. The man who reemerged from that experience for the birth of his child and the culmination of his efforts to see Bajor join the Federation. The man who then withdrew from Starfleet to settle on the world where the population venerated him.

Oh, yes, Sisko thought, *they'll remember me.* But he didn't want to be remembered, he didn't want to be recognized. He didn't want to speak with anybody. He'd come here for one reason only: to get what he needed—to get what Kasidy and Rebecca needed, what Jake and Korena needed.

Underneath the clear, concave canopy that swept from ground level up to the top floor, Sisko approached the horse-shoe-shaped desk that stood in front of a row of turbolifts. The yeoman stationed at the desk addressed him before he could even introduce himself. "Mister Sisko, the commander in chief is expecting your visit," the Caitian said. Sisko took note that the young man did not call him *captain*, indicating that Admiral Walter had processed his separation from Starfleet. "If you wouldn't mind," the yeoman added, motioning to a security scanner set into the counter.

Though Sisko had already passed through two checkpoints just to enter Starfleet Headquarters, and though he knew that automated sensors scanned every individual who entered the complex, he dutifully placed his hand in the center of the panel. It lighted up at his touch. The yeoman consulted a computer interface on his desk, then looked back up at Sisko.

"Thank you, sir," he said. "If you'll take either of the central turbolifts behind me, Ensign Ventrice will see that you're comfortable until the admiral can see you."

Sisko nodded, then circled the desk and headed for a lift. A pair of security guards stood on either side of the area, carrying no visible weapons but undoubtedly armed. Sisko passed between them and entered a car, which began to ascend without his having to specify a destination.

The lift climbed vertically to the top floor, then glided along horizontally for a few seconds. When it stopped, the doors parted to reveal a diminutive woman with short, graying hair standing there, studying a personal access display device. She looked up as he exited the lift, dropping the padd to her side. "Mister Sisko, I'm Ensign Ventrice, one of the admiral's assistants," she said with a warm smile. "Please follow me."

They crossed a foyer and passed through a door into a well-appointed reception area. Floor-to-ceiling windows at the far end of the room provided a dramatic view of the coastline and, beyond it, the Pacific Ocean. Each side wall featured a polished wooden door that obviously led to inner offices. Ventrice waved her hand toward where a sofa and several easy chairs sat arrayed around a low, square table. Hanging on the walls above, photo-realistic paintings depicted various Starfleet assets, including Deep Space 9 and *Defiant*.

"You may have a seat," the ensign said. "The admiral should be available shortly." She asked Sisko if he would like a beverage or some reading material, but he declined. The ensign left him to wait while she returned to her desk, situated in front of the windows but facing in the direction of the turbolifts.

As Sisko sat on the sofa, he debated again the reason for his visit to Starfleet Command. For months, he had considered the course upon which he had now set himself. In the wake of the terrible devastation caused by the Borg invasion, that course had become a more reasonable possibility; and since his father's death, it had transformed into a necessity. In so many ways and for so many reasons, he didn't want it to be, but he genuinely believed that he had no real choice in the matter.

The funeral had been hard. By virtue of his popular restaurant and his long involvement in the community, Joseph

Sisko had a lot of friends and acquaintances throughout New Orleans. As a result, many wanted to pay their respects and offer their condolences to the family. Sisko spent the first couple of days after his arrival receiving well-wishers at the restaurant, many of them incongruously bringing gifts of food.

As he and his siblings started to plan the memorial for their father, Sisko found himself ill-equipped to deal with the emotional strain. He ended up leaving the arrangements to the rest of his family, while he consumed his days with long walks through the city. He wandered for hours through Audubon Park, the French Quarter, and along the winding banks of the Mississippi River. One afternoon, he transported two thousand kilometers, to Babylon, New York, where he tramped across the beach on which he'd met his first wife more than a quarter of a century earlier. Indulging in self-pity, he lumbered over the sand with tears in his eyes, thinking about all the things in his life that could have been—not just for him and Jennifer, but also for him and Kasidy.

Kas had wanted to attend the funeral, but travel throughout the Federation remained problematic, and finding timely transportation from Bajor to Earth proved effectively impossible. That might have been just as well, Sisko thought, since neither he nor Kasidy knew how the experience would impact Rebecca, just four years old. It also alleviated the need for Sisko to deal with the next loss in his life—or it at least postponed that need.

The funeral had taken place yesterday, four days after his father's death. Sisko had expected a somber service in Katrina Memorial Cemetery, which already contained the remains of several generations of his father's family. Instead, his siblings arranged a jazz funeral, originating at the northeastern entrance to Audubon Park. The assembled throng marched down St. Charles Avenue to Nashville Avenue, and then up to the cemetery, with Jake carrying the crematory urn most of the way. The band played a mixture of dirges and spirituals that seemed to elevate the emotions of many, but those elegies left Sisko feeling more lost and alone than ever.

At the memorial, Sisko's sister and brothers—half-sister and half-brothers, he reminded himself—delivered eulogies, as did Jake. Sisko did not. The funeral, though perfectly in keeping with his father's personality, did not connect with him. When the band struck up rousing, celebratory songs on the way from the cemetery to the restaurant, which seemed to stir the spirits of the mourners, Sisko felt further isolated. He allowed himself to lag back in the procession, until finally he stopped walking altogether, watching as the ritual commemoration of his father's life left him behind, ultimately turning left onto St. Charles Avenue and out of sight.

He'd left a message at the restaurant so that his family would not worry, then took the afternoon to set up both his travel back to Bajor and a meeting at Starfleet Command. He returned to Sisko's Creole Kitchen late that night, hoping to avoid unwanted conversation. He didn't wish to be comforted, or reasoned with, or asked about his plans. Jake waited up for him, though, so Sisko had to prevail upon his son to permit him his solitude. Jake did, though Sisko could see both concern and a measure of hurt in his eyes. When Sisko said good night, he knew that he wouldn't see his son for a while but that at least Jake would be safe.

Sisko hadn't slept well, and that morning he'd risen early, making sure he departed without seeing anybody, knowing that Jake would make his apologies to the rest of the family. He transported to San Francisco, then after having breakfast at a local eatery, spent the rest of the morning in a library, putting his head down in a carrel and catnapping until the afternoon. Then he made his way to Starfleet Headquarters for his meeting.

Sisko had been seated in the reception area for twenty minutes when the door in the right wall opened inward. A tall woman greeted him by name and asked him to come inside. He did, entering another anteroom, with a desk to the right facing the windows and a small seating area to the left. The woman closed the door behind him.

"I'm Lieutenant Reel," she said, pronouncing it as two syllables: *Ree-el*. Because of the name and her considerable height—she stood very nearly two meters tall—Sisko suspected that she hailed from Capella IV, as did the man for whom she worked. "Before I bring you in to see the admiral, may I offer you something to drink?" When Sisko thanked her but said no, she crossed in front of her desk to the inner door, a wide slab of burnished mahogany. She turned the knob and stepped inside.

"Admiral, Benjamin Sisko to see you," she said.

"Thank you, Reel," said a deep voice from within. "Show him in."

"Yes, sir." Reel glanced back at Sisko, inviting him into the office of Starfleet's commander in chief by moving aside. Sisko walked past her, hearing her close the door after him.

The large office sat enclosed by three walls of windows, providing a spectacular one-hundred-eighty-degree view of the Presidio and beyond. Ahead and to the left, Sisko could see the unmistakable form of the Golden Gate Bridge. Glancing around, he saw the inner wall decorated with a colorful assortment of primitive crafts: carved figures and masks, cloaks and capes, scarves and coronets.

Admiral Akaar—articulated in the same manner as Reel's name, *Aka-ar*—sat behind an enormous desk, sizable enough to suit his considerable bulk. Possessed of a broad chest and shoulders, he stood up from his chair to reveal a commensurate height, at least two and a quarter meters tall. He had dark, almost black, eyes, and gray hair pulled back behind his head.

Sisko had met the admiral after returning from the Celestial Temple, during the days leading up to Bajor's entry into the Federation. He hadn't spent a great deal of time with Akaar, but he'd found him steady, somewhat formal, and forceful in a quiet, careful way. It pleased Sisko that the admiral had agreed to meet with him, particularly with such little advance notice.

"I welcome you with an open heart and hand," Akaar said, lifting his right fist to the left side of his chest, then opening his hand and holding it out, palm upward.

"Thank you, Admiral," Sisko said, mimicking the gesture. "And thank you for seeing me."

"I'm afraid I can't see you for long," Akaar said. "Even though we're still assessing the damage done by the Borg, we're already trying to move forward, trying to formulate a plan to restore Starfleet."

Sisko nodded. He knew that it would likely require

years of effort to return the fleet to its former strength. Not only would Starfleet need to construct new ships and train new personnel, but it also would have to renew the infrastructure supporting both of those activities.

Akaar pointed to the chairs in front of his desk, and Sisko took a seat. The admiral sat back down and folded his hands together atop his desk. He said nothing more, apparently waiting for Sisko to tell him why he'd requested a meeting.

"I'll get right to the point," Sisko said. "I've decided that I want to rejoin Starfleet."

Akaar nodded. "I see," he said evenly. "May I ask why?"

Sisko blinked, surprised. Considering the terrible losses suffered by Starfleet—losses to which the admiral had just made reference—he'd expected to be welcomed back into the service, not met with questions. "Does it really matter?" he asked.

Akaar seemed to consider that. "Perhaps not," he said. He stood from his chair once more, and Sisko thought that the admiral had chosen to end the meeting. But then Akaar walked out from behind his desk, along the far wall, and turned to gaze out toward San Francisco Bay. "You weren't here when the Breen attacked Earth," he said.

"No," Sisko confirmed, a bit confused by the rapid shift in the conversation. "I was on Deep Space Nine."

"Of course," Akaar said. "But you saw the images of the bridge."

"Yes." Sisko recalled well seeing pictures of the damaged Golden Gate: the drooping cables, one of the towers bent and twisted, the deck blown apart in the center of the span.

"And do you remember what you felt when you saw those images?"

Sisko did, and said so. He'd experienced a visceral reaction at seeing the broken form of a landmark he'd known and appreciated for most of his life.

"I'm sure you're aware that the Golden Gate is known not just all around Earth, but throughout the Federation," Akaar said. "And because of its proximity to Starfleet Command, it's become associated with us." The admiral turned from the window to face Sisko. "When the images of the wrecked bridge were distributed across the comnets, the number of applications to Starfleet and the Academy skyrocketed. Not just from Earth but from Andor and Tellar and Aurelia and Betazed. There was even a spike in applications from Vulcan and Pacifica."

"People wanting to defend against the enemy who destroyed the bridge," Sisko said.

"People wanting to defend against the enemy who destroyed a part of *their* universe," Akaar said. "An enemy who attacked a home they knew, even if it wasn't precisely their home." The admiral's shoulders moved slightly in what Sisko took as a shrug. "We actually received applications from a few Gorn and Ferengi, and even one Tholian."

Sisko understood. In some regard, hadn't that been how he'd come to serve on Deep Space 9, wanting to defend the Bajorans and their home? Bajor had ultimately become his home too, but initially, that hadn't been the case.

Akaar crossed back to the desk and half-leaned, half-sat on its edge. He towered over Sisko and fixed him with the stare of his dark eyes. "Is that why you want to rejoin Starfleet?" he asked. "To help defend a Federation that's been badly wounded?"

Sisko did not respond. He couldn't, because he knew in

his heart how he really felt: that he had already done more than his share to protect and serve the United Federation of Planets. But he didn't think the admiral would want to hear the true reason Sisko wanted to return to active duty.

"Wanting to defend the Federation is a legitimate reason to want to serve in Starfleet," Akaar went on. "But Admiral Walter told me that just last week he offered you an admiralty and the posting of your choice. You turned him down. So I have to ask myself, and I have to ask you, what's changed between then and now?"

Again, Sisko felt that he lacked an answer that the admiral would want to hear. And so again, he said nothing. Akaar regarded him silently for a moment, then pushed away from the desk and returned to his chair.

"As far as my information goes," the admiral said, "what's changed for you between the time you left the *New York* and now is that your father died."

The words sent a shock, a physical sensation, through Sisko's body. It somehow wounded him to hear somebody state his loss as a fact—a loss that he supposed he had yet to fully accept. *Your father died.* His world seemed to shatter anew.

Akaar leaned forward in his chair. "I'm sympathetic about your father," he said quietly. "But I also understand how such a death can drive a person to do things they would not otherwise have done . . . that they might not want to do tomorrow." He paused, as though to give Sisko the opportunity to comprehend his point—or perhaps to refute it. When Sisko said nothing, the admiral continued. "Starfleet needs people, and it particularly needs good, experienced officers like you, Mister Sisko. What you accomplished with Bajor, and the role you played in defeating the Dominion, speak to your exceptional abilities. And I appreciate your willingness to leave your home to take command of the *New York* and defend Alonis against the Borg. But I can't have somebody joining the service today and resigning tomorrow. There's enough instability already throughout Starfleet. We need to turn that around, not contribute to it."

Sisko didn't know what to say. He briefly considered admitting the truth—that he couldn't go home, and that he had nowhere else to go—but he didn't think that would effect the result he wanted. Instead, he groped for something, anything, to tell Akaar. The moment reminded him of one he'd had a dozen years earlier.

"Admiral," he finally said, "when I was first assigned to Deep Space Nine, I objected to the posting. I was raising a teenage son, and a hostile frontier beyond Federation space didn't seem the appropriate place to do that. I even considered leaving Starfleet so that I could return to Earth." Akaar listened impassively, as though none of the revealed details surprised him. Sisko wondered if the admiral had consulted his service record before their meeting. "In the meantime, I followed orders, I went to Bajor, to Deep Space Nine, and I changed my mind." Sisko leaned forward in his chair too, wanting to emphasize his next words. "Last week, after my temporary return to service ended, and after watching the Borg kill eleven thousand Alonis and scores of Starfleet personnel, I decided I didn't want to continue in Starfleet." He paused, wanting to doubly underscore his final thought. "I changed my mind."

The admiral held his gaze for long seconds. Sisko hadn't lied—he really had changed his mind—but neither had he offered up the whole truth. Akaar wanted to know why

Sisko sought a return to Starfleet, but Sisko had no intention of divulging his reasons.

"All right," Akaar said at last. Sisko couldn't tell whether he had satisfied the admiral, or if Starfleet's commander in chief had ultimately chosen simply to allow the return of an experienced officer to a service that desperately needed him. Akaar leaned back in his chair, and Sisko did as well. "I know Admiral Walter offered you your choice of assignments, but if you're hoping to return to Deep Space Nine—"

"No," Sisko interrupted, wanting to dispel the idea of a posting within the Bajoran system. "I was thinking more along the lines of my last assignment."

"Starship command," Akaar said.

"Yes."

"The *New York* will be undergoing repairs for quite a while," Akaar said. "But we do have ships out there that need a new captain."

"Any port in a storm," Sisko said.

"I could promote you to admiral," Akaar said, "but frankly, we've got enough of those around here right now."

Sisko couldn't be sure, but he thought the admiral might still be probing for the reasons he'd asked to rejoin the fleet. He didn't know what would satisfy Akaar, so he simply told him the truth. "I don't need the rank," he said. "I just want to return to service."

"All right, then," Akaar said. He rose from his chair, this time clearly signaling that the meeting had come to an end. Sisko stood up and faced the admiral across his desk. "Welcome back to Starfleet, Captain Sisko."

12

Durjik watched as the young senator stood up in the last tier of the Romulan Senate Chamber. He rose in the same way that so many other senators had throughout the afternoon. Unlike most of those others, though, the political neophyte did not bellow out his opinion or question or whatever had driven him to his feet. Rather, he waited for Tomalak to recognize him from the floor of the chamber. That did not happen immediately.

Because Durjik had served in the Senate before, he could have claimed a position in the first tier of seats, or even on the other side of the large circular room, at one of the tables reserved for the Continuing Committee. Instead, he had eschewed both for an undistinguished place amidst his fellow senators. He would still bluster and make his views known, as people would expect of him, but he would do it in a manner that would not openly challenge the praetor. In that way, he hoped to make himself less of a threat, and therefore less of a target.

Of course, he could afford to assume a lower profile, knowing that his interests—both political and personal—were well represented on the Continuing Committee.

It amused Durjik to observe Tomalak ignoring the young legislator in favor of responding to the bloviations

of Senator Eleret, the beldam from the Remestrel clan.
Eleret doggedly asked about the dwindling foodstuffs for
the masses throughout the Empire—an understandable
concern, to be sure—but she steadfastly refused to listen to
what the proconsul had to say—also understandable, Durjik thought.

As he waited for the exchange to end, Durjik took the
time to study Tal'Aura. In the center of the opposite side of
the chamber, she sat in a high-backed chair—not quite a
throne—facing the rows of senators. Behind her, a detailed
wooden framework held an expanse of glass etched with the
symbol of the Empire: a front-on view of a raptor, its talons
clutching the worlds of Romulus and Remus. Except that a
length of black cloth had been draped in an arc from the top
corners of the glass. Durjik grasped the obvious symbolism,
the official recognition and remembrance of the senators
that Shinzon had murdered in that very room, but he wondered if the mourning cloth had been purposely hung so
that it would cover the depictions of the two Romulan core
planets. Thanks to the traitorous Donatra and the incom-
petent Tal'Aura, Remus—or at least its people—no longer
belonged to the Empire.

Still, Durjik admitted to himself that Tal'Aura not only
presented herself well in the role of praetor, but over time
had shown herself adept at consolidating and holding on to
power. Her initially stunning request of the Hundred that
they re-form the Senate, which on the surface looked like
an action that would weaken the praetor, actually insulated
Tal'Aura and potentially would draw even more power to
her. Once the new Senate had convened, she'd revealed her
negotiations with the Breen, Gorn, Kinshaya, Tholians,

and Tzenkethi, and her radical plan for the Romulan Star Empire to join them in a new entity she called the Typhon Pact. By taking the proposition to the Senate, she shielded herself from charges, or even the appearance, of overreaching, of single-handedly committing the Empire to a radical new course. At the same time, if such a pact did form, it would immediately elevate the strength of its component members, and thus of their leaders.

And Tal'Aura is already strong, Durjik thought. By calling for a new Senate, she had also brought back into existence the Continuing Committee—*the* political body responsible for the confirmation of a new praetor. In theory, Tal'Aura had sown the seeds of her own potential demise; in practice, Durjik saw, she had gathered enough power to prevent the Committee from being a threat to her.

Durjik continued to regard Tal'Aura from across the chamber. She sat silently as the debate about the Typhon Pact raged around her. She had attired herself in a deep-purple ceremonial robe, and she wore it well on her tall, slender body. Her hair had grayed considerably since she had seized the praetorship, but it suited her, her quiet maturity lending her an air of confidence and authority. She sat just behind the line of four tables that accommodated the eight members of the Continuing Committee, and with the possible exception of Rehaek, she seemed the only one on that side of the chamber comfortable with the vociferousness of the arguments being waged.

Rehaek, though, appeared not only comfortable, but almost unaccountably disinterested in the proceedings. He sat farthest right among the members of the Continuing Committee, his attention seemingly on none of the speakers, but wandering to the huge silver sculpture hanging above the circular, marble mosaic at the center of the chamber. The piece mirrored the image engraved in glass behind Tal'Aura, but rendered in imposing dimension.

The reverse of Rehaek, Durjik thought. Where the great figure of the raptor loomed above the Senate as though a menace, the young chairman of the Tal Shiar—the elite Romulan intelligence agency—looked remote, a man of no great consequence. And where the inanimate statue in reality proved a danger to no one, the seemingly uninvolved Rehaek controlled the resources to imperil every person present—including Tal'Aura.

Across the room, Vortis suddenly shot up from her seat. The head of Agricultural Affairs, she occupied a spot on the Continuing Committee along with other cabinet directors, the proconsul, and a pair of appointed senators. Not usually excitable, she shouted down Senator Eleret. "This new alliance will *bring* food into the Empire!" she yelled. "Why are you insisting otherwise?"

"Because it *is* otherwise," Eleret said. "Even if the other nations in this new alliance begin to provide the food our people need, we will be ceding to them power over our lives. What happens when those other nations want something from Romulus that we're unwilling to give? They'll withhold provisions, starve us, in order to get what they want."

"That will not happen," Tomalak said, rising from his chair as well. "While members of the Typhon Pact will be providing necessities for Romulus, we will be providing necessities for them. It will be a relationship based upon mutual benefit."

"'Mutual benefit,'" Eleret spat. "Do you truly wish to

entrust the lives of the Romulan people to the whims of the Tholian Assembly? Or to the exacting requirements of the Tzenkethi autarch?"

"Who would you rather trust?" Vortis demanded. "The president of the Federation and her council?"

Tomalak raised his arms, one hand toward Eleret, one toward Vortis. "Please, please," he implored them. "One thing we need to do is trust ourselves. The association that the Empire will share with the other Typhon Pact nations is laid out in meticulous detail in the treaty document. That association mandates monitoring of any . . . delicate . . . provisions. There will be no need for blind trust, but we will undoubtedly be able to establish verifiable trust."

Vortis assumed a vindicated posture, hands on her hips, elbows out, almost as though challenging Eleret to say more. The senator appeared ready to do so, but before she could, another voice spoke. "An association with those other powers will necessarily position the Empire for the possibilities of both rewards and dangers, but any such association would," said the young senator who Durjik had seen stand earlier. He spoke in low but confident tones, not loudly, but still able to project his voice throughout the chamber. "Perhaps of more importance, so too would isolationism."

"Are you advocating for the new alliance or against it?" Durjik barked, wanting to test the tyro. He reached for the young man's name and family, trying to picture in his mind the document he'd scanned earlier, which contained information on each member of the new Senate. *Dor,* he thought. *Xarius or Xarian Dor, of the Ortikant.*

"I am trying to decide whether or not to vote to ratify the Typhon Pact treaty," said the young man. "That is why we're here, is it not?" He paused, as though allowing an opportunity for a response, but when none came, he continued. "I am in favor of advancing our relations with our celestial neighbors in general, and I believe that the way this treaty is composed, it will benefit the Empire and the other nations."

"So you're for it," another senator called out.

"Maybe," he said. "My concern is that such a significant alliance will engender fear in the Federation, in the Klingon Empire, in the Reman Protectorate, and in the Imperial Romulan State. Rather than fostering peace in the quadrant, the Typhon Pact could bring us to the brink of war."

Let it, Durjik thought. With the losses that the Federation had suffered at the hands of the Borg, it would stand little chance of defeating the combined force that the Typhon Pact could deploy. But Durjik knew the governments of the Empire's prospective allies, and while most shared a distrust—and even a loathing—of the Federation, he knew that they also shared a reluctance to declare war on it. *That is the problem with signing on as coequals.*

As Tomalak responded to Dor and the debate continued, Durjik thought, almost wistfully, *If only Donatra had not succeeded.* By dividing the military and carving away planets from the Empire to form her own fiefdom, she had weakened the Romulan people. But if Donatra could be defeated and the Empire returned to its former glory, Durjik thought that by virtue of its renewed size and military might, it could easily become the de facto leader of the Typhon Pact. Romulus could then propel the launch of a first strike against the Federation and the Klingons.

With the right praetor in place, Durjik thought. He resented the notion of the Romulan Star Empire entering an alliance with other powers as coequals, but the possibility of at last ridding the cosmos of the Federation and their Klingon lapdogs made the ignominy worth considering. So much so that when debate finally ended late that afternoon, Durjik cast his vote in favor of ratifying the Typhon Pact treaty.

As did a majority of the senators, and all of the Continuing Committee.

13

In his cell, Spock lowered himself to his knees and interlaced his fingers. With bowed head, he closed his eyes, preparing to embrace the peace of meditation. In his mind's eye, he traveled through ancient caverns, seeing moisture glistening on stone walls, and unreadable symbols notched into solid rock.

From there, Spock envisioned pushing out of the damp, cool subterranean space and into the arid heat. The great figure of a Vulcan master, sculpted from fire-red stone, rose high above him. He descended low, amorphous rock ledges, down to pools of boiling water and churning heaps of lava. Ahead lay the Fire Plains of Gol.

Spock continued on, sweeping across the great furnace of the empty plateau. His consciousness floated above the vast plain, the heat falling away as the Vulcan ground lost what few discernible elements it possessed. Spock soared over the increasingly blank land, concentrating his will on the barren topography.

Slowly at first, and then with increasing speed, Spock felt his concerns slough away from his mind. He shed the thoughts that consumed him, peeling them away like unwanted layers of clothing. A sense of calm enveloped him, a tranquility that nestled his awareness in its quiet depths.

But then a point of color appeared in the drab stretch of terrain. Where the easy contemplation of emptiness had brought peace, the blemish in the otherwise-unfilled extent demanded focus. Spock approached it from afar, and from above, driving toward it until it began to give up its detail: a body, lying in the desert, motionless, limbs twisted into unnatural positions. As he drew closer, he saw the network of dark-green lines suffusing the flesh. Even before the face came into view, he knew the identity of the inert figure: the Reman who had tried to kill him.

Spock opened his eyes. He briefly considered making another attempt to meditate, but decided against it. Instead, he would do what he had been doing for the past five days: he would wait.

Pulling himself from his knees, Spock moved over to sit down on the sleeping surface, one of only three features in the bare cell. Other than the refresher tucked behind a screen in the corner, and the magnetically sealed door, the small room claimed no other elements to interrupt the flat planes of the floor, walls, and ceiling. Obviously designed for neither comfort nor torment, the cell served well its singular purpose of detention.

Five days had passed since Spock, Venaster, and D'Tan had attempted to convey the Reman from their custody to that of Romulan Security. During his imprisonment at the Via Colius security office, Spock had been treated fairly, receiving regular meals and few questions. The latter surprised him, as did the fact that, at least as far as he knew, he had been charged with only one crime, the relatively minor offense of residing illegally on Romulus. In his few interactions with the security staff, no one had mentioned the illegality of the Reunification Movement, or made the spurious but predictable charge of espionage.

From the beginning of his incarceration, Spock had requested to speak with the protector who headed the security office. For three days, he received no response, until the protector appeared and curtly asked why Spock wanted to talk with him. Spock explained that he possessed information Tal'Aura would consider vital, and that he sought an audience with her. The protector—who identified himself as R'Jul—scoffed at the idea of an alleged criminal meeting with the praetor, and he left as abruptly as he had arrived.

Spock wondered if he'd made a mistake in coming to the security office. His intention to advance the cause of reunifying the Vulcan and Romulan people remained, as did his conviction that the current Romulan schism provided an opportunity to foment such an advance. But if he—

Without warning, an energetic hum erupted from the door, which then retracted into the wall. Beyond the force field that evidently had been erected to keep his cell secure, a pair of sentries flanked Protector R'Jul. "On your feet," commanded R'Jul, his tone containing neither antagonism nor compassion.

Spock did as instructed. R'Jul stepped back, and the sentries—he recognized one as Sorent—trained disruptor pistols in his direction. Sorent then reached up to the side of the door, the hum fading as she deactivated the force field. The trio then dropped back to the far side of the wide corridor.

"Exit the cell," said R'Jul, "then turn to your right and walk forward."

Again, Spock followed the protector's orders. As he passed from his cell and into the corridor, he asked, "Where are you taking me?"

R'Jul did not respond.

Doors lined the corridor on one side only, all of them closed. As Spock walked forward, hearing the footfalls of his jailors tracking behind him, the tableau put him in mind of what had brought him to the security office. In the present instance, though, he had exchanged places, no longer the guard, but the guarded.

At the far end of the corridor, R'Jul instructed him to turn right again, the only option available. When Spock rounded the corner, he saw a short, empty walkway that ended at a large, open door. Beyond it stood the interior of what appeared to be a shuttle or ground transport of some sort. R'Jul ordered him inside, where Sorent manacled him to the bulkhead. She then secured the doors, and in moments, Spock felt movement, suggesting that the vehicle had started on its way.

Spock did not know his destination, but he knew enough of Romulan Security to wonder if his journey would take him only one way.

The massive wooden doors, intricately carved with ornate scrollwork and inlaid with green-veined ruatinite, dominated the courtyard. Above, sunlight shined in through the windows of the cupola, imparting a hazy, twilit glow to the circular space. Other sets of doors offered access and egress to the courtyard, but none commanded attention like the ones before which Spock stood.

When the vehicle transporting him had stopped, Sentry Sorent released him from his restraints and turned him over to a pair of armed uhlans. The two Romulan military officers conducted him through a series of tunnels, until finally climbing a flight of stairs and emerging into the courtyard. Once there, one of the uhlans pulled twice on a length of thick, braided golden rope. Several seconds passed, and then a chime sounded, though Spock could not determine its source.

One of the uhlans stepped forward and pushed open the doors. He then motioned to Spock, telling him to enter. Spock did, and found himself within a dark, opulent chamber. The black floor gleamed, while the walls appeared composed of volcanic stone, burnished to give them a rich, heavy gloss. Reaching up to a high ceiling adorned with a well-executed mural, pairs of deep-blue columns marched along the periphery of the round room. Between the sets of columns, ancient Romulan artwork, realized in various media, communicated both a sense of history and the mark of great wealth. At the far end of the regal space, opposite the doors, a raised platform contained a tall chair bedecked in gold. In it sat Praetor Tal'Aura.

"Approach," she said simply.

Spock did so, the boots of the uhlans thumping along behind him at close range. When he had neared to within several paces of the praetor, he stopped and bowed his head. "Thank you for seeing me, Praetor."

"I am seeing you because it suits me," said Tal'Aura. She glanced to either side of Spock, at the uhlans. "You may leave."

"But Praetor," one of them protested, stammering over her title, "our orders—"

"Are mine to give," Tal'Aura said sharply. She peered back at Spock. "Do not worry," she told the uhlans. "This man is a pacifist. Is that not right, Spock of Vulcan?"

"I intend to commit no act of violence against you, if that is what you mean," Spock said.

Tal'Aura once again looked at the uhlans, and this time they departed without comment. Still, Spock had little doubt that the praetor had not been left unprotected. Appropriate security measures likely had been implemented in her audience chamber, from the monitoring of the room to the secreting in it of remotely controlled weapons.

"I am told that you claim to be in possession of information vital to me," said Tal'Aura. She wore a navy suit of a severe cut, its acute features complimenting her trim body, and echoing the points both of her ears and of the tapering hair that depended along the sides of her narrow face. "Was that merely a feint employed in an attempt to speak with me, or do you truly have such information?"

"The information of which I spoke is genuine," Spock said. "But it is not data that I bring to you. It is a different perspective."

A slight smile curled Tal'Aura's lips. "A different perspective? Of that, I am quite certain," she said. "But why would I even listen to the opinion of an outworlder—of an *intruder*—let alone consider it to be of vital importance?"

"Because it is the logical thing to do," Spock said. "And

because what I relate can help both you and the Romulan people."

The praetor sat forward in her chair and seemed to study Spock. "And why would you wish to help me?" she asked, clearly not believing that Spock would.

Spock did not prevaricate. "In general, I would not," he acknowledged. "But where the cause I support shares common aims with you, there is room for cooperation."

Tal'Aura sat back, dismissing the idea with the brush of her hand. "Your cause it not licit, Spock," she said. "As praetor, I cannot share its aims."

"The criminalization of the Vulcan-Romulan Reunification Movement is arbitrary, based upon no moral or ethical precepts," Spock noted. "The elimination of such a statute is therefore easily justified and easily accomplished."

"Easily?" Tal'Aura asked, her brow furrowing.

"You are the sole political leader of the Romulan Star Empire," Spock said, stating the obvious. "Within the Empire, you essentially can do as you see fit to do."

"You so readily discount the power of the Senate?" Tal'Aura said.

The question stopped Spock. It implied the re-establishment of the Empire's legislative body, something that, as far as he knew, hadn't occurred since Shinzon's dastardly mass assassination.

"The new senators may have been selected only recently, but many have served in government before," Tal'Aura said. "Imposing my will upon them may not be as easily achieved as you think." She waited for Spock to respond, but apparently read his silence as ignorance. "Wait," she said. "You don't know about the Senate."

"No," Spock said. "But it does not alter the considerable power you must still wield. If you choose to push for the legalization of the Vulcan-Romulan Reunification Movement, it will likely happen."

"True," Tal'Aura said. "But you have not convinced me that I should. What is this 'different perspective' that you wish to convey to me?"

"I must first state that which you already know," Spock told her. "The collective disposition of the Romulan people continues to deteriorate. They have been witness to the murder of Praetor Hiren and most of the Senate, the take-over of their government by a Reman force led by a human, and your own seizure of power. They have watched as dissent has been quashed, most notably in the elimination of Admiral Braeg and his opposition movement. They have seen the Remans revolt and not only gain their independence, but become a ward of the Klingon Empire. Perhaps most damaging of all, they have lived through the fracturing of the Empire into two rival states. On Romulus and the worlds you lead, Praetor, the rationing of food and medical supplies has become commonplace." He paused, allowing Tal'Aura a moment to digest, as a whole, the series of hardships experienced by her people. "Even with a new Senate," he then continued, "I wonder how long it will be before the citizenry follows the lead of the Remans, rising up to combat a government they do not trust and that they believe has failed them."

Tal'Aura rose to her feet as though propelled from her chair. "You dare to threaten me?"

Spock lowered his head and placed his hands behind his back, a conscious display of his nonviolent intent. "I do not threaten you, Praetor," he said. "As you pointed out yourself, I am a man of peace. I merely state facts and hypothesize where they might lead."

Tal'Aura appeared to consider this. Then she descended from her platform and paced over to Spock, stopping in front of him and staring directly into his eyes. "While your manner is respectful, your words are insolent," she said. "But there is some truth in what you say."

The praetor stepped past Spock. He turned to watch her as she padded across her audience chamber. The heels of her shoes clacked along the floor.

"In recent weeks," she went on, "public displays of violence, particularly against the government, have erupted across Romulus, and even on several other worlds within the Empire." Tal'Aura reached a display table situated along the wall, where she examined a large black vase ornamented with copper filigree. After a moment, she turned to face Spock across the room. "Although you are not a part of the Romulan government, you are, even in hiding, a political figure on our world. And if you are to be believed, a Reman attempted to assassinate you, and then later, was himself killed."

Spock took note of Tal'Aura's language. She had not spoken of the Reman's death as suicide, but as murder. He did not address it, but he knew that if he regained his freedom, he would need to investigate further.

"So I will grant you the verity of your observation that the public atmosphere on Romulus has deteriorated," Tal'Aura said. "But why do you tell me this?"

"It is my contention that a public debate about the merits of Vulcan-Romulan reunification will work to focus the will of the people, both those for and against it," Spock explained. "Of particular import to you, Praetor, it will also concentrate public opinion on the uniting of the Romulan Star Empire with the Imperial Romulan State."

Tal'Aura took a single stride forward. "Because how can the Romulan people reunify with the Vulcans if the Romulan people are not themselves united," she said, crystallizing Spock's point.

"Precisely," he said. "And I will pledge to you that I will lead the Reunification Movement without its resorting to violence. What I ask in return is that the Movement be decriminalized, and that its adherents be allowed to speak and act in public—including being able to stage rallies—without fear of reprisal. I also request the release of two of the Movement's supporters, T'Solon and Vorakel."

"Is that all?" Tal'Aura asked.

Spock could not tell if she spoke facetiously or seriously. "If I may be so bold as to analyze your thoughts and actions, Praetor, I do not believe that you consider the Reunification Movement a threat to Romulus. Although you have continued the occasional search and capture of our people, that appears more a result of governmental inertia than a willful continuation of Praetor Hiren's pogrom."

Again, a smile dressed Tal'Aura's face. "You are indeed bold, Spock," she said. "But I will be forthright with you. There are far greater threats to the Empire than a relatively small group of our people with a fetish for the Vulcan way of life. And by greater threats, I mean those capable of achieving their goals within my lifetime."

With the praetor having conceded his point, Spock had nothing else to say. Tal'Aura remained silent as well, until she strode back across the room, past him, and back up to her raised chair. She sat down and said, "Mister Spock, I will consider it."

The words did not seem idle to Spock. "Thank you, Praetor," he said, again bowing his head. A moment later, he heard the doors of the chamber open behind him, followed by the march of footsteps toward him. The uhlans did not return him to the custody of Romulan Security, but did send him to another detention cell. He could do nothing but wait, his fate—and perhaps that of reunification—in the hands of Praetor Tal'Aura.

14

Off to the right, the sun set behind the mountains, throwing the land into long shadows. The distant river, just moments ago reflecting a fiery red, became a dark snake, meandering lazily across the plain. Closer in, the trees that dotted the grass-covered lowland hinted that autumn had arrived, leaves here and there just beginning their transformations from deep green to pale green, to orange and red.

Sisko loved this land. As he walked along the unpaved road that led from Adarak, he recalled vividly the first time he had ever seen this place. After he'd attended a conference in Rakantha Province, Vedek Oram Yentin had invited him to visit a monastery in neighboring Kendra. Though Sisko could no longer even remember the purpose of the conference, no detail of the subsequent trip escaped his memory.

They had traveled by runabout. Just before dusk, they crossed the mountains, revealing the valley before them. Peering through the runabout's ports, Sisko saw the late-afternoon sunlight glistering off the winding length of the Yolja River, the entire landscape shimmering as though a mirage. He knew instantly that he'd found the place he would build his dream house, the place he would call home and live with—

Kasidy.

Sisko shifted his duffel from one shoulder to the other, then looked ahead at the house peeking out from behind the *moba* trees. He would reach it in just a few minutes, and still he didn't know what he would say. He had opted to take the long walk out from Adarak to give himself time to find the right words, but he'd met with little success. Actually, striding along the old dirt road, he hadn't thought much about what would happen that evening.

That's because you didn't really walk home so you could figure out what to say, he reproved himself. He'd had plenty of time for that in the five days since he'd left Earth. He traveled on two different ships to reach Bajor. Once he beamed down to the public transporter station in Adarak, he easily could have beamed out to the house. Instead, he chose to walk. Maybe he lied to himself about needing time to resolve exactly what he would say to Kasidy, maybe he simply didn't think about it, but truthfully, he just wanted to delay the terrible moments to come.

Coward, he thought. Even in his head, the epithet sounded to him like something that might have been said by his old strategic operations officer aboard Deep Space 9. Sisko could even imagine hearing Worf tell him that, in the current circumstances, he lacked honor. Despite the harshness of the characterizations, the recollection of Worf managed to force a smile onto Sisko's face. He vowed to try to keep it there as much as he could in the coming hours.

When Sisko reached the path to the house—which he and Kasidy had only last summer gotten around to lining with flagstone—he turned off the road. He mounted the steps and made his way across the porch to the front door. As he let himself in, he felt his heart pounding in his chest.

Inside, the front rooms were empty. To his left, a pair of chairs sat in front of the stone hearth, arrayed around a small triangular table. Stacked in the firebox, logs waited for the opportunity to banish the chill that would replace the warmth of the late summer. The mantel held numerous framed photographs: Rebecca as an infant, and at various ages from her first four and a half years; a montage of Jake, and his wedding picture with Korena; Sisko's father and stepmother; and others. Sisko glanced at a photo taken of him and Kasidy at their marriage ceremony, and quickly looked away. He peered up instead at the reproduction on parchment of the historic Bajoran icon painting, *City of B'hala*.

To his right, a much larger sitting area faced large picture windows that looked out on Kendra Valley. Ahead, past the front rooms, stood a dining table and chairs, and to the right of that, a doorway opened into the kitchen. A doll lay on the table.

From past the fireplace, off to the left, voices emerged from the hallway. Sisko heard Kasidy, and then the lilt of his daughter's laughter. The dread tensing his body evaporated like dew on a warm morning. He smiled and dropped his duffel to the floor.

The two of them walked out of the hall, Rebecca dressed in pink pajamas covered with drawings of Bajoran animals: *batos* and cows, sheep and *pylchyks*. A pink bow adorned her braided hair. She looked adorable.

Kasidy saw him first. When she did, she started, raising her hand to her chest, obviously surprised at the sight of another person inside the house. She uttered a yip, and Rebecca looked up at her, then followed her gaze across the room.

"Daddy!" she yelled. She threw her arms wide and ran to him. Sisko crouched and caught his daughter as she threw herself at him. She wrapped her little arms around his neck, and he squeezed her tightly to him.

Across the room, Kasidy remained standing at the entrance to the hallway, a hand still clutched to her chest. As she looked on, a warm smile spread across her face. His eyes met hers, and they connected.

For the last time, Sisko had come home.

"How was it?" Kasidy asked hesitantly. Sisko sat with her by the windows in the front room, the lamp in the corner providing the only illumination. Outside, darkness reigned, none of Bajor's five moons yet risen to wash the landscape silver with their secondhand light.

After visiting with Kasidy and Rebecca for an hour or so, Sisko had carried his daughter off to her bedroom. She hadn't gone to sleep easily or willingly; she hadn't seen her father for a month and a half, and so she'd wanted to stay up with him. While Rebecca lay in bed, Sisko had to read three stories to her before she finally drifted off to sleep.

By the time he'd come out to the front of the house, Kasidy had prepared a light meal for him. As they sat at the dining table and nibbled together at the food, Kas told him how sorry she felt about the death of Sisko's father. She asked how he felt, and how Jake had taken the loss. Sisko answered her questions, and spoke about the rest of the family and about the funeral. They both shed some tears, and once awkwardly held each other as they sat at the table.

Just a few moments ago, they'd moved into the living room, taking their seats on opposite ends of the sofa and facing each other. Although Sisko had sent messages to Kasidy after the battle against the Borg, he hadn't offered much detail beyond the facts of his own health and survival. So it didn't surprise him when she asked about it.

"It was hard," he said. He told her about how the crews of the three Starfleet vessels had somehow destroyed four Borg cubes, but how that hadn't been enough. He told her about how *New York* and *James T. Kirk* had become incapacitated, and how *Cutlass* and its crew had been blasted out of space. He told her about the two remaining Borg ships firing on Alonis and killing more than eleven thousand people.

And he told her about Elias Vaughn.

"I know," Kasidy said with great sadness. "Nog told me. I'm so sorry. I know you felt very close to Elias."

"I did," Sisko said, then realized that he'd spoken in the past tense. "I mean, I *do*," he amended. "Actually, I don't even know if he's still alive."

"He is," Kasidy said. "At least, that's what Nog told me two days ago. Elias was moved to Deep Space Nine, since Lieutenant Tenmei is his only living relative."

"How is he?" Sisko asked. "Has there been any improvement?"

"No," Kasidy said. "There's no evidence of higher brain function. According to Nog, they've got him hooked up in the infirmary to a lot of life-sustaining equipment."

Sisko nodded absently, his thoughts suddenly far away as he visualized his vital, active friend reduced to an unthinking mass of compromised flesh. He couldn't imagine Elias wanting to have his mindless body reliant on machines to keep it from succumbing. Still, as long as

Vaughn remained technically alive, Sisko felt an obligation to him. "I should visit him before I—" He stopped, aware of what he'd been about to say.

"Before you what?" Kasidy asked. He could hear suspicion in her voice, see it written in her features. Since he'd arrived, there had been none of that—no resumption of the troubles between them, no apparent renewal of old resentments. But even in mourning Sisko's father together, they had kept their interaction close to the surface, both clearly wary of going any deeper.

All of that was about to end.

"Before I leave the Bajoran system," Sisko said.

"What?" Kasidy said, turning her head slightly and staring at him askance. "Where are you going?"

He knew of no way to soften the blow. "I'm returning to Starfleet," he said.

Kasidy stood up, driven by anger or disappointment or disbelief, or whatever emotion she felt. "You *are* returning to Starfleet?" she said. "We're not going to discuss it? You've already made your decision?"

Sisko raised his hands, palms up, as though helpless to choose otherwise. "The Borg annihilated forty percent of Starfleet. They desperately need experienced officers."

"I'm sure they do," Kasidy said. "But haven't you already done enough?"

Sisko recognized the echo of his own thoughts when Admiral Walter had asked him to return to the service after the Borg crisis. Back then, Sisko had been prepared to discuss with Kasidy the possibility of spending some time apart. At this point, the situation had become much more serious.

"Kas—"

"Don't you *Kas* me," she said, raising her voice. She closed her eyes and held her hands up for a moment, as though trying to reel in her emotions. When she opened her eyes, she peered toward the hallway, obviously listening for Rebecca, concerned that her loud words might have woken their daughter. After a few seconds, she turned back toward Sisko, then took a step and sat down in the middle of the sofa, closer to him.

"Ben, I know things have been tense between us for a while now," she said. "And I understand why you had to go help fight the Borg: you were protecting your family." She reached forward and rested her hand on his knee. "But we *are* a family. We have a daughter. We agreed that we didn't want to raise her on Deep Space Nine, and I don't want to raise her here by myself with you gone off on missions half the time. Not to mention the dangers that you'll have to face."

"I'm not going back to Deep Space Nine," he said quietly.

Kasidy pulled her hand back from his knee. "Where are you going?"

"The *U.S.S. Robinson,*" Sisko said. "I'll be taking command in two weeks. At least initially, our patrol route will be in the Sierra Sector."

Kasidy looked away. "On the other side of the Federation," she said, and stood up again. "Really, Ben, if you want to leave me, you don't have to go so far."

"Kasidy, I don't *want* to leave you," he said, unable to stop himself from telling the truth. "The *Robinson* is a *Galaxy*-class vessel. You and Rebecca could—" He hated the lie, especially since it only served as an attempt to shift the responsibility for the dissolution of their marriage.

"Rebecca and I could what?" Kasidy said. "Come with you? Live aboard a starship? You know that's not the life I want for our daughter." She paused for a moment as she saw through his dishonesty. "Wait a minute. You *do* know how important it is to me to raise Rebecca on a planet, in a real home." She shook her head, her expression one of disbelief. "That wasn't even a genuine offer, was it? It was safe for you to make it because you knew what my answer would be. But you don't really want us coming with you, do you?"

He gazed up at her, feeling lost and helpless, and angry at himself for allowing all of this to happen. He said nothing.

"Do you?" she demanded. This time when he didn't respond, she turned and walked around the sofa, over to the front door. She reached down, grabbed the strap of his duffel with both hands, and hauled it into the air. "You don't have to wait two weeks for the *Robinson*," she said. "You can leave now."

Sisko rose from the sofa and looked across the room at his wife. "Kas," he said again, but he had no more words than that. He made his way around the sofa, accepted his duffel from her, and slung it across his shoulder. "I'm sorry," he told her, and he meant it. But he could not say all of the things he wanted to say: *I love you. I love our daughter. I don't* want *to leave.* He could not tell her any of that because even though it was all true, it would require an explanation from him about why he did have to leave, an explanation that he knew she would not be able to accept.

Kasidy opened the front door. "Good-bye, Ben."

Without another word, Sisko walked into the darkest night he'd known in years.

15

The chairman of the Tal Shiar gently pushed open the doors to the praetor's audience chamber, aware that his adjutant would have thrown them open, willfully expressing his disdain for Tal'Aura, and intentionally seeking to draw the ire of her proconsul. Rehaek knew that Torath despised Tomalak, a mutual rancor that apparently went back quite a number of years. The two adversaries had both served in the Imperial Fleet, though never on the same vessel, but the chairman believed that they had first crossed paths in the military.

Regardless, Rehaek did not need his meeting with Tal'Aura derailed by the bad behavior of either his adjutant or the proconsul. Of course, the chairman could have come to the Hall of State alone, or brought a different aide with him, but he trusted nobody with his security more than Torath. For a time, Rehaek had thrived on chaos. He had utilized the Watraii affair to eliminate the allies of Praetor Neral so that his own ally, Senator Hiren, could then eradicate the weakened leader and claim the position for himself. And when Shinzon had sent the Empire into turmoil with his coup d'état, Rehaek had employed it as cover for his own overthrow, taking down the ailing chairman of the Tal Shiar. But now that he had assumed the chairmanship himself, Rehaek wanted calm to rule the Empire, and stability to become the watchword of the intelligence agency.

Rehaek marched across the chamber toward where the praetor sat in her elevated chair. Her proconsul stood several paces before her, essentially guarding her time and her safety. *As though Tomalak could best me in any type of combat,* Rehaek thought, then chided himself for such overconfidence. *In all things, intellect, observation, and caution,* he reminded himself. Whether or not Tomalak could have prevented him from snapping Tal'Aura's neck, Rehaek would have been reduced to cinders just for making the attempt. As he had an ally in Torath and in others, so too did the praetor have her supporters. In fact, Rehaek had pledged to back Tal'Aura, and she him, though he suspected that the praetor trusted his word no further than he trusted hers.

A few strides before Tomalak, the chairman stopped, as did Torath beside him. Without taking his gaze from the proconsul, Rehaek reached to his side and touched the flat of his palm to Torath's chest, a signal that his adjutant should not continue forward. He could have made the same command with merely a glance, but he wished the praetor and the proconsul to see it. Following protocol, Rehaek then approached Tomalak. "Good afternoon, Proconsul," he said. "I believe the praetor has requested my presence."

"Praetor Tal'Aura requested your *presence*—" Tomalak spewed the last word as though it tasted bitter in his mouth. "—two days ago."

Rehaek shrugged and offered an explanation, though not an apology. "I am a busy man," he said. "Busy, of course, ensuring that neither the Romulan Star Empire nor its leader fall victim to their enemies." A delay of two days had been enough for Rehaek to demonstrate his independence, his nerve, and his strength, but not enough to justify Tal'Aura's finding a means of removing him from his position.

Tomalak seemed to appraise him, and then he peered over at Torath. For a moment, Rehaek thought that the proconsul would throw a venomous comment Torath's way, which would undoubtedly provoke the adjutant, but then he looked back at Rehaek. "The praetor would like an update on the death of the Reman," he said. "Have you made any progress on determining who killed him?"

"The Reman?" Rehaek said, feigning confusion.

"The one who Spock brought into the Via Colius security station," Tomalak said. "The one who was then killed inside the station."

"Ah, yes, of course," Rehaek said. "We do have some information on him, though as with most Remans, it is rather sketchy." Without turning, he gestured back toward his adjutant.

"His name was Angarraken," Torath said at once. "He was raised on Remus and worked in the mines. When the praetor made an accord with the Remans—" Torath did not hide his contempt for Tal'Aura's decision to appease the Remans, but fortunately neither she nor her proconsul responded to it. "—Angarraken was among those who settled here on Romulus. When they later relocated to Klorgat Four, he must have stayed behind."

"That is all very interesting," Tomalak said, "but it is not an answer to the question that the praetor put to you."

"But to get to that answer," Rehaek said, "we must follow the trail of that which is known, until it leads to that which is unknown."

"Of course you must," Tal'Aura said, finally deigning to speak. Tomalak stepped to the side, permitting Rehaek an unimpeded view of the praetor. She wore a simple, gray raiment. "And I appreciate your efforts, Chairman."

He bowed to her, pretending to show her the respect that would mollify her.

"But I must ask," she said, "*do* you have an answer to my question?"

"I do not," Rehaek lied. His people had identified the culprit with relative ease, but to this point, they lacked a motive. The chairman had his suspicions, though, and he hoped that the praetor would confirm them for him.

"That is disappointing," Tal'Aura said, "and somewhat surprising."

"Surprising?" Rehaek said. "Murder investigations frequently require a great deal of time and effort to resolve."

"Even with such a paucity of suspects?" Tal'Aura said. "Clearly one of the security officers who tried to take him into custody was to blame."

"I'm sorry, Praetor, but that's simply not the case," Rehaek told her. "Although one or more of the security personnel might have murdered the Reman, there is no definitive evidence to suggest just when the toxic patch was applied to his arm. For all we know, Spock could have placed it there prior to entering the security station. Or one of his collaborators. Or anyone else on Romulus, for that matter. And we have yet to conclusively rule out suicide."

Tal'Aura said nothing for a few seconds, and Rehaek wondered if she needed the time to choose which of her own lies to tell. Instead, she seemed to reveal a truth to him—or at least a partial truth. "I did not consider that," she said. "I just assumed that one of the security officers killed the Reman." She stood up, stepped down from her platform, and walked over to face Rehaek directly. Without looking at Tomalak, she gestured to him, and he moved away.

"I may be wrong about who killed the Reman," she went on, "but I believe that whoever did kill him, did so in order to silence him."

"About what?" Rehaek asked, though he thought he already knew.

"About the identity of the person who employed him to kill Spock."

"If Spock was telling the truth about the attempt on his life," Rehaek said.

"The Vulcan is still in our custody," Tal'Aura said. "We have examined him, and he bears the evidence of recent traumatic injury and surgical repair. Nevertheless, he may be lying about the Reman trying to kill him, but it is unclear to what end he would do so."

"Perhaps to gain your trust," Rehaek suggested.

"Perhaps," Tal'Aura allowed, "but wouldn't telling me the truth provide a better, more likely means of doing that?"

Before he even knew he would, Rehaek laughed. "My apologies," he said quickly. "An enemy of the state, telling the truth to the praetor in order to gain her trust? It must be the environment in which I work, but that possibility had not even occurred to me."

To Rehaek's surprise, Tal'Aura actually smiled. "I can understand that," she said. She turned and walked back to the platform, mounting it to sit back down in her chair. "I want you to answer some questions, Chairman, not just for me, but for yourself and for the Tal Shiar."

Rehaek said nothing, but waited to hear what the praetor would ask of him.

"The obvious question is, who would benefit from the death of the Vulcan?" she said. "But I would ask a different question: who would suffer from his continuing to live?"

"That is a broad question," Rehaek said.

"Yes, it is. So let me narrow it down. If Spock lived and continued to champion the cause of reunifying Romulus and Vulcan, and if by virtue of the hardships being felt by people throughout the Empire, his movement gained traction, whom would it harm?"

Rehaek considered this for a moment. "I would argue that it would harm the Empire."

"Really?" she said. "Why, exactly? Do you truly believe that's Spock's movement can succeed? That it can drive a majority of the Romulan people, or even a significant minority, to seek a union with a Federation world?"

Rehaek didn't respond, because he didn't need to respond. Tal'Aura knew the answers to her questions.

"Isn't it possible that such a movement would more likely provoke the Romulan people to demand the uniting of *our own empires*? And isn't it possible that would spread to *all* Romulan people, even outside the Star Empire?"

Rehaek nodded. "Perhaps even probable."

"And if the Romulan people demanded such unity, whom would it harm?"

She had taken the long way around to get to it, but Tal'Aura finally arrived at her destination: "Donatra," Rehaek said.

"Donatra," Tal'Aura confirmed. "The Romulan people who have found themselves no longer a part of the Star Empire, but of Donatra's 'Imperial State,' will not look for Romulus to go to Achernar Prime," she said, naming the worlds that served as the seats of government for the respective empires. "They will look for what they have known for most of their lives. The Romulan Star Empire, Romulus, Ki Baratan, the Senate."

"And the praetor," Rehaek added.

"And the praetor," Tal'Aura said. "That is why I'm going to push the Continuing Committee to reverse the law criminalizing the Romulan-Vulcan Reunification Movement. If Donatra fears it, then we shall set it free."

"So you really think that Donatra employed the Reman to kill Spock," Rehaek said, "and when that failed, she had another agent remove her assassin."

"I think it's possible," Tal'Aura said.

"Then the Tal Shiar shall investigate, Praetor," Rehaek said.

"Then do not let me keep you from your work, Chairman."

Rehaek bowed again, then headed for the entry doors, Torath following along beside him. Halfway across the chamber, the praetor called to him. He stopped and turned back to see Tal'Aura descend once more from her platform. When she reached him, she said, "You and I have spoken before about the benefits of order within the Empire, Chairman."

"Yes."

"Neither the praetorship nor the Tal Shiar are served by disarray," Tal'Aura said. "It seems to me that publicly identifying a man who died in a Romulan Security station as a Reman might cause such disarray."

"Certainly the Remans would not like it," Rehaek said. "Nor would their Klingon protectors."

"Precisely," Tal'Aura said. "It is not as though the Klingons require much provocation to go into battle. And I think you'll agree with me that despite our new alliance with the Typhon Pact nations, it is not the time for war."

Rehaek agreed, and said so.

"Then go," Tal'Aura urged him. "Investigate."

Rehaek continued out the doors with Torath, thinking that the meeting had proven more productive than he'd expected. He would indeed have to investigate, not just the Reman and Donatra's connection to him, but the role he suspected Tal'Aura played in all of this. If he was right, Tal'Aura had found the way to bring the Romulan Star Empire back together, and once she'd done so, he had found the way to bring her down.

The transceiver, mute these many months, chirped to life.

It had been so long since she had heard from Romulus that she had taken to executing diagnostic tests on the device every day. She could not believe that the praetor had discarded her, not from any sense of friendship or loyalty, but because she had served Tal'Aura well—just as she had served praetors before her. She had not always succeeded, but she had done so far more often than not, her methods calculated, merciless, and effective. She had no doubts that in the long run, no other operative could best her abilities.

She crossed the small room, withdrew the transceiver from where she'd hidden it beneath the floor, then used a retina scan, palm print, and voice code to activate it. The device looked like nothing more than a data tablet, but then the face of Praetor Tal'Aura appeared on its small screen. The two recited sequences of verbal cues that verified their identities, their privacy, and the fact that neither acted under duress. Once all of that had been established, Tal'Aura spoke the words she had waited so long to hear.

"I need you."

"I'm ready, Praetor," she said. "When do you need me, and where?"

"I need you now," Tal'Aura said. *"On Romulus."*

She resisted the urge to exclaim her relief. She had spent too much time on the frozen wasteland of Kevratas, a Romulan subject world far removed from the political environs of Ki Baratan. "I'll find my way off this rock within the hour," she said.

"Good. I'll contact you again in five days," Tal'Aura said. *"Be ready."*

"Yes, Praetor."

The screen went blank, and she went immediately to the companel in her room. It took her less than ten minutes to book passage, and only another forty before she beamed up to a transport ship in orbit. As she sat in the passenger section and peered out a port at the retreating orb of Kevratas, she allowed herself a small, satisfied smile.

At long last, Sela was heading home.

16

As D'Tan spoke in the center of the stage, Spock sat off to the side and studied those gathered in the square. Most seemed young, though he observed people across a wide spectrum of ages. Some paid little attention, and some looked around continually, as though they expected Romulan Security to descend upon Relevek Plaza at any moment. A majority of those present, however, appeared genuinely interested in listening to the ideas being put forth. Although some probably stopped for the event as they happened by, Spock thought that most attended after reading the posting announcing it on the city's intranet.

Situated on the outskirts of Ki Baratan, Relevek Plaza provided a large open space frequently used for street fairs, art shows, and farmers' markets. A pair of obelisks marked each of the two entrances to the north and south, standing on either side of the entry paths. The small concrete stage, occasionally used for amateur productions, occupied the western edge of the brick-lined space, with several rows of flat benches arranged before it.

Spock estimated the crowd at approximately four hundred—not large in absolute terms, but under the circumstances, more sizable than he had anticipated. Although Praetor Tal'Aura had followed through on her pledge to consider decriminalizing the Reunification Movement by actually pushing such a repeal through the Continuing Committee, many citizens remained skeptical that such views would be tolerated, least of all in public. Among Spock's own comrades, most suspected that the praetor wanted simply to lure as many supporters out into the open as possible; they expected Romulan Security at some point to conduct a mass arrest—or worse, a mass extermination.

Recalling his first days of involvement with the Movement, Spock remembered similar—and ultimately well-founded—concerns. Thirteen years earlier, he'd become aware of a growing number of Romulans interested in learning about the Vulcan way of life. When Senator Pardek invited him to Romulus to assist in taking the first steps toward reunification, Spock agreed. Pardek introduced him to the proconsul at the time, Neral, who claimed a receptiveness to discussing the Movement and its ideals. In reality, the two Romulans captured Spock's holographic image and attempted to use it to mask an invasion of Vulcan. Though in the end their plan failed, many of those still in the Movement from those days retained their distrust of the Romulan authorities.

D'Tan finished his short oration, an oddly emotive presentation extolling the virtues of Vulcan stoicism and logic. D'Tan spoke, as he often did, with the passion of his youth. It did not trouble Spock, for Romulan society did not discourage the feeling or even the exhibition of emotion. The Reunification Movement, he believed, should welcome all kinds, and teach not just the worthy aspects of a Vulcan life but those of a Romulan life as well.

As D'Tan took a seat beside Spock, T'Lavent rose from

her chair and moved to the center of the stage. A computer technician by trade, she had come to the Movement only recently. Older than D'Tan but just half Spock's age, she offered a different perspective on the benefits of reunifying Vulcan and Romulus.

Spock and the other leaders of the Ki Baratan cell—including Corthin, Dr. Shalvan, Dorlok, and Venaster—had chosen the speakers for their first public rally with care. They did not want to overwhelm any who attended with too many participants or too much information. It also seemed wise to include both genders, as well as a range of ages. In the end, they settled on having three speakers, but just who they would be provided the source of much consternation and argument.

From the beginning, Spock wished to contribute his viewpoint and experience to the rally. Because many of his comrades doubted the sincerity of the praetor's intentions, none of those in leadership positions wanted Spock to speak. He reminded them that Tal'Aura could have kept him imprisoned indefinitely, or even executed him, rather than dropping all charges against him, releasing him, and granting him an unrestricted visitor's visa. He also contended that, because of the relatively high profile he carried for an underground movement, and because of his Vulcan heritage, he would supply a unique and influential voice to the assemblage.

Concurring that at least the possibility of violence existed, Spock agreed that the other two rally participants must volunteer for the task, and must not come from the leadership. Though he did not raise the point, he believed that should violence erupt, he would then be the likeliest target. It also occurred to him that in the event he had misjudged the praetor, he would still serve the cause as a martyr.

T'Lavent concluded her remarks, which provided a contrast to those of D'Tan. With a calm reserve, she enumerated not only the advantages that the Vulcan way could bring to Romulus, but those that the Romulan way could bring to Vulcan. When she left center stage, she carried herself with an air of dignity and satisfaction.

Finally, Spock rose to speak. He had launched the rally with some concise comments, explaining their purpose, introducing D'Tan and T'Lavent, and avowing that the Movement intended to hold future events. When he stepped to the middle of the stage, he sensed increased anticipation in the crowd. As virtually all talking and motion ceased, he peered out to see all eyes looking to him.

"I am Spock of Vulcan," he said. "I am a citizen of the United Federation of Planets, but I am also a legal visitor to Romulus. And thanks to the efforts of Praetor Tal'Aura, the Continuing Committee, and the Romulan Senate, I am now permitted by law—as is anybody on Romulus—to speak about reunification.

"As D'Tan and T'Lavent have so eloquently described, our goals are to promote mutual understanding between Romulans and Vulcans, to foster peace and friendship between us, to find the best that we both have to offer, and to work toward the time when our two societies can become that which they once were before the Sundering: one people."

Spock paused and looked out over his audience. Nobody moved. He saw expressions of rapt attention, but he also noted apparent anxiety in many faces. "As some of you may know," he continued, "modern Vulcan culture focuses on the individual mastery of emotion, as well as an everyday reliance on logic." He paused again, this time for effect. "This, of course, contrasts with Romulan cultural norms."

The comment drew laughter, though little more than a brief murmur drifting through the crowd. Still, it seemed to bring about the result Spock intended. He saw several fleeting smiles and a general relaxing of those listening to him.

"Humor is perhaps a ready source of cultural enrichment that Romulans can provide to Vulcans," he said. "There are others."

He spoke for twenty-five minutes, offering up his own life experience and his own outlook, comparing and contrasting the two cultures, and hypothesizing the boons to be gained from reunification of the two. Afterward, although most of the crowd departed, he, D'Tan, and T'Lavent spent an hour answering questions from those who remained. At no time did Spock detect even the threat of violence, though a number of queries came delivered in hostile words, tones, and attitudes. Overall, he considered the event a success. Only a few hundred people attended the rally, and only a few dozen stayed after that to ask questions, but Spock believed that, quite possibly, a new phase of the Reunification Movement had begun.

17

The blue-white light bathed him in its glow, so brilliant that it penetrated his closed eyelids. It surrounded him, painted his world, his universe, with its dispassionate amalgam of color. Time passed, one minute after the next.

On his knees, Benjamin Sisko, Emissary of the Prophets, opened his eyes and directly beheld the Orb of Prophecy and Change. The mysterious hourglass-shaped artifact shined intensely, its aspect one of movement and energy. It radiated power, and embodied both promise and dread.

Reaching up, Sisko pushed closed the two hinged sides of the ark that carried the Orb. The light enclosed, Sisko waited for his eyes to adjust to the dimness of the temple. By degrees, the details of the ark came into focus, its unremarkable appearance the antithesis of what it held. And yet, gazing upon the simple container, Sisko found himself beset by profound emotions: Sadness. Loss. Fear.

He pushed himself up from his knees and slowly made his way out of the empty temple. He felt staggered, as though physically beaten. For the first few steps, he leaned heavily against the wall, afraid that, otherwise, he would crash to the floor.

Outside, the temperature had risen as morning had given way to afternoon, the moderate climate of Ashalla a shield against the autumnal chill felt elsewhere on Bajor. Vedek Sorretta stood near the temple's doorless entryway, his eyes closed and his face turned upward to catch the sunbeams filtering through the clouds. Sisko tried to walk quietly past, not wanting to disturb him—not wanting to be forced into conversation with him—but as he came abreast of Sorretta, the vedek opened his eyes.

"Emissary," Sorretta said. Dressed in traditional orange vestments, he filled them out like no other clergy Sisko had ever seen on Bajor. With his well-muscled physique, he resembled a bodybuilder more than a man of the cloth. "I trust your Orb experience provided you what you needed."

"It was . . . what I expected," Sisko hedged.

"I'm glad," Sorretta said, obviously not picking up on the particularity of Sisko's verbiage. Of course, the vedek had no reason to expect him to misrepresent himself. "Will you be staying with us much longer?"

"No, I'll be leaving tonight," Sisko said. He had come to the Bajoran capital and the Shikina Monastery six days ago, after leaving Adarak—after leaving Kasidy and Rebecca. In the days prior to his scheduled departure for the Sierra Sector and his new command, he wanted to clear his mind. Alone, he filled his days with long walks through the extensive grounds of the monastery, and his nights with hours of quiet contemplation in the plain room that the vedeks had provided for him. But he hadn't found the peace that he sought. The events of the past days and weeks and months recurred to him, and with them came the question of whether or not he had made the right choices.

"We will be sorry to see you depart," Sorretta said, "but it has been an honor to have you staying here with us."

"Thank you," Sisko said. "I appreciate your hospitality." He quickly walked on before the vedek could say more, darting around the corner of the building without looking back.

Sisko marched to the back of the temple and descended the stone stairs that led to the rear grounds of the monastery. As he did, he considered—as he had numerous times since his arrival—seeking out Opaka, who he knew still visited Shikina with regularity. He hadn't seen the esteemed former kai in many months, and he missed her guidance and quiet strength—especially in the current circumstances. Though always circumspect in her counsel, she often found the words that somehow allowed him to help himself.

Even if I did reach her, Sisko thought, *I don't know if I could find the words to explain to her all that's happened.* Except that he *did* know the right words. He just didn't know if he could say them aloud to another person.

At the base of the rear steps, Sisko followed a paved path out toward the gardens. He had until almost midnight before his scheduled departure from Deep Space 9 aboard *U.S.S. Mjolnir,* a *Norway*-class vessel that would deliver him to *Robinson.* That left him several hours until he needed to take a transport from Bajor to the station, where he would still have time to stop at the infirmary and see Elias. That late at night, he hoped he would be able to make it on and off DS9, and in and out of the infirmary, without encountering anybody he knew.

With my luck these days, Quark will be camped out at the airlock. Thinking of the old Ferengi barkeep—the Ferengi *ambassador,* Sisko corrected himself—actually brought a chuckle to his lips. He latched onto the positive emotion and let it put some distance between him and his experience a few minutes earlier, inside the temple.

Sisko strolled along the path as it weaved through colorful, variegated flowerbeds, trying to let his surroundings bolster his mood further in his last few hours on Bajor. At the leading edge of the arboretum that filled the back third of the monastery grounds, pavement gave way to dirt. Sisko continued on, heading for his favorite spot on the Shikina grounds.

In just a few minutes, he came upon the brook that flowed through the arboretum. He walked along beside it, traveling upstream, until he saw in the distance the burst of pink blooms that marked the location of the undersized waterfall. It surprised him to see the vibrant *nerak* blossoms flowering so late in the season. He decided that, despite everything, he would accept it as a positive omen.

When he arrived at the spot, Sisko bent and selected a rock from the ground, then tossed it into the small pool that fed the cascade of water. He watched the ripples spread out in concentric rings, and then, impulsively, irrationally, he made a wish. *Let there be peace,* he thought, *for Kasidy and Rebecca, for Jake and Korena.*

Lowering himself down, Sisko hung his legs over the stone wall that bordered the pool. His feet dangled half a meter above the water. Closing his eyes, he breathed in deeply, taking in the fragrant scent of the *neraks.*

For a while, he sat that way, listening to the flow of the brook across the little falls. He concentrated on the pink noise of the water and tried to blank his mind. He didn't hear anybody on the dirt path until the scrape of shoes reached him from just a couple of meters away.

Sisko turned and looked up, squinting into the late-afternoon sunlight. He made out a figure standing in the path, clad in the orange robe of the Bajoran clergy, and he initially assumed that Vedek Sorretta also had come out for a walk in the arboretum. But though Sisko could not see the person's face because of the placement of the sun behind it, he distinguished a much smaller frame. He lifted his hand to shield his eyes. "Hello?" he said, though he still had no desire to speak with anybody.

"Hello, Benjamin."

He had not heard the voice for quite a while—probably not for more than a year—and it sounded softer, gentler, than he remembered, but he still recognized it at once. He clambered to his feet. "Nerys," he said. It startled him to hear the delight in his voice, simply because he hadn't felt that way for so long.

Kira stepped forward with her hands out, and he took them, then pulled her in and hugged her. When they parted, he held her at arm's length and studied her robe. "*Vedek* Kira?" he asked. "Is that even possible? From novice to prylar to ranjen to vedek in three years?"

"I know," Kira said. "This—" She gestured down the length of her robe. "—just happened ten days ago."

"Well, congratulations," Sisko said. He took a stride backward and regarded her. "It seems to agree with you. You look . . ." He peered at her face, at the beatific expression she wore. "You look at peace."

"Thank you," Kira said. "I *feel* at peace. For most of my life, I didn't think I'd ever be able to say that."

"I'm very happy for you," Sisko said. "So what are you doing here? Are you a member of the Vedek Assembly?"

"Oh, no," Kira said. "And I'm not sure I ever want to serve in that way. I respect the Assembly, but engaging in politics and staying at peace don't necessarily go together."

"No, I guess not," Sisko agreed.

"I've got a meeting this evening with Vedek Garune," Kira said. "But I've got some time to take a walk, if you'd like."

Sisko stood aside and motioned forward. Side by side, they started down the path. "So then I shouldn't expect to hear the announcement of *Kai* Kira anytime soon?" Sisko asked.

Kira laughed, the same loud, hearty guffaw Sisko had heard back on DS9. For some reason, that pleased him.

"Putting aside my complete lack of qualifications and suitability for the position," Kira said, "I think we're very fortunate to have the kai we do right now."

"You always did like Pralon, even back when she served as Bajor's minister of religious artifacts."

"She's extremely bright, a woman of strong faith and conviction, but she also has a deep empathy for others," Kira said. "And she's not as . . . political . . . as some of her predecessors have been."

"I know what you mean," Sisko said, assuming that she referred to the terribly misguided Winn Adami.

Ahead, the brook curved left, cutting from the right side of the path to the left beneath a footbridge. Their shoes thumped along the wooden structure as they crossed it. Sisko recalled walking there with Vedek Bareil, many years earlier.

"How have you managed to rise through the ranks so quickly?" he asked. "I mean, it's not that I have any doubts about your abilities, but three years isn't the typical time-frame in which to enter the clergy and become a vedek."

"Honestly," Kira said, lowering her voice in mock-conspiratorial fashion, "I think I've been credited with prior experience."

"I don't understand. What prior experience?"

"Serving directly alongside the Emissary of the Proph-ets for seven years," Kira explained. "And being his friend for . . . what? Twelve years now?"

"Something like that," Sisko said, then added dryly, "although I'm not sure we were friends in the beginning."

"No," Kira admitted, "maybe not at first."

Sisko stopped in the path, and Kira did so too. "As I recall," he told her, "you weren't in favor of a Bajoran space station being run by Starfleet officers, including me."

Kira shrugged good-naturedly. "But I learned fast."

Sisko nodded as she made precisely his point. "You've taken quite a journey, Nerys—a journey I'm not sure too many people are capable of making, Bajoran or otherwise. I'm proud of you."

The accolade seemed to embarrass Kira, but she accepted it modestly, bowing her head in acknowledgment. Then she began walking again, and Sisko did so as well. "Sometimes I find it difficult to believe myself," Kira said. "For so much of my life, all I knew was strife: hunger and subjugation and violence. It was a struggle just to survive, and so many didn't."

"You are nothing if not a survivor, Nerys."

"And that was important—it's still important—but there comes a time when you realize that there's a world of difference between surviving and living."

Sisko couldn't tell if she'd spoken with a note of regret. "You did what you had to do," he said.

Kira nodded. "And I suppose I'd do it all over again if I needed to, though probably not quite in the same way," she said. "My time on Deep Space Nine, and my time with you, and even my time commanding the station . . . all of that helped put a lot of things in the past and keep them there." This time, after they had traipsed around a sharp bend in the path, Kira stopped walking and turned to face him. "It helped me learn to cherish the present, and to accept the future as it comes."

For an instant, Sisko thought that she might be trying to advise him about his own life, that she somehow might have gleaned the events of his own present, as well the immediate future he had planned for himself. *But she can't know,* he realized, and then another thought occurred to him about what she had just said. "In many ways, Nerys, your story is the story of Bajor."

"I suppose you could say that," Kira said. "You know the old proverb: The Land and the People are One."

"I do know it," Sisko said. "But I have to admit that I was concerned when you decided to leave Deep Space Nine and Starfleet. I was worried that you might be running away."

"From everything that happened with the Ascendants."

"Yes."

"I understand why you were worried," Kira said. "Believe me, I spent quite a few sleepless nights worried about it myself. In the end, though, what all of that really did was open my mind to new perspectives."

"I think what it did, Nerys, was to deepen your faith," he said. "Not in the Prophets, but in yourself."

"You may be right," she said.

Sisko noticed a tall, square totem a bit farther along the path. A wooden bench nestled beside it. "Shall we sit?" he asked. They did.

"What about you, Benjamin?" Kira reached up and rubbed her hand across the top of his head. "What's this?" Since departing Adarak, he hadn't shaven his pate, and so his hair had begun growing back. After less than a week, he knew that it more or less looked like a shadow falling across his skull.

"I guess I just needed to change things."

"Is that why you're here at Shikina?" Kira asked. "To change things?"

Sisko took a deep breath, then let it out slowly. He cared for Kira, and he held a great deal of respect for her, but he didn't want to discuss his life, even with her. "I'm not here to change anything," he said. "I just needed some time alone, a place to clear my head."

"Has it worked?" Kira asked, in a way that reminded him of Opaka, whose questions often seemed to imply that she already knew the answer.

"Not as much as I'd hoped," he said, concerned that an outright lie might encourage more questions.

"How are Kasidy and Rebecca?"

Sisko glanced away involuntarily, and so he pretended to examine the totem. "They're both well," he said. Kira said nothing, and when he peered over at her again, he saw her gazing at him with a look of concern.

"So much tension, Benjamin," she said. "You seem so troubled, so . . . isolated."

The last word sent Sisko bounding up from the bench.

He walked a few meters away and stopped, not sure what to say, but aware that his long association with Kira gave her a special insight into his moods and behavior. On top of that, his reactions to her had obviously confirmed her concerns. He raised his arms, then dropped them against his sides. Still facing away from Kira, he said, "I *am* isolated."

"I'm sure you must feel that way," she said. "But you're not. You have your wife and daughter, your son and his wife. You've got friends, not to mention virtually an entire planetary population that treasures you. And you've got the Prophets."

"No!" Sisko yelled, whirling back toward Kira. "I don't have all that."

Kira stood up and paced over to him. She reached out and tenderly placed a hand on his arm. "What's happened?"

"The Prophets have abandoned me." He hadn't wanted to actually speak the words, and now that he had, the situation seemed more real to him.

"What?" Kira said, plainly disbelieving. "No. I'm sure it feels like that to you, but—"

"Nerys, they've left me," he said. He shook his head and walked past her, unwilling to discuss any of this but suddenly unable to stop himself from doing so. He turned back toward her. "For a while, after I returned from the Celestial Temple, I still felt their presence. I thought that they continued to communicate with me, in dreams and in visions . . . but now I'm not so sure. I think those might simply have been *my* dreams, *my* visions, with no communication from the Prophets at all."

"Benjamin, I can't believe that's true," Kira said, "but even if it is, you know as well as I do—*better* than I do—

that it is difficult to know the will of the Prophets. You've also said that they exist nonlinearly in time. Since we *do* live linearly, could this just be a . . . disconnect . . . of some kind?"

"They've left me," Sisko said. "Do you want to know why I'm really here at Shikina? I needed a place to stay, so I told myself, why not here? I told myself that I wanted to find a place of silence and seclusion, where I could rest and reflect and make sure I was making the right choices in my life. And I suppose all of that's true, to one degree or another. But really, I came here to find the Prophets."

Kira took a step toward him, her face a mask of compassion. "They're here, Benjamin. They're with you, even if you don't know it, even if you can't feel it."

"No, they're not," Sisko said. "It took me six days to summon up the courage to consult an Orb, but I finally did it today." He reached forward as if it sat in front of him. "I opened the doors of the ark and beheld the Orb of Prophecy and Change." His hands parted in midair, as though revealing the Orb. "All it did was immerse me in its light." He peered up at Kira, feeling dazed. "There was nothing else. I saw nothing. I felt nothing. That's never happened."

"It happens all the time," Kira said gently. "People often consult the Orbs without having an Orb experience."

"Not me," Sisko said. "I am the Emissary of the Prophets." A sudden realization struck him. "At least I *was* the Emissary."

"You still are."

"No," he said. "I see that now. The Prophets ensured my existence, guided my path, and eventually communicated with me . . . all for their own ends."

"For the people of Bajor," Kira said. "You helped save us from the Cardassians, and then from the Dominion. You helped us join the Federation and enter a new age of peace and prosperity."

"Yes," Sisko said. "And now that I've completed the tasks the Prophets set for me, they have no further use for me."

"Benjamin, of all people, *you* must have faith."

"I do have faith," Sisko said. He moved back over to the bench and sat down again, feeling exhausted. "I believe in the existence of the Prophets, and in their love for the people of Bajor. I trust the Prophets, and I know what they told me. *You* know what they told me."

"I'm . . . not sure what you're talking about," Kira said.

"They told me I must 'walk the path alone,'" Sisko said.

"Kasidy."

"Yes," Sisko said. "The Prophets told me that if I spent my life with her, I would know nothing but sorrow. I told you about that, and you didn't think that I should marry Kasidy."

Kira quickly returned to the bench and sat beside him. "What I thought doesn't matter. It was foolish and wrong of me to say anything. I can't know the will of the Prophets."

"But you were right, Nerys. *They* were right. They were worried about what would happen to me, and I didn't listen. Now look what's happened." Sisko thought about his father and the cold fact of his death. It seemed impossible that he would never see him again, never hear his stentorian voice, never taste his cooking.

And my father is only the latest casualty of my arrogance, he thought. "Think about what's happened since I returned from the Celestial Temple. The Sidau Massacre. Iliana Ghemor and the Ascendants. The calamity on Endalla." He paused in his litany of disasters as he recalled that, prior to battling the Borg at Alonis, the last time he'd seen Elias had been on Endalla.

"But you provided help with those events," Kira said. "You saved people's lives."

"But people did die," Sisko said. "And what about in my own life? The deaths of Eivos Calan and his wife. The kidnapping of my daughter. The brain injury to Elias Vaughn." As he mentioned Vaughn, he realized that Kira might not know what had happened to him, and that he might have insensitively revealed that to her. He knew that during the time Vaughn had served as Kira's first officer aboard Deep Space 9, the two had become good friends. "Nerys, I'm sorry," he said. "Captain Vaughn—"

"I know," Kira said. "His daughter contacted me. But you can't blame yourself for that, or for anything you've mentioned. It's a terrible truth that as we grow older, if we continue to live, then more and more of the people around us die."

"My father died last week."

"Oh, Benjamin." Kira leaned forward and put her arms around him. "I'm so sorry."

They stayed that way for a few moments, and Sisko didn't want it to end. He felt a connection in his friendship with Kira that he needed, but as with all of the connections in his life, he had to let it go. He pulled away from her.

"It's getting closer," he said. "The sorrow. If I remain with Kasidy, then someday soon it will be her death that tears at my heart. Or the death of Rebecca. Of Jake and Korena."

"What are you saying?" Kira asked. "Are you leaving Kasidy?"

"If I spend my life with Kasidy, I will know nothing but sorrow," Sisko said. "I must walk the path alone." He waited for Kira to protest, to tell him that he could not possibly leave his wife and daughter. Instead, she slowly stood up and turned to face him.

"I know that you'll do what you feel you must," she said.

"I have no choice," Sisko said. "Not when it comes to the safety of my family."

"There are always choices," Kira said, once more sounding like Opaka. "Have you told all of this to Kasidy? Explained it all to her?"

"I can't explain it to her," Sisko said. "Kasidy doesn't believe, at least not the way I do. If I told her my reasons, she wouldn't let me leave. And if I did, she would follow me."

"So you're just going to leave her with no explanation?" Kira asked. Sisko heard not only surprise in her tone, but disapproval.

"I've already left," Sisko said. "Things haven't been comfortable for a while."

"Because you made them uncomfortable?"

"At least in part," Sisko said. "It made my leaving easier for her. It's hard now, but she will get over it."

"Maybe if you did try to explain—"

"It wouldn't matter," Sisko said. "But . . . would you go to her, Nerys? You can't tell her what I've told you, but you can comfort her."

Kira slowly nodded her head. "I will," she said. "But what about you?"

Sisko shrugged. "I'll live my life," he said. "Go back to what I know."

"Starfleet?"

"Yes."

Kira walked back over to him and reached a hand toward his right ear. He put his own hand up to stop her. Kira looked him in the eye, and he felt selfish for not trusting her. He dropped his hand, and she touched his ear. He waited for her to tell him that his *pagh* was strong. She didn't.

"Your *pagh* is . . . wounded," she said.

Sisko nodded. He had no doubt of it.

Kira stepped back. "Benjamin, please be careful. If—"

Sisko saw movement past Kira, somebody coming around the bend in the path. The figure wore a hooded, loose-fitting robe, brown in color. Kira turned to follow Sisko's gaze, and as they both watched, the figure pushed the robe's hood back.

"Vedek Kira," she said in a high, musical voice. She stood quite tall, with a body covering that resembled a silvery, fluidic armor more than it did flesh. Fluted around the outer edges, her large golden eyes seemed to melt into her metallic skin. "Forgive the intrusion, but you asked to be notified when the time came for your meeting with Vedek Garune."

"Thank you, Raiq," Kira said. "I'll be there in a moment. Would you please wait for me by the entrance to the arboretum?"

"Yes, Vedek," Raiq said. She pulled her hood back into place, then disappeared around the bend in the path.

When Kira turned back to Sisko, he said, "It was good to see you, Nerys. I'm sorry to have burdened you, but thank you for listening."

"It's no burden, Benjamin," she said. "If you ever need me, to listen or to help in any other way, I'm here for you. I'm usually at the Vanadwan Monastery in Releketh."

"Thank you," he said again. They hugged, and he watched her go. He felt deeply grateful for her friendship, and for her offer of future assistance. Of course, he could never avail himself of her friendship or her help again. He could not risk putting her in danger.

He must walk his path alone.

18

Alizome Tor Fel-A, special agent to the autarch, arrived well before her scheduled meeting with the Tzenkethi leader and several of his advisors. Though Alizome had visited Autarch Korzenten's residence on numerous occasions, and though she had entered the home in a considerable number of its different configurations, she liked giving herself as much time as possible to locate the entrance. That had meant allotting herself less time earlier to satisfy her other responsibilities, but she'd managed to shave enough moments from each of her other tasks that day and still complete them.

The automated hovercraft alighted on the outskirts of Tzenketh, the capital city of Ab-Tzenketh, the homeworld of Alizome's people. The door rolled upward inside the cabin, and she stepped down onto the enclosed security platform, where a quartet of guards stood watch. Having been through the procedure often enough, Alizome knew what to do without being instructed. As she moved to the center of the space, the door behind her rolled shut.

Alizome placed the only item she carried, a data cube, atop a scanner. She then splayed her fingers and laid her hand palm-down on a standard DNA sequencer. Though she could not feel the process, she knew that the device removed an epidermal sample from her hand, then extracted and analyzed her DNA in order to confirm both her identity and her echelon.

Once that verification had completed, she stepped forward and held her arms out to the side. She contracted the sacs lining her arms and slipped quickly out of the top of the tight, black jumpsuit she wore. Making her arms rigid once more, she contracted first her left leg and then her right, removing the lower half of the flexible suit. One of the guards retrieved her outfit and took it to a scanning and inspection station, while another guard examined her fully exposed body, both visually and with a portable sensor. Finally, the leader of the security squad returned her clothing and data cube to her.

"You are cleared, Tor," the guard said, employing her title.

Alizome quickly dressed, then headed for the door on the far side of the platform, which rolled up at her approach. She walked through it and out into the evening air. Both moons had already risen, one in full phase, the other in crescent. As always, their reflected light reached the surface of Ab-Tzenketh hazily, partially obscured by the virtual shell of artificial satellites ensphering the planet. Those satellites, Alizome knew, contained a wealth of different equipment that performed a wide variety of functions, from weapons platforms and external sensor grids, to communications arrays and global-positioning systems, to transporter management and weather control. They also provided an effective multipurpose defensive shield for Ab-Tzenketh, making sensor scans of the planet surface, and transport down to it, extremely difficult.

Following a narrow, winding path, Alizome passed through a copse of phosphorescent trees, their dazzling golden leaves a lingering echo of the day's sunlight, and a close approximation of her own flesh tone. When she emerged from the grove, the grand house spread out before her. Its shimmering metal skin admitted of no straight lines, its rigid form twisting and flowing like the frozen waves of a great silver sea. To the right, the walls bowed outward, the roof above a range of moderately sized swells. Deep troughs and high crests marked the central portion of the structure, with shadows enclosing the lower regions. On the left side, the roof swept up to its highest point, its convex outline suggesting a tidal mass about to crash down on shore. The house possessed no discernible openings, or even potential openings, of any kind.

On none of Alizome's previous visits had the building been so arranged. She stopped and studied it, attempting to puzzle out both the logic and the artistry behind the new design. Mathematical terms rose in her mind and tried to parse themselves into equations that defined the architecture. Various styles of creativity and construction superimposed themselves on the edifice. The intellect and personality of the autarch suggested possibilities. But even after Alizome considered her destination for a while, its new configuration did not confess its secrets to her.

The path she'd taken from the security platform and through the trees led across an uncomfortably open space to a paved area that surrounded the home, permitting visitors to walk up to it at any point. Alizome could approach the building anywhere she chose and tap on an exterior panel, and it would either prove to be the entrance or not.

She could only make a certain number of unsuccessful attempts, though, before the autarch's staff would appear and either invite her inside or ask her to leave. With her record of successes as an agent of Korzenten, she did not believe that failing to find her own way inside would lead to her dismissal and recategorization, but at the very least, it would sow doubt in the autarch's mind about her abilities.

Alizome paced the final length of the path and over toward the midpoint of the structure. Though she often assumed other titles and echelons for her assignments—such as on her mission to Typhon I as a *vik,* a speaker, in the *Tov* echelon of government leaders—she was actually a *Fel,* a problem solver, and not one of just moderate aptitude, but a level-*A Fel.* Since she had completed her preplacement education half a lifetime ago, she had failed only a handful of the everyday tests of ability that all Tzenkethi confronted within their natural disciplines. And since she had been elevated to the position of *Tor,* special agent to the autarch, she had failed none at all.

Having time to spare before the meeting, Alizome circumnavigated the house. She examined the curve of each arc, and related it not merely to its context within the current design but to the iterations of designs past. Like Tzenkethi bodies, the fluidity of the structure allowed for great adaptation, but also faced limitations. Theoretically, the entrance could open anywhere, but in practice, the set of reasonably possible locations should narrow her search.

As Alizome looped around the building a second time, she began to take better note of the shadows. With the movement of Vot-Tzenketh and Lem-Tzenketh across the sky, some areas of the house's previously unseen exterior became visible, while others remained in the darkness still enfolded within the wavelike elements of the roof. Alizome wondered if those constant regions of blackness formed a progression of any kind.

She had time enough to make a third ring around the house, but as soon as she started to do so, she saw it. She continued walking, reading the string of shadows and fitting them neatly into a mathematical series based on their relative distances from one another. When she'd gone a third of the way around, she felt confident that she had broken the code.

Reversing course, Alizome strode back to the transitional space between the crests and troughs of the middle section and the tidal wave of the left-hand section. She reached forward, the golden glow of her flesh reflecting in the silver metal of the building's exterior. Without hesitation, Alizome placed the flat of her hand against the house.

A mechanical hum began at once. Where no seams had shown, they now appeared, delineating a roughly elliptical depression in front of her. The oval withdrew into the structure, until light poured out from around the edges. Eventually, enough of a gap formed to permit her to enter.

Inside, Alizome felt immediate relief, not only from having solved the entry puzzle, but also for the comforting closeness of the floors that now enclosed her. She stood in a foyer tastefully decorated with furniture and artwork she recognized from previous visits. All of it had been arranged traditionally, displayed for the appreciation of visitors situated on the inferior floor. She doubted that the foyer even contained more than its single, natural gravity envelope.

As the door closed behind her, one of the autarch's many servants greeted her. With a pale-orange glow and matching eyes, Narzen Nok Ren-A had always looked blind to Alizome, as though he had been born with empty orbits in his skull-sac.

"You are expected," Narzen intoned. Without awaiting a response, he turned and headed down a large elliptical hall that advanced forward out of the foyer. Alizome followed.

On the way to the autarch's office, Narzen led her past several open doorways, the rooms beyond showing off the autarch's vast fortune. Alizome stole glances into an enormous library, a parlor, an art gallery, and a gymnasium. Ahead, at the end of the hallway, the autarch's sigil garnished a large door. As she neared it behind Narzen, the servant veered left, his feet stepping onto the curve of the lateral floor. Alizome followed, feeling the slight shift in gravity as an artificial envelope supplanted the natural gravitational field of Ab-Tzenketh. Narzen continued moving left, through another alteration in gravity, until they had traveled one hundred eighty degrees and stood on the superior floor, upside-down relative to where they'd started.

At the door, Narzen said, "Alizome Tor Fel-A to see you, Autarch." Alizome did not see any communications hardware, but a moment later, the door irised open. Narzen moved aside, and she walked past him into the autarch's office.

Korzenten Rej Tov-AA sat at his sprawling desk. As always, Alizome found his bright-red skin breathtaking, his golden eyes shocking in their contrast to the rest of his face. Tall even by Tzenkethi standards, he cut a striking figure.

As one of only a small number of *AA* levels in Tzenkethi

society, Korzenten also held a classification as a Tov, the echelon of governmental leaders, making him one of only a handful of individuals qualified to serve as Rej, Autarch of the Tzenkethi Coalition. His genetic composition derived from that of the previous Coalition ruler. Upon her death during the last Tzenkethi-Federation War, Korzenten had succeeded her, his superior DNA makeup remaining unsurpassed through all the years since.

"My Rej," Alizome said as she approached the massive block of polished black stone at which he sat. Though the house had been reconfigured since her previous visit, the office looked virtually identical to how she'd last seen it. Glancing up at the inferior floor, she saw the inverted contents of the luxurious sitting area, where, presumably, the autarch entertained visiting dignitaries. The superior floor, on which she stood, had been set up as a working office, with the desk, several computer interfaces, a communications panel, and a large viewscreen. Parts of the lateral floor had been utilized as decoration for both the inferior and superior floors, with artwork such as tapestries and paintings placed for the appreciation of people in both the sitting and office areas. The rest of the lateral surface functioned as a transition zone, allowing individuals to traverse from the inferior to the superior, and back again.

As Alizome stepped forward, she acknowledged the two advisors present, who sat opposite the autarch, the polished stone blocks of their seats smaller versions of the desk. Velenez Bel Gar-A and Zelent Bel Gar-A both glowed a pale yellow, the former with green eyes, the latter with orange. "You wished to see me," Alizome said. She hadn't seen the autarch since reporting to him after her mission to Typhon I, where she'd taken the title of ambassador and finalized the agreement defining the Typhon Pact. That agreement subsequently had been ratified by the *Tzelnira*—the government ministers—and endorsed by Korzenten.

"Yes, Alizome," said the autarch. Typical of Tzenkethi culture, he began their conversation without greeting or preamble. "Now that the Coalition has consented to be a part of the Typhon Pact, we must ensure that the new alliance serves our needs." Korzenten's voice rang out in low tones, resonating like the tolling of bass bells.

"Of course, my Rej," she said. "How can I assist?"

"That is what we are trying to determine," said Velenez. "The Typhon Pact carries with it some obvious advantages, chief among them the ability to provide a check on the Federation. We want to ensure that none of the Pact's deficiencies compromise that advantage."

For an instant, Alizome grew concerned. Though she had been provided guidance by the autarch and his advisors, the responsibility for negotiating the details of the Typhon Pact had fallen to her. Despite approval by both the *Tzelnira* and the autarch, if the treaty agreement failed to provide for the best interests of the Coalition, Alizome would answer for it.

As well I should, she thought. But any anxiety she felt quickly vanished. Not only had she been bred for the specific duty she performed for the Tzenkethi, but she also knew well all of the elements contained in the final accord.

"Forgive me, my Rej," Alizome said, "but it is unclear to me what possible deficiencies there could be in the Typhon

Pact. Indeed, the terms are quite favorable for the Coalition, including the exceptional agreement by the Romulans to install their cloaking technology throughout our space fleet."

"We are not discussing the *provisions* of the Typhon Pact," said the autarch, "but its *members*."

"Our chief concern," said Zelent, "is the new balance of power with respect to the Federation."

The declaration did not surprise Alizome. The United Federation of Planets had vexed the Tzenkethi for a century, forcing them into more than one shooting war and maintaining tense political standoffs against them the rest of the time. The Federation continuously sent out starships far beyond their borders, always in the name of exploration, but often resulting in expansionism and imperialism. The number of star systems and the volume of space annexed by the UFP since the Tzenkethi first made contact with them approached the size of the entire Coalition itself.

Compounding those problems, there could be little hope that the Federation would ever change its ways. Almost inconceivably, it functioned—or *mal*functioned, Alizome thought—as a republic, and not just as a republic but as one with an unregulated gene pool. The notion that a society would allow all of its adult members, including the vast majority of those of moderate or lesser intelligence, to choose their government officials seemed beyond absurd. Giving such power to the inferior components of a nation could only produce inferior results. Those mediocre and substandard minds—uneducated, self-centered, avaricious, prejudiced, chauvinistically patriotic—would ultimately bring about the downfall of their society, but until then, they would continue to export their failures to the rest of the galactic neighborhood.

"Surely the Typhon Pact will provide a counterbalance against the Federation and the Klingons," Alizome said.

"I would agree," the autarch said, "if not for the Romulan schism."

"Tensions continue to run high between Praetor Tal'Aura's old Romulan Star Empire and Empress Donatra's new Imperial Romulan State," Velenez explained. "With the recognition of Donatra's new nation by the Federation and the Klingons, those tensions are likely going to increase. If fighting breaks out between the two Romulan states, it will destabilize the region and weaken the Typhon Pact."

"So a united Romulan Empire would redound to the benefit of the Pact," Alizome concluded, "and therefore to the benefit of the Tzenkethi Coalition."

"Yes, but not enough," said the autarch. "Under the wrong leader, the Romulans would attempt to control the Typhon Pact."

"So we need to find a way to bring their empires back together," Alizome said, "*and* ensure that an appropriate person leads them."

"As we understand it from well-placed observers within Romulan space, several competing attempts to unite the Empire are already under way," said Zelent. "What we need is to find the right person to be praetor, and to ensure that they are maneuvered into place."

"And that is where I turn to you, Alizome," said the autarch.

Alizome suppressed any outward display of emotion,

but she felt a flurry of excitement. Her DNA provided her a set of skills that made her best suited to this sort of work, and satisfying her genetic heritage fulfilled her. "I understand," she said.

"Good," said the autarch. "Then prepare for a long stay on Romulus."

II

Blood Brimmed the Curse

I am gall, I am heartburn. God's most deep decree
Bitter would have me taste: my taste was me;
Bones built in me, flesh filled, blood brimmed
   the curse.

—GERARD MANLEY HOPKINS

19

The applause did not thunder through the auditorium, but that it arose at all satisfied Spock. He stood at a lectern in the center of an otherwise-empty stage, having just concluded his remarks, the last of six speakers that afternoon. Gazing out across the house, Spock estimated that the rally had filled three-quarters of the Orventis Arena. One of Ki Baratan's primary entertainment venues, it seated fifteen thousand. Just seven months of peaceful public dialogue, with no reprisals from the Romulan government, had increased attendance at Vulcan-Romulan reunification events by two orders of magnitude. The heightened interest manifested not just within the capital city but across the face of Romulus.

"Jolan tru," Spock told the audience. Then, raising his hand in the traditional Vulcan gesture, he said, "Live long and prosper." Amidst renewed applause, Spock collected his data tablet from atop the lectern and headed offstage. The five other members of the movement who had spoken at the rally waited in the wings, as did Dorlok and D'Tan, charged with overseeing security for the event.

"Congratulations," D'Tan said at once, the young man clearly pleased with the success of the rally.

"Thank you, D'Tan," Spock said. "Do we have any reports from other cities?"

"We do," Dorlok said. "There are significant turnouts in many places. The venues in Rateg, Dinalla, and Ra'tleihfi have had even larger audiences than we have. In Villera'trel, there are—"

"Spock!"

Following the sound of the voice, Spock peered through the backstage darkness toward a rear entrance to the arena. There, he saw T'Solon racing toward him, escorted inside by a member of Dorlok's security team. Captured and imprisoned a year earlier by Romulan Security, T'Solon had been released, along with Vorakel, after the repeal of the anti–Reunification Movement law. Small in stature and well into her middle years, T'Solon normally projected an inconspicuous profile. Calling out and hying toward him, she looked more agitated than Spock had ever seen her. She carried a data tablet in one hand.

Moving through the group bunched around him, Spock met her as she came up. "Mister Spock," she said. "I need to speak with you."

Upon her initial discharge from prison, T'Solon had been wary of returning to a position of leadership within the Movement, or even to rejoining the Movement at all. With a husband and two children, she had not wanted to risk being separated from them again. Despite her freedom and the legalization of her beliefs, she had been reluctant to trust Praetor Tal'Aura's government.

As the Movement had grown, though, and as the government had continued to refrain from interfering, T'Solon had drifted back to it. Because of her prior experience with the Romulan comnet—she had worked as a technician all over the planet—Spock had asked her last month to assist T'Lavent with a research project. She had agreed, and Spock could only surmise that her obvious anxiety related to that, and he asked her as much.

"Yes," she confirmed. "T'Lavent and I—"

"Not here," Spock said. Although the praetor had agreed to meet him, had listened to his appeal, had pushed through the revocation of the anti–Reunification Movement law, and had granted T'Solon and Vorakel their liberty, he did not trust her. As long as Tal'Aura's aims coincided to some degree with his own, he hoped to continue his efforts on Romulus, but he suffered no illusions that the situation could change at any time. He also recognized that just because the government allowed the Movement to thrive, it did not mean that Romulan Security had suddenly closed its eyes and ears.

Spock started to lead T'Solon outside, intending to use the rear entrance, but Dorlok stopped them. The security chief insisted that Spock take an escort. Once the rest of the security team arrived for the other speakers, Dorlok and D'Tan accompanied Spock and T'Solon.

Outside, Spock walked up Avenue Renak and led T'Solon several blocks to Cor'Lavet Park. There, he directed T'Solon to an unoccupied bench situated within a large greensward. Dorlok and D'Tan took up separate positions nearby.

"You may proceed," Spock told T'Solon.

"As you know, Mister Spock, T'Lavent and I have been researching the death of the Reman who tried to kill you," T'Solon said. "Because you didn't want us breaking any laws, it's taken us longer than it might have otherwise."

"As long as the Romulans are permitting the Movement to exist legally," Spock explained, "we must do nothing to jeopardize that."

"I understand," T'Solon said. She held up the data tablet for him to see, and then she touched a control. "Do you recognize this man?"

Spock studied the face, which belonged to that of an older Romulan. He had strong, weathered features and a steely countenance. Gray hair dusted his temples. Spock recalled him at once. "That is R'Jul," he said. "He was the protector at the Via Colius security station when I attempted to turn in the Reman."

"R'Jul is still the protector there," T'Solon said. "At least we believe he is. He was spotted entering the station as late as two days ago."

"And why is he of interest?"

"Because of his background," T'Solon said. "Over time, we've assembled a roster of the personnel assigned to that security station." She tapped at the tablet, and a list of Romulan names scrolled down the screen. "We then searched public news accounts, unshielded comnet entries, and any related, declassified material we could find. We came upon no detail, no connection, that drew our attention."

"Obviously until today," Spock said.

T'Solon found R'Jul's name on her list and selected it. A dossier appeared on the small screen, comprising a series of photographs and documents. She chose a comnet article, which enlarged to fill the viewable area on the device. The headline read: LOCAL MAN TRANSFERRED TO WARBIRD. A picture of R'Jul adjoined the text. "We found this from before Shinzon's coup," T'Solon said. "R'Jul served in the Imperial Fleet as a security officer, mostly on transports, until he received this assignment to the *Mogai*-class warbird *Valdore*."

"The *Valdore*," Spock said. "Donatra's ship."

"Yes," T'Solon said. "R'Jul served in her crew on the security staff, eventually working his way up to security chief."

A large inflatable ball skittered across the grass toward the bench, a young Romulan girl chasing after it. Spock stood up and collected the ball, then handed it to the girl when she reached him. She could barely spread her arms wide enough to hold the ball. "Thank you," she said, then scampered off.

Spock glanced over at Dorlok, who had apparently watched the episode closely. Although the security man did not appear to be carrying anything, Spock inferred that he must have used a portable sensor to scan both the girl and the ball. If he hadn't, Dorlok would have run over and intercepted both.

Returning to the bench, Spock asked, "For how long did R'Jul serve under Donatra?"

"We haven't found enough documentation to determine a precise timeframe," T'Solon said, "but for at least two years."

"When did he leave her command?" Spock asked. "And did he move directly from the Imperial Fleet into Romulan Security?"

"We haven't been able to ascertain those details,"

T'Solon said. "But we do know that he was aboard the *Valdore* as late as five days prior to Shinzon's assassination of Praetor Hiren and the Senate."

Spock nodded, trying to make sense of the information. "Is there anything further?"

"No," T'Solon said, deactivating the tablet.

"The implication is clear," Spock said.

"Because of R'Jul's affiliation with Donatra," T'Solon said, "it seems possible, maybe even likely, that he acted on her orders to kill the Reman."

"Which would in turn imply that Donatra employed the Reman to assassinate me," Spock said, "and that once he failed—or even if he had succeeded—she wanted to silence him." He pondered the matter. "But does all of that follow?"

"I think it does," T'Solon said. "Donatra gained the loyalties of a significant portion of the military, enough to allow her to take control of a number of Romulan worlds and declare them a new nation. But while she commands a force strong enough to defend her Imperial Romulan State, she does not have enough firepower to seize the rest of the Empire. Tal'Aura also enjoys some significant advantages, in that she controls Romulus, at least a marginally stronger military, and a greater population. Also, she has rebuilt the government, even ceding political power to a new Senate that she herself reinstituted. Donatra might therefore want to minimize any sentiments championing the reuniting of the two powers, since a return to a single Romulan government would be far more likely to put Donatra's position at risk than Tal'Aura's."

"And because a popular Vulcan-Romulan Reunification Movement would likely empower a Romulan unity movement," Spock said, "she chose to weaken the cause of reunification by removing its head." Spock had argued to the praetor that *his* cause would benefit *her* cause, and indeed, that had happened to a large degree. While Vulcan-Romulan reunification rallies had drawn more and more interest across Romulus, many more voices had called out for the Romulan Star Empire to be made whole. "Logical," Spock said. "But if Donatra did employ the Reman to kill me, and if she then wanted R'Jul to kill the assassin, it would seem coincidental that I happened to deliver the Reman directly to the protector."

"Coincidences *do* happen," T'Solon said. "But if Donatra had wanted R'Jul to kill the Reman all along, I would assume that he did not simply wait for him to appear in the security station; presumably he employed a more active search. And perhaps he was just one of a number of individuals employed by Donatra to eliminate the Reman."

"Perhaps," Spock said, not convinced either way. "But if you were able to locate this information, surely the praetor's staff must have uncovered it as well. If they have, if they can make this link to Donatra, then why haven't they made that information public? Any assassination attempt by Donatra made on Star Empire soil could readily be regarded as an act of war, and perhaps of greater importance, it could sway public opinion within the Imperial Romulan State away from Donatra."

"Maybe Tal'Aura is waiting for the most opportune moment to reveal all of this," T'Solon suggested.

"Perhaps," Spock said again, "or perhaps the link that you and Vorakel found between the Reman's death and Donatra is itself a coincidence."

T'Solon remained quiet for a few moments, evidently considering the situation herself. Finally, she asked, "What are we going to do?"

"I would ask that you and Vorakel continue your efforts to learn more about Protector R'Jul," Spock said. "Also, to continue searching for anybody else who might have killed the Reman."

"We will," T'Solon said. "We'll get right back to it." After Spock nodded his acknowledgment, T'Solon stood from the bench and headed away.

At once, Dorlok made his way over to Spock. "Is everything all right?" he asked. "Have they learned something important?"

"I do not know," Spock said as he rose from the bench. "But I intend to find out."

20

Captain Benjamin Sisko sat behind the desk in his ready room, his gaze directed to the personnel file displayed on his computer interface. He read through the record, which began with Lieutenant Sivadeki's time at Starfleet Academy and continued through her postings aboard Starbase Icarus, *U.S.S. T'Plana-Hath,* and *U.S.S. Fortitude,* as well as her two years serving aboard *Robinson.* As he consumed the details of her life in Starfleet, a hand reached in and tapped at the screen.

"She's been awarded a Ribbon for Meritorious Service," said Commander Rogeiro in his lyrical accent. "Consistently high marks for performance at the conn. She's—"

"Commander," Sisko said, perhaps a little too sharply. He knew that he'd been a bit hard on his senior staff during his seven months commanding *Robinson,* but he also understood his reasons for doing so. Sitting back in his chair, he turned slowly toward the ship's first officer, forcing the younger man to take a step back. Rogeiro stood about the same height as Sisko, with an olive complexion, wavy brown hair, and dark eyes. "Commander, I've taken your recommendation under advisement. I will finish reviewing Lieutenant Sivadeki's record and make my determination."

"I know, sir," Rogeiro said. "Pardon my enthusiasm, but

it's just that Sivadeki's gone far longer than she should have without a promotion in rank."

"Maybe there's a reason for that," Sisko said.

"There is, but it's not a *good* reason," Rogeiro said. "Since I'm relatively new to the ship, and since the time that this should have come up for review more or less coincided with the ship's transition in executive officers, I mistakenly overlooked it." Rogeiro had been assigned to *Robinson* at the same time that Sisko had taken command. Before that, Rogeiro had served as Vaughn's first officer aboard *James T. Kirk,* surviving their encounter with the Borg at Alonis.

The mere thought of all those lives lost to the Borg and, closer to home, the effective loss of Elias Vaughn, tore at Sisko's spirit. He regarded Rogeiro and, knowing what he had been through, suddenly felt sympathetic toward him. Motioning to the sofa off to the left, Sisko said, "If you'll have a seat for a few minutes, Commander, I'll give you my answer."

"Aye, sir," Rogeiro said, with a smile that immediately made Sisko regret his offer. He turned away from the commander, who quickly and quietly crossed in front of the desk and sat down on the sofa.

Sisko returned his attention to his computer interface, where he resumed evaluating the appropriateness of promoting Lieutenant Sivadeki. The Tyrellian conn officer had an unblemished, if unspectacular, record. Several accomplishments did stand out, though, including several instances where her starship had encountered conditions considered virtually impossible to navigate, and yet she had somehow managed to do so.

After about ten minutes, Sisko reached the same conclusion that Commander Rogeiro had—namely that, given the steadiness and length of Sivadeki's Starfleet service, she warranted an increase in rank. Sisko made that notation in her file, then said, "Commander." Rogeiro immediately rose from the sofa and stood at attention before the desk.

"Yes, sir."

"I've approved your recommendation for Sivadeki's promotion to lieutenant commander," Sisko said. "It will take effect as soon as you notify her."

"Yes, sir," Rogeiro said, a smile again appearing on his face. "Thank you, sir."

"Dismissed."

Rogeiro headed for the bridge, and Sisko picked up a padd, intending to record the promotion in his captain's log. He waited for the sound of the doors opening and closing, but it never came. He looked up and saw that the ship's first officer had stopped, and stood peering back at him. "Commander?"

"I was just wondering if *you* might like to deliver the good news to Sivadeki, sir," Rogeiro said. "She's on shift now. I can send her in."

"No, thank you, Commander," Sisko said. "It will be sufficient for you to notify the lieutenant."

"Understood," Rogeiro said, but still he made no move toward the doors.

"Can I help you with something else?" Sisko asked.

"Sir," Rogeiro said haltingly.

He appeared to have some difficulty deciding what to say—or perhaps whether he *should* say anything. Sisko waited, offering him no help, and hoping that the commander would think better of whatever difficult subject he considered broaching. Instead, Rogeiro marched back toward the desk.

"Sir," he said, "I wonder if I might ask you a personal question."

Sisko did not hesitate in his response: "No, Commander, you may not."

Rogeiro seemed surprised by the answer, but it took him only a moment to regroup. "Then might I ask you a professional question?"

Sisko sighed, not hiding his annoyance. "Go ahead."

"Why do you refuse to answer personal questions?"

Sisko dropped his hands onto the desk, shocked at the commander's presumption. "Is that supposed to be funny, mister?" Sisko's tone left no doubt that the question did not amuse him.

"It's not *supposed* to be," Rogeiro said, "but it's a *little* funny."

"Not to me, it's not," Sisko snapped.

Rogeiro glanced down, seemingly abashed. "I'm sorry, Captain." When he looked back up, though, he said, "Permission to speak freely."

"Commander Rogeiro, I've had enough of this," Sisko said, his anger quickly rising. He leaned forward in his chair. "You don't have permission to ask me personal questions, and you don't have permission to speak freely." He stopped and tried to rein in his emotions. He took a moment, then sat back. "Commander," he said, calmer, "when you have matters to discuss with me regarding the crew or the ship, by all means do so. Short of that, I know you have other duties to tend to."

"I do have other duties," Rogeiro said, "but I'm not sure

I have any more important than this one." He turned and walked away, and for a second, Sisko thought that he might actually leave, but at the far end of the room, he turned back. "And I'm going to speak freely, because it matters to this ship and crew that I do. If you feel the need to write me up, then go ahead, but it's my duty to tell you what I think."

Sisko considered relieving Rogeiro of duty on the spot or having him removed by security, but either action would result in having to explain his actions to Starfleet Command—another conversation he didn't wish to have. "And what is it you think, Commander?"

"I think this ship isn't running as efficiently as it should be," Rogeiro said, "and it's because you have nothing to do with the crew beyond issuing them orders."

"I wasn't aware that a captain was required to befriend everybody aboard his ship," Sisko said.

"Not 'everybody,' Captain," Rogeiro said. "And it's not even friendship I'm really talking about. It's your . . . your isolation."

The word resonated for Sisko because he knew it to be true. He could command a starship, he could lead a crew, and he did. But he had chosen his path, and he walked it alone.

When Sisko said nothing, Commander Rogeiro walked back over to the desk. "We've both been here for seven months," he said, "and in all that time you've gotten to know not a single member of this crew, other than on a professional basis. And you've allowed none of them to get to know you." Rogeiro shook his head, as though he couldn't believe what he was saying to his commanding officer. "How often have we sat on the bridge through an entire shift with almost nothing to do? We're patrolling the Romulan border—the *two* Romulan borders—and we're keeping our eyes and ears open, but that doesn't require too many active shifts from us. And yet whenever any member of the crew attempts to engage you in conversation, you either offer up a monosyllabic reply or don't even bother to respond at all. I've seen you head into this ready room rather than tell Ensign Stannis whether you've ever been to Pacifica."

Sisko didn't know how to react. Rogeiro had said nothing untrue, and yet Sisko could not possibly explain to the commander why he kept to himself—why he *had* to keep to himself. He'd never anticipated this sort of problem, since command, by its very nature, carried an element of separation with it.

"Captain," Rogeiro said, "I mean absolutely no disrespect to you. I know what you've achieved in your Starfleet career, and I also know that you'd been away from it for a while before you took command of *New York* and then *Robinson*. But I don't think any of what I'm talking about has to do with your time away."

"No," Sisko said. "But I really don't wish to discuss what it *does* have to do with."

Rogeiro nodded as though he understood completely. "For the sake of this crew, Captain, and for your own sake, I think maybe you should discuss it with somebody . . . even if it's just with yourself."

Sisko looked away, trying to figure out how to deal with the situation. Maybe he shouldn't be commanding a starship. Maybe he hadn't isolated himself enough. Whatever the case, he really would have to have a conversation with himself about how to proceed. To Rogeiro, he said sincerely, "I will take your recommendation under advisement."

"Yes, sir," Rogeiro said, seemingly satisfied. "Thank you, sir." He turned toward the doors once more, and then once more turned back to Sisko. "Sir, I served under Captain Vaughn for two years aboard *James T. Kirk*. He was one of the finest men I ever knew . . . really like a father to me in many ways. It's still hard. I still miss him." He paused, then said, "I know that you and he were close. I'm sorry for your loss."

Without intending to do so, Sisko slowly stood up. He peered across at Rogeiro, but instead he saw the inert body of his friend, tucked into a dim corner of Deep Space 9's infirmary, machines technically sustaining the life of his body, though the brilliant spark of his mind had perished. At last, he said, "Thank you, Commander."

"Sir," Rogeiro said, and finally he exited the ready room.

Sisko continued to stand at his desk. Obviously Rogeiro thought that his captain's aloofness stemmed from the loss of a close friend on a mission in which both had served. Although that only began to tell the story, Rogeiro had in some sense been right.

Out of a long-standing habit that he had yet to entirely break, Sisko reached up to run a hand across his goatee. Instead, his hand touched only flesh. Shortly after he'd made the decision to let his hair grow back in, he'd done away with his beard. It had been during his brief stopover on Deep Space 9 that he'd shaven, and the psychology of it seemed obvious to him. The Prophets had left him, and so when he'd finally decided to leave that part of his life behind—on Bajor, aboard DS9—he'd made a change in his appearance too, reverting back to what he'd looked like prior to his posting as commander of the station.

Sisko sat back down at his desk. Before the ship's first officer had come in to see him about Lieutenant Sivadeki's promotion, Sisko had been about to write a letter to Jake. He'd stopped recording messages to him about a month after arriving aboard *Robinson*. He knew that he had to put some distance between himself and his son—something that being stationed on the Romulan borders helped to do—but he also didn't want to hurt him any more than absolutely necessary. He'd found it impossible to strike the right balance between love and distance when he recorded messages, but found that writing to Jake helped him with that.

He'd also considered writing to Kasidy, but had decided against it. Contacting her would likely only prolong the pain through which he'd already put her. He hoped that she would be able to move on quickly and find happiness, not just for herself, but also for their daughter. *She's a strong woman,* Sisko thought. *Perhaps she's already moved on.* Certainly he had received no word from her since he'd left Bajor.

Sisko dismissed Lieutenant Sivadeki's personnel file from his computer interface, and opened the letter he'd started to Jake. He dictated a sentence, changed it, completed a second sentence, but then stopped. He saved the letter so that he could finish it another time.

Maybe it's this damned region of space too, he thought. So far, his assignment aboard *Robinson* had proven uneventful. Though the Federation president and Starfleet had pledged to continue exploring the galaxy, such missions had been handed out to only a small number of starship crews. With so much of the fleet destroyed, few ships could be spared the critical task of patrolling the Federation's borders and protecting against an opportunistic adversary—such as the newly formed Typhon Pact. Sisko did not know the ultimate goal of the new alliance, but it relieved him to know that even with Starfleet decimated, the introduction of slipstream drive on some vessels effectively maintained a balance of power in the region.

"Bridge to Captain Sisko." The tone of Rogeiro's voice revealed not the slightest indication of their confrontation just moments earlier.

"Sisko here. Go ahead."

"Captain," Rogeiro said, *"we've got some traffic in the vicinity that you might want to take a look at."*

Sisko immediately took a swing at his melancholic thoughts, trying to chase them away. "I'm on my way," he said.

He bolted out of his chair and across his ready room. The doors opened before him, and he stepped out onto the bridge. "What have we got?" he asked as he crossed to his command chair. But before Rogeiro answered, Sisko saw for himself: three massive vessels, teardrop-shaped, feature-less while in flight, but together, more than a match for the *Galaxy*-class *Robinson*. As Sisko recalled that these were the ships he had for so long seen in his nightmares, Commander Rogeiro identified them:

"Tzenkethi marauders."

21

As Alizome Tor Fel-A and her two aides followed the Romulan through the tall, wide spaces of Stronghold Ortikant, she concentrated not just on hiding her discomfort with the largely open areas through which the group moved, but on controlling that discomfort. Her people, as a rule, did not care for such exposure. Traveling the depths of space proved the most troublesome; even within the tightly packed interiors of Tzenkethi vessels, the reality of the nothingness through which the ships journeyed harrowed even the sturdiest psyches. Medication helped, but Alizome disliked dulling her faculties at any time, particularly when embarking on a mission. When she had first come to Romulus, she had suffered through the voyage, envying the echelon of the Tzenkethi crewing the marauder; though unsuited to many aspects of everyday life, the Vel enjoyed a genetic constitution that inured them to the emotional impact of open spaces.

Though Alizome's visit to the Star Empire had lasted for some time, she had not grown desensitized to the broad pedestrian thoroughfares and the squares and parks that made up so much of the exterior areas of Romulan cities. Some of their buildings afforded nicely enclosed rooms, but others—such as Stronghold Ortikant—did not. And none of the Romulan design involved maximizing the use of available space. Instead of inferior, lateral, and superior floors, they had floors, "walls," and "ceilings."

Such a waste of space, thought Alizome, *and so unsettling.* The heels of her shoes—and everybody else's—pounded against the stone floor, the echoes reverberating loudly. She peered up at the high walls and tall ceilings, bare and unused, and repressed the urge to shiver.

Ahead, the Romulan—a man named Ritor—stopped before a set of wooden doors. Ritor had greeted Alizome and her party at the landing pad where their shuttle had touched down. He'd indicated that he would escort them to their meeting, but not what position he held at Stronghold Ortikant. She believed him likely a servant, or perhaps an aide to the senator. *But this is Romulus,* she reminded herself. *He could well be a member of the Tal Shiar.*

Ritor lifted a large golden ring attached to the center of one of the doors and rapped it against the aged wood. He did not appear to wait for a response before opening the doors inward. Alizome and her aides walked into the room after him, where he turned toward a sitting area in the far corner and announced them by name to the senator.

"Trade Representative Alizome Nim Gar-A to see you," Ritor said. For her mission to Romulus, Alizome had assumed the title of *Nim,* trade representative, in the government policy specialist echelon of *Gar.* "She is accompanied by her aides, Bezorj Nim Gar-B and Ertoz Dop Yor-C." Ritor then turned toward the three Tzenkethi and said, "Representative Alizome, allow me to present Senator Xarian Dor."

Dor and a woman stood from a long sofa that ran along

two walls in the large room. Several chairs and a low, square table completed a considerable sitting area. Alizome had hoped that the office would provide a more intimate setting, but as had been the case time and again during her stay on Romulus, she had little choice but to accept disappointment. Though outfitted with modern furnishings, the room itself appeared as ancient—and as consistently large and airy—as the rest of the stronghold.

"Representative, it is a pleasure to meet you," Dor said, bowing his head. Lean and somewhat taller than the average Romulan, he wore an expertly tailored navy-blue suit. He had a piercing gaze, his dark eyes communicating a serious intelligence. Alizome wondered immediately if, for the second time, she had found what she'd come to Romulus seeking.

It must be the gene pool of the Ortikant, she thought.

As Ritor withdrew from the room, Dor introduced his aide as Noret, then invited Alizome to sit. She took a position on the sofa, and Dor sat down on its other wing. Noret directed Bezorj and Ertoz to chairs, where she also sat down. Alizome pondered Noret's true affiliation, whether one of the senator's assistants, or an incognito security officer, or—again, as one always had to consider on Romulus—a member of the Tal Shiar. The two men masquerading as her own aides had no such nefarious connection, attending her simply as a means of reinforcing her supposed identity as a trade representative.

"Forgive me, but I'm not certain how I should address you," Dor said. "Representative seems rather awkward to me."

"You may address me by my title," she said. "Nim."

"Very well, Nim," Dor said. "And that means that *Gar* is your . . . ?" He let his question trail into silence, inviting Alizome to answer it. She didn't. Before the moment could grow uncomfortable, Dor completed his question himself. "Caste, is it?"

Alizome had heard that characterization before from outsiders, who apparently believed that the Tzenkethi employed a system of social classes. Such a notion only underscored how little others understood her people. Nobody in the Coalition found themselves relegated to a particular function in life as an accident of being birthed by members of that function. Biologists confirmed the genetic composition of every Tzenkethi *in utero,* allowing the assignment of individuals to the echelon in society to which they were physiologically best suited, and which therefore best served society. Tzenkethi culture did not prevent people from overachieving and moving beyond their echelon, nor did it allow underachievers to retain an unearned position. Because of the quality of Tzenkethi genetic examination and cultural placements, though, such repositioning from one echelon to another rarely occurred.

Alizome explained none of that to Dor. Instead, she simply said, "Essentially, yes."

"And so *Gar* would equate to what in Romulan society?" Dor asked.

Alizome looked down, wanting to imply that she felt a level of embarrassment. "Pardon me, Senator, I do not wish to be rude, but what you're asking about is considered a private matter on Ab-Tzenketh." Looking back up at Dor, she attempted to sell the lie by saying, "I think it is rather like the complex practice of naming that takes place on Romulus."

The senator did not look away, as Alizome had, but his facial expression changed subtly, and he appeared as embarrassed as she had. "My apologies then."

"None are necessary, Senator," she said, "but thank you."

"I understand that you have been—"

The doors opened, and Ritor returned bearing a silver tray. He set it down on the table, revealing a large decanter filled with a pale-yellow beverage, along with a set of glasses. As Ritor began pouring, Dor said, "I don't know if you're familiar with *carallun,* but it is a citrus drink made from Romulan fruit."

"I do know it," Alizome said, "and I like it."

"Good," Dor said. "I thought you might have tried it since you've been on Romulus for so long."

"That and many other things," Alizome said, taking note of the senator's artful means of informing her that he had looked into the details of her stay—and probably her background—before meeting her. "I was sent on this trade mission just after our governments allied in the Typhon Pact. It seemed like a good opportunity to reach out to new markets."

Ritor finished handing out glasses of *carallun* by giving one to her and one to Dor. He then left the office once more. Alizome sipped at the drink, then said, "I've spoken with a great many people all over Romulus, both on the business side and on the government side. I've even spoken to members of your own clan." Dor would know all of that, but Alizome wanted to project the notion that she had nothing to hide from the senator—though of course she did.

"And have you had much success?" he asked.

"I have had some," she said. "Small successes, mostly. Since I'll be returning to Ab-Tzenketh soon, I'm hoping that I can accomplish something more lucrative in one of my last few meetings."

"As you've already spoken with the Ortikant, then you must be aware of our extensive holdings," Dor said. "As a member of the Romulan Senate, I also have access to certain other resources."

"Then I'm sure we can find some business that would benefit us both," Alizome said. Turning to her aides, she asked for a data cube. Bezorj brought one over to her. She activated it and called up an inventory of Tzenkethi merchandise. Then, to Senator Dor, she said, "Let me show you what we have to offer."

Xarian Dor examined his data tablet, reading through the details of the transaction. Even as it had developed, its size had surprised him. He had been given to understand that the Tzenkethi could make problematic business partners, but while a determined negotiator, Representative Alizome Nim Gar-A had also been reasonable. She had balked at some of Dor's more lopsided proposals, but she'd seen value when he'd offered it. Overall, the deal would benefit both the Romulan and Tzenkethi governments, at the same time proving lucrative for the interests of the Ortikant and for whomever the representative acted.

"There is one more thing, Senator," Alizome said. "We've

had major interest in Barajian fleece. Would it be possible to acquire a significant amount?"

Dor peered up from his tablet and over at the representative. The gentle golden glow of Alizome's flesh fascinated him, as did her arresting green eyes. Rarely did Dor find aliens attractive, but the Tzenkethi representative possessed a quality that drew his attention. Even the two men who attended her, though radiating a light green color, seemed exceptional physical specimens.

"Barajian fleece, I'm afraid, is virtually impossible to acquire within the Empire these days," Dor said. "It is a commodity cultivated exclusively on Achernar Prime." He had mentioned the source of the fleece as an explanation for its unavailability, but Alizome gave him a questioning look.

"Achernar Prime?" she said.

"The seat of Donatra's illegal government," Dor told her.

"Oh, I see," Alizome said. "I take it that you do not approve of the Imperial Romulan State."

Dor felt his features harden. "Would you approve if one of your military leaders co-opted a faction within your fleet, then took control of several important worlds and deemed themselves their own nation? Would you approve if that so-called nation then threatened to cut off food and medical supplies to your people if their irrational demands were not met?"

"Forgive me, Senator," Alizome said, appearing duly chastened. "I did not mean to offend."

Dor took a beat to calm himself. "No, you did not offend," he said.

"Good," Alizome said. "It would seem to me, though,

that the Star Empire's entry into the Typhon Pact should mitigate any threatened shortages in food and medicine."

"It does," Dor said. Such considerations had actually aided him in making his choice to vote for ratification of the treaty.

"It would also seem to me," Alizome said, "that the substantial military might of the Typhon Pact could make reclaiming those seized worlds an easier matter."

Dor hesitated to respond. As an official of the Empire, the voicing of his opinions required circumspection, even in private conversation. He returned his attention to his data tablet.

"It would be unfortunate to miss an occasion for such a large profit," Alizome went on. "Barajian fleece has become a sought-after commodity within the Coalition."

The Tzenkethi representative seemed to be reaching for something—something beyond their business dealings, Dor thought. "I didn't know that the fleece was so popular on Ab-Tzenketh," he said.

"It is for now," Alizome said. "But if the demand goes unfulfilled for any length of time, I doubt that it will last."

Dor readily followed the representative's implication. "The shortage of Barajian fleece within the Empire, I am quite sure, will not last."

"How *can* you be sure?"

"Because there is growing sentiment within the Romulan Senate that such valuable commodities should be returned to the Empire in the near term," Dor explained, continuing with the metaphor Alizome had introduced.

"And if the Imperial Romulan State should resist such measures?"

"The Senate would favor assistance from our newly gained allies," Dor said. "*I* would favor such assistance."

"That is good to hear," Alizome said with, Dor thought, a visible degree of satisfaction. From his own viewpoint, it gratified him to learn that at least one faction within the Tzenkethi government—and therefore a faction within the Typhon Pact—supported military intervention to rip Donatra's rogue state from her traitorous grip.

Dor looked down again at the tablet in his hands, and at the trade agreement spelled out on it. "This appears to be in order," he said. He signed the contract with his imprimatur, then transmitted the endorsed document to Alizome's data cube.

"Excellent," said Alizome. She rose from the sofa, and her two aides followed her lead. Dor stood as well and faced her. "Thank you for your time and effort, Senator." She held up the data cube. "I am confident that our agreement will be advantageous for all involved."

"As am I," said Dor.

Alizome reached a hand forward, the loose sleeve of her gossamer outfit slipping away to reveal the gentle, golden curve of her arm. Without thinking, he took her hand in his, the gesture clearly intended to show appreciation for the work they had completed together. Only later, long after Alizome and her aides had departed, did it strike Dor as odd that a Tzenkethi would practice the human ritual of a handshake.

22

Spock descended from the personnel transport *Ragul'tora* and stepped onto the landing stage. In the terminal, he walked amidst other arriving passengers, who comprised a wide mix of species, including two of which he knew, but that he'd never before seen in person. Both subject races of the Star Empire, the Teluvians and the Innix had never been permitted, as far as he knew, to range beyond Romulan space. Apparently, though, they had leave to travel within the Empire's borders.

Among the travelers, about half of them Romulan, Spock saw Ferengi, Cardassians, and Son'a, among others, as well as a number belonging to several of the Typhon Pact signatories: Breen, Gorn, and Tzenkethi. That pleased him, as it would render his behavior less suspicious when he did what he'd come to do on Terix II. He had little doubt that he would be observed, and that he had been ever since emerging from hiding on Romulus. Tal'Aura would have kept a set of eyes on him, and if she hadn't called upon the Tal Shiar to perform that task, then the covert intelligence apparatus would likely have employed their own agent as well.

Spock followed a line of passengers through a security checkpoint, which he moved through quickly. Because of his understanding with the praetor, he possessed legal documentation to travel within the Empire. Intending to return to Romulus in just two days' time, he carried with him only an overnight bag and a data tablet.

Beyond security, signs in many languages—though in neither Federation Standard nor Vulcan—directed all passengers to the mouth of a long, wide passage. Shortly after he started in that direction, Spock saw that the ceiling and right-hand wall of the passage had been built of a transparent material. As he walked along, he peered outward to see the magnificent skyline of Vetruvis. The famed Romulan travel destination gleamed brilliantly in the yellow glow of the setting Terix sun. Every structure in the modern city—buildings, bridges, thoroughfares—had been constructed of one kind or another of polished stone. Skyscrapers soared over shorter edifices, yet all seemed of a piece, as though they all had been carved from a field of massive rocks, then buffed to a high shine. The façades came in an assortment of deep colors, from burgundy to cobalt, from hunter green to titanium yellow, many of them streaked through with veins of white. At the center of the city loomed the celebrated Three Towers of Terix, an interconnecting complex of structures of various heights, the grandest of which rose more than a thousand meters above the landscape.

The passage opened up into a huge space filled with many smaller, enclosed areas. More signs spelled out different districts within the city of Vetruvis: Urban Center, Government Quarter, Lodging, Restaurants, Performance Venues, Art Galleries, Museums, Galixori Canyon, Sterlanth River Gorge, and numerous others. Spock found one of the many enclosed areas designated as *Lodging*, entered, and took the public transporter there to a target site within Vetruvis itself. From there, he made his way to the inn where a two-night stay had been reserved for him.

Once Spock had settled into his modest room, he sat at its small companel and contacted Oloara Rintel. The young woman had graduated only recently from university, but she had held an interest in Vulcan-Romulan reunification throughout her academic years. After leaving school, she had remained on her native Terix but relocated to Vetruvis, where in addition to working in her chosen field of urban planning, she had become an activist for the Movement.

"Mister Spock," she said as her image appeared on the companel screen, *"I'm very pleased that you've made it to our beautiful city."* Rintel had a narrow face and high cheekbones, which gave her something of a regal air.

"I am pleased to be here as well," he told her. "What are your expectations for the event tomorrow?" The first major rally on Terix II for Vulcan-Romulan reunification would follow on the heels of dozens of smaller but still popular events staged all over the planet in recent months. As of ten days ago, the outlook had been for upwards of ten thousand attendees.

"Mister Spock, we have disseminated word of your planned presence at the rally and of your intention to speak," Rintel said. *"That has boosted our attendance projections, which were significant to start with. We've had to move it from Vetruvis Arena, with its capacity of fifteen thousand, to Galixori Stadium, which accommodates twice that number."* Though she maintained an even tone, the rushed cadence of her words gave away her fervor.

"Excellent," Spock said, pleased not only for the increased interest in reunification but also for the cover it would provide him. "I look forward to seeing you tomorrow, then."

Rintel provided details of who would meet him at the inn and at what time, so that he could be escorted to the event. Spock agreed, and they finished their conversation. Rintel's image disappeared as her transmission ended.

Spock continued to sit at the companel, though, elbows atop the control surface, hands folded together in front of his face. He carefully considered what he would say tomorrow, working out the words that, for the sake of security, he would neither write down nor transmit. Of course, he knew well what he would say at the rally, having spoken time and again on the subject of reunification. The words that concerned him would come afterward, beyond the confines of Galixori Stadium.

Spock exited the public transporter in the section of the city given over to eateries. A wide pedestrian walkway stretched away in either direction, a shining crimson surface marbled through with streaks of milky white. He stepped out into the flow of people, moving left down the avenue.

As he walked, Spock studied the names of the various restaurants he passed, occasionally stopping to examine the menus posted outside. It might not fool anybody watching him, but he wished to give the appearance of making an unplanned trip out for a late-afternoon meal. He had some time before his scheduled rendezvous.

Eventually, when Spock reached the cross street he needed, he set off in the appropriate direction. Three blocks down, he found the tavern for which he'd been searching, a place called *Out There*. A casual establishment, its posted menu offered a variety of off-world cuisine, including food and drink of Vulcan origin.

Spock entered the tavern, its interior dark and close. Booths lined the side walls, with freestanding tables between them. A long bar marched across the back, with what looked like the entrance to the kitchen in the far right corner. In this hour between midday and evening meals, he saw only a handful of patrons, none of them Romulan.

Making his way to the bar, Spock noted a pair of com-net screens mounted high on the back wall, above shelves stocked full with bottles of myriad shapes, colors, and sizes. It did not surprise him to see on one of the screens coverage of the rally at Galixori Stadium earlier that afternoon. Not every seat had been filled, but enough people had attended to make it the largest Movement event to date.

"What can I get for you?" asked the bartender, a Ferengi dressed in a loud jacket. As though willfully attempting to project a familiar, even stereotypical, image, he stood wiping a towel over a drinking glass. "A snifter of Vulcan brandy, perhaps? Or how about a tall glass of *kellorica*?" The bartender, whose job apparently brought him into continual contact with non-Romulans, must have recognized Spock's extraction, since he'd offered up a pair of Vulcan alcoholic beverages.

"Thank you, no," Spock said. "I would like a bowl of *plomeek* soup, with a side order of whole-grain *kreyla*."

"Coming right up," said the bartender. "Something to drink?"

"A glass of water, please."

"Just water?" asked the bartender. "I've got a galaxy of beverages to choose from." He gestured at the many bottles lining the shelves. "Are you sure you wouldn't want something a little more interesting?"

"Water is the single most important component of almost all known life-forms," Spock said. "I find that interesting. Water, please."

The Ferengi stared at him for a moment, then peered over at the only other customer at Spock's end of the bar. "Vulcans," the bartender said in frustration, rolling his eyes.

The other patron, a Gorn male, hissed in response, a sound that Spock's universal translator declined to interpret. The noise sent the bartender skittering away, presumably to deliver Spock's order to the kitchen staff. The Gorn, who wore a belted red tunic and an unbuttoned black vest, glanced over at Spock. He hissed again, which Spock heard as, "Ferengi." The Gorn could not physically roll his faceted silver eyes, but Spock thought that if he could have, he probably would have.

"Bartenders," Spock replied.

The Gorn issued a burst of air through his long, pointed teeth, his equivalent of laughter. "So true," he said. He set down the large, wide-mouthed glass cradled between his hands. "I'm Slask, from S'snagor."

"Spock of Vulcan."

The Gorn regarded him for a moment, as though trying to place him. "Spock," he finally said, then pointed to one of the comnet screens behind the bar. "The same Spock who spoke on Vulcan-Romulan reunification at the stadium this afternoon?"

"Yes."

Slask nodded. "You're either a brave man or a fool to exhort such opinions within the Empire."

"There is no reason for you to think that I cannot be both," Spock said.

Again, Slask laughed. "I disagree with you, Spock of Vulcan," he said. "A fool cannot be brave, for one must understand the danger one courts in order to act bravely in the face of that danger."

"A valid point," Spock said.

"So what brings you to Vetruvis?" Slask asked.

"I came simply to speak at the rally," Spock said. "The Movement has gained many adherents in recent days, and I am striving to do what I can to continue that trend. I will be returning to Romulus tomorrow morning."

"It looked on the comnet like you were well received."

"It seemed that way to me as well," Spock said. "In excess of twenty thousand people attended today's event. As a Vulcan and a leading voice for reunification, I have become, in some ways, the face of the Movement. But those present appeared focused not just on me and my words but on what all the speakers had to say. They also asked many questions, not just about the Movement, but about the Vulcan way of life, how it differs from the Romulan way, and how the two might be combined to form something greater."

"Do you really believe there's any way that the Romulan people could reunify with the Vulcans?" Slask said. "Especially now, with Romulus a part of the Typhon Pact? How could that possibly work?"

"It might not be accomplished easily, but that does not make it unworthy of pursuit," Spock said. "There are several practical ways in which such a reunification could take place. Both Romulus and Vulcan could withdraw from their respective allegiances, or they could spur détente, or even entente, between the Khitomer Accord nations and those of the Typhon Pact."

"It all seems so unlikely," Slask said.

"Perhaps," Spock said. "But a year ago, it might have been argued that a treaty uniting the Gorn with the Breen, Kinshaya, Romulans, Tholians, and Tzenkethi was just as unlikely."

The Gorn nodded. "You make a point," he said.

Behind the bar, the Ferengi returned carrying a circular tray, atop which sat a steaming bowl of broth, a small plate containing three brown biscuits, and a glass of water. Before the bartender could set the meal down, Spock said, "I'd like to eat in one of the booths."

"Take your pick."

As Spock started back into the room, Slask said, "May I join you while you eat, Spock? I am interested to learn more about your Movement."

"Please do," Spock said. He selected an empty booth in the corner, away from the few other customers in the tavern. He and Slask sat down opposite each other, and the bartender placed Spock's food in front of him.

"Care for another *sth'garr*?" the bartender asked Slask. Spock did not recognize the word, but assumed it named the beverage that the Gorn had been drinking.

"Not right now," Slask said. As the bartender departed, Spock heard him muttering to himself in Ferengi.

Spock picked up a spoon and sampled his *plomeek* soup. To his surprise, it actually tasted quite like the dish as made on Vulcan. He broke off a piece of *kreyla* and dipped it into the broth, again satisfied with the re-creation of the Vulcan food.

As Spock ate, Slask glanced around the room, then surreptitiously removed a small device from under his belt. The Gorn stood the cylindrical object on the table, out of sight behind Spock's glass. A moment later, a small dish unfolded from the top of the device.

"This will defeat any eavesdropping," Slask said.

"It seems improbable that the praetor or the Tal Shiar would have any listening devices in this establishment," Spock said.

"Maybe, but I've always found it's good policy to trust neither of them," Slask said. "Besides, this place is run by a Ferengi. There's a good chance he's got his own microphones hidden around the room, listening for any information on which he could turn a profit." The Gorn looked over at the bartender, who had returned to wiping down glasses behind the bar. Turning back to Spock, Slask said, "So what's this all about?"

"I have information and a recommendation I need conveyed to our mutual acquaintance," Spock said. He knew that Slask had a personal relationship with Federation President Nanietta Bacco, established back when she had served as governor of Cestus III, which bordered Gorn space. At one time, the Gorn Hegemony had claimed the Cestus system for their own, although the Federation had not known that before colonizing the third planet.

"This is obviously information you do not feel comfortable sending by subspace, or putting down in writing," Slask said.

"Indeed, I am exercising a great deal of caution." After Spock had learned of the prior affiliation of R'Jul—the Romulan Security protector—with Donatra, he had sent an unencrypted message to the Federation's Bureau of Interplanetary Affairs. In it, he had detailed the growing success of the Reunification Movement within the Star Empire, in the guise of keeping the UFP informed of his situation. He had also included his upcoming schedule. Knowing that the BIA as a matter of course passed on all of his communications to the office of the president, Spock included a trigger word in the document. The president's staff understood that word to mean that he possessed information potentially vital to the security of the Federation, but that he could deliver it neither personally nor via subspace transmission.

Spock had soon after that received a brief response from the BIA director, ostensibly acknowledging receipt of Spock's message and congratulating him on the success of the Movement. But that reply also contained a trigger word, indicating after which of the events on Spock's itinerary somebody would meet him to act as a messenger. On the major worlds within the Empire, Spock had prearranged with the president's staff the locations for such meetings. The trigger word also distinguished the identity of the messenger, one of half a dozen possibilities preselected by the presidential staff.

"Very well," Slask said. "What do you wish me to tell our mutual friend?"

Although Spock had never before met Slask, he knew of him. The Gorn had also uttered specific phrases to identify himself, which Spock had responded to with specific phrases of his own. Slask had been deemed suited to such an assignment not only because of his friendship with the Federation president, but because that relationship remained unknown to most people. Slask also remained a loyal citizen of the Gorn Hegemony, one associated with neither their government nor their military. There existed essentially no reason that a seemingly random meeting between Spock and Slask should raise the suspicions of anybody who might be watching, nor could any connection reasonably be made between the two men.

Spock explained the attempt on his life eight months earlier, and the circumstances surrounding the subsequent death of the Reman assassin, including R'Jul's prior service on Donatra's starship. "It remains unclear to me whether the Reman killed himself in order to avoid being handed over to the Romulan authorities, or whether Protector R'Jul or somebody else killed him. It is possible, though by no means assured, that Donatra might be involved, either as instigator or as victim."

"Victim?" Slask said.

"If Donatra did try to have me killed, and then eliminated her assassin, she would have done the latter in order to prevent her actions from becoming public knowledge," Spock explained. "But since public knowledge of a murder attempt would hurt Donatra's cause among the Romulan people, perhaps all of this has been done not *by* Donatra, but in order to implicate her."

Slask shook his head slowly. "The machinations of the Romulans," he said. "It's difficult to know who's hiding behind which door."

"That is why we need more information," Spock said. "We need to know what has happened and what *is* happening, so that we may determine what likely *will* happen—and if necessary, change what will happen. If there is a concerted effort, or efforts, to undermine either Donatra's government or Tal'Aura's, it could lead to a shifting of the balance of power, which could adversely impact the security of the Federation. That is why I believe it is vital that our mutual acquaintance send an envoy to speak with Donatra."

"I understand," Slask said. "Is there anything else?

"No," Spock said.

Slask immediately closed the anti-eavesdropping device with a touch, then swiped it from behind the glass and tucked it back into his belt. He stood up and, a bit loudly, said, "I still think you're a fool, Mister Spock, to expect the Romulans to let you run your Movement."

"They are already allowing me to do so," Spock said.

"For now," Slask said. "I'm just not sure that they're going to keep letting you run it. But good luck."

"And safe travels to you," Spock said.

Slask headed for the door, and Spock returned his attention to his meal. As he ate his *plomeek* soup and *kreyla*, he wondered whether President Bacco would accede to his recommendation, and if so, whether Donatra would agree to meet another Federation representative. Given her tenuous position and her need for allies like the UFP and the

Klingon Empire, he doubted that she would turn down such a request. The real issue was whether or not she knew anything about the attempt on Spock's life and the murder of the Reman, and if she did, whether she would reveal anything about the situation. That would likely depend, at least in part, on whomever the Federation sent to meet with Donatra.

As Spock finished the last of his soup, he wondered who President Bacco would choose as her emissary.

23

"Tzenkethi marauders."

Lieutenant Commander Benjamin Sisko spun toward his starboard station on the *Okinawa* bridge and punched at the controls. As quickly as he could, Sisko called up a sensor readout to replace the engineering data spread across his screen. He immediately saw the ships that Lieutenant Snowden had identified.

"Two heavies," Snowden added, her voice steady in the face of the threat. "They're on a heading for M'kemas Three."

"Have they spotted us?" Sisko asked, and he felt relieved that the question had occurred to him. Although he had drawn a promotion out of engineering and into the command division nearly a year earlier, he still hadn't grown entirely accustomed to his role as the ship's executive officer. Even so many months later, he found that his duties on the bridge did not come naturally to him, and he often had to consciously think through what queries to make, what orders to give, what actions to take. In quiet moments, of late, he'd begun reviewing *Okinawa*'s drive performance at his station, more than once thinking that a return to engineering might be best for him.

"I don't think they do see us," Snowden replied, and

Sisko glanced over to where she crewed her side of the combined tactical-and-communications console. "They're making no alterations to their course and speed."

"All right," Captain Leyton said, rising from the command chair. "Let's lay low then. If we're lucky—"

"Captain," said Ensign Orr, "we're being hailed by the *Assurance*."

Leyton looked over at Sisko. "Damn," the captain said.

Sisko stood up and strode along the raised periphery of the bridge toward Orr at communications. "Ensign," he told him, "do not answer the hail. Transmit a standard silent-running protocol to the *Assurance*." Sisko peered forward to the main viewscreen, as though he could see the *Ambassador*-class starship, but it only offered the seeming constancy of the starfield it presented.

On the lower, central section of the bridge, Leyton paced aft, toward Sisko. "Captain Walter's crew must not have detected the marauders," Leyton said. "He wouldn't have made a mistake like that."

Sisko went around Orr to the tactical portion of the console, where he studied its displays. "Captain Walter's got a gas giant between the *Assurance* and the Tzenkethi vessels," he said. "There's no way the marauders showed up on their sensors."

"No more hails, Captain," Orr reported. "And no response to the silent-running protocol."

Sisko peered down into the central well of the bridge, where he saw Leyton nod in his direction and motion him forward. Sisko skirted the railing between the upper and lower sections and stepped down to join the captain. "We need a plan, Ben," Leyton said. "There's just too much traffic in this area. This system's too close to the lanes the Tzenkethi use to travel from their space to their settlements on M'kemas and Rodon. It's a wonder that they haven't scouted these planets yet."

"If they had, we'd know about it," Sisko observed. While patrolling near the Tzenkethi border, the crew of *Okinawa* had taken the time to survey the Entelior system, where on several of its worlds, they'd discovered a significant deposit of bilitrium, a rare, crystalline element valuable as both a power source and in the manufacture of certain weapons. With the system's proximity to Tzenkethi space, the Federation couldn't set up a mining operation—at least not during a time of war—but they needed to keep it out of the hands of their adversaries. "Reinforcements will be here in five days," Sisko said. "We just need to hold Entelior until then."

Leyton nodded, then took an elbow in one hand and held a knuckle up to his mouth, a nervous habit Sisko had noticed once he'd become a member of the bridge crew. "I'm just concerned that they'll detect us here, find the bilitrium, and bring back their own reinforcements," the captain said. "Maybe we should just leave the system and hope that they don't stumble across the deposits."

"They're going to stumble across them at some point, sir," Sisko said. "Those settlements on M'kemas and Rodon are new. Sooner or later, the Tzenkethi are going to come looking here."

"And if it's sooner and we're not here to stop them," Leyton said, "then we're giving them a valuable resource to use against us."

"Yes, sir," Sisko said, but then another possible solution

struck him—an engineering solution. "Unless there's a way we can mask the sensor signature of—"

"Captain, the Tzenkethi vessels have altered course," said Snowden. She worked the controls at tactical, then added, "They're now heading directly toward us."

"How long?" Leyton wanted to know. He took the command chair, and Sisko moved to stand by his side.

"Estimating three minutes, thirty seconds," Snowden said.

Sisko ran the variables through his head, then told Ensign Orr, "Signal the *Assurance*. Let them know we've got company." The Tzenkethi had obviously detected Captain Walter's hail, obviating the need for silent running.

"Aye, sir," said Orr. "Transmitting our sensor logs of the marauders."

"Shields up full," Sisko said. "Ready all weapons."

"Shields up," Snowden said. "Charging main phaser banks, loading photon torpedoes."

"Hail the *Assurance*," Leyton said.

After a moment, Orr said, "I have Captain Walter." On the main viewscreen, Sisko saw the field of stars replaced with the image of the *Assurance* captain. Not very tall, with close-cropped brown hair and hazel eyes, Walter appeared younger than his actual years, looking as though he couldn't possibly have ascended to the command of a starship in so short a life. But Sisko knew the captain by reputation and their wartime acquaintance. Walter had led the crew of *Assurance* for a decade, and he owned numerous citations and an impressive record of accomplishment to show for it.

"George," Leyton said, "we've got a pair of type-A marauders bearing down on us."

"*We have them on sensors now,*" Walter said. "*Attack sequence epsilon-three. We need to make short work of them.*" Of the two starship captains, Walter held seniority and therefore headed the patrol.

"Two on two," Leyton said. "We should have the advantage."

"*Because of our vast wealth of combat experience and keen minds for tactics?*" Walter said dryly. To Sisko, it felt too much like whistling past the graveyard.

"Exactly," Leyton said with a half-smile.

"*Type-A marauders,*" Walter said, his tone becoming serious. "*Be careful.*"

"Yes, sir."

"*Assurance* out," Walter said. The stars replaced the captain's image on the viewer.

"The Tzenkethi are within visual range," announced Lieutenant Thiemann from the operations station.

"Let's see them," Leyton ordered.

On the screen, the starfield shifted and the two marauders became visible. From the vantage of the *Okinawa* crew, they appeared spherical, but Sisko knew them to be shaped like great teardrops, their structures' graceful curves tapering out behind them to points. With virtually no surface details, they looked less like starships and more like some peculiar astronomical phenomena.

"The *Assurance* is beginning its attack run," Thiemann reported.

"Full impulse," Leyton said. "Implement attack sequence epsilon-three."

"Aye, sir," replied Ensign Lafleur from the conn, her fingers translating the captain's orders into action.

Sisko felt the power of the impulse drive surge through the ship, heard its low hum conveyed through the decking and bulkheads. *Okinawa* leaped forward, trailing behind *Assurance* and off to port.

Sixty seconds later, *Assurance* and *Okinawa* engaged the Tzenkethi marauders.

Sisko waved away the smoke that filled the *Okinawa* bridge, the gray clouds tinted red by emergency lighting. An unfamiliar whine, keyed low, betrayed the strain of the impulse engines. Flames licked at the top of a bulkhead where one of the port science stations had exploded, until a damage-control team assaulted the fire with a chemical retardant. Pandemonium flooded the bridge, but within the turbulent waters of disarray, the captain maintained the high ground of order.

Still in his command chair, Leyton called for pursuit. On the viewscreen, Sisko saw one of the marauders veer off to port, its bulbous forward end venting plasma into the void.

"Following Ship One," called Lafleur. Because the Tzenkethi vessels admitted of no distinctions, no visibly different markings or features, the *Okinawa* crew had assigned them the most basic of identities.

From his starboard station, Sisko watched as a plasma cannon, its emitter revealed by an open hatch on the Tzenkethi hull, fired on *Okinawa*. The superheated band of filaments slammed into the shields of the primary hull. The ship shuddered beneath the onslaught.

"Deflectors down to fifty-seven percent," Snowden called out.

"Target that cannon!" Sisko yelled.

A pair of phaser beams leaped from *Okinawa* and found their objective. A brilliant nimbus of white light erupted around the plasma emitter, the energy of *Okinawa*'s weapons redirected to the Tzenkethi ship's deflectors. The plasma cannon continued firing.

"Photon torpedoes, now!" Sisko yelled. "Wide spread."

For a moment that seemed to stretch interminably, nothing happened, but then Sisko saw a series of red flashes scream toward the marauder. At the last instant, the Tzenkethi ship swung around, making a turn that should have been too tight for so large a vessel. *Okinawa*'s phasers streaked past it, off into space, before ceasing. The solar-hot beam of the plasma cannon broke off as the marauder's flight carried the weapon's emitter out of sight. The first photon torpedo went wide, and the second, but the next three traced a dotted line across the teardrop hull. The Tzenkethi deflectors flared, then faded.

"Their shields are down," announced Snowden.

Offer your surrender, Sisko thought, but he knew that the Tzenkethi could do that in only one way: by standing down completely. There could be no subspace contact, as the first attacks of *Okinawa* and *Assurance* had successfully taken out the communications arrays of the marauders. The Tzenkethi couldn't be permitted to bring more ships to the Entelior system before Starfleet's reinforcements arrived.

As Sisko watched, another dark square appeared on the hull of the marauder as a panel slid clear of whatever it protected. He hoped to see escape pods, but then a collection of white-hot strands shot toward *Okinawa*. Sisko felt the ship shake violently beneath him.

"Shields down to forty-five percent," Snowden called. *Okinawa* jolted suddenly, and Sisko turned to his console. He raised the schematics for the ship's active power matrix, and saw that they'd lost one of the impulse reactors. "Shields down to thirty-seven percent," Snowden said, and Sisko realized that the reactor must have exploded, taking out part of the hull and attacking *Okinawa*'s deflectors from within.

"All weapons, fire!" cried Captain Leyton. "Maximum spread."

Sisko heard the sounds of the ship's phasers being fired, and felt the almost imperceptible rattle of photon torpedoes being launched. On the viewer, the marauder veered sharply again, but it could not escape the massive onslaught of *Okinawa*'s weaponry. The plasma cannon halted as the phaser blasts landed, dark patches erupting on the Tzenkethi hull. The first photon torpedo sailed past the marauder, but the second exploded near the plasma cannon. The detonation ripped a hole in the ship, sending a shower of fragments spinning off into space.

The third torpedo did the same, and the fourth started a chain reaction. Explosions bloomed seemingly everywhere on what remained of the marauder's hull, until the intense light of destruction hid the ship from view. When it cleared, the Tzenkethi vessel was gone.

For a few seconds, Sisko stared at the area where a ship had just been. *Where a* crew *had been,* he thought. He had come to fear and despise the Tzenkethi, who had destroyed the *Starship Lewis & Clark,* who had wiped out the colony on Raville II, who had instigated yet another unprovoked campaign against the Federation. He understood and agreed with the need to defend against the Tzenkethi Coalition, to battle them and prevent them from sowing destruction across the quadrant. But he didn't have to enjoy being a part of that defense, being a part of the effort that took lives, even those of hostiles.

"Damage report," Sisko said, so quietly that nobody on the bridge could have heard him. He waved away the smoke again, cleared his throat, then repeated his order.

"Checking," said Snowden. "Weapons and warp drive intact. Shields at thirty-five percent. One impulse reactor down. Tractor beam and secondary sensor array offline. Hull breaches on decks seventeen through nineteen aft, structural integrity fields in place. Radiation leaks on the primary hull aft, damage-control teams responding." She tapped at her controls, and then, in a quieter voice, said, "Eleven dead, thirty-nine wounded."

Captain Leyton got up from the command chair and stepped forward, to where Thiemann and Lafleur crewed ops and the conn, respectively. Leyton put a hand atop Thiemann's shoulder. "Show me the *Assurance*."

The lieutenant worked her panel, and the *Assurance* came into view. Irregular black patches marred several locations on its hull. It hung in space not far from the second Tzenkethi marauder. The reddish form of a barren, ringed planet, the fourth world in the Entelior system, afforded the panorama a vivid background.

"Take us there," ordered the captain, and Ensign Lafleur complied. Then, to Snowden, he said, "What's their status?"

"The second Tzenkethi ship has lost shields and weapons, and their life support is functioning at minimal levels," Snowden said. "The *Assurance* has lost its impulse engines, and their shields are completely down, but otherwise they're not in bad shape."

Leyton glanced over at Sisko, and the first officer left his station and joined the captain at the center of the bridge. "We're going to be hard-pressed to accommodate hundreds of Tzenkethi prisoners," the captain said.

Sisko blinked, unsure of the implication of Leyton's statement. "We can't fire on an unarmed crew," he said, declaring the obvious.

"No," Leyton said, though he did not sound completely convinced. "Recommendations?"

"The third planet in the system is Class L," Sisko said. "Marginally habitable. We could—"

"Captain!" Thiemann cried, and Sisko and Leyton both looked at the lieutenant, who pointed forward. Sisko peered up at the main viewscreen, where the Tzenkethi marauder darted toward *Assurance* on what seemed like a weapons run.

"I thought you said the marauder's weapons systems were down," Sisko said to Snowden.

The lieutenant checked her panel. "Verified," she said.

"They're going to ram the *Assurance*," Leyton said.

The crew of the bridge stared at the unfolding scene on the main viewer. At the last moment, the Tzenkethi vessel slammed to a halt, then yawed on its axis. The tapering aft section of the teardrop-shaped hull swung around in an impossibly fast maneuver that must have overwhelmed the ship's inertial dampers. Sisko couldn't believe that the marauder didn't tear itself apart.

The tip of the Tzenkethi ship sliced through the pylon supporting *Assurance*'s starboard warp nacelle. An explosion bloomed outward, the fire and gas swallowed in the next instant by the emptiness of space. Sisko watched in horror as the nacelle went spinning off in one direction while *Assurance* tumbled away in another.

"Weapons," said the captain. "Open fire as soon as we're in range." But as soon as the Tzenkethi marauder steadied after its attack on *Assurance,* it streaked away. "Initiate pursuit," Leyton said, throwing himself into the command chair.

"Sir," said Sisko, still gazing at the viewscreen. On it, *Assurance* plunged toward the planet.

"Get me Walter," the captain said.

The scene that appeared on the main viewer contrasted radically with the one Sisko had seen earlier. Captain Walter, disheveled, his uniform sliced open down the right side of his chest, looked beaten, the bridge around him charred and smoky.

"Captain," he said, breathless, *"we're falling into the atmosphere and our impulse engines are down. My chief engineer and half her team are dead or wounded. We need assistance."*

To Sisko's surprise, Leyton hesitated, then turned toward Snowden. "Lieutenant, speed and heading of the marauder."

Snowden took a beat to find the information. "They're traveling at warp five, on a direct course back to Coalition space."

Leyton turned back toward the viewer. "Where they'll inform the Tzenkethi fleet what's happened here," he said. "They'll bring back an armada, and it's a certainty that they'll locate the bilitrium."

"*Pull us out of the atmosphere and then go after them,*" Walter said.

Again, Leyton hesitated. "Out tractor beam is down."

A shadow seemed to cross Captain Walter's face as he realized the implication. A rush of thoughts swirled through Sisko's mind. He considered the crew of *Assurance* activating their ship's tractor beam, and having *Okinawa* travel into the beam to connect the two vessels and then haul it back into space.

No good, Sisko thought. It would be too great a risk for *Okinawa,* but—

"*Go after the Tzenkethi,*" Walter said evenly, though the color had drained from his face. "*You have to prevent them from reporting back to their fleet and coming back here in force. The bilitrium . . .*"

"George—" Leyton started to say, but Sisko interrupted him.

"Captain, give me three shuttles and I can pull the *Assurance* out of there," he said. "That way, you can stop the Tzenkethi."

This time, Captain Leyton didn't hesitate.

"Go."

Sisko sat at the operations console aboard the shuttlecraft *Naha.* Beside him, Master Chief Petty Officer Kozel, one of *Okinawa*'s highest rated pilots, worked the conn. Through the forward ports loomed the ruddy form of Entelior IV, and somewhere below, the *Starship Assurance* and its crew of seven hundred plummeted toward destruction.

"*Nago* and *Chatan* signal that they're in formation and ready, Chief," Sisko told Kozel. "Take us in."

"Yes, sir," hissed the Saurian as his claws raked across his panel.

At once, Entelior IV seemed to rise outside the ports as Kozel aimed the shuttle's nose toward the planet's surface. Sisko checked the sensors and saw *Nago* and *Chatan* following closely behind, one off to port, one to starboard. Scans also picked out *Assurance,* thousands of kilometers below *Okinawa*'s trio of auxiliary craft.

Sisko reached up and opened a channel. "Shuttlecraft *Naha* to *Assurance.*"

"Assurance, *Captain Walter here,*" came the immediate reply. *"We don't have much time, Commander."* Sisko perceived tension in his voice, but not panic.

"I know, sir," Sisko said. "We're on our way. Activate your tractor beam now, at its maximum power and widest dispersal."

Sisko thought he heard Walter issue the order in the background, and then the captain said, *"It's done."*

"Hold on tight, Captain," Sisko said. "We'll get you. *Naha* out." He closed the channel, then studied the sensor readings of *Assurance.* He could see an alteration in the starship's flight dynamics—if you could call an unpowered, uncontrolled descent a flight—as the tractor beam wrestled with the atmosphere through which it passed. Temperature readings for the meteor that *Assurance* had become continued to rise, portions of the hull measuring upwards of twelve hundred degrees.

Sisko peered through the ports. "I see it," he said. Even against the red surface of Entelior IV, the blazing form of *Assurance* stood out.

Kozel did not even glance up once, his gaze fixed on his

console. As the shuttle drew nearer the falling starship, he said, "I read the tractor beam. Plotting an entry course."

Sisko pulled up a navigation readout on his own display and watched as the flight plan for the shuttle took shape, calculated by computer and manipulated by Kozel. "I'm signaling *Nago* and *Chatan* that we're almost ready," Sisko said. He waited as *Assurance* grew ever larger. Beyond it, the surface of the planet filled the ports.

As the seconds seemed to elongate, Sisko wondered about *Assurance*'s transporters. If they still functioned, they could theoretically transport the crew to safety. That would mean donning environmental suits in order to survive the hostile environment of Entelior IV. But there would have been enough time to beam down only a fraction of the seven hundred souls aboard the ship. Who would Captain Walter choose? *How* would he choose? How do you tell a young girl or a young boy that you saved somebody else's mother or father, but not their own?

Sisko could not help but think of his own son. Jake would turn seven soon, and Sisko missed him terribly. The thought of never returning to him, of his son having to grow up without knowing his father, was almost too much even to consider. And Jennifer—

Sisko squeezed his eyes shut and shook his head, trying to clear his mind. He missed his wife so much, and to imagine her having to go on without him, having to raise Jake by herself, seemed cruel. It made him despise the Tzenkethi even more for the war, which had necessarily taken him away from his family. If he should—

"Course laid in," Kozel said.

Sisko opened his eyes and examined his mirror navigation display, highlighted the course, then transmitted it to *Nago* and *Chatan*. First one and then the other signaled their receipt and implementation of the course.

Just ahead, an explosion startled Sisko. He felt as though an electric shock had coursed through his body as he imagined *Assurance* crashing into the ground. "Hold on!" Kozel yelled, and the shuttle decelerated rapidly, for a moment overpowering the inertial dampers. Sisko braced himself and kept his seat as he saw the other two shuttles shoot past *Naha*.

"What—?" Sisko said, but then another object appeared spinning through the sky. Sisko had just enough time to recognize it as *Assurance*'s other warp nacelle before *Nago* slammed into it.

The shuttle exploded.

Kozel veered to port and accelerated, outrunning the wreckage as it too now fell toward the planet. Sisko looked around wildly, finally seeing *Chatan* continuing its own flight. Quickly, it fell back into formation.

"Implementing course," Kozel said as they finally reached *Assurance*. The shuttle hove to port and headed for the blue-white light emanating from the forward section of the primary hull. As Sisko watched the tractor beam, he began to feel dizzy, and he realized that he shouldn't look at the wheeling coruscation of light. He focused instead on his console.

He felt the shuttle veer again, then jolt as it entered the field of the tractor beam. The cabin brightened within the illumination. He checked the sensors to see that *Chatan* had followed them inside.

"We're hooked," Kozel said. "Pulling up."

The sound of the shuttle's drive changed, grew labored

as it struggled against the tractor beam. Sisko's engineering background had allowed him to roughly calculate that three of *Okinawa*'s shuttles would be able to haul *Assurance* out of its fall. He didn't know if only two would.

Again he thought of Jennifer and Jake.

The sound of the engines worsened, whining under the strain. Sisko checked the sensors. *Assurance* had straightened out, its bow now pointing toward the sky, but its velocity continued unchanged. After several seconds, though, it finally began to decelerate.

But not enough.

The starship continued falling toward the planet, pulling the two shuttles with it. "Keep going," Sisko said, his eyes not leaving the velocity gauge. The three vessels, tethered together by the tractor beam, slowed more and more.

Entelior IV raced upward at them.

All at once, the light inside the cabin changed, the engines quieted, and *Naha* shot forward, up into the sky.

"What happened?" Kozel asked, obviously surprised.

Sisko examined the sensors. "They cut the tractor beam," he said, realizing that Captain Walter had not wanted to haul the two shuttles down to the planet with *Assurance*. "Turn us around," he said, even as he adjusted the sensors to scan the surface of the planet.

Kozel brought the shuttle around and headed it down toward the planet. *Chatan* came into view for a moment as it followed *Naha,* and then Sisko saw *Assurance*. It lay on an open plain, the primary and secondary hulls flat on the surface, the dorsal connector between them shattered.

Sisko keyed open a channel. "*Naha* to *Assurance*," he said. "Come in, *Assurance*."

When he received no response, his heart sank. He desperately checked the sensors and, to his surprise, read life signs within the wreckage—*many* life signs.

"*Assurance to* Naha," came the voice of Captain Walter. Beside Sisko, Kozel threw his hands into the air in an obvious expression of joy.

"*Naha* here, Captain," Sisko said, unable to keep the smile from his face. "What's your status?"

"*I don't think* Assurance *will be headed back out into space anytime soon,*" Walter said, "*but thanks to you, most of my crew will.*"

Emotion filled Sisko, and he found himself unable to say anything.

"*The hull is pretty badly damaged,*" Walter continued, "*but we still have power, and that means life support and our structural integrity field, so we should be all right here for a while.*"

"We'll put down next to you, Captain," Sisko said, finding his voice again. "I hope you won't mind a few visitors."

"*Not at all, Commander,*" Walter said. "*I daresay there are some people here who want to thank you and your team.*"

"I'll let you know when we're ready to beam aboard," Sisko said. "*Naha* out." He turned to Kozel. "Take us down," he said, and then contacted *Chatan* to inform its crew.

As the shuttle approached the broken form of *Assurance,* Sisko thought about *Nago.* Crewman Butterfield and Senior Petty Officer Lintosian'a had been aboard. Sisko tried to tell himself that they had given their lives to save hundreds of others, but he doubted that would be much comfort to the people who loved them.

Only later would he realize that their fast and painless deaths would make them among the luckier Starfleet personnel on Entelior IV.

Sisko sat on the edge of the bed in the guest quarters assigned to him aboard what had once been the *Starship Assurance,* but which now amounted to nothing more than a temporary shelter. Enough of *Assurance* remained intact and functioning to keep the crew comfortable enough until *Okinawa* returned and effected a rescue. If necessary, they could even last the five days it would take for Starfleet reinforcements to arrive in the system. For the time being, they would not risk broadcasting a distress signal so close to Tzenkethi territory, but if no Starfleet personnel arrived within the next six days, they would have to consider doing so.

Sisko looked down at the padd in his hand. Once he and Kozel and the crew of the other shuttle had set down beside *Assurance,* they'd transported to the ship, where they'd been greeted as heroes. Fortunately, Captain Walter had recognized the strain that put them under, and he'd quickly provided them quarters so that they could get some privacy and some rest.

For Sisko, though, rest hadn't come. He'd lain awake in bed, his mind refusing to shut down. He thought about Butterfield and Lintosian'a, about the forty-seven people who had died aboard *Assurance,* and the eleven on *Okinawa.* He even thought about the crew of the Tzenkethi marauder.

Too much death.

Sisko hadn't entered Starfleet to risk his life, or to see his colleagues killed, or to have to contribute to the taking of other lives. He was an engineer, not a soldier. Ship design interested him, not military tactics.

The previous year, when Captain Leyton had tapped him for a promotion to lieutenant commander, he'd been pleased. But when the captain had also pulled him out of engineering and into command, when he'd named him the ship's first officer, Sisko had been stunned. *Too stunned to say no,* he thought. In truth, he respected and admired Captain Leyton, and though Sisko hadn't planned on moving beyond the engineering division, he'd thought that perhaps the captain knew better.

His time as first officer of *Okinawa* had developed well enough, he supposed, and he had performed at a satisfactory level, but he still felt undecided. He longed to talk with Jennifer about it. She had come to know him so well, and she often could provide him a perspective he hadn't considered—even about himself.

And he missed her. And Jake.

He activated the padd, intending to record a message to his wife and son, but then the door chime sounded. "Come in."

The doors opened to reveal Captain Walter. "I hope I'm not disturbing you, Commander."

"No, not at all," he said, setting the padd aside on the bed. He started to rise, but Walter waved him back down.

"I wondered if we might talk a bit," said the captain. Without waiting for Sisko to reply, Walter pulled the chair from in front of the companel and set it facing the bed. When he sat down, he said, "I understand that you're not just a relatively new exec but also new to command."

The subject surprised Sisko, not only because he'd just

been thinking about it, but because of the current circumstances. "Yes," he said. "I'm ten months in."

Walter nodded, then seemingly apropos of nothing, said, "You know, I've played a lot of poker with your captain."

Unsure how to respond, Sisko said, "I didn't know he played."

"Oh, yes," Walter said. "Not particularly well, but that's one of the reasons I like playing against him." He chuckled before continuing. "Captain Leyton and I go back to our days at the Academy together. We're friends, and we stay in touch. I'm telling you this because he's talked about you from time to time, Commander."

Sisko felt his eyebrows lift. It didn't surprise him that his commanding officer had discussed him, but he didn't understand why Walter had brought it up. "Well, I might have told a few people about Captain Leyton too," he said, more just to contribute something to the conversation than for any meaningful reason.

"I'm sure," Walter said. "What I want to say, Commander Sisko, is that I'm aware that Captain Leyton plucked you out of engineering and set you down onto the bridge. I'm also aware that your captain thinks that you're considering leaving the bridge to go belowdecks again."

"I haven't told him that," Sisko said.

"No, I know that," Walter said, "but he thinks he knows you pretty well, and that's what he believes is in your head right now."

"I . . ." Sisko began, but he didn't know what to tell Captain Walter. He didn't want to lie to him, but neither did he want to discuss the issue with him.

I want to talk with Jennifer.

Walter held out his hands in a placatory gesture, obviously sensing Sisko's distress. "You don't need to say anything, Commander," the captain told him. "I don't expect you to tell me anything. But I wanted to tell you something, especially in the context of what I've just mentioned. You may be thinking about going back to engineering, and if you really want to do that, that's perfectly fine. Starfleet needs good engineers. But what I want to say to you, I say as a Starfleet captain: we need you, Ben. I saw your performance today—your ability to solve problems quickly, to implement solutions quickly—and I saw your willingness to take calculated but reasonable risks for the good of your fellow officers."

Walter stood up, not waiting for a reply, and set the chair back before the companel. "Thank you for your time, Commander," he said. "And for everything else."

Just as he turned to leave, the red alert klaxon blared to life. The captain turned to the companel and activated it. "Walter to bridge," he said. "What's—"

The sound of a phaser blast pierced the air. Walter reached for his own phaser, hanging at his hip, then glanced at Sisko. Stranded on a planet so close to Tzenkethi space, the captain had ordered the entire crew to carry weapons, Sisko included.

Sisko opened a drawer beneath the bed and pulled out his phaser. Together, he and Walter headed toward the door. The captain reached for the control beside it, toggled it off, then stepped up and placed his ear to the door. After a few seconds, he signaled to Sisko, then reached again for the control. The door glided open with a whisper.

In the corridor, the intermittent red glow of the alert continued to flash, and the klaxon still called out its warning. In the distance, Sisko could hear voices and more weapons fire. Walter cautiously looked out into the corridor, then stepped out of the cabin. Sisko followed.

"We need to find out what's going on," Walter said, moving over to a computer interface in a nearby bulkhead. As he reached to activate it, Sisko heard something and turned.

The last thing he saw before he lost consciousness was the greenish-yellow glow of a Tzenkethi, pointing a weapon in his direction.

24

Federation President Nanietta Bacco stood behind the desk in her office at the end of yet another long day at the Palais de la Concorde. Exhausted, she gazed out through the windows that formed the curve of the outer wall, looked out across the River Seine, to where Tour Eiffel rose with artistry and grace from the Left Bank. Night had fallen hours ago, and La Ville-Lumière earned its nickname: bright white lights outlined the city as far as she could see, keeping the international metropolis alive and thriving in the darkness.

For an idle moment, Bacco thought about Paris. Steeped in history, the ancient city still held sway over important events, serving as the seat of government of the United Federation of Planets. More than that, though, Paris seemed to embody the promise not just of humanity, and not even just of the Federation, but of life itself. Nature and civilization, art and architecture, science and industry, joy and romance, remembrance and expectation, all permeated a place occupied for virtually all of Earth's recorded history.

And all I want is to take a turbolift down to the Champs-Élysées and go out for a little walk, Bacco thought. She didn't want a security detail attending her, she didn't want tomorrow's decisions weighing her down, she didn't want much of anything beyond hearing the heels of her own shoes on the pavement as she strolled from one pool of lamplight to another. *That's not too much to ask, is it?*

Except she knew that it *was* too much. She did not for one moment believe herself indispensable to even the smallest segment of the universe—not even to her daughter—but she owned the responsibility of her position. She had taken office in crisis, after the disastrous Tezwa affair, and in the two years since, there had been essentially no ebb. Against all odds, the Federation and its neighbors had survived the Borg invasion earlier that year, but at a cost that would have to be repaid for years to come.

At least there is *a Federation,* she told herself, a phrase that, if not exactly her mantra, then at least a fact of which she continually reminded herself. Once, when she said as much to Esperanza Piñiero, her chief of staff suggested wryly that they'd found a ready-made slogan for her reelection campaign in 2384. Of course, although she had yet to make a decision two years out, Bacco often found it impossible to envision running for office again. *Most of the time, I want to run* from *office.*

Peering from the top floor of the Palais de la Concorde, Bacco refocused her eyes, pulling her gaze from the great city spreading before her to the image of her own face reflected in the window. With her short white hair pulled back from her face, and the lines in her flesh etched ever deeper, she thought she looked severe. Approaching her ninetieth birthday, she felt that the job had aged her, that it had scooped her up and carried her summarily past her middle years—well, her *late* middle years. When she'd taken office, she'd felt at the height of her abilities, at her prime, but these days, she felt constantly fatigued.

Even if I really wanted to run from *office, I'd be too weary,* she thought. In truth, though, Bacco didn't really know how to run from difficulties, only how to face them head-on. *Why else would I be in my office at midnight on a Friday?*

"And why the hell am I here alone?" she asked aloud as she turned from the window. She gazed past her desk at the large, semicircular space, at the various chairs and tables and other pieces of elegant furniture scattered throughout the room. She liked the office. When she needed to think, she could move about without feeling restricted, and when she needed to work, it provided a comfortable environment conducive to her productivity. But when required to wait by herself—which didn't happen often—she found the area too big, its many empty chairs an accusation of lost time—of *wasted* time.

Glancing over at the chronometer, Bacco saw that the hour had actually slipped past twelve. She strode over to her desk and reached for the intercom. "Sivak," she said, "where in hell is the secretary?"

"Madam President," replied her assistant at once, *"your question lacks both specificity and meaning."* Prior to Bacco's relocation to Paris, Sivak had assisted her for three years during her time as governor of Cestus III, and she had come to rely on his organizational abilities and keen mind for detail. At the same time, she had never entirely warmed to the Vulcan's decidedly sardonic wit. *"If you are referring to Secretary Shostakova, I can assure you that she is not in 'hell.'"*

"Thank you for that information, Sivak," Bacco said

crisply, "but I'm more interested to know where the secretary *is*." She knew that her secretary of defense had been touring various sections of the Federation over the past half-year, examining rebuilding efforts as they tried to fully recover from the Borg invasion. That day, the secretary had to travel to Earth from Rigel IV for their meeting, but the ship ferrying her should have arrived an hour ago.

"Right now, she's on a turbolift," Sivak said.

"A turbolift?" Bacco echoed, surprised. "Where?"

"Somewhere between the second and fifteenth floors," said Sivak.

"Here, at the Palais? Why didn't you say so?"

"I believe I just did, Madam President."

Bacco rolled her eyes, wondering how Sivak would react if she fired him on the spot. Then she wondered which three people she could hire to replace him. "Send the secretary in as soon as he arrives," she said. "And have my chief of staff, Admiral Abrik, and Secretary Safranski join us in my office immediately."

"Yes, Madam President."

Bacco took a seat behind her desk and picked up the padd she had been studying earlier. It detailed reports of former Ambassador Spock's efforts on Romulus—or at least the results of those efforts. Bacco still found it difficult to believe that he had persuaded the praetor to grant him a legal visa and to allow him to openly advocate for Vulcan-Romulan reunification.

Perhaps of more importance, though, the padd held the contents of a communication sent from Spock through her old friend Slask. The Gorn had conducted the message through another trusted intermediary to Bacco, but she didn't quite know what to make of it. As if the division of the Romulans and the advent of the Typhon Pact had not been enough to keep the Alpha and Beta Quadrants spinning in uncertainty, Spock seemed to think that the currently stable relationship between the Romulan Star Empire and the Imperial Romulan State might not last.

Bacco heard a knock at the leftmost of the three doors that lined the inner wall of her office. It then opened to reveal not only Secretary of Defense Raisa Shostakova, but Chief of Staff Esperanza Piñiero; Esperanza must have met Raisa at the transporter bay. The two women approached the desk, a study in contrasts. Esperanza, though not especially tall, appeared to tower over the defense secretary, owing to Raisa's short stature and poor posture—both traits the result of her hailing from a human colony on the high-gravity planet of Pangea. As well, Esperanza had an olive complexion and black hair, while Raisa had much lighter coloring.

"I am sorry for the delay, Madam President," Raisa said with a slight Russian accent. "The *Altair* made an unscheduled stop at Mars."

"The *Altair*?" Bacco asked. "That's one of the new vessels, isn't it?"

"Yes, ma'am," Raisa said. "They're still on their shakedown cruise, and they needed some parts for the engine room."

"Well, you're here now." Bacco understood that even though Starfleet had made great strides in renewing their force after the Borg invasion, the speed with which rebuilding efforts took place could also lead to problems. "Have a seat," she said, pointing toward the sitting area.

As Bacco walked out from behind her desk, there came another knock. The door opened again, this time admitting Federation Security Advisor Jas Abrik and Secretary of the Exterior Safranski. "Gentlemen," Bacco said, "join us."

Once everybody had taken their seats, Bacco explained that Spock had sent a clandestine request for an undercover courier to deliver a message to her office. She then detailed the events Spock had described in that message, and his recommendation that the president send an envoy to speak directly with Donatra. "We need to discuss whether or not to send such an envoy, and if we do, exactly how we should approach the empress."

"Pardon me, ma'am, but it's unclear to me exactly what Spock thinks is going on," said Safranski. The Rigelian sat alone on the sofa to Bacco's left, with Raisa and Jas in separate chairs to her right. Esperanza had taken a seat at the far end of the conference area, opposite the president.

"It doesn't sound as though he knows what's going on," Raisa offered. "Only that something *may* be transpiring on Romulus."

"That's how I read it too," Bacco said. "Jas, can you tell us what we know about Tal'Aura and Donatra right now?"

The security advisor leaned forward in his chair. "As best we can tell," said the Trill, "neither of them want the Romulan people divided, but neither want to surrender their positions of authority. Some months ago, Praetor Tal'Aura strengthened her hold on the Star Empire by reconstituting the Romulan Senate, but she still lacks the military might to forcibly take control of Empress Donatra's Imperial State. At the same time, Donatra not only doesn't have enough military might to take control of the

Star Empire, she doesn't even have enough to occupy the planets of her own nation. Because of that, it stands to reason that the people on those planets must more or less support Donatra."

"According to Professor Sonek Pran," Bacco said, "Donatra's plan was basically to wait out Tal'Aura." Months prior, Pran had successfully lobbied the empress to offer food to the Star Empire, an offer that Tal'Aura had rebuffed after allying with the Typhon Pact nations. "Donatra believed that the support of her people would grow and spread all the way to Romulus, where a popular uprising would ultimately take Tal'Aura down."

"That made more sense when the people of the Star Empire were facing shortages of food and medicine," Jas said. "But now that Tal'Aura's joined the Typhon Pact, that's no longer the case."

"Since the Star Empire is now allied with the Typhon Pact," Safranski asked, "doesn't that alter the balance of power between the two Romulan states?"

"It could," said Raisa, "but so far, we've seen no indication that the other members of the Pact have any inclination in getting involved in a civil war. That's particularly true since both the Federation and the Klingon Empire have formally recognized the Imperial State. Although there's no formal treaty, the Pact might not be disposed toward opening hostilities with Donatra if they believe that the Federation and the Klingons might get involved."

"So it remains a stalemate," Bacco concluded.

"Romulan leaders in general don't like to lose," Jas said, "but there's one thing they might dislike more: inertia."

"And with Tal'Aura and Donatra, it's not just political, is it?" Safranski asked. "They despise each other."

Bacco considered all of the comments, as well as Spock's message. "So it seems to me that we have to ask ourselves whether it's likely that either Tal'Aura or Donatra is taking actions to undermine the other, to compel the uniting of the Romulan people under her own leadership."

"I think it's a virtual certainty that *both* are acting," Jas said, "but I think it's likely that other factions are also maneuvering to take control of a united empire. Although Senator Pardek was murdered, his so-called war hawk contingent—which favors confrontation with the Federation—still exists, driven by Senator Durjik. There is also the Tal Shiar, under control of the ambitious Rehaek, as well as the militaries of both Romulan states, and various members of the Hundred. And I don't think we can discount Spock's Reunification Movement either, which has grown more popular since coming out of the shadows."

"Wait," Esperanza said. Bacco's chief of staff had yet to contribute to the conversation, instead doing what she often did, sitting back and allowing the principals to work through an issue. She spoke up when something arose that she either didn't understand or that didn't seem right to her. "Are you suggesting that Spock's Reunification Movement is seeking political power within a united Romulan state?"

"There's no question," Jas said. "Spock may not wish an official role in such a government, but that doesn't mean that the Romulans who believe in his cause don't want a role—or that some of them don't actually want Spock in a role."

"So is that how this involves the Federation?" Safranski asked. "Through Spock?"

"I think it's more than that," Bacco said. "The point Spock has made is that we need to know what's going on, because whatever happens could mean trouble for the Federation. I mean, what happens if the Romulans unite under Durjik, who then convinces the Typhon Pact to launch a preemptive strike against the Federation? They know that we're still rebuilding from the Borg invasion, more so than they need to."

"They also know that we have the slipstream drive," Raisa said.

"For now, that might provide a balance of power," Jas said. "But technological secrets can be fleeting, and you can be certain that the Typhon Pact nations have initiated their own slipstream research-and-development efforts."

For a moment, silence descended in the president's office, the sobering notion of a technologically equal Typhon Pact giving pause to Bacco, and she thought probably to the others. With their six members, the Pact would pose a major military threat—as well as an economic and political threat—to the Federation. For that reason, Bacco had already reached out to the Ferengi Alliance, the Cardassian Union, and the Talarian Republic as possible new allies in an expansion of the Khitomer Accords. She had also invited Donatra to discuss having her Imperial Romulan State join the fold—a discussion the empress had agreed to have, but which she had so far delayed.

"So what is it we're proposing here?" Safranski asked. "That we try to find out what's happening among the

Romulans? What if we do, and what if we don't like what we find out? What are we going to do then? Assassinate their potential leaders that we don't like?"

"Wouldn't that be preferable than going to war again?" Jas asked. "Haven't we seen enough bloodshed recently?"

The secretary of the exterior jumped to his feet and pointed at Jas. "You're actually advocating murder as a means of avoiding bloodshed?"

"Sometimes," Jas said carefully, "good, important ends justify normally unpalatable means."

"Not for me, they don't," Safranski said, his voice rising. "We would be no better than the Romulans if we took such an action."

"Hold on," Bacco snapped. She looked up at Safranski. "Sit down, Mister Secretary." Once he sat down again, Bacco said, "*I* am not suggesting that the ends justify the means, or that we should involve the Federation in Romulan politics. But we are debating all of this in a partial vacuum. We know of the various factions on Romulus and Achernar Prime. What we don't know is what all of those factions are doing, and how the Romulan political situation is likely to play out. It seems eminently reasonable to me that we take steps to keep ourselves informed."

"So that we can then manipulate events to suit our own needs?" Safranski asked.

"Manipulate?" Bacco said. "No. But we may be able to offer opinion and advice. We have recognized Donatra's government. We have had an ongoing dialogue with her. I see no reason not to continue that dialogue by sending another envoy to meet with her."

"I don't think we can expect her to tell us just how she's planning on conquering Tal'Aura and taking control of a united Romulan government," Raisa said.

"Of course not," Jas said. "But that doesn't mean that she won't reveal information to us, or that we won't learn things we don't already know."

"But what if Donatra *did* send the Reman to assassinate Spock?" Safranski asked. "And what if she then had the Reman killed to cover it up?"

"Then we need to send somebody to speak with her capable of gleaning that information," Bacco said.

"Somebody familiar with the Romulans," Jas said.

"The Federation diplomat most experienced with the Romulans is Spock," Safranski noted.

"Perhaps somebody from Starfleet," Jas suggested.

Bacco nodded. "I'll contact Admiral Akaar and get his recommendation," she said. "So are we all in agreement?" She turned toward the secretary of the exterior. "Mister Safranski?"

He looked over at her with a dissatisfied expression. "If all we're talking about is data-gathering, and possibly offering some advice, then yes, I'm in agreement."

"I'll accept that," Bacco said. Rising to her feet, she said, "Thank you, everybody," signaling the end of the meeting. Everybody stood and thanked the president, and as Esperanza joined Bacco, the others headed for the door. Before departing, though, Safranski stopped and looked back. "I truly hope you know what you're doing, Madam President."

Bacco didn't hesitate to reply. "So do I, Mister Secretary," she said. "So do I."

25

Spock moved along the edge of Victory Square, skirting the crowd even as he observed it. Located within Ki Baratan, the majestic plaza celebrated the history and successes of the Romulan Star Empire. Defining the square, great columns climbed high along its periphery, interspersed with towering statuary. Colossal likenesses of praetors and senators, of military leaders and heroic soldiers, stood with their backs to the outside, as though standing guard over the grounds within.

At the four corners of Victory Square and at its center, grand fountains usually sent plumes of water soaring high into the air, but Spock saw that they had been shut down, obviously to accommodate the day's event. At the far end of the plaza, broad stairs led up to a platform on which stood the largest of all the statues, an image sculpted in stone of the first Romulan praetor, Pontilus. As Spock looked in that direction, a man began to ascend the steps, presumably to address the crowd, just as two other speakers had already done.

"How many people do you think are here?" asked Venaster, raising his voice. The ambient noise of the people massed in the square made communicating at a normal level impossible.

Spock did not know the dimensions of Victory Square, nor could he adequately gauge them from his position along the perimeter of the space. Still, he cast his gaze from the front of the plaza to the rear, doing his best to conservatively estimate the number of those present. After a few moments, he leaned toward Venaster and said, "I would approximate a minimum of a quarter of a million."

Venaster's eyes widened, and Spock understood why. The figure dwarfed the number of people who had attended any single rally for Vulcan-Romulan reunification. Although the popularity of those events had continued to trend upward, Spock could not reasonably expect that his voice or those of his comrades would draw enough people to fill Victory Square any time in the near future. The size of the crowd at that moment did not surprise Spock, nor did its fervor, but he thought that the fact of both likely signaled a coming change in the status quo. He did not know how long it would require for that change to take place, but it pleased him that he had forewarned President Bacco— though he did not know if she had heeded his advice.

At the top of the stairs, the man reached the platform and turned toward the crowd. Behind him, the titanic statue of Pontilus provided a dramatic backdrop. *So dramatic,* Spock thought, *as to ensure its widespread distribution across the Romulan comnet.* It did not escape Spock's notice that Victory Square had been the location where Tal'Aura had captured Donatra's ally, Admiral Braeg.

"My name is Veltor," said the man, his voice collected and amplified by a sound system that Spock could not see but that he noted would serve to enhance all records made of the event. *"My name is Veltor, and I am a Romulan."* The

man threw his arms into the air as though he had achieved some sort of triumph. The people in the square cheered, supporting that impression.

When the volume of the crowd had dropped enough, the man continued. *"My sister lives on Virinat,"* he said. *"She's a schoolteacher, an honest, hardworking woman with a family and a home of her own. She is and has always been a loyal Romulan, and yet I haven't seen her—I haven't been permitted to see her—for hundreds of days."*

A rumble of discontent snarled through the square. Spock glanced around and saw seemingly genuine anger on many faces. He found the differences between the current gathering, and those in support of Vulcan-Romulan reunification, pointed. Where Spock and his comrades advocated for the positive benefits that the rejoining of two civilizations would bring, the speakers he had witnessed that day had consistently articulated their anger, emotion that appeared to engage the people assembled.

"Why?" the man called out to the crowd. *"Why have I not been allowed to visit my sister on Virinat?"*

Although such a question seemed an obvious rhetorical flourish, Spock heard numerous people exclaiming in reply. Donatra's name flew across the plaza, accompanied by epithets: Egotist. Traitor. *Veruul.* And like weeds sprouting in grass, hand-lettered signs suddenly popped up throughout the crowd, decrying the empress of the Imperial Romulan State.

But Spock did not hear and see only the name of Donatra. He also heard and saw that of Tal'Aura, though not with nearly as much frequency. And somewhere, someone called out, "Shinzon!" To Spock, all of it seemed calculated to give the impression of proletarian unrest, though clearly the gathering had not arisen as a spontaneous aggregation of concerned citizens. The setting, the extinguishing of the fountains, the sound system, the overly amateurish nature of the handheld signs, all of it indicated to Spock a controlling interest.

"We must not be divided," Veltor went on. *"We must not allow ourselves to be divided. We are all Romulans. We must take back our Empire. We must be one."*

The crowd roared its agreement. Veltor raised his arms once more, then started back down the stairs. As he did so, a woman headed up the stairs, no doubt to continue the shared screed against the sundering of their people.

"Spock," somebody called. "Venaster."

The two men turned together toward the sound of the voice. Spock did not feel particularly comfortable being identified by name amidst an angry throng, but nobody appeared to take notice. As he looked for the source of the voice, Spock saw D'Tan struggling to push his way through the crowd. When finally the young man reached them, he said, "You need to see something." He reached into his jacket and pulled out a data tablet.

Venaster looked to Spock. "We can go," Spock told him. "We've seen enough here." Venaster nodded, then pressed past D'Tan and headed for the nearest exit, forging a traversable path for them.

Outside the square, Spock took the lead, directing Venaster and D'Tan away from the exit and down the avenue, until the flow of people around them had thinned. Then he stepped to the side of the pedestrian thoroughfare and addressed D'Tan. "What is it that we need to see?"

D'Tan held up his tablet and activated it, then handed it over to Spock. Venaster leaned in to look at it as well. On the screen, a large crowd of people listened to somebody urging the rejoining of the Romulan people.

For just a moment, Spock thought that D'Tan had handed him a recording of the event they had just seen for themselves. But then other details became visible, and he saw that the event depicted on the tablet had not taken place in Victory Square, or in any other location that Spock recognized. "D'Tan, where did you get this?" Spock asked.

"It's all over the Romulan comnet," he said.

"Where did this take place?" Spock wanted to know. He continued to watch the recording, picking out familiar details: the large crowd, the single speaker, the slapdash signs.

"On Artaleirh," D'Tan said. "But that's not the only place something like this has happened. There have been at least half a dozen protests throughout Romulan space."

Spock peered up from the tablet. "Where else?"

"Abraxas, Devoras, Xanitla—"

"Xanitla," Spock said. "There have been protests within the Imperial Romulan State?"

"Yes," D'Tan said. "There was even one on Achernar Prime."

The homeworld of Donatra's empire. "Do you have a recording of that event?" Spock asked.

"Not yet," D'Tan said. "We've only read accounts of it."

"Tell me," Spock said. "On Achernar Prime, did they denounce Donatra or Tal'Aura?"

"From what we've read so far," D'Tan said, "the protests have all been similar: there are complaints about both the praetor and the empress, but far more about Donatra."

Spock nodded. He wondered how much of the sudden public call for the two Romulan states to become one could be laid at the door of the Vulcan-Romulan Reunification Movement. He had convinced Tal'Aura to allow him and his comrades to bring their cause out into the open because it would also serve the praetor's own interests. He had argued to her that one call for reunification could beget another. That appeared to have happened, though nothing he had seen or heard suggested to him that the abrupt communal outcry for one Romulan empire had arisen naturally. He could readily envision Tal'Aura setting the wheels of civil unrest in motion, seeking to grind down Donatra through the mill of public support.

But is that too simple a solution? Spock asked himself. He understood well the Romulan penchant for cunning. For all he knew at this point, Donatra could be driving the protests in order to spur a backlash against Tal'Aura. Spock still didn't even know whether or not the empress had been behind the assassination attempt made on him.

Misdirection is the key to survival, went an old Romulan maxim. *Never behave as your enemy expects, and never reveal your true strength. If knowledge is power, then to be unknown is to be unconquerable.*

"What's it mean?" Venaster asked.

"I don't know," Spock answered honestly. He had little knowledge about the current state of Romulan politics, and therefore little power to do anything about it. "I don't know, but I am concerned about our Movement." Spock handed the data tablet back to D'Tan. "I wish to convene the leadership, but not in the open."

"You want to return to the tunnels beneath the city?" D'Tan asked, but Venaster was already nodding.

"I'll make sure none of us is followed," he said. "When do you want this to happen?"

"Tonight," Spock said. "Two hours past sundown."

"What should I tell everybody this is about?" Venaster asked.

"The future," Spock said. "Tell them it's about our future."

26

Ben Sisko sat in the command chair on the bridge of U.S.S. *Robinson*. Around him, the crew worked at their stations, the only sounds the chirps and tweets of their controls, mixed atop the low thrum of the warp drive that pervaded the ship. In that silence lurked the truth of Sisko's isolation, identified a month ago by *Robinson*'s first officer. The captain set the tone for his crew, and most especially for his senior staff.

On the flip-up panel set into the arm of his chair, Sisko studied the continuous sensor readings appearing there. An overlay on the readout of local space demarcated the boundaries of the Federation and the two Romulan nations, along with the established Neutral Zone. As had been the case for most of the time that the crew of *Robinson* had been tasked with patrolling the borders, nothing moved out there.

How do you know? Sisko asked himself. *Maybe there's a fleet of cloaked ships heading your way right now.*

Except that he *did* know that nothing moved out there. Starfleet had long ago established a host of technologies along the Federation side of the Neutral Zone to unmask cloaked Romulan vessels: subspace listening posts, gravitic sensors, tachyon detection grids. And not only did the crew of *Robinson* continually check those monitoring stations for breaches and breakdowns, but during the eight months of their guard duty, they had deployed a new array of probes along the territory they patrolled, and at random intervals, they activated their own tachyon network.

No, Sisko thought. *Nothing's moving out there.*

Which was not to say that there had been no activity at all during their time along the border. Scans had frequently distinguished the warp signatures and impulse wakes of numerous Romulan sentries watching their own side of the Neutral Zone. Additionally, more than a dozen times, the *Robinson* crew had identified other starships making their way through Romulan territory, and on a couple of occasions those vessels had been close enough to one or another of the listening posts to capture a visual of them. They'd detected Breen, Gorn, and Tholian ships, and twice they'd actually seen Tzenkethi marauders.

Sisko instinctively glanced up at the main viewscreen. The starfield there remained empty, but he had no difficulty at all imagining the distinctive teardrop-shaped Tzenkethi battleships. When a listening post had first caught sight of a trio of the fearsome vessels a month ago, the image had brought him back to those terrible days fighting in the last Federation-Tzenkethi war. Since then, those memories had invaded his dreams.

Deactivating his display, Sisko folded it back into the arm of his chair. He had enough troubles without fixating on the Tzenkethi. Oddly, though, the nightmares that had become a regular part of his life over the past few weeks somehow comforted him, at least in retrospect. He abhorred reliving in his dreams those horrible days, the experience of jerking awake in the middle of his sleep cycle, with his heart racing and his bedclothes drenched in sweat, more than just a little unpleasant. At the same time, the relief he felt in the moment after waking, in the instant that he realized he had left those experiences far back in his past, always struck him as profound. In some sense, it seemed as though he not only had survived those dark days but had survived the bad dreams of them as well.

It's more than that, though, isn't it? Sisko thought. In a perverse way, the nightmares filled a void in his life. For years, his existence had been punctuated by steady, if irregular, surreal visits from the Bajoran Prophets. Those had vanished from his world, and so the dreams, as ugly and upsetting as they were, substituted one set of visions for another. It didn't sound healthy, and he knew that it shouldn't continue, but for the time being, it worked for him.

Sisko rose from his chair and walked to the center of the bridge, his eyes still on the main viewer. It had taken some time for him to become accustomed again to seeing a moving starfield. During his years on Deep Space 9, he had commanded *Defiant* on a significant number of missions, but he had spent far more time on the station. And for more than four years after that, he had lived his life planetside, beneath a more or less fixed view of the stars. He could peer up of an evening in Kendra Province and pick out the Bajoran constellations: the Forest, the Temple, the Chalice, the Orb, the Flames. . . .

Sisko thought to say something to the crew, or maybe just to Commander Rogeiro. Over the course of the past month, ever since his set-to with the ship's first officer,

Sisko had made a concerted attempt to spend less time in his ready room during his duty shift. He had also endeavored to appear less remote with the bridge crew, though the pattern had become too well established to break through easily: the captain and the ship's senior staff spoke when necessary and not otherwise. But Sisko thought that Rogeiro saw his efforts, and that truly had been the captain's goal: to assuage the concerns of *Robinson*'s exec. He neither wanted nor needed to receive questions from some admiral somewhere about the dissatisfaction of the ship's first officer.

Before Sisko could think of something to say, he heard the doors of the upper, portside turbolift whisper open. He glanced up in that direction and saw a crewperson he didn't recognize walking down the ramp to the lower section, a padd in hand. *Status report,* Sisko thought, and realized that he should complete another entry in his log before the end of the hour.

"Captain Sisko?" The crewperson stepped up to him in the center of the bridge, holding out the padd toward him. "I need your signature for the engineering status report. I've already had it signed off by Commander Relkdahz." *Robinson* had inherited the Otevrel chief engineer from *New York*.

Sisko reached out and accepted the padd, and as he did so, he noticed two things: the wide smile on the crewperson's face, and the familiar ridges at the top of his nose. "Crewman . . . ?" Sisko asked.

"Scalin, sir," said the young man. "Crewman Scalin Resk."

"All right, Mister Scalin," Sisko said as he perused the

engineering report. Without looking up from the padd, he said, "Is there a reason for your smile?"

"Oh," said Scalin, lifting a hand up to his mouth before self-consciously dropping it back to his side. "No, sir. I'm sorry, sir," he said, stumbling over his words as he worked to suppress his smile. "I mean, yes, there's a reason, but I didn't mean to, sir."

"I see," Sisko said. He took a moment to read through the rest of the report, then pulled out a stylus from within the padd and used it to append his signature. He handed both back to Scalin. "And what is that reason, Crewman?"

"Well, sir, it's just an honor to be in the presence of the Emissary of the Prophets." The young man's smile returned.

"Crewman," Sisko said sharply, and he paused, pulling himself back before he merited another admonishment from the first officer. "Crewman Scalin, I understand your appreciation, but I am *not* the Emissary of the Prophets."

Scalin looked down. "I've heard how humble you are, sir."

"I'm not being humble," Sisko said, knowing that he failed to mask his irritation. More quietly, he said, "I may have been the Emissary at one time, but I no longer am."

Scalin looked back up at Sisko, and though the young man's smile had lessened, it had not completely disappeared. "I've heard that might be how you feel now," he said. "But that's all right; the rest of us still believe."

Sisko's frustration threatened to boil over, but before he could say anything, somebody else did. "Mister Scalin," snapped Commander Rogeiro. The first officer stood from his chair and paced quickly over to Sisko and Scalin. "Mister Scalin, Captain Sisko has informed you that he is *not* the Bajoran Emissary. But he *is* the commanding officer of this vessel. You will treat him as such, and *only* as such. If you cannot keep your smiles and your beliefs to yourself, then perhaps I can find you another starship where you can. Do I make myself clear, Crewman?"

"Yes, sir," Scalin said. No hint of a smile remained on his face. "Very clear, sir."

"Good," Rogeiro told him. "Then carry on with your duties."

"Yes, sir." Scalin looked down at the padd and painstakingly slid the stylus back into storage. He then headed back to the turbolift. Once he'd gone, Sisko turned toward Rogeiro.

"Thank you, Commander," he said.

Rogeiro shrugged, but a bit of a smirk played across his own features. "Just trying to keep the ship running smoothly," he said.

Though Rogeiro had never mentioned it, Sisko knew that he must be aware of his captain's status among the Bajoran people. In his own experience with members of Starfleet, Sisko had run into a great deal of skepticism about his role as a major figure in the religion of Bajor's people. He recognized the expression on Rogeiro's face, but he didn't—

"Captain," said Lieutenant Commander Uteln from the tactical station. Sisko peered up at the Deltan security chief. "We're receiving a message from Earth." His brow furrowed as he worked the controls on his panel. "It appears to be in real time."

Sisko and Rogeiro exchanged a look. "Real time?" said the first officer. "They must have ships halfway across the Federation boosting the signal."

"It's eyes-only, Captain," Uteln said.

"All right," Sisko said. "Route it to my ready room."

"Aye, sir."

"You have the bridge, Mister Rogeiro," Sisko said before heading into his ready room. Once he'd sat down behind his desk, he tapped a control on his computer interface to accept the incoming message. The screen blinked to life, revealing the image of the Starfleet commander in chief and a middle-aged, white-haired woman who looked familiar to Sisko.

"Admiral Akaar," Sisko said. Because of the context, it took him a moment to recognize the leader of the Federation. He immediately wondered what could be so important that it required the heads of both Starfleet and the United Federation of Planets to contact him.

"*Captain Sisko,*" Akaar said in his deep voice. "*Obviously you recognize President Bacco.*"

"I do," Sisko said. "It's a pleasure to meet you, ma'am."

"*Captain,*" the president acknowledged. She seemed quite serious, as did Akaar.

"*Captain Sisko, you were assigned to the Federation embassy on Romulus as a junior officer, were you not?*" asked Akaar.

"Yes, I was."

"*And I know you had quite a lot of contact with the Romulans during the Dominion War,*" the admiral added. "*In fact, it was you who finally convinced the Empire to join our efforts against the Dominion.*"

The statement, though true, recalled the uncomfortable manner in which the Romulans had been brought into the war. To Akaar, though, he simply said, "Yes, Admiral."

"All of that would lead me to believe that you have as good a firsthand understanding of the Romulans as anybody in Starfleet," Akaar said, an assertion Sisko found almost hyperbolic.

"I don't know about my experience with the Romulans relative to anybody else," Sisko said, "but yes, sir, I do feel I know something about the Romulan mind-set."

"I'm delighted to hear that, Captain," said the president, *"because we need you to talk to them and try to get some information that could be extremely important to the Federation."*

Hearing and seeing President Bacco speak to him seemed peculiar to Sisko. He tried to shake off his feeling of awe, though, and respond directly to what she'd said. "You want me to go to Romulus, ma'am?" he asked.

"Not Romulus," the president said. *"Achernar Prime."*

27

Durjik sat in the Senate Chamber and listened with satisfaction as his colleagues argued about the Imperial Romulan State. Ever since the Hundred had re-formed the Senate, Donatra's illegal regime had been a topic of debate. But while nobody believed that the Romulan people should live divided into two separate political entities, never before that day had the senators come so close to a consensus regarding what to do about it. For so long, with no clear military advantage and no taste for war among the people, the Senate had been content to stay the course.

But circumstances had changed.

Despite the reluctance of the other Typhon Pact nations to involve themselves in a Romulan civil war, the alliance at least theoretically provided enough firepower to overcome Donatra's forces. Of greater interest to Durjik, the widespread public protests on Romulus and throughout the Empire—and even within Donatra's rogue state—would undoubtedly convince the holdouts among his colleagues to reconsider their resistance to a military option.

Most important of all, the inevitable consensus would ultimately bring about an end not only to the woman who had proclaimed herself empress but also to the one who had proclaimed herself praetor. *And once the Romulan people have been united and both leaders deposed,* Durjik knew, *a new praetor will rise to renew the Empire.* After that, the time would finally come to take on the hated Federation. With its Typhon Pact allies, Romulus would not be denied.

"We cannot take military action against the Imperial Romulan State," said Senator Eleret, the old woman speaking as though her words carried the weight of truth. She stood on the floor of the chamber, addressing her concerns to the rest of the Senate. Behind her, the praetor's chair and the tables that accommodated the Continuing Committee all sat empty. Either when the Senate finally reached agreement on a course of action, or when Tal'Aura ordered it, the full government would meet to decide on a way forward.

"Why can't we attack Donatra?" demanded Mathon Tenv from the first tier of seats. An old ally of Pardek, Tenv thought about galactic politics in much the same way that Durjik did, believing that diplomacy could best be accomplished at the emitter end of a disruptor.

"Donatra might have broken the Empire in two," Eleret said, "but the Romulan people on the worlds she has claimed did not. They are already paying a steep price by being torn from their true government and the rest of their people. We cannot undo that injustice by causing them to part with their lives."

"It's what those people want themselves," contended Tenv. "Haven't you seen the protests? Tens of thousands taking to the streets on Achernar Prime."

Durjik smiled to himself. *Rampant public dissent within the Romulan Empire,* he thought. Unpunished *dissent.* It would have amazed him had it not come about as the result of a political calculation. When Tal'Aura had first pushed

to decriminalize the Vulcan-Romulan Reunification
Movement, Durjik had fought against the idea; the very
notion of permitting treasonous ideas into the public dis-
course seemed not merely foolish but abhorrent. But after
the death of Pardek, his friend and political confederate,
Durjik had chosen a new ally well, and the chairman of the
Tal Shiar had explained the praetor's reasoning in allowing Spock and his followers out of the shadows. Rehaek
had kept Tal'Aura under surveillance, and so had learned of
her intention to have Vulcan-Romulan reunification drive
a call for Romulan unity. Once that had begun to happen,
Tal'Aura's minions had spread throughout Romulan space
to organize enormous protests.

Soon enough, Durjik believed, the Senate would vote to
launch an attack on Donatra's Imperial Romulan State. But
they wouldn't need to, because before then, Tal'Aura would
continue the second part of her plan to topple Donatra.
And once the Empire had been made whole again, the time
would come for new leadership on Romulus. Durjik felt
more than capable of assuming that mantle. He could then
turn whatever bloodlust had been directed at the Imperial
Romulan State to an even better target: the Federation.

On the floor of the Senate Chamber, Eleret concluded
her remarks and returned to her seat. Durjik waited to see
if anybody else would rise. Many of the senators, himself
included, had already spoken. He couldn't believe that anything new remained unsaid, except possibly for political
statements intended to forge new coalitions.

Durjik peered down toward the first tier, to where Senator T'Jen sat. As vice-proconsul, she administered sessions

that lacked the presence of the praetor and the Continuing Committee. Durjik waited for her to stand and declare the senatorial assembly at an end, but then somebody spoke from the last tier.

"I would make my position known."

Durjik turned to see Senator Xarian Dor on his feet. Dor quickly extracted himself from his tier and made his way down to the chamber floor. "My fellow senators," he said, "I think we can all appreciate the differing points of view put forth here today. I cannot imagine anyone sitting in this august body who does not wish the Romulan Star Empire to regain its full power and glory. I also cannot imagine any senator willing to risk the lives of our fellow citizens if there is some other way to achieve our aim of uniting the Romulan people."

Durjik suspected he knew where Dor would take his argument. The young man had been a vocal advocate for peace, when fighting would be hard, but more open to battle when the odds favored his side. In time, Durjik thought, he of the wealthy and powerful Ortikant could make a valuable new ally.

"I have been reluctant to plunge our people into battle against each other," Dor continued. "But the situation has changed for the Empire. We are now part of a major alliance that can bring us prosperity for generations to come, through peaceful means if possible, and through force if necessary. But I fear that unless our people return to a single, strong Empire, we will become subsumed within the Typhon Pact. We welcome new allegiances, but as Romulans, we must always be first among equals."

Yes, thought Durjik. *I must get to know this man.*

"If public protests and pressure fail to move Donatra," Dor said, "then it is incumbent upon the Senate—"

With no warning, Dor collapsed.

Durjik shot up from his chair, stunned by what he had seen. Dor had not fallen forward or back, or to one side or the other, but had crumpled where he stood. As other senators raced to the chamber floor, Durjik frantically looked around, searching for somebody who might have done this. But the doors remained closed, and Durjik had heard nothing, had seen nothing. Convinced that nobody but the members of the Senate had been present, he hurried down to the floor.

In the distance, Durjik heard an alarm signaling a medical emergency, which one of the senators must have initiated. As he stood with his colleagues over the unmoving form of Dor, he saw Vice-proconsul T'Jen hurrying toward the main entrance. Unsealing the chamber, she threw open the doors, allowing a medical team to enter. To get Dor to a hospital, the doctors would have to carry him out on the antigrav stretcher they had brought with them, since shielding prevented transport into or out of the Senate Chamber.

The medical technicians worked on the fallen senator for some time. In the end, they did carry him out of the chamber and transport him to the nearest hospital. But it didn't matter.

Xarian Dor was dead.

28

The single lighting panel leaned against a stone and battled the darkness of the cavern, winning in part but unable to penetrate into the many crevices lining the walls, or past the rocks and formations littered about the small space. Spock sat on the uneven ground, his back beginning to ache. The dank air penetrated the cloak he wore, contributing to his discomfort. More than any physical distress, though, what he had witnessed that day in Victory Square troubled him.

"I have called you here because of the many massive protests throughout *both* Romulan empires," Spock said. The leaders of the Reunification Movement's Ki Baratan cell sat and stood arrayed about him in the cavern: Corthin, Dorlok, Venaster, and Dr. Shalvan. D'Tan had accompanied Spock as well, and remained by his side. "Although I expected that the open discussion and espousal of our cause would likely help focus the attentions of many Romulan citizens on the division within their own empire, it seems extremely unlikely to me that what we saw today can be explained as such a consequence."

"We *have* seen rallies in support of uniting Tal'Aura's and Donatra's realms," Dorlok said. The former military officer, ever watchful, stood beside the entrance to the cavern.

"A *few* rallies," Corthin noted. "All smaller than ours, and only in a few places on Romulus. Nothing like today."

"What do you think it means?" Venaster asked Spock, just as he had outside Victory Square. He sat across from Spock, seated between Corthin and Shalvan.

"I am not certain," Spock said. "But because I believe it improbable that our rallies sparked the protests today, and because of the obvious organization of those protests, it seems reasonable to conclude that somebody *did* organize them."

"You're talking about somebody other than random citizens, or even a network of citizens," Shalvan said, more a statement than a question.

"Yes," Spock confirmed. "While it is theoretically possible that some Romulan citizen or group of citizens staged the protests, the similarity of all the events and their far-flung distribution suggest a managing force with considerable reach. Because none of the protests met with official resistance, the government itself seems a likely candidate."

"Actually, we have some new information," Corthin said. "Government security did try to shut down one of the protests on Achernar Prime. The one nearest to Donatra's fortress."

"They were not successful?" Spock asked. He felt another section of his back begin to hurt, and so he shifted in his position to relieve it.

"The reports are mixed," Corthin said, "but there are no reports of violence."

"So does that mean you think Tal'Aura is behind the protests?" Venaster asked.

"Perhaps," Spock said. "If either Tal'Aura's government or Donatra's is behind the protests, then the intent appears evident: to foster considerable public support for the uniting of the two Romulan states. With such support, the range of acceptable methods to achieve unity becomes broader."

"You're saying that people in general who want unity might not support the use of the military or other methods under normal circumstances," Corthin said. "But with a sizable and vocal portion of the populace calling for unity, military action might become more acceptable to people."

"Yes," Spock said.

"I understand what you're saying, but you've called us together under what amount to emergency procedures," Dorlok told Spock. "I'm not sure why."

"My concern is that because some powerful entity is pushing for Romulan unity, that may be more likely to occur in the near term," Spock explained. "Once it does, the primary reason I employed in petitioning Praetor Tal'Aura to decriminalize the Reunification Movement—namely that it would drive public calls for Romulan unity—becomes moot. That being the case, I have no expectation that our Movement will remain legal."

Nobody responded to Spock's concern immediately, a thick quietude suddenly filling the cavern. But as the others appeared to consider the implications, D'Tan spoke up. "Our group has been illegal before," he said. "That's never stopped us."

"No, but it has put all of us at risk, and some of us have lost our freedom because of it," Spock said. "Others have lost their lives."

"But my point is that we've all risked that before," D'Tan said.

"It would be different now," Corthin said. "Many people who support reunification have done so in public. Romulan Security—and probably the Tal Shiar—now know who many of us are, and most are everyday citizens who do not skulk through the Ki Baratan underground to avoid detection. It would be a simple matter to arrest large numbers of people."

"But they would come for us first," Dorlok said, stepping away from the door and deeper into the cavern. "They would want to take you in, Spock, and the rest of us who lead the cause."

"There's an old Romulan adage," said Venaster. "'Remove the head of the serpent, and though the serpent lives, it is a threat no longer.'"

Spock pondered for a moment about the apparent Romulan preoccupation with serpents—so many of their aphorisms seemed to mention the creatures—but then he pushed the thought aside. "What we must decide is how to proceed."

"What can we do?" Shalvan asked. "They know who we are."

"Not all of us," Spock said. Unwilling to fully trust the praetor, he had successfully convinced the other leaders of the Ki Baratan cell that none of them should speak at any of the rallies. "What we can do is return underground."

Dorlok laughed, showing signs of frustration. Lifting his hands to include their surroundings, he said, "We seem to have returned to the underground already."

"You want to stop holding the rallies?" Corthin asked,

plainly ignoring Dorlok's comment. "Shut down our com-net presence?"

"I think it would be wise to consider doing both," Spock said.

D'Tan hauled himself to his feet. "What you're suggesting is giving up," he said, his voice rising with emotion. "After all we've done . . . after all our efforts . . ."

"D'Tan," Spock said calmly. He rolled onto his side and pushed himself up, until he stood facing his young friend. "I am not proposing that we *abandon* the cause of reunification. One does not take action in support of a moral obligation because it is easy; one does it because it is a moral obligation. And that is what reunification is for me."

"And for me as well," D'Tan said.

Across the cavern, Corthin stood up, followed by Venaster and Shalvan. "For all of us," Corthin said.

Spock peered around at his comrades, taking a moment to appreciate them, before looking back at D'Tan. "Because we all want the Movement to survive, we must nurture it in ways that make the most sense for that survival. For now, I think that means reducing our profile."

D'Tan looked away, clearly still upset. When he gazed back at Spock, he said, "Even if Romulan unity happens tomorrow, we don't know whether Tal'Aura or Donatra will lead the new Empire."

Spock did not bother to point out that with regard to the future head of a united Romulan government, numerous other possibilities existed. "If we are to ensure that the Reunification Movement continues, then we must wait to see if this call for Romulan unity succeeds, and once it does or does not, we must then evaluate how to proceed from there, based upon the identity of the Romulan leader."

"If it's Tal'Aura," D'Tan said with almost childlike optimism, "then she might permit the Movement to continue legally."

"She might," Spock agreed. "But we will have to wait and see."

D'Tan lifted his hands and opened his mouth as if to say more, but then he dropped his hands to his sides and said nothing. Instead, Dorlok said, "So we're not going to arrange any more rallies, and we're not going to continue our comnet presence. What *are* we going to do?"

"I think the first thing is to try to figure out who's behind the Romulan unity protests," Venaster said.

"I agree," Spock said.

"I'll contact T'Lavent and T'Solon," Corthin said, naming the two women who had tracked down the connection between the protector in the Via Colius security station and Donatra. "They can start scanning the comnets for more information." She strode across the cavern and through its lone entrance.

"Dorlok and I will see if we can find anything out from our military contacts," said Venaster. "Somebody had to tell them to keep their distance from the protests."

Spock nodded, and Venaster and Dorlok exited.

A sudden twinge gripped Spock's back, and he reached to massage the spot for a few seconds. "Are you all right?" asked Dr. Shalvan.

"I am old," Spock said, "but given that fact, I am well."

"Good," Shalvan said. "You know, if Romulan unity

is achieved, it's possible that neither Tal'Aura nor Donatra end up leading the new government."

"I am aware of that possibility," Spock said.

"Good," Shalvan said again, "because you now have a lot of supporters on Romulus." The doctor turned and walked toward the mouth of the cavern, leaving Spock speechless. The mere suggestion of any Vulcan becoming praetor of the Romulan Empire seemed ludicrous on the face of it. But before Shalvan left, the doctor looked back and said, "What better way to champion the cause of reunification than by being the top official in the Romulan government?"

After the doctor exited, D'Tan peered over at Spock and smiled. Again, Spock could find no words to say.

29

Captain Sisko stood at the top of a high promontory overlooking the Verinex Sea. The wind howled above him, obviously redirected away from ground level by the low wall at the edge of the cliff. Beyond that wall, white-capped blue waters stretched to the horizon. In the sky above, the oblate form of Achernar shined a cool bluish white.

Sisko turned away from the top of the bluff and saw that the surface of polished stone beneath his feet formed a wide circle that reached from where he stood to a fortress that looked centuries—if not millennia—old. The walls of the massive edifice drove into the ground at an angle in such a way that it caused the captain to turn around again and pace over to the low wall. Peering over it and down to the sea, he saw that the fortress had been built into the face of the cliff, the highest section of the continuous structure emerging from the land behind him.

Between Sisko and the summit of the fortress stood a cylindrical projection, about three meters tall and two wide. He walked over to it, and as he drew near, a door in its side arced open to reveal a waiting turbolift. *Quite a reception area,* he thought. The door glided closed as soon as he stepped inside, and the lift immediately began to descend.

Before he had transported to the surface of Achernar Prime, Sisko's choice to beam down alone had been challenged by Commander Rogeiro. As much as he could, Sisko explained to *Robinson*'s first officer the sensitive diplomatic nature of his mission. The justification didn't appear to sit well with Rogeiro, but the commander stopped short of calling security to physically prevent the captain from leaving the ship.

Maybe he's hoping I'll get carried off by one of Achernar's pterosaurs, Sisko thought, though he knew that the great flyers had been hunted almost to extinction, and that they resided in territories far from Romulan-inhabited areas. *Or maybe he's just hoping that Empress Donatra will shoot me on sight.*

Though simply joking to himself, Sisko felt ill at ease about Rogeiro. The commander had performed his job well since coming aboard *Robinson,* despite the obvious discomfort he felt with his captain. Sisko had wanted—and still wanted—to keep to himself, but he hadn't wished to cause anybody any trouble.

Tell that to Kasidy, Sisko reproached himself. He closed his eyes and tried to put such thoughts out of his mind. Over the past eight months, he had become far more adept at compartmentalizing the past and the present, the people who'd been in his life and—

The turbolift door slid open with a soft release of air. Sisko opened his eyes at once, then stepped out into a long, rectangular space. Made of dark stone, with low ceilings and cluttered side walls, the place felt confining. At the far end, Empress Donatra sat in what amounted to a throne, raised onto a dais. A pair of uniformed officers—a man and a woman—stood in front and to either side of her, both holding disruptors in their hands and aiming them in Sisko's direction.

The captain waited for a moment, and when nobody said anything, he started forward. As he approached the empress, he glanced left and right, examining a collection of swords and shields hanging on the walls. Barely legible Romulan runes marked some of the dulled silver surfaces, giving the impression of great age.

When he had come within just a few meters of the throne, Sisko bowed his head, as he had been instructed to do when given his assignment. "Empress Donatra, I am Captain Benjamin Sisko of the Federation *Starship Robinson*. Thank you for granting me an audience."

"I do so as an act of reciprocity," Donatra said. "Your Federation President Bacco recognized my government and my empire when asked to do so."

Sisko raised his head. To his surprise, Donatra had styled her look like no Romulan woman he had ever seen. Her dark hair reached past her shoulders, framing an attractive face that had high cheekbones, full lips, and beautiful green eyes. She wore an elegant black dress, with a narrow wine-red sash draped across her right shoulder.

"I understand that I am not the first Federation envoy to visit you," Sisko said. Behind and above Donatra's throne, he saw a stylized image of a raptor, shown in profile, only one of its talons visible.

"In the first seventy-five days of this new empire, I welcomed several visitors from the Federation, including several Starfleet captains," Donatra said. Sisko noticed the hint of dark circles beneath her eyes, the only real blemish in her appearance, and a suggestion that she had not been sleeping well. "They had been charged with the unenviable task of attempting to persuade me to provide food to Tal'Aura's illegal and immoral government."

Donatra's characterization of Tal'Aura's praetorship struck Sisko as a possible challenge. Did the empress wish to gauge his reaction? Did she wish to see if he would either defend Tal'Aura's position, or state the obvious fact that many believed Donatra's own position bereft of legal and moral standing? If so, he had no desire to rise to the bait, and if not, there seemed little point in telling the empress what she already knew. Instead, he saw a way into the conversation he needed to have with Donatra. "As I understand it, you actually agreed to supply food to the Star Empire."

"I did," Donatra said, her expression hardening, "but my largesse was rebuffed."

"I imagine the praetor didn't have to accept food from you once Romulus joined the Typhon Pact."

"The Typhon Pact," said Donatra derisively, her voice rising. The two guards each took a pace toward Sisko, their disruptors still trained on him.

"With all due respect, Empress," Sisko said, "I come in peace and unarmed." He raised his empty hands, palms up.

"So you claim," she said. "I trust that you are not here to negotiate with me for the benefit of Tal'Aura."

"Tal'Aura who?"

Surprising Sisko once again, Donatra threw her head back and laughed. The captain smiled, pleased with the way the meeting had begun. Looking to her two guards in turn, she said, "Stand down." Both guards holstered their weapons, then fell back to the edge of the dais. Donatra rose from the throne and stepped down to the floor. Not as tall as Sisko had thought, she stood a dozen or so centimeters shorter than he. "If not Tal'Aura," she said, "then what did you come here to speak with me about?"

Sisko knew that he should not hesitate, and so he made an instantaneous calculation. "The Typhon Pact." He had been given a great deal of latitude on how to conduct his conversation with the empress, as long as he focused on finding out from Donatra what President Bacco needed to know.

The empress appeared to take his measure. "Come with me, Captain," she finally said, walking past him. The guards remained where they stood. Sisko turned and followed the empress, who headed back toward the turbolift, but then moved left to the wall, to a door that Sisko had not seen on his way to the throne. Donatra reached forward and took hold of a handle that Sisko hadn't seen either. She pulled the door open and the two went through it.

Inside, a small room mixed the functions of a basic kitchen and a dining area. A brazier stood in the center of the space, with a large, hooded vent reaching down from the low ceiling above it, obviously to carry away smoke. Off to one side, two chairs had been set around a small table. As Donatra moved toward the table, a man walked over and pulled a chair out for her. "May I offer you something to eat or drink, Captain?" she asked as she sat down.

"Thank you, no," Sisko said, taking the seat opposite her.

"That will be all," Donatra told the attendant. As the man withdrew to the far corner of the room, Sisko noted a revealing prominence on the man's hip. It appeared that Donatra did not believe in leaving herself unguarded.

"So tell me, Captain, why I should be interested in discussing Tal'Aura's alliances."

"Because even without Tal'Aura's own military capabilities," Sisko said, "the Tzenkethi and the Breen and the Tholians and the Gorn and the Kinshaya can take the Imperial Romulan State from you and return it to the Star Empire."

Donatra's eyes narrowed, the idea of such an event clearly not enthusing her. "They can," she allowed, "but will they?"

Sisko thought the question rhetorical, but she appeared to wait for a response. "The last thing I want to do is get inside the mind of a Tzenkethi," he said. "But since it's evident that Tal'Aura wants to unite the two empires, it seems to me that she might lobby her newfound allies to that cause."

"I'm sure the traitorous Tal'Aura will try to lobby anybody she can to her cause," Donatra said. "That does not mean that she will succeed. She may have thrown away the dignity of her Empire by aligning it with other powers, but that does not mean that those powers would be interested in involving themselves in a Romulan civil war. In fact, I think it unlikely that any of the Typhon Pact member nations would want to strengthen Tal'Aura's position. Nor would they want to risk hostilities with the Federation and the Klingons."

Sisko felt his eyebrows rise. "There are no mutual-defense agreements between the Khitomer Accord nations and the Imperial Romulan State, Empress."

"Not yet," Donatra said. "But the Federation is well known for coming to the aid of its friends. Besides, I don't think that President Bacco likes or trusts the Typhon Pact any more than I do, and I cannot imagine that she would want to see it strengthened by allowing Tal'Aura to take control of this nation and its resources."

Sisko held up his hands as though warding off the turn in the conversation. "I am not a diplomat, Empress, nor am I an admiral in Starfleet Command," he said. "Not only am I not authorized to discuss the views of the Federation president or Starfleet's commander in chief, I don't know their views."

"Not a diplomat?" Donatra said, her words filled with disbelief. The empress rose from her chair and crossed to the center of the room, to the brazier. "Not *exclusively* a diplomat, no," she said, "but you are obviously *many* things."

Sisko took the implication as a reference to his time as Emissary of the Prophets. He did not doubt that Donatra had checked his background before meeting with him. "We are all many things, Empress," Sisko said.

"Indeed," Donatra said. She picked up a metal poker and jabbed it in the brazier, which sent up a flurry of glowing embers. "One thing I imagine you to be, Captain, is a patriot. For Earth, for Bajor, for the Federation."

Wanting to avoid any discussion of his own past, Sisko simply reiterated Donatra's own words. "As you say, Empress, I am many things. As, I'm sure, are you."

"I am," Donatra said. "And I am a patriot. For the Imperial Romulan State, but also for the Romulan people in general. That includes those unjustly resigned to living under Tal'Aura's rule." She tossed the iron into the brazier, where it landed with a metallic clank. Peering back over at

Sisko, she said, "Come with me, Captain." She skirted the brazier and walked toward the wall to the right of the one through which they had entered. Her attendant strode over and opened a door there for her, revealing a long, narrow passage beyond it. "Remain here," Donatra told the man.

Sisko followed Donatra through the straight corridor until they reached another door. She pulled it open, then walked through. Sisko did as well, and found himself standing on a balcony lodged along two rock faces that met at right angles. The balcony described a quarter of a circle, an elaborately carved marble railing at its edge. Sisko peered upward and saw the precipice atop which he had stood before descending in the turbolift. Below, the Verinex Sea dashed itself against the base of the cliff, the roar of the encounter between water and stone constant and loud.

"This is a spectacular view," Sisko said. Though he found the air a bit cold, the sheer rock walls apparently protected the balcony from the wind.

"So much of Achernar Prime is beautiful, Captain," Donatra said. She had moved to the railing, where she stood gazing out at the sea. "But this is not home." She turned to face Sisko. "Vela'Setora is home," she said, offering up the name of a major Romulan city. "Romulus is home."

"I understand," Sisko said.

"Do you?" Donatra asked. "You said it was 'evident' that Tal'Aura wants to unite the two Romulan empires. I infer from that statement that you do not believe I want the two empires united."

"I did not mean to imply that, Empress," Sisko said. "But because yours is the—" The word *breakaway* occurred to him, but he discarded it. "—newer nation, that would suggest that any uniting of the two would favor Tal'Aura's government."

"That is what she would have people believe," Donatra said. "Do you know of the unity protests throughout the empires?"

"I learned of them just this morning," Sisko said. "I understand that they've been going on for a couple of days now."

"They have been *staged* for a few days, yes," Donatra said.

" 'Staged'?"

"By Tal'Aura," Donatra said. "The protests call for one empire, under her rule."

"I understood that the protestors spoke out against both you and Tal'Aura."

"There are token objections to Tal'Aura, but most of the remonstrations target me," Donatra said. "Even within the Imperial Romulan State, where most of the people have supported me. Even here on Achernar Prime."

Sisko knew that he needed to tread lightly. He did not want to anger Donatra enough that she sent him back to *Robinson* without learning what he had come here to learn. "Is it possible," he asked carefully, "that public opinion has changed?"

"Of course it's possible," said Donatra. "But it's not what's actually happened. Public opinion didn't change to support Tal'Aura; she's using these protests to *drive* public opinion."

"So you're opposed to such dissent?" Sisko asked.

"I am opposed to Tal'Aura's political agenda masquerading as public dissent," Donatra said.

Something occurred to Sisko, and he thought he could follow it to where he needed to go. "Empress, do you recall a man named R'Jul?"

A puzzled expression dressed Donatra's face. "R'Jul?" she said. "No, the name does not sound familiar."

"He was a security officer in the Romulan Imperial Fleet," Sisko said, studying Donatra's reactions. "He served aboard the *Valdore,* eventually getting promoted to chief of security."

"As the commander of *Valdore,* I would know my own crew, Captain," she said. "I had two chiefs of security during my command of the ship, both of them women, neither of them named R'Jul." She paced over to where he stood and looked him in the eyes. "Why do you believe otherwise?"

"That is the information I was given," Sisko said.

"Obviously," said Donatra. "But why is it important that you convey that information to me?"

Sisko looked away from the empress and moved past her, walking over to the edge of the balcony. Farther from the cliff walls, the wind felt stronger. Sisko gazed out at the waters of the Verinex Sea and debated how he should proceed. He found that he judged Donatra's reactions as genuine, and so he opted to tell her the truth. "A man named R'Jul may have killed an assassin some months ago on Romulus."

"And because you believe this R'Jul connected to me," Donatra reasoned, "you naturally think that I am also connected to the assassin . . . that I had the assassin silenced in order to prevent that connection from becoming known."

"If you knew R'Jul," Sisko said, "it would logically follow, yes."

Donatra shook her head, an aura of melancholy suddenly about her. "Assassination has played a strong role in Romulan politics for a long time," she said. "Too much of a role, and for too long." She paused, as though considering something. "Believe me when I tell you that I would not shed a tear if Tal'Aura died tomorrow. But the violence and self-interest plaguing the Romulan government must end. I did not order an assassination of Tal'Aura, or the killing of the assassin."

Again, Sisko believed her, and this time he said so. "But the assassin did not attempt to kill Tal'Aura," he said. "He attempted to kill Spock."

"Ambassador Spock?" Donatra said, seemingly surprised. "Of the Federation?"

"Yes."

"Why would somebody want Spock dead?" Donatra asked. "It was my understanding that Tal'Aura had decriminalized his Reunification Movement."

"The praetor did so to allow the public discussion of reunifying Romulan and Vulcan societies," Sisko explained, "in order to impel the public discussion of uniting the two empires."

"That is logical, but—" She stopped as something apparently struck her. "If you believe that public dialogue of uniting all Romulans favors Tal'Aura, and if you believe that Spock's Reunification Movement would aid such dialogue, then . . . are you accusing me of plotting Spock's assassination?"

"I am accusing you of nothing," Sisko said. "I am simply trying to understand what's happening on Romulus."

"Will there be repercussions for the death of a Federation citizen?" Donatra asked. "Is President Bacco considering revoking the Federation's recognition of the Imperial Romulan State?"

Sisko could see that the possibility of losing the amity of the Federation troubled Donatra. *And why wouldn't it?* Sisko thought. Without the Federation, she would be left with no major supporters beyond the Klingons. "I am not privy to the policy making at the Palais de la Concorde. But Ambassador Spock survived the assassination attempt."

Donatra nodded. "That's good, but . . . yes, that must be it," she said, visibly upset now. "Details are being manipulated to make it look like I had something to do with trying to kill a Federation ambassador. Tal'Aura is trying to discredit me, to weaken the Imperial State so that she can reclaim it for her own. That is why she's driving these protests: to ease the transition."

The argument made sense to Sisko, predicated on whether or not Donatra spoke the truth. He continued to believe that she did. "I'll make a report of what you've told me," he said.

"Check whatever records you can find on R'Jul and the *Valdore,*" Donatra said. "You should be able to discover that they've been falsified."

"I'll make a note of that," Sisko said. "Thank you for your time and candor, Empress."

"Thank you, Captain."

Sisko started toward the door, but Donatra stepped into his path. "Captain Benjamin Sisko," she said, her manner extremely serious, "please understand that I *do* want a united Romulan Empire, but under just leadership. I will not do what is unjust to make that happen."

"But what *will* you do?"

"I don't know," Donatra said. "Even if they're driven by Tal'Aura, these protests will eventually undermine my support. I don't have enough resources either to occupy all the worlds of the Imperial State, or to launch an attack on Tal'Aura."

"You also just said that you would not do what is unjust to bring about unity," Sisko pointed out. "Neither occupying worlds nor attacking Romulus is just."

"No," Donatra agreed. "But without additional military aid, I will not be able to keep the Imperial State intact."

Sisko understood what the empress wanted, but he could not provide it for her. "I have no authority to offer military aid," he said. "But even if I did, I can tell you, because President Bacco told me, that the Federation will under no circumstances engage itself militarily in a Romulan civil war."

"Then the Imperial Romulan State will fall."

"There's nothing I can do."

"Would you at least report the situation to President Bacco?" Donatra asked. "Will you tell her what I need?"

"I will," Sisko said, "but I wouldn't wait for military assistance."

Visibly distraught, Donatra turned and walked toward the edge of the balcony. For an instant, Sisko envisioned her throwing herself into the sea, and he took a step toward her to prevent that from happening. Instead, she simply stood there with her hands on the railing, her hair blowing in the wind, her gaze fixed on the vast ocean before her.

His mission complete, and with nothing more he could

do, Sisko headed for the door. He would return to the reception area at the top of the cliff, transport back to *Robinson,* bring the ship back to Federation space, and make his report. He left Empress Donatra of the Imperial Romulan State standing there, unsure how much longer either would last.

30

Gell Kamemor, designated elder of the Ortikant clan, entered the library of her family's ancient stronghold. When she had done so almost two hundred seventy-five days ago, she had held on to a sense of hope, a feeling that the praetor's appeal to reconstitute the Senate could mark a positive turning point for Romulus. As she crossed the threshold into the library this time, though, personal sadness filled her, along with an overall despair that her people would never find the right leadership to guide them out of the wilderness.

Inside, she saw far fewer than the seventeen members of the clan she expected. Several of those who had deliberated previously about who the Ortikant should send to the Senate had clearly been asked to return this time: Ren Callonen, Roval D'Jaril, and Anlikar Ventel, the grandson of Kamemor's sister. She could describe the other six present as genuine clan elders, all of them much farther along in years than she. While Kamemor welcomed the voices of experience, it made little sense to her that she had not been invited to stand aside so that one of the true elders could preside over the gathering.

As Kamemor stepped up to the head of the large conference table, the two people not already seated quickly took their places. At the far end of the room, the great stone hearth functioned as static decoration only, the warm temperatures outside making a fire unnecessary. The air inside the library felt close, despite the room's large size. As always, the scent of old paper filled the space.

"Jolan tru," said Kamemor after she had taken her seat. Then she bowed her head and offered the family benediction. *"Ihir ul hfihar rel ch'Rihan. Ihir ul Ortikant. Ihir dren v'talla'tor, plek Rihannsu r'talla'tor."* When she raised her gaze to the others, she saw each of them waiting expectantly.

"We have come together today in the face of tragedy," she said, her voice low and even. Although everybody present surely knew what had happened, if not all the details, tradition and her own sense of decorum dictated that she honor the lost by recognizing the terrible events. "Three days ago, Senator Xarian Dor collapsed on the floor of the Senate. The Hall of State's medical staff arrived immediately and administered life-saving techniques, without result. Senator Dor was rushed to Ki Baratan Medical Center, where he was pronounced dead upon his arrival." Kamemor felt pressure behind her eyes as she fought not to weep.

"An autopsy confirmed no sign of violence perpetrated against him," she continued. "Death occurred as the result of *Velderix Riehn'va.*" The virulent disease, often called *The Usurper,* struck at the arteries in the brain, weakening their walls and resulting in multiple aneurysms. Left undiscovered and untreated, ruptures typically occurred and resulted in instantaneous loss of life. "The doctors report that death for Senator Dor was immediate. All other members of the

Senate, as well as their staffs, have subsequently been tested for the disease. Fortunately, Senator Dor's appears to be an isolated case."

Kamemor paused to take a breath and settle her emotions. "This loss is a tragedy not just for our family but for the Romulan people. This young senator, with his sharp mind and absolute dedication to duty, held within him the promise of a brighter future for all of Romulus. Many, myself included, expected that he would rise quickly through the Senate, and then through the Continuing Committee, and that he might one day lead the Romulan Star Empire as its praetor. His loss, in our hearts and in our government, leaves a void not easily filled." Kamemor saw a dazed expression on the face of Anlikar Ventel, and suspected that she wore a similar visage.

"As difficult as it may be," Kamemor said, "it now falls to us to find a suitable successor for Xarian Dor in the Senate. Though it will be impossible to replace his—"

"Gell."

Kamemor stopped, but so quietly had her name been uttered, she could not even tell if she had imagined it. She peered at the members of the Ortikant around the table, and when her eyes found Minlah Orfitel, the grande dame of the family spoke again. "Gell," she said, "I would ask that you voluntarily stand aside so that I may lead the clan representatives through our obligations."

Kamemor required no further prompting than that to relinquish her duties. She stood up, her chair scraping loudly against the stone floor as she pushed it back. "I withdraw at once," she said. She stepped aside and waited for Orfitel to take her place. The revered old woman, three-quarters of the way through her second century, with a heavily lined face and a mass of thinning gray hair, rose slowly from her seat. When she arrived at the head of the table, Kamemor helped her into the chair.

Once Kamemor had taken her own place, Orfitel began to speak. "I want to thank Gell for presiding over the gathering to this point, and for taking over such duties when we first needed to name a new senator." She looked over at Kamemor, who forced a wan smile in return.

"As Gell has said, we must choose another member of the Ortikant to serve as senator," Orfitel went on. "A number of significant issues face Romulus. Tal'Aura and Donatra have divided our empire, and public opinion continues to grow that we must take action to unite all Romulans. We also must meet the challenges of dealing with our new alliances as a member of the Typhon Pact. And of course, there are always the interests of the Ortikant." Orfitel peered down the table to another of the elders. "Velephor, would you address that last point?"

Velephor, nearly as old as Orfitel but without a touch of gray in his hair, nodded. "Over the past three days, I and other members of our clan have met with business partners old and new. The general consensus among them leans heavily toward stability. They would eschew war with the Klingons and the Federation, as well as martial engagement with our own people, even should they remain under Donatra's control. The Typhon Pact presents us with strong alliances both military and economic, but since the governments manage, fund, and supply the various fleets, we stand nothing to gain if we go to war, and much to lose."

When Velephor finished, Orfitel looked over at Kamemor. "What do you think of that, Gell?"

The question nonplussed Kamemor for a moment. She did not understand why she was being singled out among those assembled, but then realized that Orfitel sought to relieve any slight Kamemor might have felt when the elder had taken charge of the gathering. "I concur," she said, "but for more than simply economic reasons. I think that the actions of government possess a moral component. I am well aware that the history of the Empire is rife with violence, much of it justifiable, but we do not necessarily have to kill in order to provide an environment in which our citizens can have full, satisfying lives. From a practical standpoint, it is impossible to keep people satisfied if they have lost their lives in battle."

"So you would leave the Empire divided in two," Orfitel asked, "rather than risk the lives of Romulans?"

"I would, but not because I don't desire a united Empire," Kamemor said. "But I judge that all that will be required for unity are vigilance and patience. We have already seen citizens filling public squares across *both* Romulan states. It seems inevitable that a time will soon come when no choice will remain but that of a single Empire. Our people will see to that themselves."

"And what of the Typhon Pact?" Orfitel asked.

The elder's continued attention made Kamemor feel uncomfortable, but she could hardly refuse to respond. "I am in favor of the Pact," she said. "I believe that the alliance will benefit Romulus in many ways. Certainly, the strength of a large coalition brings with it robust military and economic protections, but in addition, our people—and even our government—will find opportunities for new relationships, new experiences, and new challenges. We can teach our new partners many things, and from them, we can also learn many things."

Orfitel nodded, apparently satisfied with Kamemor's replies. The elder stood up once more, her hands steadying her along the edge of the table. "Gell Kamemor has lived her life in service of the Romulan people. She has served as a diplomat, as a teacher, as a military liaison, and as a governmental leader, managing both a city and then a territory. She is a Romulan loyalist, but not an apologist, and forthright in her politics." She gazed over at Kamemor, who felt as though she'd suddenly been caught in the headlamp of an oncoming maglev. "There can be no better choice for the Ortikant, and for all of Romulus, than to select Gell Kamemor as our next senator."

The maglev in Kamemor's imagination proceeded to run over her. "Elder Orfitel," she said, but her words went unacknowledged.

"I ask for an appointment by acclamation," Orfitel said. "Is there any opposition?"

Kamemor looked up and down the table, almost willing somebody to speak. Nobody said a word. She opened her own mouth to object, to say that she had retired from public life and that she had no desire to return to government. She wanted to vow that even if appointed she would not serve. But then she stopped short of doing so. She felt the weight of her societal obligation, but more than that, she understood that serving as senator would provide her the opportunity and the responsibility to set the agenda for her people—an agenda that, some time ago, had gone badly awry.

"There is no opposition," Orfitel said. "Senator Kamemor, may you find the right proportions of Soil, Water, Air, and Fire within you that you may succeed."

So saying, Elder Minlah Orfitel ended the gathering.

31

Spock sat in front of the companel in D'Tan's small apartment. It had been ten days since he had witnessed the Romulan unity protest in Victory Square, ten days since the leadership of the Ki Baratan cell had chosen for the near term to return underground. Word had been disseminated throughout the Reunification Movement, and overnight, its public presence on Romulus and throughout the Empire had vanished.

On the screen of the companel, Spock watched another massive assemblage of people, another large protest in support of Romulan unity. In the days since the first event in Victory Square, the protests had continued unabated, growing in size and spreading farther afield throughout both the Romulan Star Empire and the Imperial Romulan State. Criticism expanded for the two governments, and especially for their leaders, but consistently in the same ratios, with disapproval and disparagement developing into condemnation in far greater numbers for Empress Donatra.

Spock's judgment that circumstances would soon change on Romulus and throughout the empires remained, more certain than ever. Hour by hour, pressure mounted for Praetor Tal'Aura to take action against the Imperial Romulan State, to do something to unite all Romulan people under one banner. More and more, citizens at the protests characterized their call to the praetor for action as a demand for the Empire to proceed militarily. Any expressions of doubt or concern about incurring the deaths of innocent Romulans had disappeared. *Romulus for Romulans* had become a constant refrain.

Spock touched a control surface and shut down the companel. He found the increasingly mob-like mentality of the unity crowds unnerving. He thought again about what he or the Reunification Movement could do to quell the rising anger, or at the very least to avert bloodshed.

The uniformity of the protests with regard to their structure and content still pointed to a single organizing force, an assessment borne out by the fulfillment of Spock's recommendation to President Bacco. Spock rose from the chair before the companel and crossed to the low table at the center of D'Tan's small living area. He picked up a Romulan data tablet from the tabletop, then removed a storage chip from a pocket inside his cloak. He inserted the chip into the tablet and again reviewed the response he'd received from the president.

On the small screen of the slate, the face of a Vulcan male appeared, nominally an acquaintance of Spock from his days at the Vulcan Science Academy. The storage chip had arrived from the Federation four days ago, carried to Romulus by an intermediary, a trader known to do business throughout the Alpha and Beta Quadrants. The message seemed innocuous enough, the greeting of one former colleague to another, a brief review of current projects and personal circumstances. Though not precisely in code, when juxtaposed with Spock's request that President Bacco send an envoy to speak with Empress Donatra, the communication responded to that request.

Spock watched the message again, wanting to ensure that he had missed no nuances of meaning. But the content seemed clear. The Federation president had received his recommendation and acted upon it. The envoy sent to meet with the empress had judged her as innocent of driving the attempt on Spock's life, and desperate over the growing unity protests and the dawning of the Typhon Pact.

Watching the message play through to completion, Spock detected no detail that he had previously missed. More and more, he considered leaving Romulus and traveling to Achernar Prime to seek an audience with the empress. Given the circumstances, he felt confident that she would see him. But what could he say to her, what could he tell her, that would make a difference? Inaction on her part would eventually invite action by Tal'Aura, but what actions could Donatra reasonably take? Though her military resources matched up evenly with those of the praetor, they could not stand against a force mounted by the Typhon Pact, and even if they could, the cost in lives would be far too great.

Spock considered contacting Corthin to check on the progress of T'Solon and T'Lavent, who continued to search for evidence of the identity of whoever was orchestrating the unity protests. He could seek out Dorlok and Venaster as well, who hunted for similar information. But there seemed little point to doing either, since if anybody learned anything, they would certainly—

The door to D'Tan's apartment slammed open. "Spock!" cried the young man as he raced inside. He appeared breathless, his eyes wide, his face flushed. He peered around frantically until he saw Spock across the room. "You're not on the comnet," he said, then quickly headed over to the companel, where he hurriedly worked its controls.

Spock walked over. "D'Tan, what is it that has you—"

Spock halted his words in midsentence as he saw the companel screen wink to life. On it, he saw the face of Empress Donatra.

"—have endured together many of the same things," Donatra said. "Together, we suffered through the assassination of Praetor Hiren and most of the Romulan Senate. Together, we—"

Spock reached forward to the companel and paused the images. "What is this?" he asked D'Tan.

"Donatra has accessed the Romulan comnet and is broadcasting a message live," D'Tan said.

"Do you know the scope of the transmission?" Spock said.

"It's everywhere, Mister Spock," D'Tan said. "She's speaking to every Romulan throughout her empire and Tal'Aura's—at least to anyone who will listen."

And nobody's stopping her, Spock thought. Nobody's blocking her transmission. Not Tal'Aura's people, not the Tal Shiar.

Spock tapped a control and restarted the feed. Donatra's message ran back a few seconds, then continued. "Together, we faced the uprising of the Remans, their relocation to Romulus, and their move to the Klingon Empire. Together, we battled for the soul of the Romulan people.

"And then we divided.

"Praetor Tal'Aura—"

Spock noted the respectful use of Tal'Aura's title.

"—and I have significant political differences. We want to take the Romulan people down different paths. But I do not doubt that the praetor wants the same basic things that I do, the same things that all Romulans want.

"We want peace and prosperity for all our people. We want one Empire, undivided. And we want to accomplish this without risking the lives of innocent Romulans."

Spock did not know if Donatra would take to the field of battle against Tal'Aura if the empress believed victory even a possibility, but he understood that in stating her desire not to risk the lives of innocent Romulans, she wanted to seize the high ground in the debate, and thereby preclude Tal'Aura from initiating military action.

"Because we are at an obvious impasse, and because the Romulan people have these past days so eloquently made clear their desire for unity, I am stepping forward to pledge my efforts to once again make the Empire whole. To that end, I invite Praetor Tal'Aura to Achernar Prime for a summit. I promise her safety and a willing audience to hear her proposals for bringing us all back together. For it is together that we are strongest.

"I await the affirmative response of Praetor Tal'Aura."

Donatra stepped back and offered the Romulan salute, bringing her right fist to the left side of her chest, then straightening her arm outward. "Romulus for Romulans," she said. The transmission ended.

D'Tan looked at Spock. "What do you think?" he asked.

"I think that Donatra's appeal is the result of desperation," Spock said. "It is also possible that it is an example of the type of leadership that would most benefit the Romulan people."

"Do you think Tal'Aura will accept Donatra's invitation to a summit?"

Spock inhaled deeply, than exhaled slowly, meditatively. "The praetor did not stop Empress Donatra's transmission," he said. "That suggests that there is at least the possibility that Tal'Aura will agree to a summit."

"And what then?" D'Tan wanted to know. "How can that possibly end well?"

Spock thought for a moment, searching for an answer to D'Tan's question—an answer that might define the course of the Romulan people for generations to come. In the end, he could only offer up the truth. "I do not know."

32

Ben Sisko woke up in hell.

The lieutenant commander regained consciousness quickly, but his mind felt dulled. He opened his eyes in dim light, the right side of his face resting on a hard surface. Another surface, looking equally hard, rose up before his eyes just a few centimeters away.

Sisko's body burned. His flesh felt as though it had been doused with an accelerant and set aflame. Worse than that, his muscles ached in the same way, without his even attempting to move. The simple act of opening his eyes had sent bolts of agony through the top of his face.

He lay there like that, his eyes open but his body still, for some period of time he could not estimate. His head pounded with the beating of his heart, as though the pulse of his blood sent freshets of pain overflowing his veins. No thoughts entered his mind beyond the recognition of his agony and the desire for it to cease.

Eventually, a scent reached his nose, and the perception made it all the way to his brain, providing the first minuscule decrease of what to that point had been his all-encompassing physical suffering. Somehow, the odor pushed through, demanding the slightest bit of his focus.

At first, he welcomed it, grasped for it, tried to use it to pull himself away from the pain.

And then he recognized the smell: burnt flesh.

Sisko gagged, the involuntary reflex engaging some of his muscles. Fire ripped through his body, forcing tears from his eyes. When he lay still again, though, the pain had diminished, as though actual movement had broken a spell.

Sisko thought. He couldn't remember his location or how he'd arrived there, or many other relevant details. He just knew that he wanted very badly to go home, to Jennifer and Jake. He could barely recall his own name, his own position—

Executive officer, U.S.S. Okinawa.

Rescuing the crew of Assurance.

The Tzenkethi.

Sisko had never been shot with a Tzenkethi weapon before, and he hoped he never would be again. He remained motionless, but no longer to avoid the pain. He concentrated, opening his mind to his senses. Past the odor of smoldering flesh, he heard noises, little noises, and he attempted to isolate and identify them. A hum in his ear pressed to the floor: the engine of a starship. A soft rustle from somewhere behind him: somebody stirring from unconsciousness. A murmur from above . . . he could not place.

With care, Sisko turned his head and looked up, grateful to find the pain declining further. What he saw, though, made no sense to him. Across the overhead stretched a mass of color: the reds and golds and blues of Starfleet uniforms, the myriad flesh tones of humans and Andorians and Orions and other species.

And he saw faces.

Sisko pushed himself up onto his elbows, and then to a sitting position, the wave of pain flowing through him at least bearable. The surface in front of him when he'd woken up—*When I regained consciousness,* he corrected himself—turned out to be a silver cylinder embedded in the deck, a meter or so tall and perhaps a dozen centimeters in diameter. He leaned against it, then peered into the dim light.

He seemed to be in a large space, like the hold of a starship. All around, he saw what he thought he'd seen above him: the uniformed bodies of Starfleet officers. Here and there, some of them stirred, and he heard the low moans of physical distress. Intermingled with the bodies, Sisko saw more of the silver cylinders.

Turning to his left, Sisko looked for the bulkhead that marked the extent of the hold. Instead, he saw more bodies. Shocked, he peered upward again, and saw the same thing. It made no sense to him, and he wondered if—

An electronic whir began somewhere above him, and then he heard the sound of soft bells. It took him a moment to recall that the voices of Tzenkethi sounded like that. He immediately threw himself back onto the floor—his body protested, but complied. He lay not on his side, though, but on his back. He closed his eyes, but not fully.

The hold brightened considerably. Through his almost-closed eyes, Sisko again saw the bodies of Starfleet officers on the overhead. Movement caught his attention, then, and he shifted his gaze to see a circular opening far up in the bulkhead. Two Tzenkethi walked inside—directly onto the overhead. The opening behind them irised closed.

Between them, they dragged the body of a human,

dressed in a blue Starfleet uniform. The Tzenkethi hauled the unmoving body across the overhead, then threw it down—or up. It flopped onto the overhead, and Sisko saw that part of the uniform had been burned away, the exposed flesh mutilated, as though seared by exposure to hot metal. And again, the smell of burning flesh reached him.

Sisko realized that the body the Tzenkethi had just thrown down was dead. He realized that a lot of the bodies in the hold were dead.

The two Tzenkethi—both of them glowing a greenish yellow—moved back toward where they'd entered, when the door dilated open again. Another Tzenkethi, this one radiating more of a golden color, walked inside and waited for the other two. Then, as a group, they walked toward the bulkhead—and then onto it. They walked normally, making their way down to the floor on which Sisko lay.

As he watched them through his squinted eyes, they drew nearer, peering down at the bodies they passed. Then one of them looked in Sisko's direction, and Sisko suddenly felt terrified. The golden Tzenkethi pointed, and the other two started toward Sisko.

I'll fight them, Sisko resolved. He would overcome his pain and do as much damage as he could.

Stepping past other bodies, the two Tzenkethi had come within three meters of him when one of the Starfleet personnel grabbed for them. He wrapped his arms around one of the Tzenkethi and pulled him down. In the flurry of motion, Sisko saw the attacker: Captain Walter.

Sisko suspected he would get no better opportunity, and he hauled himself up by grabbing hold of the silver cylinder. He felt suddenly light-headed as he got to his feet, but he lurched forward. As he did, the golden Tzenkethi drew a weapon.

"No!" Sisko yelled, but too late. The orange beam struck both Captain Walter and the Tzenkethi with whom he grappled. Both dropped to the deck, either unconscious or dead.

Then the Tzenkethi trained the weapon on Sisko.

In the moment before she fired, the remembrance of the terrible pain he'd experienced led him to just one thought: *I hope this shot kills me.*

When Sisko came to again, his pain did not approach what he'd felt previously. He opened his eyes to find himself on the deck of a small room. Before him stood a beautiful Tzenkethi woman, a soft golden glow emanating from her body.

Sisko heard a gentle metallic tinkling. The Tzenkethi reached to the wall and touched a control. When she did, Sisko saw another silver cylinder embedded in the deck. Then, from a panel in the bulkhead, strangely inflected words spoke in Federation Standard, and Sisko realized that she'd activated a translator.

"Why are you here?"

Sisko pulled himself up and leaned against the bulkhead. "I don't even know where I am," he said. He heard a deeper set of chimes, obviously his own words translated into the language of the Tzenkethi.

"You are aboard a Tzenkethi marauder," she said. *"But I am not asking you why you are aboard. You were seized from a planet near the border of the Tzenkethi Coalition. You were aboard the remains of a Federation starship that crashed on a*

planet. Sensor scans show the residual energy effects of Tzenkethi weaponry on the hull of that starship, but there is no Tzenkethi vessel in this planetary system and none reported destroying a Federation ship here.

"*So I ask you again: why are you here, in this planetary system, on this planet, after battling a Tzenkethi starship?*"

"We're at war," Sisko said. "Ask the autarch why that is and you'll have your answer."

The bottom half of the Tzenkethi's right leg shot forward in a way that would have been impossible for a human. It kicked Sisko in the side. Where it struck him, he felt a sensation like something between electricity and heat, through his uniform and that of the Tzenkethi.

"*You encroachers have caused this war,*" the Tzenkethi said, moving away. "*Do not look to blame us for your transgressions. Why are you here? In this planetary system? Did you destroy the Tzenkethi vessel that fired on you?*"

"We did not start this war," Sisko said. "But we defend ourselves."

The Tzenkethi stepped quickly forward, and Sisko threw his hands up to ward off another kick. Instead, she strode past him and onto the bulkhead. He peered up to see her walking upward, past another silver cylinder, and then onto the overhead. There, he saw another heaped body in a Starfleet uniform. The Tzenkethi took a small device from somewhere in her formfitting clothing and touched it to the outside of the officer's arm.

Sisko watched as the officer came to, and he saw that it was Captain Walter. The Tzenkethi touched a control in the wall, and then the translation of her lyrical sounds spilled from a panel in the bulkhead there. *"Why are you here?"*

"To convince the Tzenkethi to stop waging war," Walter said.

"We do not wage war," she said. *"You do!"* She reached for the captain, grabbing him by the hair and pulling his head back, forcing him to look up. He saw Sisko.

"You," the Tzenkethi said, pointing at Sisko with her free hand. *"Why are you here?"*

Sisko repeated Captain Walter's words.

"Why are you here?" she said again, and then the Tzenkethi reached up and pressed her fingers to the captain's forehead, as though trying to reach *through* his head.

Walter screamed. But even over the sound of his voice, Sisko could hear his flesh sizzling beneath the Tzenkethi's golden touch. The raw odor of burning meat filled the room. And still the captain screamed.

And then a siren split the air, a moment before the deck beneath Sisko pitched forward. Sisko slammed into the cylinder, and crashed to the floor. He felt momentarily nauseous, and he realized that the embedded cylinders functioned as field nodes, generating gravitational envelopes within the Tzenkethi vessel, possibly even reinforcing the ship's structural integrity.

He peered upward and saw Captain Walter struggling with the Tzenkethi. The lighting flickered, the Tzenkethi glowing brightly in the instants of darkness. Sisko looked at the bulkhead before him, then rushed forward and stepped onto it. He felt momentarily disoriented, but he did not fall back to the deck.

Quickly, he strode forward, and then onto the overhead—which became the deck for him. He felt woozy once more, but did not hesitate. He rushed forward and threw himself at the Tzenkethi.

Sisko felt a jolt, like an electric shock, but the Tzenkethi flew backward and into the bulkhead. Sisko followed, raised his foot, and thrust it forward into whatever joint passed for her knee. His boot connected, and he felt the sensation of something giving way, like a water-filled balloon popping.

The Tzenkethi opened her mouth and a sound like gravel falling on metal came out, clearly a scream of pain. Not knowing if he had sufficiently incapacitated her, Sisko raised his foot to strike a second time, but the deck beneath him rocked again, and he lost his footing, sending him onto the deck, hard. He landed beside the captain, and Sisko saw the flesh of Walter's forehead hanging in tatters, blood seeping down his face.

The room shook again, and over the siren, Sisko heard the sounds of battle. *Phasers,* he told himself, though he could not really tell. He looked back at the Tzenkethi, but she was gone. He glanced up, and saw her pulling herself up the bulkhead with her arms, her leg dragging uselessly behind her.

Sisko let her go. Instead, he reached up to his uniform and tried to tear a strip from it. When he couldn't, he peeled off his uniform shirt and applied it gently to Captain Walter's forehead, wanting to stanch the bleeding. Walter winced when the fabric made contact with his wrecked skin, but the captain reached up and held it there.

The room continued to shake and rattle for ten minutes. At one point, Sisko looked up again and saw the Tzen-kethi woman nowhere in the room. She must have left, but no one else entered.

Finally, Sisko stood. "I'm going to go try to find something of use for us," he told Captain Walter. "A weapon . . . a shuttlebay . . . something."

Walter said nothing, but he nodded.

Sisko saw a flanged metal circle in the wall, which resembled the opening through which the Tzenkethi had entered the hold. He moved toward it, but before he reached it, his vision began to cloud. He thought the Tzenkethi vessel and its various internal gravity envelopes had affected him again, but then he recognized the sensation of being caught in a transporter beam.

He and Walter materialized aboard *Okinawa.*

They were two of only eleven survivors recovered from the Tzenkethi vessel.

33

Praetor Tal'Aura of the Romulan Star Empire—an empire soon to be made whole—sat down in the gilded chair in her audience chamber. Months of planning perched on the threshold of fruition. She found it nearly impossible to contain her satisfaction, though she knew that she must.

As she waited to play out one of the final acts of her complex plan, she gazed around her chamber. She relished its regal splendor: the beautiful artwork, the stately columns, the dazzlingly glossy floor and walls. For too long, this place had felt temporary, as though the means by which it had come into her possession lessened the legitimacy of her claim to it. But Romulan politics had a long and rich history of advancement by assassination. And she had not plotted the demise of Praetor Hiren and the Senate; Shinzon had. Tal'Aura had merely escaped her own death by agreeing to assist Shinzon in his plot—had escaped her own death, and contributed to the removal of a praetor and his sympathetic Senate, all of whom preferred to appease the Federation and the Klingons rather than stand firm and face them down. She had taken control of the Empire to strengthen it, to make it *the* power in the region, to return it to a position worthy of respect and even awe.

And I would have succeeded, she thought, *if not for*

Donatra escaping the Empire and forging her own base of power. "'Empress' Donatra," she said aloud, her lone voice sounding hollow in the large space. *But now I've cornered that* veruul, *and there will be no more escaping.*

The enormous wooden doors that permitted visitors into her chamber began to swing open. Her proconsul, Tomalak, entered, closing the doors behind him. His boot heels clicked along the floor as he approached her dais. "Praetor," he said, bowing his head, "I bring news."

"Tell me."

"The chairman of the Tal Shiar and his loyal pet have just entered the Hall of State," Tomalak said. "They will be here shortly."

"Very good," said Tal'Aura. "Make sure that our friend is prepared."

"Immediately," said Tomalak. He bowed as he withdrew a step, then made his way around the dais to one of her chamber's private entrances. He returned only a few moments later, informing her that the necessary arrangements had been made. Then he turned and stood before her, to her left, facing the visitors' doors and waiting along with her.

When Rehaek entered, Tal'Aura for the first time felt pleased that he had brought his bilious servitor. Torath's constant display of disrespect for anything not directly associated with the Tal Shiar rankled her. Even as he crossed Tal'Aura's audience chamber with Rehaek, he moved with an air of pomposity impossible to miss. The Tal Shiar chairman, on the other hand, walked unhurriedly, almost carelessly, at least not wearing his arrogance for all to see.

Rehaek stopped several strides before Tomalak, Torath at his side. While the Tal Shiar chairman kept his gaze trained on the proconsul, his aide haughtily peered up at the praetor, as though looking upon a mere servant girl. "Good evening, Proconsul," Rehaek said with polite formality. "I understand that Praetor Tal'Aura has requested my presence." In the past, Rehaek had often taken days to respond to such requests, but that night, knowing the current state of affairs—as he most assuredly did—he had made his way to the Hall of State within an hour.

"Thank you for coming so quickly, Chairman," Tomalak said, and Tal'Aura cursed him for his courtesy. A change in behavior would certainly not go unnoticed by a man of Rehaek's ilk. But then Tomalak regarded Torath with a disdainful look, and Tal'Aura calmed herself. "The praetor wishes to inform you of a political undertaking that will at the very least demand your notice, if not your attention."

"I see," Rehaek said, and Tal'Aura knew that he did. She could scarcely eat a meal without the chairman being informed of her every bite. His spies had infiltrated so many places throughout the Empire, and his surveillance devices even more. But Tal'Aura had her own methods and agents, and few actions could Rehaek take without the praetor finding out about them.

"You are aware, I trust, of Donatra's plea two days ago," Tal'Aura said, "for a summit between us."

Rehaek looked up at the praetor. "I would imagine that there are few enough citizens throughout the Romulan realms that are not aware of it," he said. "It seemed a desperate attempt to ask you to help bail water from her sinking ship of state."

"Perhaps," Tal'Aura said, actually appreciative of the

chairman's turn of phrase. "But I have chosen to take Donatra at her word. She said that she wants a united Empire, as do I, and clearly the Romulan people want that as well. I have therefore agreed to her offer of a summit."

"I . . . am surprised," Rehaek said, and Tal'Aura waited to hear what more lies he would tell her. The praetor's own sources had already confirmed the chairman's knowledge of the summit. "It may prove difficult for the Tal Shiar to do any advance work on a meeting held within Donatra's so-called Imperial Romulan State. She has tightened security considerably on her world."

Another lie, Tal'Aura thought. "The summit will not be on Achernar Prime," she said. "I have agreed to host Donatra here. This is, after all, the homeworld of the Empire."

"Ah, I see," Rehaek said. "I am pleased with your decision, Praetor. It will make what I am about to tell you much easier for us both to deal with."

Tal'Aura waited for Rehaek to tell her the greatest lie of all. Instead, the chairman motioned to Torath, having his aide do it.

"We have just learned that the man who attempted to assassinate Spock," Torath said, "was himself assassinated by a protector in Romulan Security named R'Jul."

"And that is important why?" Tal'Aura asked, presenting her own falsehood. The praetor's people had hired the Reman to kill Spock, and when that had apparently failed, they had put out the word to protectors throughout the city to execute any Remans on sight. Once R'Jul had done that, it had been a simple matter to plant enough false information to link him to Donatra. *But then, Chairman Rehaek knows all of that too.*

"It is important because R'Jul was in the employ of Donatra, and in killing Spock's assassin, acted on her behalf," Torath explained. "Donatra wished to silence the failed killer after having hired him to eliminate the leader of the Reunification Movement. She apparently wanted Spock dead so that his ideas of reunifying the Romulans and Vulcans could not stir people's desires to unite the two Romulan empires."

"These are extraordinary charges," Tal'Aura said, playing her part. "Do you have proof enough?"

"We do," Torath said.

"And when Donatra arrives on Romulus for the summit," Rehaek said, "it will be a simple matter to make public her complicity in both acts—in the attempt on Spock's life, and in the murder of Spock's would-be killer. After that, we will have no choice but to arrest her."

"Thus dissolving the only real government of the Imperial Romulan State," Torath added.

But neither Torath nor Rehaek added the subsequent part of their plan, which Tal'Aura's own agent had uncovered. Once Donatra had been arrested and put to death, the chairman would reveal that Tal'Aura actually had framed Donatra, which would provide more than enough cause for the Senate to remove her from the praetorship, imprison her, and possibly even execute her. Rehaek then would call in favors in the Senate to have his own puppet installed as the leader of the Romulan people: Durjik.

But Tal'Aura disclosed nothing. "You have clearly earned your position on merit, Chairman Rehaek," she said, summoning up the spirit of magnanimity. "Donatra will arrive on Romulus, in Ki Baratan, two days hence.

Once she is within the city, you are authorized to release the information and see that she is taken into custody."

Rehaek nodded. "It shall be done," he said. "Is there anything else with which I can assist you today, Praetor?"

"I asked you here to inform you of the summit," Tal'Aura said, "and to direct you to coordinate with Romulan Security on the logistical details for Donatra's visit. I ask now that you still take on that task. All must appear normal."

"Of course," the chairman said. "Is there anything else?"

"No," Tal'Aura said. "Thank you, Chairman."

"Thank you, Praetor."

Spinning easily on his heel, Rehaek headed back toward the great doors, pulling Torath along behind him like a planet hauling around a lightweight moon. Before they exited the audience chamber, Torath glanced back over his shoulder at Tomalak. The two men exchanged a final harsh look.

Once they had gone, Tal'Aura felt an enormous sense of relief. She had never liked nor trusted Rehaek and Torath. It pleased her greatly that she would never have to deal with them again.

Chairman Rehaek of the Tal Shiar permitted himself a small smile. As he and Torath sat in the cabin of the automated airpod on the way to Rehaek's home, it pleased him that he would not have to deal with Tal'Aura for much longer. When she had first come to power—when she had first *seized* power—he had embraced her. In his field of expertise, chaos made for too short a life expectancy, and challenges to Tal'Aura's praetorship would have brought chaos. He had seen to the dampening and even elimination of such challenges.

Outside the cabin windows, Rehaek saw the densely clustered lights of central Ki Baratan slip behind as the air-pod sped toward the purlieus of the city. He looked forward to a sound sleep that night, as he doubted that he would have much time at home over the next three or four days. Chaos would arrive with Donatra, and it would leave with Tal'Aura. After that, life in the Romulan Star Empire—in *the* Romulan Empire—should return to a relative calm.

The chairman glanced over at Torath, his trusted and exceedingly useful adjutant. In his mind, he could see his aide in the courtyard that surrounded the Hall of State, producing a curved steel blade in his hand faster than even Rehaek himself could follow. He recalled the dizzying speed with which Torath had struck, opening a gaping, blood-green wound across Pardek's throat.

An exceedingly useful adjutant, indeed, he thought.

At the time of Pardek's demise, just after Tal'Aura had taken the reins of what remained of a government decimated by Shinzon's thalaron weapon, circumstances on Romulus threatened to spin out of control. The agenda of Pardek and his compatriots concentrated not on the best interests of the Empire—let alone on its stability—but on a desire to strike at the Federation. It mattered little to those so focused that Shinzon had plunged Romulus into turmoil following a similar campaign. To restore constancy to the Empire, Rehaek had developed his own program of actions aimed primarily at quelling dissent within and without the government. And for the most part, he had succeeded.

But circumstances had changed since then. Donatra had taken the military assets under her control and maneuvered a division of the Empire. Even that had been manageable, until Tal'Aura had begun her intricate plot to bring down her rival. Joining the Typhon Pact, allowing Spock and his Reunification Movement out of the shadows and into the public eye, and then steering massive Romulan unity protests, all had subverted the steadiness Rehaek had worked so hard to reestablish. Tal'Aura, a fool blinded by her thirst for power, did not even understand that Donatra's imprisonment and death would not mean the end of the Imperial Romulan State. The empress had supporters, and her death on Romulus, even after being charged with capital crimes, would not convince all of those supporters to abandon their new nation. The only thing that would do that, Rehaek had realized, would be the subsequent imprisonment and death of Tal'Aura.

But that would bring about another power vacuum, one which, if not properly controlled, could lead to even more disorder. Rehaek needed a new praetor, somebody whom he both understood and could manipulate. Senator Durjik had been an easy, if ironic, choice.

Durjik had been one of Pardek's compatriots, one of those dedicated to the military extermination of the Federation. But though Durjik had not altered his attitudes, he would, as praetor, find himself limited by the Empire's new alliance. Rehaek knew from his sources inside the governments of the Typhon Pact nations that, with the possible exception of the Kinshaya, none of them had a taste for war. They all despised the Federation to one degree or another, and for a variety of reasons, but they had also had their fill of battling an enemy with massive resources and a strong collective will to survive. They still wished to bring the Federation low, but their newfound alliance would provide far more options for them than that of the military. Several believed that they could defeat the Federation utterly, without even firing a shot.

Up ahead, Rehaek spied the scattering of lights that marked the extent of Leri'retan, the neighborhood on the outskirts of Ki Baratan where he kept a home. Torath appeared to notice their location as well, and he tapped the button that would begin an automated security sweep in and around Rehaek's property. Two security officers kept watch there at all times, but Rehaek trusted in an overabundance of caution.

Except that when Torath touched the control, nothing happened. Normally, the small screen at the front of the airpod would begin listing the security procedures being performed in the house, along with the result. In this instance, the screen remained dark.

"Trouble with the security system," Torath said. Rehaek himself reached for the button, but also received no response. "I'm aborting our approach, Chairman," Torath said. "I'll contact the team at the house and have them—"

That was when the airpod fell out of the sky.

Sirens cried out in the night, their plaintive wails growing closer. Though the outer districts of Ki Baratan offered open stretches of land, the crash of an airpod could not escape notice. The fiery wreckage threatened no homes, but it marked well the site of the accident.

Sela hurried through the field and neared the twisted debris quickly. Consulting the scanner in her hand, she saw no risk of the pod's batteries exploding. An electrical surge in the fractured equipment interfered with her bioscans, but even if it hadn't, she always, whenever possible, liked to check on her work directly.

The airpod had come to rest canted partially onto its nose. Flames reached up its left side and flickered toward the sky. Stepping up to the mangled door on the right-hand side of the small craft, Sela saw an arm hanging down from within the cabin. She poked her head inside to see which of the pod's two passengers the arm belonged to, but discovered that it was no longer attached to a body. Inside, the smell of copper mixed with that of charred equipment.

Shifting her upper body so that she could see the entire cabin, Sela spotted a shoe upside-down beneath a fallen panel. She followed the line of it down to where a leg should have been, and a torso, until at last she caught sight of a bloodied face on the floor. It belonged to Torath. Sela reached her gloved hand to his neck and felt for a pulse, lingering only long enough to confirm his death. Then she peered around the rest of the cabin.

It was empty.

Sela quickly extracted herself from the airpod and spun around, prepared to see the half-burned, half-contorted figure of Rehaek bounding at her. Instead, she saw only the dark field. In the distance and getting closer, she now saw the flashing lights that accompanied the sirens.

Moving cautiously around the pod, she skirted its bow, walked around the left side, past where flames still crackled along the hull, and then around the back. She saw nothing, and so she made a second circuit, farther away from the craft. On her third trip around, she found Rehaek.

The Chairman of the Tal Shiar sprawled facedown in the mud, his neck bent at an unnatural angle. Still, she squatted down beside him and felt at his neck for any indication of life. She found none.

Satisfied, she turned and quickly headed back the way she had come, from a nearby path that would go unused by the emergency equipment. She walked for a while, utilizing her scanner to ensure that she met nobody along the way. She passed several houses, but her dark clothes would have made it impossible for anybody glancing from a window to see her.

When she felt she had gone far enough that any residual traces of her transporter beam would not be singled out for attention by Romulan Security, she activated her automatic recall. She materialized on the other side of Ki Baratan, out in an uninhabited area of the countryside. From there, she activated her recall again, and then again, bounding around the outskirts of the capital. Finally, she removed her dark clothes and turned them inside-out, dressing herself in moderate colors before beaming back to the city.

Tomorrow she would wait for the praetor to call for her. When eventually she visited the Hall of State, Sela would be both humble and grateful. She knew that she would enjoy her new position as Chairman of the Tal Shiar.

34

Tall ceilings topped a wide space filled with row upon row of shelves, intermingled with an assortment of carrels. Skylights ushered in the midmorning light, the bright rays of the sun alive with the dance of dust motes. A sense of quiet saturated the room.

Spock sat at one of the carrels, a hardbound volume of Romulan philosophy open to a chapter on Vorkan Trov, a famed existentialist who had lived two hundred years earlier. Spock read the book with interest, but found it difficult to concentrate. He had too much to think about at the moment, and not enough to do.

The old section of the Alavhet Public Library in outer Ki Baratan reminded him of his youth. During his childhood days in Shi'Kahr, he had spent many after-school hours in a similar facility. His mother, a teacher, had educated him on the value of books—actual physical books, with hard covers and paper pages. Of course, logic dictated the superiority of books stored on automated media, owing to such characteristics as their searchable nature, their greater portability, and their ability to include hyperlinks. Spock's mother had not availed herself of logic when espousing her views about books; she had preached instead about how they felt when held in the hands, how the paper delivered a distinctive and somehow special scent, how words appeared somehow more alive when seen on a page instead of a screen. Completely illogical, and yet she had still managed to pass on to him her appreciation of physical books, something he had retained throughout the rest of his life.

Spock had come to the Alavhet Library essentially as a distraction. With the Reunification Movement still underground and maintaining its lowest profile in years, he had little to do but ponder the route forward. He strongly believed that the disposition of the summit between Praetor Tal'Aura and Empress Donatra would greatly impact the future of him and his comrades. While he knew that neither woman personally supported reunification, he did not know if either would be willing to allow their fellow Romulans the right to their own views. Tal'Aura had done so already, but with an ulterior motive; it remained to be seen if she would recriminalize the Movement after the summit, since she would at that time have exhausted the usefulness to her of the unity protests. Donatra, on the other hand, appeared reasonable enough that Spock thought he might be able to negotiate with her, though he could not be sure until he approached her.

For his part, Spock did not know what to expect from the summit. Other than Donatra's initial entreaty delivered on the Romulan comnet four days ago, and Tal'Aura's conditional acceptance two days ago, little information existed to allow an estimation of how the conference would resolve. Spock knew from speaking with his comrades and from observing comnet coverage of the coming event that a sense of anticipation infused the whole of Romulan society. He had noticed, though, that a significant segment of the population expected the summit to result in a resolution, with one or the other of the two leaders standing aside. There had been conjecture in some quarters about Donatra serving as Tal'Aura's proconsul, or about the reverse. Spock had even heard some calls for the institution of some form of bipartite praetorship, but that seemed to him both unworkable and unlikely.

Knowing that the summit would not begin until that evening, and unwilling to engage in unsupported speculation, Spock returned his attention to the Romulan philosophy text. He had read through the chapter on Vorkan Trov, and then through three more chapters on different Romulan philosophers, when he became aware of a disturbance in the library. Voices reached him, where only moments ago the place had been wrapped in silence. Spock listened, and while he could not make out individual words, he noted more and more people speaking, louder, in shocked tones. He rose from the carrel and started to follow the sounds, as did several other people in that section of the library.

In a room given over to companels and computer terminals, a crowd had gathered, their backs to the door. Spock entered and approached the people, realizing that he heard not only *their* voices, but that of a commentator on the comnet. He moved forward until he could hear clearly.

"—this startling development. To repeat, Romulan Security forces have arrested self-styled 'Empress' Donatra on charges of conspiracy to commit murder, and murder. According to a spokesperson for Romulan Security, the crimes were committed some time ago, but Donatra's complicity in them has only just become known. She has been taken into custody and presumably will soon be faced with an arraignment. There has so far

*been no word from the Hall of State or Achernar Prime about
these developments.*

"*Donatra arrived on Romulus—*"

Spock headed for the door, knowing what he had to
do. He also knew precisely how the standoff between the
Romulan Star Empire and the Imperial Romulan State
would end.

It required hours of effort, as well as the assistance
of Dorlok and Venaster, before Spock learned where
Romulan Security had detained Donatra. As night fell
across Ki Baratan, Spock made his way to the security
office on the D'deridex Arc. The long, low building
followed the curve of the avenue, its frontage black, the
emblem of a silver raptor holding a shield emblazoned
above the front door.

Spock entered the office and passed through its narrow, enclosed foyer, then walked through the second,
inner door. In the lobby, he recognized the layout of three
tall counters rimming the space, with a wall of monitors
observing numerous public sites. A pair of sentries immediately accosted him, one of them—a man whose name read
Neritel on his dark-gray uniform—demanding that he state
his business.

"I am here to visit a prisoner," Spock said.

The man gestured toward the center counter. "Step up
and speak to a defender."

Spock moved forward, where a woman—T'Vakul—
asked him once more to give the reason for coming to the
security office.

"You are detaining a prisoner in this facility," Spock said. "I would like to visit her."

"Very well," T'Vakul said. She reached for a data tablet, and then said, "Prisoner's name?"

"Donatra."

T'Vakul froze as though she'd been suddenly trapped in amber. Spock waited for her to say something, and finally she asked him to repeat the name, which he did. "Sir, I can neither confirm nor deny that a prisoner named Donatra is in this facility."

"I am already aware that Donatra has been imprisoned here, and I wish to see her," Spock said. He took a pace back from the counter and held his arms wide. "I am unarmed. In fact, I have nothing with me other than the clothes that I am wearing."

T'Vakul peered blankly at him for a moment, and then repeated her earlier statement, refusing even to admit Donatra's presence at the security office.

"I wish to speak with your superior, then," Spock said. Before T'Vakul could even reply, Spock felt a hand on his elbow. He turned to face a tall man with a well-muscled build.

"I am Protector Vikral," he said in a deep voice. "May we talk in my office, Mister . . . ?"

"Spock."

Vikral did not react to the name, but Spock thought he saw a glimmer of recognition in his eyes. "Mister Spock," he said. "Please accompany me."

Vikral led Spock off to the left and down a long corridor. At the end, he opened a door on the right and stepped aside so that Spock could enter. Inside, a large desk filled most of the floor space of a modest office. Vikral invited Spock to have a seat in front of the desk, then sat down opposite him.

"I won't insult your intelligence, Mister Spock, by asking you to repeat your request or by coyly suggesting that Donatra may or may not be in my security station," Vikral said. "I also won't pretend that I don't know who you are, since your name is mentioned prominently in the charges against Donatra. But the fact of her incarceration here is not generally known. In order to preserve Donatra's own safety, I ask that you not divulge her location to anyone."

"I have no intention of doing so," Spock said. "I merely wish to speak with her."

"I have no particular reason not to permit you to do so, Mister Spock," Vikral said, "other than the fact that I have been ordered not to let anybody see her at this time."

"That is contrary to Romulan law," Spock said.

"You have been here on Romulus a long time, Mister Spock," Vikral said, "so you probably know that we have many laws that take effect only in extraordinary circumstances. Regardless, I have my orders, and I intend to follow them."

Understanding that he would achieve nothing by continuing his conversation with the protector, Spock stood up. "To whom would I speak to reverse this order?"

"As protector, I answer directly to the office of Internal Security," Vikral said. He came out from behind his desk and escorted Spock back to the lobby.

Outside, Spock headed for the Hall of State, where he would request a meeting with the head of Internal Security.

It struck him that he did not know exactly why he wanted to speak with Donatra. He understood that he didn't trust Tal'Aura, and he had the report of the Federation envoy, who believed that the empress had nothing to do with the attempt on Spock's life or the murder of his assassin. Spock decided that he wanted to hear about that from Donatra's own lips.

And suddenly he knew why: it concerned him that, of the two Romulan leaders, the wrong one would continue to rule.

35

The computer interface on the desk displayed an image of the Romulan Senate Chamber, in preparation for the broadcast of an address by Praetor Tal'Aura. As far as Sisko knew, it marked the first time that an appearance by a sitting praetor would be transmitted from the Hall of State. Thanks to *Robinson*'s proximity to Romulan space, the captain would have a front-row seat.

As Sisko sat in his ready room, waiting for Tal'Aura's speech, he thought about Donatra. When he had met with the empress on Achernar Prime, he had genuinely believed her innocent of the crimes for which she had ultimately been arrested. He didn't know whether he had misjudged her, or whether she had managed to dupe him, or if he'd actually correct in his assessment. But guilty or not, it didn't seem to Sisko as though Donatra had received a fair opportunity to plead her case. A month after she'd been taken into custody, her trial had not yet been set, and so, at least in theory, she might ultimately prevail, but at that point, would it matter to her?

Since Donatra's imprisonment, Tal'Aura's government had released the evidence allegedly tying the empress to an attempt by a Reman on Ambassador Spock's life, and to the ensuing murder of the would-be assassin. As Sisko understood it, President Bacco had needed to expend a great deal of effort to convince Klingon Chancellor Martok not to attack Romulus for the murder of a Reman by a Romulan, given that the Reman state existed as a Klingon protectorate. According to Admiral Akaar, the president had finally threatened to dissolve the Khitomer Accords based on the incidence of a Klingon citizen—the Reman—trying to kill a Federation citizen. Martok had then relented, claiming that the Reman had never lived on Klorgat IV and so did not qualify as a Klingon citizen, thus invalidating both assertions.

The evidence against Donatra, whether authentic or manufactured, convinced Romulans everywhere of her guilt. The public unity protests throughout the Star Empire and the Imperial State transformed into denouncements of the empress. Those disillusioned by the accusations against Donatra vilified her, easily drowning out the voices of her few remaining supporters. Sisko thought that the haste with which people in the Imperial State abandoned the empress suggested that they had long been ready to latch onto anything that would result in uniting all Romulans.

Also of major significance, Donatra had lost the backing of many of her military forces. Though the empress could never have achieved a martial victory over the Star Empire, and though she could never have persevered against a combined Typhon Pact offensive, her fleet of starships had still provided a measure of security for those in the Imperial State. Once Donatra's military capabilities fractured, her people had grown fearful, pushing them to more strongly support Romulan unity.

Watching the computer screen, Sisko saw the members

of the Romulan Senate rise as one, along with the individuals making up the Continuing Committee. Praetor Tal'Aura then appeared, moving with grace and confidence, resplendent in a dark ceremonial robe of reddish purple. Rounded, block-like glyphs tumbled down the right side of her garment in a lighter purple color. Sisko had to reach back to his days stationed at the Federation embassy in the Star Empire to decipher the meaning of the characters: *Romulus for Romulans.*

Praetor Tal'Aura bowed her head to those assembled in the Senate Chamber. As a group, they sat. Into the silence that followed, Tal'Aura began to speak.

"Worthy members of the Senate, honored members of the Continuing Committee, people of the Romulan Star Empire, and people of the Imperial Romulan State, I bid you greetings." She had short gray hair, with only a few small patches of dark color here and there. Her bangs came to a shallow point in the center of her forehead, with locks that mimicked the inverted line of her upswept ears hanging down the sides of her face.

"The road the Romulan people have traveled together has been a winding one, weaving through pitfalls and perils, through exultations and expectations," she continued. *"We have endured war and loss, and we have celebrated peace and victory. For millennia, we have experienced all of this, and more, together, as one nation, as one people, united in the strength of our common heritage, and in the joyous hopes for our shared futures.*

"Until recently.

"This is not the time to debate the circumstances that led to

the sundering of our Empire. Nor is this the proper setting in which to pass judgment on the actions of Donatra that led to our division. In due course, she will face a trial that will weigh other of her alleged actions, and that test of her character and her deeds will stand on its own."

It seemed impossible to Sisko that Donatra could confront criminal charges without her founding of the Imperial State coloring the ruling.

"What we do know about Donatra is that she served the Romulan Star Empire and its people for many years, with tours of duty aboard warbirds such as the Vel'reger *and the* T'sarok,*"* said Tal'Aura, with a generosity that, considering the circumstances, seemed almost noble. *"Eventually, she commanded her own ship, the* Valdore, *and then the entire Third Fleet, all with distinction. However we may disagree with Donatra's choice to hold Achernar Prime and Xanitla and other worlds under the banner of a new nation, there is no question that she has been a true Romulan patriot."*

Sisko could not measure the sincerity with which Tal'Aura spoke, but regardless, she had clearly chosen to speak in accordance with her high station. Such kind words also could not help but woo some of the remaining Donatra supporters.

"In that spirit," Tal'Aura went on, *"I say to you that the time for our divisions has passed. Indeed, we have expanded our ties by joining the Typhon Pact, and I have spoken with representatives from each of those governments, and each has pledged their support for what I must now do."* Tal'Aura paused and seemed to pull herself up straighter. *"From this moment, I declare that the Imperial Romulan State is no*

more. All territory, all matériel, all property, and most important, all people, within the former state are once again part of the Romulan Star Empire.

"Tonight, and forevermore, we are one."

The senators and the members of the Continuing Committee leaped to their feet, their applause thunderous. Tal'Aura appeared to bask for a moment in the adulation heaped upon her, but she did not tarry. After just a few moments, before the ovation could fade, she withdrew from the chamber. *She doesn't want to spoil her performance with a show of ego,* Sisko thought.

The captain reached forward and thumbed off the screen. *So one of the Federation's enemies has gotten stronger tonight,* he thought. *Wonderful.* And then he realized that not only had the Romulan Empire grown stronger, but so too had the Typhon Pact.

Sitting back in his chair, Sisko suddenly thought about the plight of the Bajorans. The Romulan people, as a group, had certainly not suffered as the people of Bajor had, had not lived for decades fighting the oppression of a brutal occupier, but Sisko nevertheless saw similarities between the two. The citizens of the Imperial Romulan State—even those who supported Donatra—surely had not wanted to live divided from Romulus and the other worlds of the Star Empire. When the Cardassians had finally left, Bajorans had felt that they'd finally gotten their home back. For the people of the Imperial State, returning by way of a single declaration to the Star Empire must feel comparable, like going home.

Home.

The echoes from Sisko's recent dreams, from his past,

reverberated in his thoughts and in his heart. The concept, the emotion, had been taken from him—or he'd abandoned it himself. Either way, the realization of his circumstances, phrased just so, struck him hard, and he said it aloud.

"I have no home."

36

The data tablet sailed through the air, spinning like a propeller. It struck the blank wall with a satisfying thud, then fell to the floor with a clatter. Unfortunately, it did not appear to break.

Of course not, Donatra thought. *The damned things are indestructible.*

Donatra sat on the lone sleeping surface in her cell, her back against the wall, her knees pulled in tight to her chest. When the guard asked her—with no apparent malice—if she wanted to watch Tal'Aura's address, she had declined. Later, though, when her evening meal had arrived, a data tablet had been left with it. Donatra had dismissed it, but at the appointed time for the speech, she had found herself unable to resist her curiosity, morbid though it might have been.

Watching Tal'Aura deliver her oration in the Senate Chamber, wearing the robes of office, speaking to the Romulan people and about them, had been even more difficult for Donatra than she'd imagined it would be. But when that self-serving harpy had condescended to mention Donatra's own service record, when she had pretended to honor that record, Donatra felt that she could have choked the life out of her right there in the Senate Chamber, in front of enough witnesses to guarantee that she would then be summarily executed.

That would be one way to do what's right, wouldn't it? Donatra thought. *First Tal'Aura's death, and then mine.* In that way, Donatra wouldn't have to go to her grave, or live any longer, with what had become the daily agony of her regret.

Once, uncounted seasons ago, Donatra had made a choice—one terrible choice—from which she had essentially never recovered. She had thrown in with Shinzon, seduced by his strength, his intellect, his confidence. He had said the right things to her, at the right times and in the right ways, and she had lost herself.

Or maybe I lost myself before that, she thought, *and Shinzon had provided the light that seemed as though it would let me find my way back.*

"What difference does it make now?" she asked the empty cell. Tal'Aura had taken away the very last thing of value that Donatra had, the very last thing she had done to atone for her sins with Shinzon.

But not just with Shinzon, she reminded herself. Tal'Aura herself had been a part of their cabal, had actually deployed the awful weapon that had razed Praetor Hiren and the Senate like ocean waves tearing down a castle in the sand. And then once Shinzon had also perished, Tal'Aura, unrepentant and power-mad, had taken the Empire for her own.

How can I ever forgive myself for that? Donatra asked herself. It was not the first time she had posed the question.

Dropping her legs to the floor, she reached to rub at her side. The dull aches there, all along the right side of her torso and down her leg, had never quite subsided. The result of shallow plasma burns, the scars there remained because of her unwillingness to have them treated. She had suffered them on the day that Tal'Aura had executed Braeg—a man Donatra had first admired, and then loved. She left the scars to remind her of what she had lost, and of who had taken it from her.

And now Tal'Aura's taken away the Imperial State. In some ways, founding a new Romulan nation had been the finest achievement of Donatra's life. She had done it neither for glory nor for sacrifice—though she had hoped the act would, in some way, allow her a measure of expiation. More than any other reason, though, Donatra had simply wanted to save Romulan people from the catastrophe that Tal'Aura's praetorship surely would become. Donatra had not been able to rescue the whole of the Empire, but she had liberated the populations of as many worlds as she could. In the back of her mind, she had always imagined the day that Tal'Aura would be forced from office, or perhaps even die, and on the next day, how Donatra would lay down the standard of the Imperial Romulan State and restore the Empire to its totality.

But now that possibility, and the accomplishment that would have permitted it, stood in ruins.

I was a fool to offer Tal'Aura a summit, she thought. Still, there had been few other avenues open to her, and none of them appealing. Her support had been seriously undermined by the unity protests. As well, she understood the reality that even if Tal'Aura's fleet couldn't bring the Imperial State to its knees, those of the Typhon Pact could. Donatra had reached out to the United Federation of Planets and to the Klingon Empire, but while they had recognized the sovereignty of the new nation, they had not become full-fledged allies. She had stood alone, growing weaker, and she'd had little choice but to approach Tal'Aura in an attempt to salvage . . . something . . . anything.

Her intention had not been to try to convince Tal'Aura that she should allow Donatra to be praetor, or that the two of them should devise some form of power-sharing arrangement. Rather, Donatra had been prepared to argue that both leaders should step down, and that they should permit the Senate to select a new praetor. Tal'Aura could even have gone back to the Senate herself, perhaps with the goal of one day *earning* the praetorship.

And if all of that had failed, if Donatra had been unable to free the Empire of Tal'Aura's grasp, then Donatra would have found Tal'Aura's throat after all. It would have been suicide, but that wouldn't have mattered. Under the circumstances, Donatra would have done it gladly.

But the summit had never come. Donatra had been aware, thanks to the Starfleet captain, of the spurious speculation about her possible involvement in an assassination attempt and an actual murder, but because there had been no truth to that speculation, she had not let it concern her. No charges had been filed against her, nor had she even heard the rumor of such charges being filed, something she would have expected, given that the crimes had allegedly taken place hundreds of days earlier. When she had arrived on Romulus, there had been no indication of trouble, but before midday, she had been arrested and indicted, and it had all taken her by surprise.

Foolish, she rebuked herself. But she could not undo

what she had done; otherwise there would have been no coup d'état by Shinzon, nor any of the lamentable consequences that had followed.

So what now?

She had been incarcerated for thirty days, and she believed that would continue for another thirty days, and thirty more after that, with no relief and no trial, until the day finally arrived when Tal'Aura decided that Donatra had lived long enough. She considered escape, but even if she could find a way to make that happen, then what? What would she do? What *could* she do? Where could she even go? It would not be as though she could readily hide anywhere within the Empire, and she had no intention of living out her days in the Klingon Empire or the Federation or the Ferengi Alliance or anywhere else.

Donatra was a Romulan. She had always been a Romulan, and she would always be a Romulan. At this point, there was nothing else she could be.

The charges are false, she told herself. She had never sent anybody to kill Spock, had not then had the assassin killed. If she could somehow overcome the false accusations, overcome the counterfeit prosecution that Tal'Aura would surely see mounted, maybe she could secure her freedom. Or maybe she could find proof that the evidence against her had been falsified . . . or even that Tal'Aura had herself perpetrated the crimes of which Donatra had been accused . . .

Donatra stood from the sleeping surface and walked over to the other side of the cell, where she bent and picked up the data tablet. She carried it with her back to the bunk, sat down again, and thumbed on the device. Then she restarted Tal'Aura's speech from the beginning.

Even before Tal'Aura reached the end of her second sentence, Donatra threw the tablet back across the room. It skittered to a stop on the bare floor, undamaged by her frustration, her anger, her disappointment, her sorrow.

The only thing damaged was Donatra herself.

37

Spock stood at the central counter in the lobby of the D'deridex Arc security office, waiting for the arrival of Protector Vikral. A sentry waited with him. It had taken a month, but Spock had at last received authorization from the Office of Internal Security to see Donatra. As far as he knew, other than legal counsel, he would be the first person to visit her since her arrest. He wondered if Donatra knew that Tal'Aura had officially dissolved the Imperial Romulan State last night, and if she did, then what her spirits would be like.

He stood peering at the wall of monitors behind the counter. He felt impressed by the scope of Internal Security's efforts to watch and protect the residents of Ki Baratan, and dismayed by the Romulan proclivity for surveillance. It would not have surprised him to see his own image on one of the screens, observed while observing.

As Spock waited, he considered again information that he had learned during the course of petitioning Internal Security for the privilege of seeing Donatra. A month earlier, just after Donatra had first proposed a summit with Tal'Aura, an airpod accident had claimed the lives of the chairman of the Tal Shiar and his adjutant. That much, Spock had known from comnet accounts at the time.

What he and his comrades had been unable to ascertain since then was the identity of Chairman Rehaek's replacement—at least until he had discovered during one of his many appointments at the Office of Internal Security that Sela had taken over the post. Spock hadn't even known that Sela—

"Mister Spock?"

He turned from the counter to see Vikral. "Protector," he said, "thank you for your time."

"Not at all," Vikral said. He held up a data tablet for Spock to see. "I have the order from Internal Security permitting your visit." He turned to the sentry. "Rivol, you have processed Mister Spock?"

For *processed*, Spock read *searched*. The sentry had already checked him for anything he might employ in an attempt to free Donatra, or anything else he might pass to her during their visit. For that reason, Spock once again had brought with him only the clothes he wore.

"I have," Rivol said. "Mister Spock has been cleared."

"Very good," Vikral said. "If you will accompany me then, Mister Spock." Vikral motioned to two sentries, who fell in behind them.

Spock followed the protector down a side corridor, until their group reached a security checkpoint crewed by a quartet of guards, a pair on each side of an active force field. As he passed through with the protector and other sentries, Spock noted the physical door off to the side, which no doubt would slam into place should the checkpoint completely lose power.

Farther into the facility, Spock followed the protector through a second security barrier. The layout of cells along the corridor echoed what he had seen during his own incarceration nearly ten months ago, after he had attempted to turn the Reman over to the authorities. He saw indicator lights active at only one cell, and he wondered if other prisoners had been removed to another section, or even to another security station entirely.

When the group arrived at the closed cell, Vikral reached up to a panel set into the wall, placing his hand flat against a security scanner. An indicator light blinked on, and then a red beam played across the protector's face, clearly confirming his identity via retina scan. A second light came on, and Vikral worked a control. An energetic hum signaled the operation of a force field.

Even before the door had completely retracted into the wall, Spock saw the ribbon of green that extended almost all the way to the force field. He followed it with his gaze back to its source, to where Donatra lay sprawled in the middle of the floor, in a spread of blood, her back to the entry. At once, Vikral reached up to the panel and said, "Security alert, priority one. This is Protector Vikral. Send a medical team to maximum security, cell one."

"Lower the force field," Spock said. Vikral hesitated for a moment, glancing at the pair of sentries behind Spock, then operated the panel once more. The hum faded, indicating the deactivation of the field.

Spock raced into the cell, sidestepping the pooled blood and moving past Donatra so that he could see her from the front. He smelled the metallic odor of copper. As he squatted down, he saw the ragged gashes that had been ripped into the flesh of her wrists and across her neck. Blood had flowed freely, but did so no longer. He reached a hand up to the side of her neck. He detected no pulse.

From a distance, the beat of rapid footsteps approached the cell. Spock glanced up to the entry for a moment, to the protector and the two sentries peering over at him. "She's dead," he told them. Then he looked around. Lying on the floor a meter or so away, he saw a small object he could not immediately identify. But then he recognized it: half of a data tablet, the device rent in two. Green blood covered its jagged edge.

Spock gazed down at Donatra's face, at her glassy, unseeing eyes. A great sadness washed over him. And then he wondered for the first of many times about the last thing Donatra's eyes had ever seen.

38

The Ravingian Mountain Range climbed high into the clouds, its snowcapped peaks vanishing into the mist, the dividing line between land and air impossible to discern. Reaching downward, the steep land bathed itself in solitude, the surface barren between the dusting of snow above and the trees below. From the timberline, a heavily forested slope descended to the foothills and beyond, down into a verdant valley.

Sisko leaned against the railing of the small, private balcony, taking in the magnificent view. The dichotomy of the landscape struck him, with the lush, living countryside downslope, and the cold, dead wastes upslope. He didn't care to draw any metaphors for his own life out of the vista, but they seemed obvious enough.

The range also reminded him of the Janitza Mountains on Bajor. But then so many things these days pulled his mind back to the world that, at least for a time, had been his home. And thoughts of Bajor always brought thoughts of the house he had planned in Kendra Province, outside Adarak, which Kasidy had completed during his time in the Celestial Temple.

Did that even happen? Sisko asked himself. The Prophets had not spoken to him in so long, they had been gone from his life for so long, that it often felt to him as if every experience he'd ever had with them had been a dream. Some days, he almost managed to convince himself of that. In those moments, with the reality of the Bajoran Prophets a myth, with their existence a collective delusion of hope and fear, faith and need, he told himself that their promise to him, their threat, had been not even a lie, but something illusory. And if that declaration—that if he spent his life with Kasidy, he would know nothing but sorrow—had come to him as a chimera, then he could dispose of the idea that his marriage had anything to do with all of the misery and death that had come to surround his life.

Ridding himself of that concept would change everything. He would be able to resign his Starfleet commission and go back to Bajor, and if she would have him, back to Kasidy as well. Sisko would be able to visit Jake and Korena, and to watch Rebecca grow up. Dismissing one idea would be the only thing required for him to go home—for him to *have* a home.

Except that Sisko couldn't quite do that. He couldn't quite make himself believe that he had imagined all of his communications with the Prophets, and all of the time he had spent with them. Denying the truth would not cause it to cease to exist.

Sisko pushed back from the railing and paced around the balcony. Relieved at the Romulan border for a week by *U.S.S. Fortitude*, *Robinson* had arrived at Starbase 39-Sierra that morning. The crew had been due a rest-and-recreation break for some time, and circumstances had finally allowed it.

Sisko had initially thought to remain aboard ship for

the week, but when Admiral Herthum had asked for a briefing on *Robinson*'s months on patrol, the captain had little choice but to transport down to the surface. Before he did, though, he decided that after the meeting he would remain planetside and take some time away. He glanced at the small travel bag at the end of the balcony, which he'd brought with him from the ship. Once the admiral's aide came out and told him that Herthum was ready to see him, and once that meeting had concluded, Sisko intended to find a place where he could actually relax. He needed to blank his mind for a few days, perhaps give himself some time so that he could then come at things from a different perspective.

It occurred to Sisko that the new year had arrived on Earth almost two weeks ago, that 2381 had finally and mercifully come to a close. He didn't know what 2382 would bring, but already there had been rumblings. Fifteen days had passed since Praetor Tal'Aura had officially disbanded the Imperial Romulan State, which had apparently led directly to Empress Donatra's suicide. Freed from the restraints of a divided empire and a reduced military, Tal'Aura had offered some pointed statements about the Federation and the Klingons—statements ignored by President Bacco, and challenged by Chancellor Martok. Although the bellicose Klingons actually seemed disinclined to commence a shooting war—probably because of the considerable firepower of the Typhon Pact nations—there had been indications that Romulus and its new allies might be plotting different forms of combat: diplomatic, economic, intelligence-related.

In a very real way, that was all right with Sisko. He wanted the best for the people of the Federation, of course, but he felt confident that without a hot war, the UFP would survive just fine. He knew he could live with that.

All Sisko wanted was peace.

39

Proconsul Tomalak sat in the shadows of an alcove outside the Senate Chamber, a tiny audio monitor pressed to his ear. He had listened for some time to the deliberations of the senators as they discussed trade agreements. Many of the conversations involved members of the Typhon Pact, and most especially the Tzenkethi, who were emerging as a major economic partner for Romulus.

Having heard enough, Tomalak pocketed the monitor and left the alcove. He walked through the arcing corridors of the Hall of State, his footfalls echoing through the large, empty spaces. He felt intensely satisfied. In the thirty days since the dismantling of the Imperial Romulan State and Donatra's consequent death, life inside the praetorship had become a good deal easier.

Or if not easier, he decided, *then at least a good deal simpler.* Concerns about uniting the Empire, which had so plagued Tal'Aura and Tomalak, no longer applied. As well, any questions about the place of the Romulan Star Empire in the Typhon Pact had disappeared. Though the alliance remained in its infancy, its hierarchy had become well defined with the reintegration into the Empire of the worlds and resources that Donatra had taken. Once all of Romulan space had united, it ensured that the Empire would possess the largest population, the strongest military, and the most planets of any of the Pact members.

As Tomalak turned into a radial corridor, he thought about the deaths of Rehaek and his sycophantic lackey, Torath. With one of their own, Sela, in Rehaek's stead at the head of the Tal Shiar, a valuable new tool had replaced a dangerous old burden. The Elements, it seemed, had realigned back into their natural order. Romulus for Romulans. The Typhon Pact for Romulans. The *galaxy* for Romulans.

Tomalak reached the courtyard, the brilliant sunlight beating down through the cupola windows a perfect reflection of his frame of mind. He strode to the great doors that led to Tal'Aura's audience chamber, knowing that the praetor would be waiting for his report on the Senate. Tomalak leaned into the doors and slowly pushed them open.

Tal'Aura sat in her raised chair, and Tomalak greeted her. "Praetor," he said, "I bring news." He turned and closed the doors, then crossed the wide black floor toward the dais.

Tomalak had gone halfway across the chamber when he realized something was wrong. Tal'Aura sat in her chair, but slumped, her head hanging sideways in what must have been an uncomfortable position.

Or would have been, if Tal'Aura had been conscious.

Tomalak sprinted the remaining distance and vaulted onto the dais. He saw no wounds or injuries on Tal'Aura. Her eyes were closed, and the proconsul convinced himself that she had merely fallen asleep, no matter how radically out of character that would have been. "Praetor," he said, and when he received no response, he raised his voice: "Praetor!"

When Tal'Aura didn't respond, Tomalak reached up to her hand. Her flesh felt warm to the touch, which lifted Tomalak's hopes, but when he searched for a pulse, he found none.

III

The Sea Took Pity

The sea took pity: it interposed with doom:
'I have tall daughters dear that heed my hand:
Let Winter wed one, sow them in her womb,
And she shall child them on the New-world
    strand.'

—GERARD MANLEY HOPKINS

40

The list of people who wanted to meet with the new praetor must have been considerably long, so it pleased Spock that he had been granted an audience in less than a month. He stood in the central courtyard of the Hall of State, a pair of uhlans—a man and a woman—as his escorts. One of them pulled twice on the braided golden rope that hung beside the ruatinite-inlaid doors that led into the praetor's audience chamber. Spock awaited the answering chime, but it never came.

Instead, the doors opened inward, revealing a man of medium height and build, wearing a dark suit. Deep lines incised his face beneath a mop of unruly gray hair; Spock put his age at about a hundred, perhaps a few years higher. He had gray eyes, an unusual iris coloration for a Romulan. "Ambassador Spock, I presume."

"I am Spock, though not an official representative of the Federation at this time."

"Mister Spock, then?" the man asked.

Spock bowed his head in both reply and greeting.

"Very good, then, Mister Spock," the man said. "Please come in." He moved to the side of the doors and beckoned him into the dimly lit chamber with a wave of his arm. Spock entered, followed by the two military officers. "I am Anlikar Ventel," the man said. "Proconsul to our new praetor."

"I am pleased to make your acquaintance, Proconsul Ventel," Spock said. He had known that Ventel's predecessor had not been kept on by the new praetor, whose judicious statement about the appointment had suggested a personal decision by Tomalak to return to the Imperial Fleet.

"Thank you," Ventel said, bowing slightly. "I am pleased to meet you, Mister Spock. I am particularly pleased to see that you are well, obviously recovered from the unfortunate attack on you."

"Yes, thank you." Though the assassination attempt had occurred a year earlier, it had certainly become well known throughout the Empire just three months ago, when Donatra had been charged with planning the attack.

"The praetor is looking forward to meeting you," Ventel said.

Spock glanced across the chamber toward the raised chair and saw it sitting empty, undermining the veracity of the proconsul's claim. But then Spock heard a voice from off to the left.

"I am over here."

Spock looked in that direction and saw the praetor along the perimeter of the room, her body turned toward a sculpture set atop a short column. Like Ventel, she wore a suit, though of a lighter hue. Though Spock knew her age to be almost one hundred twenty-five, her fit body and black hair gave her the appearance of a woman much younger.

"Please join me, Mister Spock," she said. "And you as well, Proconsul." As the two men started toward the praetor, the uhlans trailed behind them. Apparently the praetor saw this, because she said, "Uhlan Preget and Uhlan T'Lesk, you may leave us."

The two uhlans stopped, but the woman said, "I'm sorry, Praetor, but we have our orders. By mandate of the Continuing Committee, no one other than the proconsul and members of your cabinet are permitted to see you without the presence of at least two armed guards."

The praetor looked at Ventel. "Unlimited power is not quite as unlimited as it used to be."

"Nobody ever said that the praetor has unlimited power," Ventel noted with a wry smile.

The praetor appeared to feign indignation, her eyebrows rising. "I knew I shouldn't have allowed the Senate to vote me into this position." To Spock, she said, "I think everybody is concerned about when the next praetor or empress is going to be found dead."

Spock knew that an autopsy of Praetor Tal'Aura had shown her cause of death as *Velderix Riehn'va,* otherwise known as The Usurper. Several months earlier, a Romulan senator had died from the same malady, a rare disease that resulted in the formation of brain aneurysms. Speculation on the comnet had suggested that the praetor had perhaps contracted the disease from an intimate relationship with the similarly afflicted senator, though former Proconsul Tomalak had strongly denounced the notion.

To the uhlans, the praetor said, "Would you please at least stand your watch over me by the door?"

"Yes, ma'am." The uhlans withdrew as they'd been requested, and Spock and Ventel walked the rest of the way over to the praetor.

"May I present Praetor Gell Kamemor," said the proconsul. "Praetor Kamemor, this is Mister Spock, of the planet Vulcan and the United Federation of Planets, though he is here in no official capacity."

Spock bowed his head again in a show of respect. "I am honored," he said. "Thank you for agreeing to see me." From his time as a Federation ambassador, Spock knew of Kamemor, though he had never met her. She had served a similar function for the Empire—at least up until the Treaty of Algeron in 2311, at which time the Romulans withdrew from galactic politics for a lengthy period.

"Tell me, Mister Spock, what do you think of this piece?" Kamemor said, obviously referring to the sculpture by which she stood.

Spock stepped forward and examined the bronze. It featured a bird of prey in flight, its talons wrapped around a serpent, which had twisted around in such a way that it appeared about to strike its fangs into the raptor from above. "With all due respect to you, the artist, and the Empire," Spock said, "I find it rather uninspiring. Both the bird of prey and the serpent are exceedingly common icons in Romulan culture, and this piece really adds nothing to the oeuvre. I can appreciate the skill of the artist, but I do not appreciate the work itself."

The praetor exchanged a glance with the proconsul. "I like it," Ventel said.

"Just another thing about which we disagree, Proconsul," said Kamemor. "I think I dislike it even more than you do, Mister Spock." As she gestured toward the other side of the room, Spock noted that she had the same unusual gray coloring in her eyes as Ventel. "Why don't we sit down and you can tell me why you wanted to see me."

Spock and Ventel followed the praetor to the other side of the room, to where a small table had been placed, along with three chairs. An elegant silver set sat atop the table. "May I offer you some tea, Mister Spock?" Kamemor asked. "It is from my home planet of Glintara."

"Thank you." Spock and the proconsul sat down after the praetor did, and then Ventel poured out two cups of the tea. Spock sampled his, and found that it had a pleasing aroma and flavor. "It is not unlike *relen* tea, from Vulcan, a personal favorite."

"I shall have to try some Vulcan teas," Kamemor said. "Now, then, Mister Spock, for what reason have you asked to see me?"

"I wish to speak with you about the Reunification Movement," Spock said.

"What about it?" Kamemor asked. "I have seen very little from the Movement in some time."

"That is correct," Spock said. "Nearly a year ago, I petitioned Praetor Tal'Aura for the right of Romulans to publicly support and further the cause. As I'm sure you know, the praetor granted that request, but it is my belief that she did so only to advance her own agenda. When it became evident to me that she had achieved that agenda, it seemed equally clear that she would likely revoke that right. Because such a revocation could have been followed by mass arrests of citizens involved in the Movement, whose identities had become known, my comrades and I ceased promoting our aims in public."

"I see," said Kamemor. "But I am unsure what it is you wish of me. Neither Praetor Tal'Aura nor the Senate revoked the right to openly champion the reunification of the Romulan and Vulcan people."

"I would ask you what your views on the Movement are," Spock said.

"My views?" Kamemor said. She sipped at her tea, then set the cup down. "Frankly, Mister Spock, I find the idea of attempting to bring together two cultures that diverged millennia ago not only unlikely to succeed but unnecessary. From a political standpoint, the fact that the Vulcans belong to the Federation makes the possibility of their reunification with Romulans extremely dubious—especially now that the Empire has joined the Typhon Pact. At the same time, I just do not see the point of it, other than perhaps as an intellectual exercise. The Vulcan culture and people have valuable qualities, to be sure, as is true of the Romulan culture and people. I see nothing wrong with individuals or groups of either society who wish to cross-pollinate their beliefs and customs for their own benefit, but why does it require a movement?"

Spock nodded. He had not known Kamemor's views on reunification, but he had wanted to seek an opportunity for those who believed as he did to be able to continue following their aspirations. Needless to say, he found the praetor's stance unsatisfying. "I am sorry to hear that," he told Kamemor.

"Why?" the praetor asked. "Why should your happiness . . . or satisfaction . . . require me to believe as you do?"

"It does not," Spock said, "but I assumed from what you communicated that you would not then be in favor of keeping the open discussion of reunification decriminalized."

"That seems to me less of an assumption and more of a *pre*sumption," Kamemor said. She turned to Ventel, who had remained quiet but attentive during the conversation. "Proconsul, how often do you and I disagree on matters of policy?"

"Um, well . . . I'm not sure, Praetor," Ventel said. "Twenty-five percent of the time? Thirty?"

"And we've only been in office twenty or so days," Kamemor said. "I have every confidence that the percentage of our policy differences will increase." She regarded Spock quietly for a moment, then said, "That's one of the reasons I wanted Anlikar as my proconsul. I'm an intelligent, experienced, well-read woman, but I don't know everything, and some of the ideas I hold true are probably incomplete, inaccurate, or wholly incorrect. I don't want people around me who will simply agree with me. I want people like Proconsul Ventel, who will disagree with me when they think I'm wrong. I want people to convince me that their way is better than my way. That is, I think, what a good leader does."

"I would agree," said Spock. "May I ask precisely what that means for the Reunification Movement?"

"It means that I have no intention and no desire to see public speech of any kind criminalized," Kamemor said, "including with respect to your Reunification Movement."

"I am gratified to hear that, Praetor," Spock said. "Thank you."

"Let me also add that your visitor's visa will remain in force," Kamemor said. She paused, then added, "At least as long as you obey Romulan law."

"I have no intention and no desire to violate Romulan law," Spock said, paraphrasing her own earlier statement.

"Very good." She stood up and said, "Is there anything else you need to discuss with me?" The meeting had clearly come to its natural end.

"No, Praetor," Spock said, rising as well. The proconsul also got to his feet. "It has been most illuminating to speak with you. *Jolan tru.*" Kamemor bowed her head, and Ventel stepped away from the table and escorted Spock back toward the doors.

Outside the Hall of State, on the avenues of Ki Baratan, Spock considered his meeting with Gell Kamemor. So early in her praetorship, he could not know what kind of a leader she would be for the Romulan people, but he thought that she would be a good one. From everything he knew of Kamemor, and from what he had just seen of her, he believed her far more thoughtful and far less militant than either Tal'Aura or Donatra. She also seemed less interested in power than in doing what was best for the citizens of the Empire. Spock suspected that would include taking a much less antagonistic posture toward the Federation.

Walking along Via Karzan, Spock headed for the home of his young compatriot, D'Tan. From there, he would contact the leaders of the city's Reunification cell—Corthin, Dr. Shalvan, Dorlok, Venaster—and inform them of what Praetor Kamemor had told him. After that, they would spread the word to their supporters across Romulus, and then to others throughout the Empire.

41

Benjamin Lafayette Sisko, husband, father, Starfleet captain, starship commander, and erstwhile Emissary of the Prophets, paced back and forth across his quarters on *U.S.S. Robinson*. Outside the large ports of the living area, the stars blurred into streaks of light as the ship traveled at warp. He had the lights down low, adding to the impressiveness of the display.

It had been five weeks since the crew had departed Starbase 39-Sierra and resumed its patrol route along the Romulan Neutral Zone. Five weeks since Sisko had camped along the foothills of the Ravingian Mountains, had breathed the fresh air of an almost-pristine world, and stopped thinking for a few days. By the end of his shore leave, he had been able to decide exactly what he needed to do next.

Sisko hadn't delayed taking action since then because of any uncertainty he felt, or because of any desire to rethink his choices one more time. He knew what he must do. He just wanted to make sure that he used the right words.

Today, finally, he thought he'd found them.

Sisko sat down in front of the companel at one end of the living area in his quarters and activated the device. The familiar Federation emblem—a starfield partially encircled by a pair of stylized laurels—appeared on the screen. "Computer, transmit file Sisko-One-Nineteen to the Incoming Records Administrator of the Adarak Courthouse, Kendra Province, Bajor." Electronic tones signaled that the file had been sent, and the word TRANSMITTED replaced the UFP sigil.

"Computer," Sisko continued, "record a message to Kasidy Yates, Kendra Province, Bajor." Again, he heard the electronic tones, and then the word RECORDING appeared on the screen.

"Kasidy, it's Ben," he said. "I know that in a few weeks it'll be a year since I left. Before I say anything more, I want to tell you that I'm sorry. I know that I've hurt you, and I've done so in a way that's probably unforgivable.

"In many ways, I know that I can't possibly understand what you've gone through, and what you're still going through. But in some ways, I can. It's not the same thing, but my first wife left me too. It's different, of course, because Jennifer died, but the truth is that after the last moment of her life I never saw her again, never got to share time with her again, and I was suddenly the single parent of an eleven-year-old boy.

"I'm telling you this because I want you to know that I do have some idea of what I've put you through. What I endured with the loss of Jennifer, I would not wish on anyone—least of all on someone I love.

"And I do love you still, Kasidy, and I imagine that I always will. And it's because I love you, and our beautiful Rebecca, that I had to leave.

"Kas, I know that you don't believe in the Bajoran Prophets, at least not in the way that I do. But I have conversed with them, I have communed with them, and they have guided me on a journey that allowed me to help, and even save, the people of Bajor. I don't regret that. I *can't* regret that.

"But I do regret how my relationship with the Prophets has impacted us . . . how it has impacted you and Rebecca. I told you before we got married that the Prophets had let me know that if I spent my life with you, I would know nothing but sorrow. And you said that it sounded like a threat. But it wasn't.

"It was a gift.

"The Prophets do not exist in time the way that we do. And neither did I in the time that I spent with them in the Celestial Temple, so I have some firsthand understanding of this. The Prophets live a nonlinear existence, but more than that, they live a *continuous* existence. It's how they can generate accurate prophecies, how they can know the future: they *live* in what we call the future, and in the past, and in the present. They are aware of every moment in their lives at all times. And they also see potential moments in uncountable possible timelines.

"I don't think I can explain it any better than that. But I lived that way, and even though I can't remember the details of it, of a future that was the same as my present and my past, I do remember how overwhelming it was. And I recall the nature of it . . . the *reality* of it.

"My point is that when the Prophets told me that I would know only sorrow if I spent my life with you, they weren't threatening me. They were telling me what they had already seen . . . what they were seeing at that instant. They saw me marry you, and they saw my life inundated by sorrow. They also saw an existence where I did *not* spend my life with you, and where I was *not* inundated by sorrow.

"For you, Kasidy, for your love and because I love you, I could suffer many things. But this isn't about making things better for me; it's about saving *you*. And Rebecca. If I stayed with you, I would know nothing but sorrow, and at some point, that sorrow would include something terrible happening to you, and something terrible happening to Rebecca. That would be my greatest sorrow.

"In the time before I left, it had begun. Eivos Calan and Audj died in the fire. Rebecca was kidnapped. Elias Vaughn suffered a massive brain injury and is essentially dead. My father died.

"I saw it happening. The sorrow was getting closer, and deeper. I couldn't let something happen to you and Rebecca. It was hard enough when we almost lost her the first time.

"I didn't tell you all of this before I left because I know that you don't believe in the Prophets, and I knew you wouldn't believe in the truth of their prophecy. But that's what this is: a prophecy. And unless I heed their advice, it will continue to come true.

"I love you, Kasidy. And despite what I've put you through, I suspect that you still love me too. I think it's okay for you to love me, at least in the way that I still love Jennifer. But I was eventually able to let go of Jennifer enough to fall in love with you. I think it's okay for you to let go of me in that way. When you're able, I want you to be open to love again.

"I'm sending this message to you because I think it will help you—today and, I hope, tomorrow. I hope you'll let it help Rebecca too, when she's ready to know all of this.

"Right before I started recording this message, I transmitted a petition to the courthouse in Adarak to dissolve our marriage. It might have been the hardest thing I've ever done. But it will be the best thing for you.

"I love you. And I'm sorry."

Sisko tapped a control surface to end the recording. He didn't know if it would help Kasidy as much as he wanted it to, but he hoped so. He didn't know what else he could do.

"Computer," he said, "transmit message." Once more, he heard the tones that indicated fulfillment of his order, and the word TRANSMITTED appeared on the companel. Sisko thumbed off the device, stood up, and headed across the living area to the replicator. He needed a drink.

Before he reached the replicator, though, the door chime sounded. "Come in," he called. The doors parted and the ship's first officer stepped inside.

"Captain," he said. "I hope I'm not disturbing you."

"No," Sisko said. "What can I do for you?"

Rogeiro held up a padd. "You wanted those figures on shortening the duty shifts and increasing their frequency," he said. "I finished them, and I was on the way to my quarters, so I thought I'd drop them off."

Sisko walked over and took the padd from Rogeiro. "Thank you, Commander. I'll take a look at what you've come up with." He leaned over to his desk and deposited the padd atop it.

"Have a good night, sir." Rogeiro turned and headed for the door.

"Commander," Sisko said on an impulse, and the first officer stopped. Sisko had no right to expect a positive response to the question that rose in his mind, but he asked it anyway: "I was just about to get myself a drink. Would you like you stay and have one with me?"

Rogeiro looked more than puzzled; he looked as though he thought that *Robinson*'s captain might have been taken over by some errant, noncorporeal life-form. "Sir?"

"Maybe we could chat a bit, Commander," Sisko said. "Get to know each other a little better."

Sisko thought that Rogeiro would have been justified in reaching back and slugging his captain right in the jaw. Instead, he smiled. "Thank you, sir. I'd like that."

"What can I get you?" Sisko asked, and he walked over to the replicator.

42

Alizome Tor Fel-A balanced on one of the smooth stone blocks in front of the autarch's expansive black desk. With her legs twisted around her torso and a full report stored in the data cube in her hand, she felt more comfortable in the presence of Korzenten Rej Tov-AA than ever she had before. Alizome had been summoned to his home, to meet with him on the superior floor of his office, but by herself, without even any of his advisors present. In times past, she might have grown concerned that she had been called to the autarch's residence to explain some failure on her part or, worse, to suffer a repositioning to another level or echelon because of that failure. That had never happened, though, and she thought that she had finally become accustomed to her continued successes.

And her mission to Romulus had been a considerable success.

"So your report is ready, Alizome?" the autarch asked, the deep ringing of his voice almost hypnotic. As she did each time she saw him, Alizome found his bright-red flesh stunning to behold.

"Yes, I've prepared my report," she said. Alizome reached forward—she had to unfurl one leg and brace it against the floor—and placed her data cube atop the autarch's desk. Korzenten picked up the cube but did not examine it.

"It is complete through the first twenty days of Praetor Kamemor's rule?" he asked.

"It is."

"Excellent," he said. "I've already received preliminary reports from our observers in Romulan space and from my advisors, and I want to congratulate you on doing an excellent job."

"Thank you, my Rej," said Alizome.

"We may have to retest your level," the autarch said. "Results like this suggest that you just may be a double-A."

"Thank you, my Rej," Alizome said, accepting the accolade even as she knew that Korzenten did not truly intend to reassess her level.

"You posed as a trade minister?" the autarch asked.

"I did," Alizome said. "Employing the Coalition's many contacts on Romulus, I met numerous people, some of them inside the government, some of them outside it, but always making sure that they were a member of the Hundred. The Hundred are the wealthiest, most powerful groups in the Empire, who effectively control the populace through economic and governmental means.

"Through those meetings, I identified the individual best suited to lead a united Romulan Empire. I maneuvered her into place by dispatching the senator that had been representing her group in the Senate, then lobbied her group to select her as his replacement."

"How did you dispatch him?" Korzenten asked.

"I passed a disease on to him through casual contact," Alizome said. "The disease was naturally occurring, untraceable, and not harmful to Tzenkethi. It took a month for it to incubate and cause his death.

"After that, I had intended to remove Praetor Tal'Aura and Empress Donatra from the equation, but as you suggested might happen, my Rej, Donatra was eliminated without my assistance. It was then a simple matter to pass on the same disease to the praetor, whom I met with as she prepared to bring an end to the Imperial Romulan State."

"After Tal'Aura's death, you must have had to lobby quite a few senators to have your selection voted into the praetorship," Korzenten said.

"Actually, my Rej," Alizome said, "I chose so well that I didn't need to do so. A quick poll showed me that the Romulans would vote Kamemor in on their own."

"And so they did," said the autarch. "So now we have a unified Romulan Empire, under the rule of a leader whom you believe will not attempt to control the Typhon Pact."

"That is correct, my Rej."

"And now that the Romulan Star Empire has regained its former strength and been made stable under a new regime, the Typhon Pact is in turn at its strongest and most stable," said Korzenten.

Alizome agreed. "The Tzenkethi and the Typhon Pact therefore need fear nothing from the Federation."

"Rather," said the autarch, "it is the Federation who should now fear us."

Acknowledgments

My first exposure to the Typhon Pact came in a Midtown Manhattan restaurant, over lunch with editor Marco Palmieri. Quite unexpectedly, Marco described to me the conceit and genesis of an idea for the literary *Star Trek* universe upon which he had been working. The Typhon Pact, a new coalition of *Trek* antagonists, would provide a counterpart to the United Federation of Planets and its Khitomer Accords alliance—a twenty-fourth-century version of the Warsaw Pact and NATO. For starters, Marco intended to publish a book series, with each volume focusing on a different Pact member, and he invited me to pen the Romulan entry. For that offer, for his creativity and first-rate editorial skills, and for his friendship, I am grateful.

After Marco had to leave our endeavor, Margaret Clark nimbly picked up the ball, shepherding the story within these pages from conception through final form. Margaret provided a couple of parameters for the tale, hoping to accomplish some specific developments in the overarching *Trek* meta-story, but then allowed me a great deal of latitude in developing the novel I wanted to write. I am thankful for her supportive direction, for her remarkable endurance, and for her friendship.

Once Margaret also had to depart the project, Jaime Costas and Emilia Pisani signed onboard. I want to thank both of them for their generous assistance, their patience, and their good natures.

Thanks as well to my fellow *Typhon Pact* writers: David Mack (*Zero Sum Game*), Michael A. Martin (*Seize the Fire*), and Dayton Ward (*Paths of Disharmony*). Fine writers all around, scholars and gentlemen, and a thoroughly enjoyable group with which to work. I am particularly grateful to Dave Mack, who graciously allowed me exclusive access to one specific bit of the *Deep Space Nine* milieu.

In choosing to work with the heretofore unseen, mostly unexplored Tzenkethi, I had cause to seek out the assistance of two other writers who had at least touched upon the mysterious aliens. Keith R. A. DeCandido kindly answered some questions about the Tzenkethi from his *Articles of the Federation* and *A Singular Destiny,* as did James Swallow with respect to his *Day of the Vipers.* Keith also provided a roster of Federation government personnel and a description of the Palais de la Concorde, which I found quite useful. Thanks, guys.

I also tapped William Leisner for some information from his *Losing the Peace,* and Una McCormack from her *Hollow Men.* Once more, fine writers and nice people, willing to help when asked. Thank you.

Turning to my crack staff of knowledgeable *Star Trek* fans, Deborah Stevenson, Alex Rosenzweig, and Ian McLean also helped with some literary *Trek* research. Thanks to each of them for giving of their time and effort. I appreciate it.

And then, of course, there are my regulars, the people whom I always thank because they are always there for me. Walter Ragan, Anita Smith, Jennifer George, and Patricia Walenista help me with everything. I am privileged to enjoy such warm, loving, happy people in my life.

Finally, as always, there is Karen Ragan-George. Whenever I get to this point in my acknowledgments, I wonder what I can possibly say about the woman of my dreams that I have not said already. This time, for my beautiful, redheaded, albino Polynesian, I opted for Hawaiian: Aloha wau ia ʻoe, e kuʻu wahine no na kau a kau.

About the Author

Born and raised in New York City, David R. George III currently resides in southern California with his enchanting wife, Karen. Their wildly busy lives include many things: reading and writing (and some 'rithmetic), national and world travel, art and history, movies and music, swing dancing and hula, playing baseball and following the New York Mets, and livin' and lovin'.

Please do not try this at home. Void where prohibited. Your actual mileage may vary.

David can be found on the Internet at http://www.facebook.com/DRGIII.